CRUEL TO BE KIND

CRUEL TO BE KIND

A BAD CHOICES NOVEL BOOK 2

JOSEPH SOUZA

To Allie, my beautiful daughter.

Chapter One

GWYNN

Gwynn separated the kids into two equal teams and made herself the designated pitcher, the player who rolled the ball to each kicker. Her phone rang as she took to the mound.

We have a problem, Gwynn, the text from Peters read.

I told you never to text me on this phone, she texted back

Sorry, but this is important.

What? she typed back.

Nguyen just woke from her coma.

She ended the text chain and considered the news. What if Nguyen eventually recovered her memory and started recounting that fateful night, and identified her as the person who'd chased her out into the street? Would the police even believe Nguyen, knowing that her memory had been compromised?

Gwynn rolled the ball toward the plate, reflecting on all that she'd been through in the last year. And what a year it had been, seeing how she hadn't been arrested or thrown in jail. Tom had taken her back after their brief separation. Although this was not the outcome she'd desired, she had agreed to get back with him for Jack's benefit, her son being the most precious thing in the world to her.

Eduardo kicked a grounder to the mound. She scooped the ball up and underhanded it to Aisha for the first out. Luis flied out to the shortstop.

Martin then drubbed a double to center field. The last kid, the newest client to The Loft, lined the ball right into her hands. End of inning.

While waiting for the teams to switch sides, her mind rewinded to when she wrapped that wet plastic bag over Townsend's head, his eyes nearly exploding out of their sockets. Then to the bay when she strangled Sandra while she was out on her morning swim, only to return to the woman's home and practically bump into William as he walked through the front door. Spiking his coffee had been the easy part. Once he was out, she'd dragged his body into the back of her SUV and drove him up to the quarry, pushing him over the edge. She'd dispatched her biological mother by setting fire to her sundress while she lay unconscious in her trailer. Nearly killed Officer Janet Nguyen, too, but that was an accident—or so she wanted to believe.

She rolled the ball toward the plate. Jose keyed it up and toed a booming home run over the right fielder's head. As he rounded the bases, he trash-talked the other players and would have gotten into a scuffle with Anderson playing third if she hadn't interceded.

The contest continued, inning after inning, the kids cheering and getting into the flow of the game. After a long and brutal winter, everyone at The Loft looked forward to being outside. A Maine spring could go either way as far as the weather was concerned. She remembered one day in April when it snowed seven inches, and they had to cancel school. And another when she was in high school, and the temperature hit eighty-six degrees. It had been so hot inside the classroom that day that the teachers had to open up all the windows to let in some fresh air. The week after that, she pushed that rapist high school teacher to his death.

An hour later, the game ended, and the winning team cheered. The smaller kids ran up and clung to her, not wanting to let her go. Happy, she escorted them back to their classrooms. Once all the kids were safely inside, she returned to her office in the admin building and grabbed her bag and nylon jacket, trying not to think about the unsettling news of Nguyen waking from her coma.

Her phone rang. She glanced at the screen and saw Tom's number.

"Hey, hon. What's up?" she said.

"I want you to be ready when I come home tonight."

"Ready for what?"

"Tonight we play." The line went dead.

A sense of dread filled her upon hearing these words. She needed to bide her time and be a dutiful wife a bit longer. Someday, she would be free from her husband and his abusive ways. This marriage wouldn't last forever. Nothing ever did.

Chapter Two

GWYNN

Gwynn stood in the dark bedroom, snapping two ends of the rope in her hands in anticipation of Tom's arrival. The POP, POP, POP sound of the rope sent an electric jolt up her arms and biceps. At another time, she might have appreciated the way this braided nylon felt in the palms of her hands, but these were not normal times, so she didn't take any pleasure in preparing to inflict pain on her husband. In fact, she hated herself for what she was about to do, even if she wanted more than anything to kill him.

Trish had picked Jack up earlier in the day, and the two of them planned to spend the night at her place watching movies and eating copious amounts of junk food. As much as she and her sister-in-law had been at odds with each other these past few years, Trish adored her son.

How her life had changed since Tom walked in on her and Peters as they made love in that cabin. How that one moment in time had changed the trajectory of her life. Her future seemed so bright back then that she could barely contain her excitement. In Peters she'd met the love of her life, a man who respected her and treated her as an equal. More importantly, he knew the crazy things she had done and had accepted her in full.

The front door opened and closed downstairs. All the muscles in her body tensed in anticipation of Tom entering the room. She snapped the rope in her hands as he made his way up the stairs. Placing the rope down on the nightstand, she grabbed the knife and gripped it by its beechwood handle. The silver knob rotated, and the door opened, and in walked Tom. He draped his suit jacket over the armchair in the corner. After a few seconds passed, she crept up behind him, sticking the tip of the blade into his back so that it penetrated his Oxford dress shirt.

"Don't move, Tom."

"Gwynn? What are you doing?"

"You try anything stupid, and you're dead. And you know I'll do it," she said, following the lines he'd scripted for her.

"Are you going to kill me?"

"What do you think?"

"But why?"

"Shut up and take off your clothes."

"What?" He turned his head ever so slightly.

"Do as I say."

"And if I don't?"

Gwynn cracked him in the head with the knife handle before delivering three swift blows to his kidney. If only her mother-in-law had known what these steak knives would be used for, she might have given them a different wedding present. Tom dropped to his knees, groaning.

"Stand up," she said, lifting him by the collar.

"How can you do this to me? I'm your husband."

"And a great husband at that. You threatened to turn me into the police that day you caught me and Peters fucking."

"I said I wouldn't if you took me back."

She cuffed him over the ear. "Shut up and get undressed."

Tom unbuttoned his shirt and let it fall to the floor. Then he kicked off his shoes and undid the button on his pants.

"The underwear too."

"Really?"

"Do it."

"You can be such a bitch!"

"Trust me, Tom, you have yet to see the real bitch in me."

Gwynn nudged the tip of the blade into his back. A teardrop of blood stained his T-shirt as Tom pulled the shirt over his head and tossed it aside. Blood leaked from the tiny wound on his lower back, and his spare tire hung like a jowl over his boxers. Gwynn grabbed the elastic band and cut the material down over his posterior until his underwear fell away. She stared at his pink flesh, remembering how slim and attractive he'd been back at Brooks College.

She remembered a day, near the end of the spring semester, when a bunch of them skipped class and drove over to the lake for a swim. The day was hot and muggy. Someone brought a Styrofoam cooler filled with beer and passed them around to everyone. The guys ripped off their clothes and jumped naked into the water. She'd glanced over and saw Sandra trying to make small talk with Tift, but Tift was having none of it and looked the other way. As Gwynn applied suntan lotion over her arms, Tom popped out of the lake, his long blond hair dripping with water and his stomach ripped like a washboard. His penis dangled like the neck of a steamer clam, the kind her father used to dig up at Scarborough Beach during low tide.

She would always treasure those college days, even her memory of Tom back then.

Blood trickled into the crack of his butt. Holding the knife and rope in the same hand, she shoved him facedown onto the mattress, watching as his two hundred plus pounds bounced up and down on the bed. The freckles that had once dotted his skin had long ago faded into his pasty complexion, the result of bad diet, too much alcohol, and the extremely long hours he'd been putting in at his CPA firm.

She sat atop his backside, pressing the tip of the blade into the base of his neck. He groaned, the left side of his face smushed up against the pillow. Reaching back, she tugged off one of his socks, grabbed his wrists, and lassoed the rope around them. So tightly, in fact, that his fingers began to turn purple.

"That hurts," he grunted.

"Serves you right," Gwynn said, pressing the blade deeper into his neck.

"Please, Gwynn. I'm begging you not to kill me."

"Keep it up, Tom. I so love hearing you grovel."

She lifted the remaining length of rope toward his head and forced all of her weight down onto the small of his spine. Within seconds, her fists began to pummel his back, leaving red welts over his skin. Tom howled and begged her to stop, which she did, but only to stuff the balled-up sock into his mouth. Using the remainder of the rope, she wrapped it around his throat and twisted the knot against the base of his neck. Tom's scream, muffled by the pillow, echoed throughout the room. She leaned back and pulled with all her might. His spine arched, and his warm blood dampened the backside of her thigh. How much longer would this take before Tom stopped breathing?

Chapter Three

DETECTIVE PETERS

Peters stood on the banks of the Presumpscot River, hungover and tired after a late flight home, mentally preparing to examine the body of a teenage girl. It was the second victim in three months to have been found along this stretch of the river. The first girl had been discovered on the Portland side, not far from the third tee box at Riverside South Golf Course. The girl had been found naked under a thick canopy of ferns.

His phone dinged. A text message from his bookie, reminding him that he owed him money for his bet on the Celtics game last night. It had been his third loss in a row and another setback to his once robust savings account.

Just yesterday, he'd been sitting in the offices of *30 Rock* getting schmoozed by an important producer. The network was thinking about producing a true crime show based on the Muddy River Killer, and they had offered him a nice sum, assuming the project got green-lighted. He hoped it would because he badly needed the money. The show would not only fatten his bank account, but it would give him another opportunity to confirm the false narrative of who really killed those girls. Only he and Gwynn knew that her father was the culprit, not Vinny Lazzara, the poor sap he'd set up to take the rap.

He squatted, holding the wet ferns aside, and studied the corpse. The odor was like nothing else he'd ever smelled before: rank vegetables and decaying fish. Above him stood a team of technicians, waiting for him to finish viewing the body. Despite the fact he hadn't really solved the Muddy River Killer case, he'd gone back and studied all the murders Gwynn's father had committed, putting the details to memory. Now he knew as much about that case as anyone.

Staring at the girl's unmoving face, Peters estimated the time of death to be roughly four days ago. Burn marks and bruises peppered her bloated body. These were old wounds, indicating a childhood filled with abuse and neglect. Foam bubbled from her bluish lips, and her gaze appeared heavenly, as if she'd been transported to a Renaissance painting. He didn't think it would take long before they identified her. Judging from the ligature marks around her neck, he could confidently report back that the girl had been asphyxiated.

Sticking his head beneath the canopy of ferns, he picked up a twig and angled it under the girl's purplish hand. He lifted one of her fingers and wiggled off the silver ring, careful so that none of the others could see him doing this. Cupping it in his hand, he eased the girl's finger down onto the soil. The ring, depicting an arrow pointing toward a hollow heart, rested in the palm of his hand. He slipped it into his pocket and stood to leave.

The river below flowed gray and silent, the banks caked from two years of lower than normal rainfall. Across the river, he saw a small opening in the tree line. Two Adirondack chairs faced the water, and a thick line of rope dangled from an overhanging tree branch, the loop at the bottom used for a foothold come summer. Had someone on the other side of the river witnessed the girl being murdered?

The cops and evidence techs watched as he trudged silently up the bank and disappeared into the woods. He didn't care to stand around and make small talk with the same people who once talked shit about him behind his back.

He walked along the trail and through the woods, his mind returning to Gwynn. Everything in his life currently revolved around that fateful day when Tom walked in on them while they were making love next to that fireplace in Gwynn's cabin. Peters recalled the sense of dread he'd felt when he looked up and saw Tom at the top of those stairs, a shitty grin over his face. He'd thought they'd crossed every obstacle to clearing their names, especially with Nguyen lying in a coma at Maine Medical. He'd 'solved' the Muddy River case and had become a minor celebrity in town. The possibilities for a happily ever after seemed endless—until Tom walked in and ruined everything.

As soon as he emerged from the woods, he noticed the girl who had discovered the body. A golden retriever sat on the ground next to her with its shaggy head resting on her lap. Parts of the dog's mane had been twisted into knots and stuffed into colorful hair tubes. Two police officers stood a few feet from the girl, their arms crossed and talking in whispers. The girl's clothes screamed hipster, and her hair fell in serpent-like dreadlocks around her shoulders. Two Chinese letters had been tattooed on her neck. The dog lifted his head as Peters approached. He squatted next to the girl, scratching the Golden behind its ears.

"Thank you for your patience, miss."

"It's Darby."

"Miss Darby?"

"Just Darby." She wiped a tissue over her eyes.

"Remind me again how you found the body."

"Xen got loose and ran down into the woods. It was so horrible when I saw that poor girl."

"Xen?"

She patted her dog's head. "My dog."

He scribbled the word "idiot" in his notes.

"How long do you think she's been there?"

"Not sure," he said, staring intently at the Chinese characters.

"Do you know who she is?"

"Not yet, but we'll find out." He tapped his pencil against the page of his notepad. "Is there anything else you can tell us?"

"No, that's it. I found her and then called you guys."

"My sergeant will take down your name and information if we need to get ahold of you. Thanks for your help."

As he headed back to his vehicle, he saw Annabelle standing among the other reporters. Amazing how fast news got around here, especially in a small town like Portland. He should have felt blessed to have such a stunning and accomplished girlfriend, but he didn't. Not when he was still in love with Gwynn. Despite 'solving' the Muddy River case, he'd been an emotional wreck these last few months. Her absence from his life had been far more traumatic than he could ever have imagined.

Annabelle smiled at him, and a pit grew in his stomach. It was rare that an anchorwoman of her stature would venture out into the field to cover a news story, but this was not any old story. And Annabelle was the highest-rated news reporter in the city. The discovery of this second victim would bring in a massive viewership, and the various media outlets would label this a copycat killing. Because of that, he felt an obligation to answer all their questions.

He'd met her three months ago at a dinner held in his honor, and although he'd recognized her immediately (who wouldn't have recognized her?), he hadn't even noticed when she started to hit on him. He'd begun dating Annabelle in the hopes that she might help him forget about Gwynn, but it hadn't worked; he couldn't get that woman out of his head. So he bided his time and hoped for the best, praying that someday Tom would be out of the picture and they could get back together.

Annabelle asked the first question, and he answered quickly and without emotion, giving no indication that they were an item. Of course, all that would all change tonight when they appeared together at the Dirigo Awards banquet. Annabelle and a few other people were being recognized for their civic contributions to the community. He had no desire to announce their relationship to the world, but she'd forced the issue, making it impossible for him to say no. What if Gwynn found out they were dating? Would she write him off? He cursed himself for ever hooking up with Annabelle. If it weren't for Tom blackmailing them, he and Gwynn would be together now. Maybe even married with a child of their own on the way.

"Do you think the girl's death is the work of a copycat?" another reporter asked.

"It's only two girls at this time, so it's way too early to speculate. Once we get the victim identified, we'll have a better idea where we stand with these two murders."

"Have you heard the latest about your partner, Detective Nguyen?" another reporter asked.

"No. Is she alright?"

"She woke from her coma an hour ago."

"That's wonderful news," he said, forcing a smile over his face. "Has she said anything yet?"

"Nothing yet, but the doctors are saying it's a good sign."

"Good to hear," he said, knowing he had to tell Gwynn about this. "Well, that's all I have for now. Gotta run."

Annabelle headed back to the news van with her cameraman in tow. Any straight guy would have given his left arm to be with her, he kept telling himself. If only he could erase Gwynn from his memory, maybe he could move on in life and finally be happy. But Gwynn was like a parasite that had wormed its way into his brain and wouldn't let go.

He walked back to his car, thinking about his date with Annabelle tonight. Their appearance together would be fodder for all the gossip columns, as they were probably the two most eligible celebrities in town. Annabelle's romantic status had been a hot topic ever since she started at the station thirteen years ago. She'd dated athletes, movie stars, politicians, and once even had a brief, volatile fling with her co-anchor on the news desk.

Once inside his car, Peters removed the dead girl's ring from his pocket and rolled it around in his palm, allowing the sunlight to reflect off the surface. He studied it closely, noticing the small gap between the arrowhead and the heart.

The bodies of two teenage girls had been discovered along the Presumpscot River in the span of three months, and he could already hear the nervous whispers around town about a copycat killer stalking the streets. After 'arresting' the Muddy River Killer and helping convict Sam Lazzara, he knew the pressure would be on to solve this case.

But as he drove back into town, he couldn't help but think about Gwynn.

What would her reaction be when she heard the news of this second dead girl? Could solving this case help finagle his way back into her good graces? At this point, he'd do just about anything to hold her in his arms. Or hear her voice in his ear. He remembered making love to her on that sheepskin rug, the fire crackling just behind them. Gwynn had resurrected his career and shown him the true meaning of love, and because of that, he wanted nothing else but to be with her.

A bit extreme, yes, but it was the main reason he'd killed those two girls. Well, not totally. Admittedly, he did love all the attention he'd received for solving those cases. It felt amazing to be appreciated and respected by the public and his fellow officers in the department, and he wanted badly to experience that same feeling again. And make more money so he could pay off all his debts.

Killing the first girl proved easier than expected. She'd practically jumped into his passenger seat when he offered to give her a hundred bucks and a bottle of wine. When she passed out, he drove to an abandoned lot and covered her nose and mouth with his hands and watched with surprised delight as the girl's life slipped away from her. When he was certain the girl was dead, he put her body in his trunk, waited until nighttime, and then deposited her body along the river.

Before he went inside Headquarters, he texted Gwynn to tell her the news about Nguyen. Hopefully, she'd want to meet with him and sort everything out. If not, he might have to kill again in order to get her attention.

Chapter Four

GWYNN

Gwynn counted to forty before loosening the knot. Below her, Tom lay unconscious, looking corpse-like. As soon as she flipped him over, she crab-walked toward his ankles, lifting them up so that the blood could rush back to his brain. His eyelids fluttered, and he shook his head. She let go of his legs and bounded over to the nightstand, grabbed the tube of smelling salts, and stuck it under his nose. His eyelids shot open, and he sat upright, gasping for breath. Hopefully, the red mark around his neck would soon dissipate. Tom stared at her, his face breaking out into a giant smile.

"Holy shit, Gwynn. That was one of your best ever," he said, still breathing hard.

She stared at him, trying to hide her disgust.

"You didn't leave any bruises on my face, did you?" he said, reaching up and patting his cheeks.

"Please, Tom. I'm not that careless."

"Just making sure," he said. "Did you like our game?"

"I suppose."

"You suppose?" he said. "You'd better learn to like it if you know what's good for you."

"I will. You just need to be patient with me."

"Fine, but my patience is wearing thin."

"It's just so…" She struggled to find the right words.

"Different from what we've done in the past?"

"Yes."

"They say that this kind of role-playing spices up a marriage."

"Who's they?"

"Marriage counselors. Psychologists. I don't know."

"This is dangerous behavior, Tom. I'm afraid I'm going to hurt you."

"That's the beauty of our game; we're walking right up to the edge of the cliff."

"Okay. Just give me some time to get used to it," she said.

He patted the mattress next to him, and she lay down so that he could spoon up against her. "Didn't I tell you that you'd love me again?"

"You did, but I didn't believe you at the time."

"That's because you were being a very naughty girl that day I found you screwing you-know-who in our cabin."

"That will never happen again," she said, thinking about Peters.

"Better not," he said, kissing her neck. "I was a little nervous at first, thinking you wouldn't like playing these games, but then I remembered how much you enjoy killing people."

"You don't have to do all this for me."

"Oh, I'm not." He pulled her into him. "Truth be known, I've always liked it a little rough."

"Really?" This was the first time she'd heard this. "Did you want to do this sort of thing back at Brooks?"

"I wasn't about to ask you, the girl I hoped to marry."

She remained still, feeling his belly rubbing against her backside.

"Do you remember the first question I asked you before we started dating?"

"How could I forget? You quizzed me on who I liked better in Van Halen: David Lee Roth or Sammy Hagar."

"I knew it was meant to be when you answered David Lee Roth," he said.

"Who in their right mind would date a Sammy Hagar fan?"

"Exactly," he said. "Isn't it wonderful that we can share our deepest, darkest secrets."

She didn't reply to this, fearing she might say something that might piss him off.

He massaged her neck. "But next time, I want you to go further."

"Further than we did tonight?"

"Hell yeah."

"How much more can I go without…"

"…killing me?"

Gwynn gulped.

"You know exactly how long it takes before I pass out, and then when to wake me with the smelling salts."

"Aren't you afraid that I'll go too far?"

"Like that's stopped you before."

"But you're my husband, and hurting you scares me."

"It really turns me on when you're scared," he whispered in her ear. "And if you do end up killing me, my friend will send those videos to the police, and you'll be up shit's creek."

"I love you, Tom. I would never kill you," she said with a straight face.

"I know, my little murder bug. Because if you do, you'll go away to prison and never see Jack again."

"Honey, we really need to start getting ready for the awards ceremony tonight," she said, changing the subject.

He sat up on the bed and stared down at her. His expression darkened, and his eyes glazed over. She'd seen this look on him before and knew it meant trouble.

"Why should I go? Just so you can bask in the limelight and make me look like shit?"

"What? No, you're being silly."

"I think you should stay home and help Jack with his homework," he said.

"But your sister is watching Jack tonight, and the two of them are planning to watch *Star Wars*."

"They can watch movies some other time. As you always say, his homework comes first."

"But Trish will be so disappointed if she has to bring him home."

"What my sister needs is a piece of ass."

She bristled at such coarse language. "But the people at The Loft expect me to be there tonight. I'm representing the organization."

"What's the big deal? You'll see them all at work tomorrow."

"Please, I'm begging you. This means so much to me."

"Didn't you listen to the pastor's sermon on Sunday? The husband is the head of the household. It's why I forbid you to go."

"You forbid me?" She couldn't believe her ears. Part of her wanted to grab the steak knife and slice it across his throat.

"Yes," he said, standing off the bed.

She laughed. "You can't forbid me."

"I most certainly can."

"Don't be an asshole, Tom." Tears formed in her eyes.

"Don't force me to keep Jack from you."

She fell to her knees, unable to stop the tears. Doing this made her feel weak and worthless, especially knowing what she could do to him if given the chance.

"I'll do whatever you ask, Tom. Please just let me go."

"Get up," he said, watching her stand. "Look at you. You're all skin and bones."

"I can eat more if you want," she said, knowing he'd been eating enough for the two of them.

He bit his thumbnail and appeared to think it over. "I don't care. Go to your stupid event."

"Thank you, honey. I'm so grateful."

"I have a busy day at work tomorrow, so you better be quiet when you come home."

"I swear to you that I won't make a peep."

He put his face next to hers. "Why haven't you called the handyman and gotten that closet door fixed? It still squeaks when you open it.

"I'll call him first thing in the morning. Unless you want to fix it," she said, knowing this would piss him off.

"I'm way too busy to fix things around here," he said. "You need to return home no later than eleven."

"Of course," she said, knowing he often tracked her whereabouts on his phone app. "Does that mean you're not coming?"

"That's exactly what I mean," he said. "And remember, if you come home late, there'll be a price to pay."

"I won't be late."

She hated when his mood switched so drastically from hot to cold. His whimsical and unpredictable behavior frightened her, and she never knew what Tom to expect. He now had all the leverage in their marriage and reveled in the power, using it whenever the mood struck him.

How she would truly enjoy hurting him if she knew it would end his life. But she couldn't kill him right now, and he knew it, which was why he could make her do whatever he wanted. She was mentally stronger than him. Smarter too. If it weren't for those damning videos he'd taken of her and Peters in that parking lot, trying to convince Nguyen to work with them, she would have ended his life a long time ago.

Tom stared into her eyes. She considered herself a thoroughly modern woman, educated and urbane, and dedicated to helping the children in her care. While attending Brooks, she never would have imagined her future husband to be the kind of man who enjoyed degrading women. Nor did she ever imagine that he would one day force her to reenact all the murders she'd committed—on him.

"Thank you for letting me go, Tom."

He took a few deep breaths before saying, "I will never let you go, Gwynn. I'd be lost without you."

Chapter Five

Gwynn pulled over to the side of the road to collect herself. The relief she experienced at being away from Tom, even if temporary, made her realize what a horrible marriage she'd been stuck in all these years. Rather than dwell on the negative, she took a deep breath, gave thanks for her brief moment of freedom, and pulled back on the road.

She turned on the radio and heard a Dave Matthew's song, which helped her forget about all the bad stuff that had happened. The last year with Tom had been a nightmare, like living under a fascist regime, forcing her to think about every little thing she did and said while in his presence. Tom had assumed complete control over her life and Jack's life, as well. He'd forced her to step down from the job she loved and take a lesser-paying one. It devastated her to give up the title of director and let someone else make all the decisions, but so be it.

At first, he didn't want her to work outside the home, but she begged and pleaded with him, explaining how important it was to maintain her dignity by helping the children in her care. Only when she told Tom that she'd rather kill herself than be stuck at home all day did he finally give in. His only stipulation was that she work six hours instead of her normal nine. He wanted her there in the morning before he left for work and home at night when he returned after a long day of filling out tax returns. She was not to leave The Loft's campus unless it was work-related, and he'd made her download a tracking app on her phone so he could keep tabs on her at all times. Aside from hanging out with Jack, being at work was the happiest part of her day.

Fortunately, he had no idea that she'd been writing in her spare time. Apart from her job, these stories were the only thing she did completely for herself. Oftentimes, she wrote at the kitchen island while he lounged on the sofa watching TV, ignorant as to what she was doing. Once she polished these scripts, she sent them off to Tift with no expectation that her friend would even read them. It didn't matter; writing gave her direction and purpose. It provided her with something to do in her spare time, and the only thing she could genuinely call her own.

More than anything, she wanted Tom out of her life. And yet she couldn't take action until she discovered whom he had sent that incriminating video to. Not that she hadn't been doing all she could in the last year to expedite Tom's health woes. She'd been adding more salt and trans fats to his meals, which was probably why he loved her cooking so much. And she made sure to purchase twelve-packs of his favorite beer, making sure he had a cold one in his hand as soon as he walked through the door. In the past, he complained when he noticed all the beer in the fridge, but then when he ran out, he would throw a fit, and she had to run out and buy him a six-pack at the mini mart. Recently, she'd taken to buying extra cases and hiding them in the garage, and then secretly replacing the bottles in the fridge when he was at work. She'd replaced all his blood pressure and cholesterol medicines with generic vitamins and bought cookies and chips at every opportunity, leaving the packages in places where he could easily find them. Switched from butter to margarine—the worst kind of fat—and cooked all his meals in it. Despite all that, she knew that a heart attack or stroke could take years to happen, but at least she was making a conscious effort to end his life. The problem was, she didn't have that long to wait.

She turned into the parking lot of the Italian Heritage Center. A John Mayer song came on, and it reminded her of her first 'interview' with Peters as they noshed on pizza and sipped beer. As much as she missed her previous life, she put him out of her mind and stared at herself in the rearview mirror. Everything about her screamed TOM, from her hairstyle to the wardrobe he'd picked out for her. Whatever she did these days, he found fault with. Her relationship with him felt like a debilitating sickness; she pleased him with pain and suffering, and he allowed her to remain in her son's life.

The John Mayer song ended, and the news came on. A second girl had been found along the banks of the Presumpscot River, eerily similar to the crimes her father had committed over thirty years ago. She listened to Peters talk about the murder, wishing she could meet with him to discuss these cases, even if just for a few minutes. How wonderful it would be to fall into his arms and kiss him with the same passion she did before this all went down. She desperately wanted to believe he missed her, only wishing she felt the same way about him.

While listening to Peters talk, she wondered if these two murders were the work of a copycat killer. A twisted individual who got off on killing young girls like her minister father once did. At least she'd abided by a strict code when it came to that sort of thing. When, and if, she ever killed again, and she sincerely hoped she wouldn't, she'd do it to someone wholly deserving of death.

She took out her phone and punched in Ivy's number. Instead, she got directed to Ivy's voicemail, leaving a detailed message for the girl to call her back.

The news finished just as more cars pulled into the lot. People got out, dressed to the hilt, and made their way up to the entrance. Gwynn looked at her watch, took a deep breath, and tried to muster up the courage to get out of her car. The ceremony would start in ten minutes, and now, for some reason, she felt embarrassed to go inside by herself. What would people think when she showed up without Tom? How pathetic would she look, especially if she won an award and had no one to share the moment with? If only they knew the depraved things Tom forced her to do behind closed doors, they'd understand.

Gwynn exited the vehicle and made her way toward the entrance, queuing up behind three other well-dressed couples. Trying to look invisible, she glanced down at the boring blue blazer and skirt Tom had picked out for her. He'd instructed her to tie her hair into a ponytail, not wanting her to look too sexy for the men in attendance. While waiting in line, she undid the elastic band and let her hair fall down to her shoulders.

As soon as she entered the lobby, a host handed her a name tag, which she taped to the breast of her jacket. She received instructions where to sit, walked into the main hall, and saw a jazz trio playing off to the side. Circular tables appeared throughout the hall. Gwynn moved quickly past the tables and toward the front of the room where she'd been directed to sit. Name tags appeared on the tablecloths. An elderly Asian man and his wife sat quietly next to her. Gwynn put her hands in her lap and tried not to look like a lost soul.

The table filled up quickly until only two empty seats remained. Seconds later, the emcee walked to the podium and started the night's activities. The band stopped playing, and the lights dimmed. Two people behind her pulled up to their seats. Upon turning, she saw Annabelle Grace, Portland's most beloved anchorwoman. Someone behind Annabelle pulled out her chair, and a pang of jealousy shot through her when she looked up and saw Peters standing there. She felt like sprinting out of this hall and never coming back. Peters appeared as surprised to see her as she was to see him. She smiled, fighting back the tears, and returned her attention to the speaker on the podium, trying to forget that Janet Nguyen had just woken from her coma.

How will I ever make it through this evening?

Chapter Six

I sit in the back of the Italian Heritage Center, far enough away so as not to be seen. The jazz band to my left plays a little too loudly. Thanks to my diminutive stature, it's highly doubtful she will see me here. Even more so once the lights dim.

The news of this latest dead girl worries me. It's the second body in the last three months to be found along the Presumpscot River, and it's starting to look eerily similar to the crimes committed by Gwynn's father.

I see Gwynn walking past the tables and toward the stage, and it surprises me that she's come here by herself. As usual, she looks ravishing. The last time we spoke, I came away with the impression that Tom was treating her badly, knowing all the terrible things she'd done. Did he not want to attend this event with her? Maybe he didn't want to watch her bask in the limelight. Maybe not attending this ceremony was his way of punishing her.

Gwynn makes her way to the front of the room and sits next to an elderly Asian couple.

Then I see something that surprises me. Judging from Gwynn's expression, it surprises her, too. Peters walks in with Annabelle Grace and sits at the same table as her. Gwynn nods at them before turning back around. I wonder what she's thinking, knowing that the love of her life is a seat removed from the most popular news anchor in town. Who knew that

Detective Peters, a celebrity in his own right, had been dating her?

If the ceremony hadn't already started, I'd head to the bar and order a bourbon. But I can't take my eyes off my ex-patient, especially after not seeing her for the last few months. I'd already decided that I will not be the one to initiate contact. If she's not planning on returning to therapy, I'll need to wean myself off Gwynn Denning once and for all.

Chapter Seven

GWYNN

After a lengthy and eloquent introduction, Gwynn heard the emcee at the podium present the first award to Detective Janet Nguyen. It felt as if a thunderbolt had come out of the sky and struck her in the head, especially now that Nguyen had woken from her coma. The elderly Asian couple stood from their chairs and bowed in gratitude as the crowd applauded and stood to their feet. She stood along with them and glanced uneasily at Peters, who returned her gaze with a quizzical shrug. Nguyen's parents remained standing, without expression, until the woman walked down off the stage and handed them their plaque. Once the applause died down, the presenter returned to the podium. She then proceeded to detail the incredible journey Detective Nguyen took to becoming Portland's first Vietnamese female detective.

Gwynn studied Nguyen's parents, knowing that they had no idea that their daughter's attackers were sitting at the same table with them. She experienced a brief pang of guilt while staring at them, knowing she was to blame for their daughter being in a coma. But what other choice did she have that night? It was either Nguyen's life or hers, and she had no intention of getting arrested and being separated from Jack.

When Nguyen's mother placed the plaque down on the table, Gwynn glanced at the detective's face imprinted on the brass plate. As bad as she felt about what had happened that night, it had been necessary. She recalled that car slamming into Nguyen. And then Nguyen flying through the air, landing with a sickening thud along the pavement, her body mangled beyond repair.

Annabelle's name got announced over the loudspeaker. Did she really expect Peters to remain single after she'd unceremoniously dumped him back in her family's cabin? He was a good-looking guy. Famous now, too. Was it serious between them or just a fling? Had Peters already forgotten about their passionate lovemaking by the fireplace? Or their rendezvous at the edge of that quarry?

Annabelle strolled up to the podium and began to deliver a speech so polished and funny that even she had to laugh. Speaking in public must have come easy to someone used to delivering the news each night. Not only was Annabelle beloved by her audience, but she was drop-dead gorgeous. During the speech, Gwynn turned and met Peters's gaze, and he raised his eyebrows as if helpless to do anything.

The crowd stood and applauded once Annabelle finished her speech. Annabelle stood at the podium, waving like the Maine beauty queen she'd been sixteen years ago. She clutched her plaque and flashed that plastic smile she'd patented during her many years on-air. It took Gwynn a second to realize that she was the only person still sitting, so she stood and tapped her fingers against her wrist. Once the applause died down, Annabelle returned to her seat. A murderous rage filled Gwynn as she watched Annabelle lean over and kiss Peters on the lips. Had he brought her here to make her jealous? Her mind went to a dark place, and she fantasized about luring Annabelle up to that quarry and pushing her over the edge.

She snapped out of it at the sound of a young man's voice. She stared up at him, standing at the podium, suddenly taken with his youthful good looks and smooth voice. He had wavy, dark brown hair that tapered down to smallish ears. His skin glowed a gorgeous caramel hue, and he possessed the most dazzling blue eyes she'd ever seen. A silver earring dangled from one ear, and when he smiled, it completely lit up the room. He was dressed head to toe in black: black suit jacket over black shirt buttoned all the way to the neck, and wearing Fendi sneakers. He looked to be well over six feet tall. Although he appeared almost young enough to be her son, she couldn't take her eyes off him, momentarily making her forget about Peters. She became so intrigued by him that it took her a few seconds to realize that he was talking about her. Who was this guy, and why was he talking about her in such glowing terms?

"Had this wonderful woman not interceded in my life when I was a young child, who knows if I would even be alive today. My parents were alcoholics and drug addicts, mired in a destructive lifestyle that left me to fend for myself. Gwynn happened to walk into my life when I needed her most. My father lay dying from a drug overdose, and my mother was nowhere to be found. I was five at the time, suffering from malnutrition and neglect. Most of the nurses who treated me that day believed I was much younger than I looked. I might have died in that squalid apartment if not for Gwynn. Instead, my guardian angel appeared out of nowhere and whisked me away from that dangerous situation, and eventually, I moved into a good home with loving parents. I stand here today because of this generous and giving woman, this amazing angel who has helped the lives of so many children in our city. I can't tell you how proud I am to present this award to the most deserving person I know, Gwynn Denning."

Gwynn heard the thunderous boom of applause and realized she needed to go up to the podium and receive her award. An award presented to her by the young man she'd rescued nearly sixteen years ago from his heroin addicted father. She stood, recalling the day she had entered that dilapidated apartment. The young boy had looked to be no older than three, neglected and abused, and she vividly remembered the rage that filled her upon seeing the family's living conditions. And because of that, she'd taken matters into her own hands and delivered a lethal dose of heroin to that scumbag. Not a person in this world would have blamed her. Looking at the young man now, handsome and well-spoken, she knew that she'd made the right decision.

She made her way to the podium as he held the plaque aloft for the audience to see. Then he presented it to her. She took it in hand, gazing at her profile affixed to the brass plate. Then he held his arms out, and she fell into his embrace, hearing the nonstop applause filling the room. His lips pressed against her ear, the ear facing away from the crowd.

"I know the truth about you, Gwynn Denning. You murdered my father."

Chapter Eight

GWYNN

Dinner arrived, but Gwynn had no appetite. Servers brought out platters of chicken parm, baked rigatoni, meatballs, and glistening salads in wooden parquet bowls. She made herself a small plate as the platters got passed around and then proceeded to push the food from one side of her plate to the other, thinking about what that young man had whispered to her while onstage. Every so often, she glanced at him, sitting two tables away, and wondered what he wanted from her.

Had he actually remembered her injecting heroin into her father's veins? Although he looked to be three at the time, he was actually five when it happened, old enough to make lasting memories.

She learned that his name was Callum Frye and that he'd taken his adopted parents' last name. Despite Peters sitting next to her and Detective Nguyen's parents sitting quietly to her right, she couldn't take her eyes off him. At one point during the meal, while he held forth with some guests seated around him, she glanced over, and their eyes met. He stopped talking and smiled, causing her to look away in embarrassment.

"That was such a beautiful introduction," Annabelle said to Gwynn. "It must feel wonderful knowing you saved that boy's life."

"I only did what anyone else would have done."

"You're too modest," Annabelle said, touching her forearm. "As a reporter, I've always believed that the best stories are the ones that make people feel good."

"I couldn't agree more," Gwynn said. "So how long have you two been an item?"

Annabelle grabbed Peters's hand. "How long has it been since we started dating, hon? Three months now?"

"Yeah, that sounds about right," Peters said, averting her gaze.

"I can't believe I'm sitting next to two bona fide celebrities," Gwynn said. "And two celebrities who are dating each other."

"Our personal histories didn't matter when we met. It was love at first sight," Annabelle said, lifting Peters's hand and kissing it. "Not only is he the cutest cop in town, but he's the sweetest and most caring man I've ever known. I'm one lucky gal."

"I'll say," she said, looking over at Peters. "Life must have really changed when you solved that Muddy River case."

He stared at her. "You could say that."

"How in the world did you solve it all by yourself, Detective?"

"A lot of hard work with a little luck thrown in for good measure."

"Sometimes it's better to be lucky than smart," Gwynn said, her eyes shooting a laser beam through him.

Peters took a sip of his water.

"I imagine there'll be many long nights now that this copycat killer is on the loose."

Annabelle turned toward Gwynn. "It's only two girls at this point. It could just be a coincidence."

"Could be, but I doubt it," Gwynn said, turning to Nguyen's elderly parents.

"Your daughter is an amazing woman, Mr. and Mrs. Nguyen. I'm sure she'll recover quickly now that she's woken from her coma," she said, knowing that would be the worst outcome for her.

"We pray every day that she gets better," Mrs. Nguyen said. "That is the most important thing to us right now."

"Yes, that it *is* the most important thing," she said, patting the woman's wrinkled hand.

Annabelle stood and made her way to another table to schmooze. Gwynn watched the woman, hoping she might trip and fall on her face. A few admirers came over to Peters and shook his hand, asking for an autograph, and he obliged with a quick scribble. She mouthed for him to meet her out back when he got the chance. After standing, she moved past all the tables, receiving congratulations and accolades as she passed, until she arrived at the rear of the facility. A few minutes passed before Peters made his way to the back of the hall. Nodding for him to follow, she turned and made her way down to the basement. Seconds later, he appeared. She opened one of the doors and let him in. Used kitchen equipment sat on tables all around them. As soon as the door closed, he rushed over and kissed her on the lips.

"Annabelle? For real?" Gwynn said.

"She means nothing to me," Peters said. "You don't know how much I've missed you."

"You're just saying that."

"I swear to you I'm not," he said, caressing her cheek.

She walked away from him and stood next to an industrial coffee urn, trying not to act like a jealous girlfriend, especially since she wasn't even sure how she felt about him.

"I read in the newspaper about your father passing, Gwynn. I'm sorry."

"Thanks," she said. "I left a few important details out of his obituary."

"So I noticed."

"No one deserves to live the rest of their life like that."

He walked over to her and reached for her hand. "I wish we could stay like this forever."

"Well, we can't. Not until we find that video Tom made of us in that parking lot with Nguyen."

"Don't worry, we will."

"We have no other choice or else go to prison, especially now that she's woken from her coma."

"I despise that husband of yours. If there was only a way you could dump his ass, then we could finally be together."

"I can't just yet."

"I know, but it's a nice thought."

"Is it serious between you and Annabelle?"

"It may be for her, but not for me."

"Then why are you with her?"

"I'm a grown man, Gwynn. You can't expect me not to see other women, especially when you so unceremoniously dumped me back at that cabin."

"You know why I had to do that."

"Maybe so, but I still have needs."

"You men are all alike."

"That's not true. I'd give anything to be back with you."

"Once we find out who Tom sent those videos to, we can start considering our options. But until that time comes, we need to stay away from each other."

"Is that asshole mistreating you? Because if he is—"

"If he is, what? What are you going to do about it?" She laughed.

"I'm going to make him pay."

"Easy, killer. We both know you're not built for that sort of thing."

"Don't be so sure. I'll do anything to get you back in my life."

"Looks like you'll be too busy searching for this new killer."

He stared down at her. "This case is proving more difficult than I expected. Is there any way you can help me with it?"

"Just because I know a thing or two about murder?"

"Maybe I just want to see you on a more regular basis."

Gwynn pushed away from him and walked around the room, running her hand over all the equipment. "Can you believe Nguyen's parents were sitting at the same table as us?"

"What are the odds they would be at the same event? Or that the committee would actually give that miserable woman an award?"

"It concerns me that she woke from that coma," she said. "What if she starts talking?"

"If only Nguyen would drop dead, it would make our lives so much easier."

"As a mother, I do feel sorry for her parents."

"Okay, but they have no idea what a backstabbing bitch she is."

"The longer she stays quiet, the better our chances are of staying out of trouble," she said, returning to Peters's side.

"I've got to get back to my table, or else Annabelle might suspect something," he said, kissing her one last time.

"Is she the jealous type?"

"Oh yeah. The poor girl is going to be heartbroken when I break up with her."

"Good luck with that."

"Wait a few minutes before you head upstairs," he said.

"Give me your phone number," she said, taking her throwaway phone out of her purse.

He told her the number, and she called it.

"This is my new burner phone. Call me, but only if it's an emergency. And never at night or on the weekend."

"Okay."

He kissed her and left the room. She paced back and forth among the used kitchen equipment, thinking about all that had transpired in the last twenty-four hours. After a few minutes, she headed upstairs, slipping anonymously back into the crowd. Rather than return to her table, she headed to the bar and ordered a glass of Chablis. An elderly gentleman congratulated her on winning her award and picked up the tab for her drink. She thanked him and left the bar. With glass in hand, she stood at the back of the room until she caught sight of him.

Portland was a small town, but how many surprises could this night hold? Did Kaufman come to this event because of her? He had many friends in Portland. Should she go over and say hello? But then she decided against it. He knew she was here. He'd seen Callum speak, and then had watched as she received her award. If he wanted to come over to her table and pay his respects, then that was up to him. But watching him now, she felt a twinge of regret. And she missed her weekly therapy sessions. If only she could return to his office and pour her heart out to him, she'd do it in a heartbeat.

"You look lovely tonight," someone next to her said.

She turned and saw Callum Frye standing next to her, and suddenly the words he whispered in her ear came rushing back.

"That was a lovely introduction. Thank you so much."

"You really liked it?"

"It was far better than I deserved."

"I meant every word of it, even what I said to you afterward."

"Might you have been mistaken about what you saw that day? After all, you were only five at the time."

"Oh no, I remember it like it was yesterday." He leaned down and whispered in her ear, "You killed my father."

"It was meant to be merciful," she said, looking around to see if anyone could hear them.

"For me or for him?"

"Both," she said.

"Seemed like you knew exactly what you were doing. And you did it with a smile on your face."

"Do you really think I was going to let CPS put you back in that house with those two monsters?"

"We need to meet sometime and talk about what happened. Here is not the place."

"What is there to talk about? I saved your life, and you turned out to be an amazing young man. I'm not asking you for anything in return."

Callum shook his head. "I'd hate to tell everyone what really happened that day."

Gwynn laughed. "I doubt anyone would believe you."

"Maybe. Maybe not. But then, when I bring up that high school teacher who fell to his death, they might reconsider. Or that Boston man who disappeared last year. Didn't he attend the same corporate event you and Sandra Clayborn were at?"

She stared into his eyes, wondering how he knew all this.

"I have no intention of making any of this known, Gwynn. All I'm asking is that we sit down and talk."

She laughed. "You're a real piece of work, Frye."

"Believe me, I know."

She sized him up. "Okay, it looks like you and I will be having a friendly chat."

"Be seeing you soon," he said, handing her his business card before walking away.

Gwynn returned to her table and saw that the Nguyens had taken their plaque and gone home. Annabelle snuggled up next to Peters, staring at him like a puppy dog as he talked to the person seated next to him. On the other side of the room, Kaufman stood conferring with the elderly man who had paid for her drink. Rather than stay, she bid everyone goodnight and headed for the exit. She downed the rest of her Chablis in one swallow and left the empty glass on the bar. Then she sprinted to her car, got in it, and sped home, planning to arrive well before Tom's curfew.

She slipped quietly into the house so as not to wake him. Made her way upstairs and into the bedroom and saw Tom sitting back against the headboard, watching TV with a family-sized bag of chips resting on his belly. Crumbs dotted his chest. She'd hoped he would be asleep by now, and she could forego any conflict, but she wouldn't get off so easy.

"How was your awards thingy?" he asked without taking his eyes off the screen.

"Okay."

"Just okay?"

"Nothing special."

"Oh, nothing special, huh?"

He turned and glared at her. "You lying bitch. Give me that thing."

She walked over and handed him the plaque. On the nightstand next to Tom sat a half-empty bottle of scotch. He flung the plaque across the room, and it landed with a crash against the dresser before resting on the floor.

"I'll be tossing that in the trash come morning."

"What's wrong, Tom? I did exactly as you said and came right home."

"Big deal. You want another award?"

"I thought you'd be pleased with me."

"Pleased? You didn't tell me that *he* was going to be there."

"Who?"

"Who do you think? That corrupt pig you were fucking behind my back."

A shudder of fear passed through her. How did Tom know about that?

"It was on the news, dumbass. The fucker was sitting next to you and that hot news anchor the entire time."

"I had no idea he would be there. Swear to God."

"Is that why you let your hair down? To look all sexy for him."

She knew she'd been caught.

Tom pointed his finger at her. "You want to kill me now, don't you? I can see it in your eyes."

"No, Tom. I don't want to kill you."

"The hell you don't." He placed the bag of chips down, stood off the bed, and put his face close enough to hers so that she could smell the scotch on his breath. "Admit it. You'd like nothing more than to wrap that plastic bag around my head and finish me off, just like you did with that Townsend guy. That way, you could be with your cop friend."

"You're drunk and acting crazy."

"I may be drunk, but I'm not crazy. Maybe crazy in thinking I could be a good husband and make you happy."

She started toward the bed, but he held his arm out, preventing her from moving.

"I should have released that video months ago and let the two of you lovebirds rot in prison. That way you'd never get to see Jack again."

Gwynn tensed. "You do that, and I'll kill you for real."

"Is that a threat?"

"Don't push me, Tom. You know Jack means the world to me."

He ogled her, whiskey dribbling down the side of his mouth. "Think you can keep me alive the next time we play? Or are you going to make your son an orphan?"

"As long as you play fair and keep your word."

"Like you did when I found you cheating on me in our cabin? How fair was that?"

"I made a mistake, but I swear it won't happen again."

"We'll see about that." He pushed her away. "Now get in bed and don't make a peep. I've got a busy day tomorrow."

"I won't."

"Trish is more than happy to take Jack for a few days if you piss me off."

"I'll do whatever you want, Tom. Just don't take our son from me."

Tom turned and staggered back to the bed.

Relieved, she lay down and disappeared under the blanket, hoping he wouldn't spoon her. She'd do just about anything to keep her son in her life, even if it meant following Tom's crazy rules.

Chapter Nine

Gwynn struggled to keep her eyes open as she sat at her desk. The computer screen appeared fuzzy in her vision, and she found it difficult to concentrate, especially after that bizarre encounter with Callum Frye last night. What did he want from her? Simply to give thanks for rescuing him from the two monsters who brought him into this world?

Her back ached from spending all night curled up and away from Tom. His snoring proved deafening, and he had an annoying habit of spreading out over the bed. The next morning, she had to set out his clothes and prepare his coffee and breakfast the way he liked. It pained her to be nice to him after his drunken behavior the previous night. But it pained her even more when he treated her with kindness and respect. The Jekyll and Hyde nature of his behavior left her constantly on edge, and she never knew from one moment to the next which Tom she would be dealing with. She'd have much preferred him to stay in character and be an asshole twenty-four seven. At least that way it would be easier to hate him.

Since stepping down as The Loft's director, per her agreement with Tom, she'd accepted a part-time position as assistant to the manager. She now worked twenty hours a week so she could be home for her family. But she missed her old job and her old office, located two doors down from the small office she now occupied. She missed all the space she once had and the massive windows that let in the early morning light. The responsibilities of the new job paled in comparison to her old one, and she often found herself with large swathes of free time on her hands. Time for writing stories and wondering if Tift liked them or not. She'd also been trying to figure out who possessed the videos that put her and Peters at the scene of Nguyen's 'accident'.

Besides Jack and the children at The Loft, the stories she'd been sending to Tift were the only thing keeping her sane. There was something to be said for the therapeutic effects of writing. And Tift encouraged her to keep sending them. She'd written many stories and plays during her years at Brooks, and they'd obviously left a mark on her old college roommate. For all she knew, Tift had been tossing her work in the trash whenever she received them. Yet she continued to write them, day after day, more for her own benefit than anything else.

While she liked Tift and respected her talent as an actress, she had no illusions about her friend's sincerity. Tift had been a drama queen in college, always wanting to be the center of attention. She often believed that her friend acted this way for her own benefit. She'd perfected the dumb blonde to a tee, and her various personalities were like characters in her movies, all designed to achieve a desired outcome.

Why had she still maintained a friendship with her old college roommate, knowing that this friendship was in part what had led her down this rocky path? Had Gwynn ended up rooming with someone else her freshman year, Townsend might still be alive today. As would Sandra and her husband. Maybe she wouldn't even have murdered her biological mother. Surely, Nguyen wouldn't have ended up in a coma. Everything, it seemed, had emanated from Tift's singular encounter with Sam Townsend that fateful night at Brooks. Aside from how it had affected her marriage, Gwynn never regretted killing that scumbag. She had no doubt he'd assaulted Tift while on their date. Or at least she kept telling herself this. And yet his death had scratched that deep existential itch that had nagged her ever since she was a little girl.

Tift had texted her earlier this week, saying she needed to chat with her this morning. She took a break and sipped her coffee. What in the world could Tift want? Hopefully, it was not another request to visit her out in LA. Tom would never allow it. Not just because he wanted to keep her under his thumb, but because he hated Tift and always talked badly about her. She thought that Tom hated Tift more than anyone she knew. But why? For a while back in college, they'd appeared to be on friendly terms. Maybe Tom and Tift had been competing for her attention.

So many lies and secrets seemed to be hidden from her. Gwynn thought about Tom and his predilection for rough sex. How long had he been wanting to do such twisted and sick things? This obsession of his couldn't have developed overnight. He must have desired this for years, similar to the way she'd been forced to keep her own secrets hidden—until he eventually found out about her penchant for murder. She thought it perverted of him to take such pleasure from pain, but no more depraved than her own desire to kill.

The irony of their evolving relationship never ceased to amaze her. It would almost be funny if she weren't so miserable ALL. THE. TIME. And yet the chains of oppression rarely, if ever, subsided but for the few hours a day she came to the office to work. How long would she have to live in this draconian marriage? Following his harsh rules? Pleasuring him with both pain and simulated acts of murder? At some point, when Jack got older, she feared her son might catch them in the act. If that happened, she might actually have to kill Tom. Not a day went by when she didn't fantasize about killing him. It was one of the few things that gave her any pleasure. And yet the thought of never seeing Jack again was all the incentive she needed to keep him alive.

Seeing Kaufman at the awards ceremony made her miss him more than she realized. Why hadn't he congratulated her on winning? Had he washed his hands of her once and for all and moved on in life? Was he really prepared to move forward, knowing all the grisly murders she'd committed in the name of justice? She badly wanted to tell him about her twisted marriage to Tom and all the terrible things he'd been forcing her to do.

A knock on the door startled her out of her thoughts. She gazed up and saw The Loft's new director, Denise, who started working here a week ago after a nationwide search. Today was her first real day on the job, seeing as how she'd been required to attend various training sessions before starting. But from the moment they'd met, Denise had taken a visceral dislike of her. Despite Gwynn's seven successful years as director, Denise treated her like a lowly staff member. Maybe they'd just gotten off to a bad start, but Gwynn suspected that Denise harbored some underlying resentment toward her for preceding her in the job. Jealousy? Maybe. Hopefully, they could work everything out going forward, especially since she had no desire to ever be The Loft's director again.

"Good morning," Denise said.

"Morning."

"What are you working on?"

"I'm filling out an intake report on a potential client. Do you need something?"

Denise took a few steps into her office. "I was going over the books this morning and noticed that this place was way over budget last year."

Gwynn smiled at this subtle dig. "We had some unexpected costs last year, including a new roof at the Atlas House and some electrical issues that needed immediate repair."

"All the same, I'll be performing a comprehensive audit of the program and going through every penny this organization has spent."

"Sounds good."

"I'm also trying to raise additional funds so we can update the facilities and get them up to code. That way, we can make sure cost overruns never again hamper our mission."

"Great," she said, waiting for the next ball to drop.

"I've also written up some guidelines for staff to follow."

"Such as?"

"Every employee will be mandated to keep a logbook and record their hours and what they've been working on."

"Record our hours?" Gwynn laughed. "We're not a law firm, Denise. We don't bill out every minute of our day. We work with children."

"Good record keeping is the most efficient way to keep employees on task and be accountable for their performance." Denise crossed her arms. "The culture here at The Loft needs to change."

"You do realize that I ran this place for seven years?"

"I'm well aware of that."

Gwynn stared at her new boss.

"I asked the board to hire someone full-time for your position, but for whatever reason, they insisted that you fill it."

"I'm more than qualified for this job."

"There's a lot of work that needs to be done here, and a part-time assistant just isn't going to cut it."

She tried to remain calm and not say anything she might regret. "I just want to do my job and help these kids the best I can."

"Good to hear." Denise walked back toward the door and grabbed the knob. "One of my other priorities will be to hire more staff."

"Fantastic. It was also one of my goals as director."

"It's something that should have happened a long time ago."

How much more of this could she take? "Finding good employees—any employees at all—is extremely challenging in this job market," Gwynn said.

"I understand, but we need to do a much better job recruiting in the neighborhoods we serve."

"I couldn't agree more."

"Many of the children in our care come from marginalized backgrounds. For that reason, I want to make sure that they have people here they can relate to."

"Understood."

"Implementation of these programs should be your number one goal from here on out."

"Look, Denise, I have no desire to be the director of The Loft again, if that's what you're worried about. I'm here to help you in any way I can, so you don't need to feel threatened by me."

"Threatened by you?" She laughed. "That'll be the day."

"I'm just saying."

"I want these programs up and running by the end of the month."

"Okay, I'll get started on them immediately."

Denise stood in the doorway. "I'm glad we had this talk."

Gwynn's cell phone rang, saving her from further humiliation.

"If you'll excuse me, I really have to take this call."

Denise turned and walked away.

Gwynn glanced down at her phone, visibly shaken from the encounter. Would her relationship with Denise always be this contentious? She knew she couldn't quit this job just yet; Tom would never allow her to get another. He'd insist she stay home and be a dutiful housewife and mother. Besides, no other job would allow her to work such flexible and accommodating hours. And with children she loved and cared for. This job had been her only saving grace, and now it appeared that her new boss would be making everything more difficult for her. Maybe Denise was trying to get her to quit. If she wanted to stay at The Loft, she'd need to toe the line, no matter how compassionate and qualified she believed herself to be.

Her phone pinged. It was a text message from Ivy, the girl who used to live at The Loft.

Ivy: Hey u. I'm no longer living at home. Needed to get away from those crazy parents of mine.

Gwynn: I'd like to see you, Ivy. Can we meet tomorrow morning and talk?

Ivy: Sure. Not too early tho. I like 2 sleep n. Let's meet somewhere near the teen shelter.

Gwynn messaged her back, and they agreed to meet tomorrow at a coffee shop on Cumberland Avenue. If Tom discovered that she'd left the office, it could possibly set him off. But she could handle Tom, within reason. There were times when she had to leave the campus and meet with a client. On the other hand, Denise might be more problematic. Her new boss wanted to know what she was up to every second of the day. Make her log everything she did while on the job. She had no doubt that Denise would be riding her like Elizabeth Taylor on National Velvet. A dictator at home. And now a dictator at work. What more could go wrong?

Chapter Ten

Gwynn slipped out of the office the next morning and drove over to Cumberland Ave. The further down the street she traveled, the more homeless kids she saw loitering about. It left a bad feeling in the pit of her stomach. Ivy was barely sixteen, a runaway, and she feared for the girl's safety out on the streets where violent predators and sex traffickers lurked around every corner. And now, quite possibly, another serial killer.

She parked on a narrow side street and walked around the corner to the coffee shop. Three homeless people shuffled past her. Up ahead, she saw some girls standing on the sidewalk and smoking cigarettes. Below one of them sat a ratty dog with a red bandanna around its neck. Although teenagers, they hadn't yet possessed the look of chronic drug addicts. Almost immediately, she saw Ivy waving at her, her long hair dyed to a shimmering platinum. She looked thinner and had grown a few inches since the last time she'd seen her. It always amazed her how fast these kids grew up, and she often wondered what her own son would look like when he became a teenager. Would Jack be tall or short? Thin or husky? The closer she got to the girl, the more she noticed signs of neglect: the yellow pallor of her skin and the weight loss due to self-neglect. There were blotches over her once smooth face, and her eyes had that vacant look of someone who'd been using.

"You made it," Ivy said, hugging her.

"Of course, I made it. I wouldn't miss seeing you for the world," she said, feeling the girl's spine beneath her shirt. "Let's go inside and get something to eat."

They walked into the café, and Ivy ordered a sugary iced coffee and a pastry. Gwynn ordered a coffee. Once seated, Ivy began to wolf down the sticky bun on her plate, licking the frosting off her fingers.

"Someone is hungry."

"Dude, I haven't eaten since yesterday."

"Enjoy, then."

"Me and my homies love this place," she said, now looking like a young girl. "Sometimes they give us free leftovers."

"That's nice of them."

"Especially since the food at the teen shelter sucks."

"Is that where you've been staying?"

"For the time being." Ivy shrugged. "When I'm not couch surfing."

"What prompted you to leave home?" As if she had to ask.

Ivy sipped her drink, broke off another gooey layer of sticky bun, and stuffed it in her mouth. "Take a wild guess."

"Your father?"

"You're pretty smart for a social worker." She pointed a half-painted nail at her. "You shoulda been a detective."

"Did he hurt you?"

"He'll never stop hurting me, even when he's dead and buried." Ivy averted her eyes and stared out the window. "But I don't want to talk about that right now."

"Okay." Gwynn sipped her coffee. "What are you doing to support yourself?"

"What's with all the questions today? Can't we just hang?"

"I'm just concerned about you, is all."

"Well, don't be. I'm perfectly fine. It's all these other dumbass kids out here who really need the help."

"Who are you referring to?"

"I saw on the news this morning that the cops identified the girl they found down by the river. Her name was TammyRae."

"You knew her?"

"Of course, I knew her. Every kid on the street knew TammyRae."

"What was she like?"

"A complete psycho. Girl'd go off with anyone if it would get her some smack."

"She prostituted herself?"

Ivy laughed. "You make it sound so…official."

"You don't do that sort of thing, do you?"

"Turn tricks?" She smiled. "Why? Would you hate me if I did?"

"You know I could never hate you, Ivy, but I'd feel much better knowing you weren't engaging in such risky behavior."

"You were always my favorite staff member at The Loft. I loved you more than you know. But then I realized there's a limit to how much someone will love you back."

"I've always tried to be there for you as best I could."

"That's true, but you were getting paid to help me. At the end of the day, it was your job, and then you went home to your family and forgot about screwups like me."

"Believe me, I never forgot about you. Not for one second."

Ivy wedged a piece of sticky bun in her mouth and stared down at the table. "But you never would have considered taking in a kid like me. And I don't blame you. I wouldn't adopt a creep like me, either."

"I would if I could, Ivy, but I'm dealing with my own issues right now."

"What issues could you have?"

"Too many to mention."

"Which is more reason why I have to look after myself."

"Just be careful out there."

"Don't you worry about me," she said, wiping her fingers on a napkin. "Remember that day when we were standing on the playground, and I told you I felt like killing everyone around me?"

Gwynn nodded.

"Remember what you said to me?"

"I said that I often felt that way when I was a kid."

"Yup. And that helped me more than you know."

"I'm happy I could help."

"I still feel that way about my father, but the feelings are not as bad as they used to be."

"I'm glad to hear that, too."

"Don't get me wrong. There are times when I still feel like killing the asshole."

"He should be in prison for all the things he did to you and your family."

"Yeah, he should be, but we both know that's never gonna happen."

She sipped her coffee, thinking about what she would like to do to Ivy's father, given the chance.

"I can tell you one thing: there's no way I'm ever going back to that house while he's still there. I'd rather live on the streets than be around him."

"Can't say I blame you."

"And if I did return home, I'd most likely end up on the streets, anyway. Or in prison."

"We certainly can't let that happen." Gwynn reached into her pocketbook, pulled out a wad of cash, and handed it to her. "Take this and put it to good use."

The girl snatched it out of her hand without even a thank you.

"Did you happen to see TammyRae before she disappeared?"

"No, but my homey did. Said she saw her get into some dude's car. No one saw her again after that."

"Did your friend tell the police about it?"

"Hell no. The po-po would only return her home, or else try to put her in foster care. Better to live on the streets and do our thang."

"Did your friend recognize the car or write down the license plate number?"

"Hell no." Ivy began to tear the napkin into strips and place them down on the table so that the formation resembled a ladder. "You think the guy who picked her up was the same dude who killed her?"

"It's possible." Gwynn grabbed the girl's free hand. "Please be careful out there, Ivy. I'm begging you."

"Why do you care about me so much?"

"I don't know. I just do."

"You should worry more about yourself, Gwynn. You don't look too good right now."

"As I told you, I've been dealing with some issues."

"Not giving the hubby enough loving?" She laughed. "It's why all these old pervs keep coming around here and handing us money. To get some of what their old lady ain't giving them at home."

"You're better than that, Ivy."

Ivy grabbed her coffee and stood. "You don't know me well enough to say that."

"You're right. I don't. And I'm sorry."

"I've always looked up to you, Gwynn, but you should probably look in the mirror before you start judging others," the girl said before storming out of the coffee shop.

Gwynn felt terrible. More than anything, she wished she could track down Ivy's father and make him pay for all the terrible things he did to his daughter. And maybe someday she would. But not today. Not when her own life was falling apart.

It occurred to her that she should pay Dr. Kaufman a visit and get her head straightened out. But how? She'd practically written him off the last time they parted ways. He must be really upset with her if he hadn't even bothered to come over and say hello to her at that awards ceremony. But he did say to come see him whenever she felt the need.

She knew one thing. The next chapter in her life would begin once she was free from Tom. Whether that be by death or divorce had yet to be determined, but she couldn't go on living this way. And she saw no other way out of her troubled marriage until she found those videos he'd taken of her and Peters. Then she would destroy them and make plans for her husband to disappear.

Chapter Eleven

DETECTIVE PETERS

Peters heard the girl's name announced over the news the next morning as he sat in his waterfront condo, sipping his coffee. TammyRae Lynn. Seventeen, a habitual wild child and troubled soul. She'd been living on the streets and turning tricks for the last year now to support her habit. Now he had to go into the station and 'investigate' this most recent murder, and he found himself eager to do so. Killing those girls made him feel important again. And relevant. More importantly, it would help him get back together with Gwynn.

He thought back to the Muddy River Killer case. Solving those murders was the greatest thing that had ever happened to him, even if he hadn't really solved them. It had bolstered his reputation in the department and made him a star, allowing him to move out of that ratty apartment on St. John Street and put a down payment on this sleek, modern condo on the waterfront. But lately his old bad habits had been creeping back into his life: gambling, drinking, yearning for Gwynn. Now he could add murder to that list.

He showered and dressed, happy that he hadn't stayed over Annabelle's last night. Seeing Gwynn the other night, and feeling his love for her, he couldn't possibly have had sex with Annabelle. Just thinking about her now brought him back to that day when she'd taken him to the quarry near her camp, tugged down his trousers, and pleasured him as he stood perilously on that cliff. And all the while, he had wondered if she'd push him over the edge.

That kiss in the basement of the Italian Heritage Center had sealed the deal. Now he knew for sure that she still loved him. How could he possibly continue dating Annabelle after that, knowing Gwynn was willing to help him solve these murders? It was the reason he'd decided to break up with Annabelle. She'd be heartbroken when he uttered the dreaded words, but so be it.

He walked into the police station, his shoulders held high. Although most of the staff and fellow officers treated him civilly, he knew they resented him for solving the Muddy River murders.

"Did you hear the news?" Officer Romano said, one of the few cops on the force who still remained friends with him. He often wondered if she had a crush on him or if she was just being nice.

"Yeah, Nguyen woke from her coma."

"Not that news. The news about what the divers found?"

"What divers?"

"William Clayborn's parents hired a team of deep-sea divers to search the bay where Sandra went missing."

"Why would they do that?"

"Supposedly, they were upset that William's name got dragged through the mud. They never believed he killed his wife and went on the lam."

"Why hadn't I heard about this?"

"They kept it all hush-hush, afraid of the bad publicity that might come their way if people found out what they did."

"So what did the divers find?"

"Sandra's boot, which was part of her wetsuit. And here's where it gets interesting. There was a section of rope tied to the loop on the heel."

"Wow. And they concluded from this that it belonged to Sandra?"

"One hundred percent. Same design and everything."

"That means Sandra was definitely murdered. And most likely by William."

"Oh yeah," she said a little too cheerfully. "All that money spent on divers, and it ended up backfiring on them. You were right again, Detective. William Clayborn definitely drowned his wife and fled the state."

"Finally, someone believes me," he said with a straight face, knowing Gwynn was in the clear now.

"I always did."

"Thanks, Romano."

"Everyone else will now believe you. Too bad you got your hands full with this copycat killer."

"We're not sure yet if it's a copycat, but between you and me, it sure looks that way," he said before walking away.

No sooner did he get to his desk than he realized that nothing would be accomplished with him sitting around and thinking about how he would break up with Annabelle. He would need to let her down easy. But if she decided to badmouth him in public, it could make his life more miserable than it already was.

He stared down at his cluttered desk, knowing he'd been offered a choicer one since solving those murders, but he didn't want to jinx his run of good luck. Besides, staring at Nguyen's empty desk kept him on his toes and reminded him of what was at stake. He needed to do everything in his power to shore up his name in the public's eye in the unlikely, and catastrophic, event that Nguyen regained her memory and started spilling the beans.

His phone chirped. He looked down and saw a text message from someone he'd hoped to never hear from again. Ruby wanted to meet him in a dive bar two streets up from the Preble Resource Center. After five minutes of procrastinating, he got up and headed toward the exit.

He made his way to the garage until he arrived at his car and drove the short distance to the Bayside. As soon as he walked into the bar, he saw her sitting in a booth in the back. She looked much worse than the last time he'd seen her, when he'd made that proposition to her less than a year ago. Her teeth were discolored and chipped, and the skin over her face was covered with sores. He should have been grateful that she'd lied under oath and testified against Sam Lazzara in court, but he'd had a feeling that it would someday come back to bite him in the ass—and now that time had come.

"How you been, Mikey?"

"Can't complain, Ruby. Who'd listen?"

"Not this ho."

"Exactly."

"Bet you ain't complaining about all the fame and fortune been coming your way."

"Trust me, I'm not that famous or fortunate."

"Could have fooled me."

The waitress appeared and stood over them.

"Double Jack," Ruby ordered. "My boy here's picking up the tab."

Peters ordered a root beer and thought about the money he owed his bookie.

"Thought you'd at least check in on me from time to time, Mikey, seeing as how I did you a solid. But I know you got other important matters to deal with these days, especially with this new creep on the street killing young girls."

"Glad you're keeping up on current events."

"Sure, I seen how busy you been getting on TV and such." She downed half her drink in one gulp and then wiped her nose with a napkin.

"Can't hold it against a guy for bettering himself."

"Hell no. Don't blame you for that one bit," Ruby said, flagging down the waitress. "American way, right?"

"Exactly."

"In fact, that's the reason I called you here."

He laughed, knowing what was coming next.

She knocked back the rest of her drink and, when the waitress arrived, said, "Another one of these, doll."

"So why'd you call me here, Ruby?" he said.

"I got to thinking. You should be spreading the wealth around for the way I helped you out with that case. Wasn't for old Ruby here, you never woulda put ole Vinny away. Or been able to buy that expensive pad on the water."

"We paid you two thousand bucks."

"We? You mean you in cahoots with someone?" She laughed and took her second drink from the waitress. "Hate to tell the judge that I made all that stuff up about Vinny on account you paid me."

"Come on, Ruby. We both know that Lazzara killed those girls."

"I don't know shit, Jack. I told the judge exactly what you paid me to tell him."

"We didn't have enough evidence to convict him without your testimony, but everyone knew he did it."

"Can't blame a woman for bettering herself." Ruby laughed. "And I'm sure that news lady you're all hot and bothered over would love to learn that Vinny's an innocent man, and that the real killer's still out there—maybe even still killing."

"No offense, Ruby, but you think anyone's gonna believe a junkie whore like you?"

"I suppose we gonna find out, then, huh, Mr. Bigshot Detective."

"How much you want to keep your mouth shut?"

"Five Gs plus a date thrown in for good measure."

He cringed at the thought of a 'date' with this woman. "Five Gs? Are you out of your mind?"

"Like the car salesman says, take it or leave it."

He sipped his root beer and thought about it. It was not like he didn't have the money. He had some savings left, even if his account was rapidly dwindling. And he'd earn a lot more if that documentary about the Muddy River killer got green-lighted. But with someone like Ruby, the blackmail would never stop. And the stakes would keep getting higher and higher for as long as she lived, although, judging by the looks of her, her days seem numbered. Still, he couldn't afford to let her go public with this information.

"Need a few more minutes to think about it?"

"When do you want the money?"

"Soon as possible, sugar."

"Gimme a few days, and I'll have it for you."

"What's the holdup? You got to cash out some stocks and bonds, Mikey?"

"Something like that."

"Okay, I'll give you two days."

"You're not going to keep blackmailing me, are you?"

"Blackmail? Oh no, Mikey, you got it all wrong. What we have is a business proposition. Capitalism at its best."

"We all good after this?"

"We good as gold, homes." She downed the rest of her drink and stood. "Best of luck catching this new killer. You don't find your man, let me know, and I just might be able to help you again—for the right price."

He watched Ruby saunter out of the bar, half tempted to knock back a few shots himself before heading back to the office. Instead, he pulled out his phone and made a call.

"Hey, Gwynn. I know you said not to call you unless it was an emergency, but it looks like we have another situation on our hands."

Chapter Twelve

GWYNN

After receiving the call from Peters, Gwynn couldn't concentrate on her work. She worried about Ivy living on the street. She worried about all these new work rules and regulations that would make her job more difficult. Helping children was the reason she got into this profession, and she refused to sit at a desk all day and be a paper pusher.

Now she had this old prostitute to worry about. Peters had the money and could pay her off, thanks to what she had done for him. Let him deal with her.

A staff member walked in while she contemplated all this and said that Denise had been looking for her. Great. It appeared that she and her new boss would be squaring off once again.

The little money she'd inherited from her father's estate had gone right into her and Tom's joint bank account, and now Tom controlled all of it. He provided her with a measly allowance that made her feel like an indentured slave. If only she could find another revenue source, she could sock away some money for her future. But that didn't seem possible, especially when Tom monitored every penny she spent.

Her mind spun like a roulette wheel. Where would it stop? Ivy? Denise? That mysterious young man she rescued as a young boy? Now she had this new obstacle with the prostitute? She couldn't afford to let the woman talk and ruin her well-thought-out plan. Her father was dead and buried, his name unsullied by the terrible things he did, and she hoped to keep all that hidden. No way she wanted to burden Jack with that ancestral baggage.

Her phone chimed. She answered and was surprised to hear Tift's voice. With all these problems stacking up, the thought of listening to her old roommate complain about her glamorous life was the last thing she wanted to hear right now.

"How are you, girlfriend?"

"Fine, Tift, but I'm really busy at the moment."

"I know you're keen on making the world a better place, but there are other ways you can do good without having to slave away nine to five."

"Not everyone has your fat bank account. Some of us have to work for a living."

"That's why I'm calling. I have some exciting news to tell you."

Gwynn couldn't handle any more of Tift's exciting news after all she'd been through in the last year. It often felt as if her friend was continually rubbing her success in her face.

"What amazing thing has happened to you now?"

"Not just to me, Gwynn. To us. And by us, I mean you and me," she said. "The producers loved the work you've been sending me so much so that we've been secretly shooting the first episode."

Her mind got blown upon hearing this. "They loved my stories?"

"Yup. We had to make a few changes here and there, but the initial footage looks amazing."

"Why didn't you tell me about this earlier?"

"I would have, but I was bound by secrecy. Not that I don't trust you, hon, but if word of this show leaked out, the producers threatened to shut down the entire production."

"How closely did they follow my storyline?"

"Like I said, we changed the location and some of the characters' jobs, but they loved the story of a vigilante, serial-killing housewife," Tift said. "There is, however, one slight issue."

"What's that?" Gwynn looked up and saw Denise standing in her doorway. She held up a finger, and Denise rolled her eyes and walked away.

"Please don't be upset, but I'll be the one getting the credit for this show. But don't worry, you'll be receiving a nice check in the mail."

Gwynn felt her cheeks go hot. "So you're getting all the credit for writing the story that I wrote? How is that fair?"

"I'm sorry about this, Gwynn. Attaching my name to the project was the only way the powers-that-be would agree to move forward. Those snobs at the studio won't even look at a script from someone who's not in the Screen Writers Guild."

She considered this and thought it a plausible explanation.

"I'll be sending out your first check soon. I know it's not much, but one hundred thousand dollars will have to do for now."

She nearly lost her breath. Did she hear Tift right?

"I know it sucks," Tift said, sounding apologetic. "But if the show does well, they'll want more scripts, which means more money for you."

"One hundred thousand dollars?"

"Sure, but there'll be more where that came from if this show takes off like I expect it to."

"Who is playing my…" She caught herself mid-sentence. "Who's starring in the main role?"

"Yours truly. And Garth Fuller is playing the role of detective?"

"Garth Fuller? He's a great actor."

"He's okay," she said. "I'm also one of the show's executive producers. Me and Max Frankel."

She'd never heard that name before. "When is it to air?"

"The first episode comes out in a few months, assuming all goes well. I can't wait to see what you think of it."

"You said the location changed?"

"We moved the story from Maine to LA," she said.

"That could work."

"Please tell me you have more ideas, because I couldn't possibly write a second season if they asked. You know what a terrible writer I am."

"Don't worry, Tift, I have plenty more ideas in the pipeline," she said, not able to process this amazing news.

"Would you be able to get away for a week and come out to LA? We could toss around some ideas and catch up on everything."

She thought about Tom and his draconian restrictions. "I'm way too busy right now."

"Come on, girl. We'd have so much fun waxing nostalgic over tacos and margaritas."

"How about we talk about this later."

"Okay, we'll figure something out. Whatever else you do, keep sending me your work. If the show gets picked up for a second season, we'll certainly need them."

"Can you do me a favor? Would you mind sending that check to my work address instead of my home address?"

"Sure. Text it to me."

Gwynn said goodbye and ended the call. She sat in a state of shock, unable to process the news just delivered to her. One hundred thousand dollars was certainly not enough to retire on, but it was a pretty substantial sum for when she was ready to move on from Tom. And she needed an exit strategy for when that day came. It meant opening a secret bank account and squirreling away the money. Investing it for her and Jack's future, although she knew virtually nothing about stocks, bonds, or investing. How she would do that without Tom's knowledge, she didn't know, but she'd figure something out. Like she'd figure everything else out.

It suddenly hit her: she had a talent for something other than murder. And by the sheer force of her friend's ego, Tift had managed to keep her name out of the limelight. It couldn't have worked out any better, seeing as how she'd modeled the scripts on her own life.

As much as she appreciated Tift's friendship, she knew she had to watch out for her friend. The woman had proved to be a backstabbing snake dressed in sheep's clothing. She stole all the credit for her stories and lied about it. Good thing it had played out that way, because if someone connected her life to this show, they might put two and two together and figure out that she'd committed multiple murders. Hopefully, the Hollywood writers had changed enough of the script so that no one would ever suspect her.

She needed to get the ball rolling if she wanted to start her life anew. A serial killer was roaming the streets, and Nguyen had woken from her coma and threatened to tell the cops everything she knew. If a new life out in LA awaited her, she needed to act fast.

Filled with newfound optimism, she walked over to Denise's office and peeked her head inside.

"You wanted to see me, Denise?"

"Where did you disappear to this morning?"

"I went out for lunch. Tangiers makes the best chicken shawarma in town. Let's you and me go there sometime."

"Last I checked, you're paid to be at your desk."

Gwynn did a double-take, trying to maintain her composure. "I'm allowed a lunch break."

"You can't just come and go here like you did when you were the director. Things are different now."

"For real?"

"I've never been more serious."

"We're grown women, Denise. Is all this drama necessary?"

"I won't tolerate employees wasting time when vulnerable young lives are at stake. Everything we do here is for the children. Do you understand?"

"Yes."

"Good. Now I need you to go through all the case files for the last ten years and put them in chronological order. It appears that the filing system has been in complete disarray for some time."

Gwynn turned to leave, trying to keep herself from responding in kind.

"And please close the door behind you."

If not for her current situation with Tom, she'd tell Denise where to shove it. Then she'd move her and Jack out to LA and start their lives anew. But Gwynn understood she couldn't move away from Maine until she wrapped everything up here. She had to find out whom Tom had sent that stupid video to before she could be free of him. Of course, she'd have to kill him for that to happen. He knew way too much about all that she had done.

She'd been thinking about it for a while now, devising novel ways in her head to make him disappear. But none seemed plausible if she wanted to stay out of prison.

* * *

She arrived home from work and parked in the driveway. An oddly colored green Jeep sat parked in front of her house. As soon as she exited her car, the door to the Jeep opened, and Callum Frye got out and strutted in her direction. The possibility of a neighbor seeing them together and telling Tom filled her with dread.

"What are you doing here? My son will be getting off his school bus any minute now."

"Nice house for someone who earns her keep as a social worker," he said, stepping back to take it all in.

"My husband makes the money in our family."

"What does he do?"

"He's a CPA."

"Certified professional asshole?"

She burst out laughing. "Why would you say that?"

"He must be an asshole if he couldn't even show up to see you win your award."

She stood on her toes and glanced over his shoulder. "Mommy and daddy buy you that Jeep?"

He turned and looked at it. "You obviously didn't check out my website."

"I will when I have the chance, but now is definitely not the time." She glanced down the street. "Please, Callum. You can't be here."

"Then when can we talk?"

"Any other time but now. My husband will kill me if he sees us talking."

"Tom the jealous type?"

"You could say that." It surprised her that he knew his name. "Most husbands would be jealous if they saw a handsome young guy talking to their wife."

"So you think I'm handsome?"

"And completely full of yourself." She cursed herself for complimenting him. "You've got ten seconds to tell me why you're here."

"Remember, girl, I know all your secrets," he said, taking a hit off a vape pen.

She craned her neck, looking for Jack's bus, waving the smoke out of her face.

"Does anyone know about the dead guy in Paris they found washed up along the Seine?"

This stunned her that he knew about this. "What guy in Paris?"

"The summer you were there. They discovered the body of a convicted rapist along the banks of the Seine. His throat was cut with a jagged object. Supposedly, he liked to find his victims late at night while they were walking along the river, only this time, he messed with the wrong person. I read somewhere that walking along the Seine late at night was one of your favorite things to do in Paris."

She remembered that interview she'd done with the Brooks's alumni magazine when she'd mentioned that. Had this kid looked into her entire past? She glanced down the street and finally saw Jack's bus turning the corner and barreling toward them.

"I have no idea what you're talking about. Now, if you wouldn't mind getting lost, I'd like to get my son off his bus."

"I'd love to meet the little tyke."

"Well, you can't."

"Why not?"

"Because you just can't."

"We really need to talk, Gwynn."

"What else is there to talk about?"

"You saved my life, and for that I'm eternally grateful."

"You're welcome," she said, waving him away as the bus got closer. "Now get out of here."

"Please don't make me tell the world how you killed my father."

"Okay, okay, we'll talk. You happy now?"

"Very much so, because I need you to help me with something."
"Help you with what?"
"I was hoping you'd teach me about murder."

Chapter Thirteen

GWYNN

Jack sat at the kitchen island, forming his letters with crayons while she prepared dinner. The tranquility of domestic life always astounded her compared to all that she'd done. Tom required his meals plated and served as soon as he came home from work each night. If not, he would throw a fit and be miserable all night. But Jack needed help with his letters, and she was already ten minutes late with dinner and frantic. She'd noticed lately that Jack struggled to sit still and concentrate on his homework. The teachers had noticed this, too, and planned on testing him for any learning disorders.

Tom had called earlier in the day and changed the menu he'd scribbled out at the beginning of the week. Instead of pork chops, he wanted enchiladas tonight—and enchiladas took much more time to prep than did pork chops. After wiping the sweat from her brow, she cut up all the vegetables while the ground sirloin sizzled in the pan, occasionally glancing at her laptop where the recipe glowed onscreen. She and Tom had once dined on enchiladas in Cancun, and he swore that he'd never tasted anything better.

Tom would be home in thirty minutes, and she couldn't be sure she'd finish everything in time. Then she remembered that there was no beer in the fridge. She dashed over to the kitchen faucet and rinsed her hands with soap and water, then headed to the garage and brought back six bottles of Heineken. Before leaving, she saw Jack holding his crayon aloft like a nuclear warhead until it landed on the granite countertop. He made an explosion sound, raising his arms up to emphasize the point. How crazy that her home life was so different from her secret life that it seemed surreal at times.

"Jack, you're supposed to be tracing your letters."

"I don't want to do my stupid letters," he said, continuing to play.

"Then there'll be no video games after dinner."

Jack buried his head in his arms.

"I want to see all your uppercase Cs finished by the time I return."

He lifted his head. "Where are you going?"

"To the garage," she said, placing the crayon in his hand. "Now start tracing."

"No!" He put his head back down on his arms.

"Are you talking back to me?"

"Daddy doesn't make me trace letters. He lets me play video games and have fun."

"Are you going to trace your letters or not?" she said, anxious about getting dinner plated on time.

Jack lifted his head and shook it vigorously back and forth.

"Go to your room, then."

"You're a meanie. Daddy will come up and play with me once he gets home."

She pointed toward the stairs, half tempted to swat him on the behind to emphasize her point. But she'd sworn a long time ago that she would never lay a finger on her child. If she had to resort to corporal punishment to discipline him, then she'd already lost the battle.

Jack bolted upstairs and slammed his door shut. She couldn't deal with a temper tantrum right now, although she noticed that they were happening on a more frequent basis lately. Was it because of her and Tom's one-sided relationship? Or did Jack intuit that his father was a controlling and sadistic freak? If not now, then he certainly would the older he got. It was the reason she needed to get Tom out of the picture as soon as possible.

She sprinted into the garage, grabbed a six-pack out of the case, and dashed back into the house. Tom preferred bottles to cans, and he liked his beer ice cold, which meant she needed to put the bottles in the freezer so that they got chilled enough by the time he arrived home. Twenty-five minutes left to prepare dinner, and she feared she wouldn't make it. Would Jack get over his little temper tantrum and return downstairs to finish his letters?

Smoke billowed out of the frying pan as she thought about Callum's request. Why would he want to learn about murder? She glanced down and saw that she'd burnt part of the hamburger. Using a metal spatula, she broke it up, removing the charred pieces, and threw them in the trash. Fortunately, the rest of the meat appeared salvageable. She took out the large glass baking dish and arranged the enchiladas in neat rows, finishing it all with shredded cheese and store-bought enchilada sauce. Once it was in the oven, she grabbed the bottle of Chardonnay out of the refrigerator, poured herself a large glass, and rested momentarily against the kitchen island. Sweat dripped from her forehead, which she wiped away with a terry towel. It might piss Tom off to see her drinking a glass of wine before dinner, so she told herself to finish it before his car pulled up in the driveway.

Now caught up with everything, she went over to the computer and deleted the recipe from the website. She typed in Callum Frye's name. What she saw surprised her. He had his own website, professionally done and slick as ice. She scanned his bio and learned that he had been a nationally ranked figure skater as a kid before injuring his knee. He'd foregone college to teach himself software coding. But his primary occupation had been investing in cryptocurrencies. He claimed on his website that he'd purchased Bitcoin at a young age and then added to his portfolio throughout the years. She read on and learned that he'd cashed in some of his Bitcoin to purchase other altcoins. His favorite movie was The *Silence of the Lambs*. His favorite book is *American Psycho*. Clearly, he was fascinated with serial killers.

Maybe Callum could prove useful. He obviously knew all the things she'd done, although he had no hard evidence to prove it. Still, she didn't want any of this to come to light. If he wanted to learn how to kill, then so be it. She'd teach him what she knew, and in return, maybe he could teach her how to invest her one hundred thousand dollars in cryptocurrency and become independently wealthy like him. She'd need to be financially independent once Tom was gone.

A car door slammed outside, and she realized that Tom had arrived home a bit early. Her stress level began to spike knowing he'd be walking through the door any second now. But which Tom would she have to deal with tonight: the nice version or the cruel one? She checked on the enchiladas in the oven and saw that they needed only a few more minutes. The beer in the fridge was not yet cold enough to suit his tastes, so she took one out and placed it directly on a tray of ice cubes. Seconds later, the door opened, and in walked Tom. For some reason, he looked heavier than usual.

"Hi, honey," she said with a straight face.

"You don't know how good it feels to be home." He passed her his suit jacket and then kissed her on the lips.

"Tough day at work?"

"You don't know the half of it. Every asshole wants their returns done yesterday. And Jerry put in his notice today and is taking a job with a firm across town."

"Jerry? That's too bad. I know how close you guys are."

"We started at the firm the same week."

"Well, all is good now that you're home and with your family. And dinner is almost ready."

"The stress of that job is killing me. And now with Jerry leaving, it's going to get a lot harder."

"Relax, hon, and leave your work at the door."

"Yeah, you're right. Where's my little panda bear?"

"In his room. I sent him up there for not tracing his letters."

Tom laughed. "You're way too hard on the kid. I'm going upstairs and bring him down."

"What kind of signal does that send? We should be on the same page in that regard."

"I hated tracing those stupid letters when I was his age, but I suppose you're right," he said. "Would you grab me a beer out of the fridge?"

"Of course. I'll even pour it in your favorite mug."

"No need. Just give me the bottle," he said, moving over to her. "Do you know how much I love you?"

It creeped her out when his thick arms enveloped her. "I love you more."

"Didn't I once tell you that I would?" he said, and she believed he really meant it. He slapped her playfully on the butt and squeezed one cheek. "Now go get me a beer. I'm going to unwind for a bit and watch some TV."

"What about dinner?"

"It can wait."

"But I spent so much time preparing it for you."

"And I appreciate all that you do around here, including getting me that beer."

She went to the freezer and took out the bottle she'd placed on the ice tray, praying it was cold enough. One wrong move could potentially set him off. After capping it, she put on the oven glove and took out the enchiladas, placing them on the stovetop to cool. Then she brought the bottle over to him. He took it in hand and swallowed half of it in one gulp. She stood over him, praying the warm beer wouldn't ruin his mood.

"Taste so good." He patted his hand on the sofa next to him. "I was hoping that you and I could play our game tonight."

"Sure. Maybe after Jack goes to sleep," she said, sitting next to him, knowing that was the last thing she wanted to do.

"Would you mind using the plastic bag this time? The see-through one like you used on Townsend?"

"Sure, hon, whatever you want." She bristled at the thought of draping that bag over his head like she did to Sam Townsend. "How hungry are you? Because I made a whole tray of enchiladas."

"Actually, I grabbed an Italian and some chips on the way home. Hope you don't mind."

"No, it's all good. The enchiladas will make a nice lunch for you tomorrow." She wanted to throttle him for making her work so hard preparing dinner, and now he didn't want it.

"Just put it in some Tupperware, and I'll eat it whenever." He reached up and put his hand on her cheek. "You're so beautiful. Much more so than when you were at Brooks."

"Thanks."

"What an amazing journey we've taken together, huh?"

She smiled, trying not to gag.

"Our love story is like something out of a movie."

Yeah, a horror movie.

"Okay, I'm going upstairs to get Jack."

"I told you he's on a time-out."

"He'll be fine. Besides, with computers running things these days, who the hell writes letters anymore?"

"Yes, but—"

"Me and the little rugrat need to finish the video game we started last night." He downed his beer and held the empty out to her, the signal for her to get him another. Lately, he'd been drinking at least four or five beers each night, and more come weekends. Sometimes, a twelve-pack throughout the course of a lazy Sunday.

She moved to the freezer and got him another beer while he ran upstairs to get Jack. She knew she wouldn't win this battle. And even if she did, she'd end up losing later in the evening. But what worried her most was Jack's bad attitude. What message was this sending him by not making him finish his letters? By letting him do whatever he wanted, he'd grow up to be a spoiled brat. Entitled and privileged. She needed to hang in there a bit longer until she and Peters figured out whom Tom had sent those videos to. As soon as they destroyed them, they could discuss a way to make Tom disappear. A car accident? Fake suicide? She'd think of something. After all, killing was her talent. Oh, and now writing stories too. Stories that got made into a TV series.

Chapter Fourteen

DR. EZRA KAUFMAN

I receive a call from my mother's nursing home, informing me that she had suffered a major stroke. I jump in my car and drive south. As much as I knew that her days on earth were numbered, the news devastates me. At her age, a stroke of such magnitude means it's unlikely she'll ever recover.

I can barely process my thoughts as I speed down to Massachusetts, hoping that I can be there if and when she passes, and hold her hand until she moves on from this world.

Before receiving the call, I'd been holed up in my study, reading about the two girls found along the Presumpscot River. Is it the work of a copycat killer, or did Gwynn actually have something to do with these deaths? I don't for one minute believe she did, but after everything that's happened, I can't be sure of anything. I know her too well, having counseled her since she was a teenager. But I can't help wondering if there's a tenuous connection between her and the deaths of these girls, especially since her father turned out to be the Muddy River Killer.

I race over the Piscataqua Bridge, which separates Maine from New Hampshire, thinking about Gwynn's father. He passed away six months ago in his sleep, although he didn't deserve to die in such a dignified way. Gwynn mentioned that she had just visited him that evening and left him in good spirits. By that point, his disease had advanced to the point where he could barely do anything on his own. Even the most basic conversational skills had left him. One of his caretakers at the wake told me that they no longer had been able to look after him and that Gwynn had been looking into memory care facilities. I wouldn't blame her if she did what I think she did. Right or wrong, it would bring her death count to a total of eight people—and that's only the ones I know about.

I still can't believe that Nguyen's elderly parents were sitting next to their daughter's attackers at that awards ceremony. If they only knew the truth about what Gwynn and Peters had done to their daughter. What were the odds that Peters and his anchorwoman girlfriend would also be there, and sitting at the same table? I watched them all closely, observing their body language and reactions. Gwynn attempted to be civil when she shook Annabelle's hand, but I could see the anger in her eyes.

More surprising was the handsome young man who introduced Gwynn. His eloquent introduction wowed the crowd. After all these years, how had he found her? Or had the committee found him? And did he have any idea that Gwynn had administered the fatal dose that killed his father? From all indications, he's done well for himself. I Googled him with no expectation of finding anything and learned that he's a prodigy of sorts. A champion figure skater in his youth and an early investor in cryptocurrencies. As a young boy, he convinced his parents to buy Bitcoin for him.

I pull into Mass General's parking lot and check in at the front desk, and they tell me where my mother is. I race up to her room, praying that she can hang on a bit longer. Making my way out of the elevator, I head toward her room. A nurse greets me before I go inside.

"Are you a family member?"

"I'm her son."

"Are you aware that your mother has a no-resuscitate order?"

"I am. How's she doing?"

"Not well, I'm afraid. She suffered a massive stroke."

I fight back the tears. "Can I go in and see her?"

"Of course."

"Thank you," I say before heading inside.

I pull up a chair alongside her bed and grab hold of her wrinkled hand, thinking about all the wonderful memories I have of her. My only hope is that she goes peacefully in the night and joins my father, wherever he is now.

While holding her hand, I realize that life is too short to hold grudges. I need to speak to Gwynn and convince her to return to therapy, assuming her husband will let her. I want to help her get through whatever struggles she's going through at the moment. Maybe I'll even tell her how I really feel about her.

Three hours later, my mother takes her last breath. That familiar flatlining sound fills the room. A nurse rushes in and stares down at me as I squeeze my mother's hand. Then I stand from my seat and kiss her one last time. A tear falls from my eye; I can't remember the last time I cried.

Chapter Fifteen

DETECTIVE PETERS

The teller had the five-thousand-dollars ready for him when he arrived. He hoped, for Ruby's sake, that this would be the last time she attempted to extort money from him.

He returned home and stuffed the cash-filled envelope in one of his bedroom drawers, planning to give it to Ruby later. Then he headed back to the office, dreading having to go on his dinner date with Annabelle. As painful as it would be, he knew he couldn't continue to see her as long as he still loved Gwynn. That meet-up in the basement of the Italian Heritage Center had cemented his decision.

He drove down to the teen shelter and interviewed two girls standing against the building and smoking cigarettes. They acted all sassy and bold, pretty little things in their own way. Both claimed to have known the two dead girls. The girls looked to be sixteen or seventeen, both runaways and drug addicts, judging from their jittery demeanors. He studied them, wondering if either one would be the killer's next victim—his next victim. And he couldn't help but notice how nonchalant they appeared about living on the streets, without a care in the world, knowing that a predatory shark was out there and hunting them like seals. Then again, they acted no different from most kids. At one time in his youth, he too felt immortal. It was the reason these young girls had no problem jumping into a stranger's car and performing sex acts for short money, money they used to buy drugs and alcohol.

He jotted down their names, even knowing that they had probably lied about their identities. They broke out laughing when he walked away, the sting of ridicule something he'd never quite gotten over since his high school days. Then he headed to Maine Medical for his scheduled meeting with the media.

* * *

Annabelle had set this publicity stunt up a month ago, and as much as he'd complained about it, he finally agreed to help her out. The PD also thought it a good idea. A male cop supporting his injured Vietnamese partner would make for great publicity. It would also help boost the GoFundMe page that Jimmy Nguyen, Janet's brother, had set up in her name.

As he got out of his car, he wished he hadn't agreed to this stunt. Butterflies fluttered in his stomach at the prospect of seeing Nguyen's parents. The entire spectacle seemed a farce, but Annabelle insisted that it would help the family, as well as show the world what a big heart he had.

He approached the entrance to the hospital and saw Annabelle standing with her crew, a big smile on her wrinkle-free face. It was obvious that she'd undergone Botox treatments and a facelift in the last few years. Behind the crew sat the news van with the station's logo affixed to the side panel. Annabelle rushed over and kissed him, free now to show PDA after their first appearance together as a couple. The prospect of breaking up with her made him want to put it off as long as possible, but he knew he had to do it sooner rather than later, no matter how painful it might be.

"You're late," she said, looking up at him with those big brown eyes.

"Yeah, I've been busy working on these murder cases."

"It's okay, Mike," she said, which made him miss the way Gwynn called him Peters. "The Nguyens are waiting over by the van. I want you to go over there so we can get the four of you in one shot."

"You never told me I would be appearing with them."

"I thought it would be a nice touch."

"Okay, let's do this as quickly as possible. I need to get back to work."

"You're not mad at me, are you? You seem upset."

"No, just tired."

"I promise I'll make it up to you after dinner tonight," she said.

He walked over to where the Nguyen family stood, the elderly couple's expressions unchanged from the last time he saw them. They nodded as he approached. Before he knew it, the crew started filming. Nguyen's parents spoke first. Then Peters spoke, and he talked in platitudes about what a great partner Janet Nguyen had been and what a bright future she had in law enforcement. After they finished the interview, they all went upstairs to Nguyen's room to pay her a visit. It spooked him to see his former partner lying there in that condition. She looked so different from her former self that it creeped him out. Having lost a considerable amount of weight, she was now all skin and bones. It made his skin crawl to see her glaring at him, as if she'd remembered what he'd done to her. Various machines beeped and glowed, and her skin appeared like cellophane wrapped tightly around her body. If it were him in that bed, he would have wanted someone to pull the plug a long time ago.

Nguyen's mother started to cry. Her husband wrapped his arm around her shoulder and tried to comfort his wife as best he could. He remembered Nguyen telling him that her parents had fled Vietnam by boat before finally arriving in this country. Annabelle shouted out directions, and he snapped out of his fog, doing as instructed. The camera rolled. Despite his chagrin, he felt slightly guilty knowing that his partner lay there because of what he and Gwynn had done. Still, he didn't for one moment regret what had happened, and he stared back at her as if to say, 'bring it on, bitch!'.

He felt guilty about his plans to break up with Annabelle tonight. She was clearly infatuated with him and believed he felt the same way about her. Then again, it would be much worse to continue on in a relationship that he knew stood no chance of surviving. It had reached the point where he couldn't even get hard at the sight of her naked. All he could think about was Gwynn. Gwynn on her knees at the edge of that quarry. The two of them making love on that sheepskin rug next to the roaring fireplace.

Hanging out in his shitty old apartment while drinking Coronas with limes wedged over the rims. She consumed his every waking thought, which was both a blessing and a curse, seeing as he now had killed two girls in order to be with her.

Once they finish filming, he informed Annabelle that he had to get back to the station. After saying goodbye to the Nguyen family, he approached Annabelle.

"We good now?"

"Thanks so much, hon. That went way better than I expected."

"Glad I could help." He couldn't stop staring at her smooth, shiny forehead.

"You did an amazing job. I'm going to make sure you get rewarded big time after dinner tonight."

"I'm going to be working late, Annabelle. How about we just do dinner?"

She appeared taken aback. "You feeling alright?"

"Yeah, just tired from all the hours I've been putting in on these two murder cases."

"Okay, babe, dinner it is. I'll give you a rain check on all that extracurricular activity."

"Sounds good." He forced a smile, thinking about the news he would deliver this evening. "Gotta go."

She gave him a peck on the cheek before he turned to leave, and he could smell the perfume she used, a fruity scent he found almost too much to bear.

Chapter Sixteen

DETECTIVE PETERS

Annabelle sat across from him on the outdoor deck, chatting nonstop. She talked endlessly about nothing in particular while at the same time making it sound as if her words were of the gravest importance. In some ways, he thought it nice not having to initiate conversation. It took all the pressure off him. Had he genuinely liked her, he might have found it an endearing trait, and he actually had when they first started dating. But the more time he spent with her, the more his mind tended to wander when she spoke, and he would lose track of entire blocks of conversation, and she'd laugh and ask him to repeat the last thing she'd said, which, of course, he couldn't.

He'd picked a casual restaurant on the waterfront that served fried fish and onion rings with homemade tartar sauce. No sense going somewhere fancy and spending a lot of money when he planned on breaking up with her. The waitress brought over a Corona for him and a glass of Chablis for her. He took a sip of his beer while she told him about her day in mind-numbing detail. His thoughts meandered to Gwynn and the two girls he killed. It occurred to him that Annabelle had taken the night off from the news desk in order to dine out with him. But that made him feel even worse, knowing what he was about to tell her. For a brief moment, he thought he might put it off for another day, but the longer he stayed in this stagnant relationship, the harder it would be to break it off with her.

The food came out quickly, hot and glistening. A crab slider on a toasted bun for her. A fried haddock sandwich with coleslaw and fries for him. She talked on and on, occasionally stealing some of his fries, a habit that irked him, seeing as how she could order her own fries. Annabelle covered her mouth with her hand while she talked, making it hard for him to hear her. He squeezed a lemon wedge over his sandwich, putting off the inevitable. The clouds turned pink as the sun set behind them. A reggae band played Bob Marley's "Buffalo Soldier" somewhere on the pier.

"You're awfully quiet tonight, Mike."

He chewed his sandwich before wiping his mouth off with the napkin. "I think we need to talk, Annabelle."

She lifted the glass to her lips and froze. "We are talking."

"I mean about us."

Annabelle smiled, but not in a good way. "Wait. Are you about to say what I think you are?"

He stared at her.

"Mike, please don't."

"It's not you, Annabelle."

"I can't believe you just said that shitty line," she said a little too loudly, causing a few heads to turn. "Do you know how many guys would kill to be with me?"

Peters wanted to be anywhere but here. Maybe he should have done this back at her place so as not to cause a scene.

"Are you seeing someone else?"

He shook his head as a seagull squawked overhead. Did Gwynn count as seeing someone else?

"Why are you doing this to me, Mike?" A tear trickled down her pancaked cheek. "I thought we had something good."

"It's the work, I suppose. I'm married to my job and not yet ready for a serious relationship."

"Are you kidding me?"

"Do I look like I'm kidding? This is a difficult thing for me to do."

"You fucking prick," she said, throwing her scrunched-up napkin at him.

She stood and leaned over the table. "Do you know how badly I could ruin you?"

He glanced over at her, surprised by the aggressive tone. He had hoped she'd tear up, hug it out, and then the two of them would go their separate ways.

"Please don't make this any harder on me than it already is."

"You selfish bastard." Everyone on the deck turned their heads and stared at them.

"I was hoping we could do this civilly and remain friends."

"That sure as hell isn't going to happen," she said. "You probably don't remember, but I reported on that civilian shooting you took part in. Maybe I'd overlooked all the messy little details because I fell in love with you, but in the back of my mind I've always wondered if you killed that gangbanger and planted the gun on him."

"I didn't."

"You really think that solving one big murder case will absolve you of murdering a civilian?"

"You weren't there that day, Annabelle, so you have no idea how dangerous a situation I was in."

"Maybe a detailed investigative report might be warranted. Throw some shade on that glossy reputation of yours."

"You're doing this just because I broke up with you?"

"What do you think?" she said. "I'm not the kind of woman who gets tossed to the curb like a piece of trash."

"I'm not tossing you to the curb. I'm merely being open and honest with you."

"Honesty goes two ways, pal. I'm going to make your life a living hell from now on."

"Good luck with that. Everyone will know you're being vindictive just because I broke up with you."

"I'll put one of my best reporters on the story and make sure they dig so deep into your past that it'll be coming out your ass."

"For god's sake, Annabelle, can't we behave like adults?"

"Furthermore, how does a cop who never solved a major case in his life end up solving one of the greatest murder mysteries in this town's history? None of the other cops even knew you were working on it. In fact, no one had any idea you were such an industrious sleuth in your spare time."

"I didn't want to make waves."

Annabelle shook her head. "I can't believe I let my feelings for you cloud my judgment," she said, turning to leave. "You better watch yourself, Mike, because I'm coming for you."

"No, Annabelle, you should watch yourself. Maybe you don't know me as well as you think you do," he said, thinking about those two girls he had killed.

She stormed out of the restaurant, and he felt nothing but relief now that he'd finally ended their relationship. The breakup didn't go as smoothly as planned, far from it, but breakups were never easy. And most of the time, he was on the receiving end of getting dumped. Women had always turned on him first, which made it easier when it came to killing those girls, knowing they were all part of the same wrecking crew.

Rather than walk back to his condo, he ordered another beer and stared out at the harbor, listening to the faint echo of the reggae band playing on the pier. It was a beautiful evening, and the view of the boats bobbing in the bay soothed him. He had nothing else to do and nowhere to go. No one waiting at home for him to ease his pain. Come tomorrow, he'd spend most of the day at his desk, working on the cases of those two girls, all the while knowing that he'd been the one who'd killed them. He wished he could relax and enjoy the quiet of his own company, but he felt a deep sense of longing. Instead of Tom, it should have been him returning home each night to Gwynn. How he loathed Tom. Just the thought of Gwynn's husband brought out the worst in him.

He started to think of inventive ways to kill the bastard. If given the chance, he knew he'd do it. Then he'd celebrate Tom's death with an elaborate and elongated toast. While not a killer in the same vein as Gwynn, he could do it under the right circumstances, because he had done it. Three times, in fact. Gwynn might even be proud knowing that he'd killed those two girls to win her over.

Finally, he sauntered home, carrying his doggy bag containing Annabelle's uneaten crab slider. He debated whether to call Gwynn, but then remembered how she warned him not to call her unless it was an emergency. No sense pissing her off. Besides, an error in judgment could put his relationship with her in jeopardy, especially if Tom found out.

Once inside his condo, he collapsed on the sofa. He needed a fresh start. Stop drinking so much. Put an end to his gambling. Hopefully, that documentary would get green-lighted and help replenish his meager bank account. Winning back Gwynn's love demanded he be more proactive in everything he did. He had most everything he needed now: celebrity status in town, a new car, and a nice place to live. She was the only piece of the puzzle missing from his life. It meant he needed to double down and find whoever Tom had sent those videos to and destroy them as soon as possible. Then, and only then, would he be able to get rid of his nemesis and have Gwynn all to himself.

Around midnight, he got up off the couch and put on his shoes. He'd not sleep tonight, his mind too busy tossing and turning. He left his condo, got into his car, and cruised the streets. Somehow, he needed to release the rage now threatening to overwhelm him. Tonight, he'd find another girl and make her his next victim. Then, place her near the river, under a bed of ferns, positioned the same way as the others. Maybe that would get Gwynn's attention and force her back into his arms.

Chapter Seventeen

GWYNN

A week had passed since Callum showed up at her door, and Gwynn still hadn't contacted him. Nor had he sought her out. Although intrigued by his request, she couldn't see where she'd ever find the time for him in her hectic schedule. But she knew she had to, or else he might tell the world everything she'd done. She'd pored through his website several times now and believed it a mistake to underestimate this young man she saved from a life of destitution and neglect. She'd even checked out a few YouTube videos of him figure skating as a young boy and came away amazed at the grace and strength he projected on the ice, especially for someone so tall. As far as teaching him what she knew about murder, she wasn't sure how that was going to happen.

She kept her door closed this morning so Denise wouldn't interrupt her. But thus far, her plan hadn't worked as Denise continued to barge in and pile more paperwork on her desk. And filling out that dreaded logbook every fifteen minutes seemed the worst part of her job.

Someone knocked on her door, and she bristled at who it might be. Instead, it was a staff member dropping off her mail. She sorted through it until she found it: the check from Max Frankel Productions. Smiling, Gwynn ripped it open and saw five zeros after the one. What an amazing development. Now she needed to find a bank to stash the money in, away from Tom and his prying eyes. And seeing as how he controlled all their finances, including the proceeds from her father's estate, she would need to find her own tax specialist. Maybe Callum would give her a few tips on how to invest the money, and it would set her and Jack up for life. But that would only happen if she taught him the ins and outs of murder.

A text came in while she stared in disbelief at the check. She opened her phone and saw that it was Ivy.

I'm in a bad way, Gwynn, Ivy texted.

What's wrong?

I'm sick and desperately in need of a fix. Could you come over and help me?

Where are you?

I'm staying at a friend's house on Grant Street. I'd rather kill myself than keep living this way.

If I give you the money, will you promise to check yourself into rehab afterwards?

I promise. Just come over and help me. Please.

Text me the address, and I'll be right over.

After receiving the address, Gwynn grabbed her bag and headed out of the office, almost bumping into Denise on the way out. Was it her imagination, or was her boss watching her every move, looking for any excuse to fire her?

"Where do you think you're going?"

"I need to go out and help a former client of The Loft who is in crisis."

"You have way too much work here to finish."

"This girl is in trouble and needs me."

"I'm warning you not to leave, Gwynn, or there will be consequences."

Furious, Gwynn stepped into her boss's face and glared at her. "Do you really want to do that, Denise? Because if this girl dies, I'll put the blame on you. Then I'll tell the newspaper and the board of directors how you refused to let me help a former client in trouble: a client who was beloved by all the teachers and staff."

The woman's expression changed ever so slightly. At that moment, Gwynn realized that this woman didn't care about the children in her care, but about grabbing power and control.

"Fine. Make sure she's okay and then come right back. We have a lot of work to get done today."

Gwynn rushed past her without even a goodbye. She jumped in her car and drove over to the apartment on Grant Street, thinking about the events of last night. Despite her pleas that Jack finish his letters, Tom had dismissed her concerns, choosing instead to play video games with his son until almost ten. She was the one who had to put Jack to bed each night and then get him ready for school. And she'd struggled mightily to wake him up this morning. Jack had barely been able to keep his eyes open. Not that Tom cared one way or the other. He had already gone off to work by the time she'd started to get Jack ready for his school day. One of her greatest fears was that Tom's obnoxious behavior would rub off on their son and Jack would turn out to be a chauvinist pig, abusing women and controlling them like he did her.

After she'd carried Jack upstairs to bed, Tom stood waiting for her on the landing, a beer in hand. Five empty bottles sat on the coffee table, which she later had to pick up and put in the recycling bag. He reached out and grabbed her hand and started to slow dance with her, his hand moist from the cold bottle. His breath reeked of stale beer and garlic from the Italian he'd wolfed down on his way home, but she did nothing to resist him.

After shutting off the lights, Tom led her upstairs. The beers made him unsteady on his feet, and she'd wondered if he'd be able to stay awake long enough for them to do anything. Instead, he lay down and snuggled up next to her, telling her how much he loved her. His breathing was heavy and labored, as if he'd just finished running a marathon. Then he'd fallen asleep, his arm like a tree trunk over her body. It took at least thirty minutes before she felt safe enough to wiggle away from him. His loud snores filled her ears all night and made her vigilant lest he wake up. Because of that, she now felt exhausted.

She searched around the Bayside until she found a parking space. Congress Street was the divide between the glamorous version of Portland and the gritty reality not meant for the tourists to see.

She got out of the car and walked to the address Ivy had given her. A few shady figures loitered around on the street, but she wasn't worried.

Once she found the house, she bolted up the rickety steps. The apartment complex had seen better days. After going inside, she took in the grimy interior and headed upstairs. The door to Ivy's apartment was slightly ajar. She opened it and moved inside. Not the cleanest place she'd ever been in. She went from room to room until she found Ivy lying in bed and under a child's blanket decorated with fishes. Gwynn sat on the mattress next to her, running a hand through the girl's sweaty hair. Ivy looked completely different from the sweet, sassy girl she'd met for coffee days earlier. Her skin had an ashen color to it, and she gave off a foul odor.

"I can't do this anymore," Ivy moaned, reaching for her phone.

"You need to go to rehab," Gwynn said, putting her hand on the girl's leg.

"I promise I'll go after this fix."

"Do you swear?"

"Swear to God, Gwynn. I'm done feeling sick and tired all the time."

Gwynn sat back and watched as Ivy called her dealer. After hanging up, she buried her head under the blanket and sobbed in pitiful gasps. Gwynn felt for the girl, knowing the abusive and dysfunctional family she'd been raised in. She tried to comfort Ivy and give her reasons to live. A few minutes later, a skinny, tattooed guy walked into the room, wearing a red tracksuit and a baseball cap askew on his shaved head. She moved aside and paid him his money. Upon receiving the drugs, Ivy sat up, ravenous for her fix. Then the dealer pocketed his wad and left.

Practically frothing at the mouth, Ivy swung her feet onto the floor. She grabbed the yellow rubber band and wrapped it around her bicep, and then stuck the end in her shivering teeth. Her skin revealed small puncture wounds up and down her arm. She lit the powder before sucking it into the hypodermic needle. Although horrified, Gwynn couldn't look away. She'd seen this ritual done so many times now that she had it down to memory.

Ivy searched in futility for a good vein, crying in desperation. Finally, she located one and plunged the tip of the needle into it. Her face looked haggard and older than her sixteen years. But then all her muscles relaxed, and her expression melted away. Her eyes rolled back in her head, and she fell back onto the comforter, the needle still protruding from her arm.

"Are you feeling better now?"

"Oh yeah," Ivy moaned. "You're the best, Gwynn."

"You promised you'd check yourself into rehab if I helped you."

"I will." She flicked her hand in the air and extended two fingers. "Scout's honor."

"I have to get back to the office now."

"Run along, chicky," she said, giggling.

"Take care, Ivy."

"Love you."

"Love you, too."

Ivy closed her eyes, and a peaceful expression settled over her face. Gwynn kissed the girl on the forehead and left, comforted by the fact that Ivy was no longer in pain. But she couldn't keep buying her drugs and bailing her out like this. The girl needed professional help. And Ivy did promise to check herself into rehab afterward. Hopefully, she'd keep her word. She couldn't keep getting involved in the girl's troubled life, especially when she had her own problems to worry about.

What would she do if Jack ended up like this? She knew she'd do everything in her power to save him, and that was the difference between the children in her care and her own blood.

Chapter Eighteen

GWYNN

Sitting in her car, still reeling from that meeting with Ivy, Gwynn took out the business card Callum had given her and called him, expecting to leave a message. Instead, he answered after the first ring.

"I've been waiting all week for you to call. What took you so long?" he said.

"Sorry, but I've been extremely busy."

"So do you agree to my terms?"

"Sure, if you teach me everything you know about cryptocurrency and how to invest in it."

He laughed. "I see you've done your homework."

"Didn't take you for a figure skater."

"I was tall for men's singles, which is why my knee eventually gave out."

"Your résumé is quite impressive."

"Are you free right now?"

"I could be."

"There's a coffee shop on the back side of Marginal Way called Ground Zero. Can you meet me there?"

"Sure."

"I'm here now. I'll wait for you."

She ended the call and headed over to the coffee shop. It was so far off the beaten path that Tom would not be upset that she went there—or so she hoped.

***

She parked in the back and walked toward the front of the building. As soon as she turned the corner, she saw Tom standing on the sidewalk and conversing with three other men. It forced her to jump back behind the brick wall and wait for him to leave. Had he seen her? Her breathing accelerated, and her heart thumped in her chest. What the hell was Tom doing here? She took a deep breath and glanced around the corner, and saw Tom still conversing with the group. Were they clients? Coworkers? Hopefully, Callum wouldn't bail on her.

She peeked out again and saw them heading in her direction. Frightened, she turned and sprinted back to the parking lot, noticing that the lot was surrounded by a chain-link fence. Only a few other cars were parked here. She ran behind the furthest vehicle, an old pickup truck, and hid behind it. She waited a few seconds before glancing out past the front bumper and saw the four of them settle into a Lexus. A few seconds later, the car took off and disappeared down the street.

After waiting a few seconds to compose herself, she made her way toward the coffee shop. As soon as she entered, she saw Callum sitting at the back of the room, typing on his laptop. Behind him was an exposed brick wall, aesthetically distressed and decorated with three abstract paintings. Callum didn't look up as she walked toward him. When he did, he smiled and stood out of his chair.

"Sorry I'm late. Something came up," she said.

"I'm just glad you could make it."

"Did I have a choice?"

"You always have a choice in life. Unfortunately, some choices are better than others."

"I didn't save your life so you could lecture me."

"Unfortunately for you, I was a very observant child, blessed with a memory like an elephant." He tapped his index finger against his head.

"Something tells me not to underestimate you, Callum."

He smiled. "I wouldn't if I were you."

"Can I ask you something?"

He nodded.

"Did you have a happy childhood after I handed you off to CPS?"

"I did. And I was able to experience things I never would have had I been raised by my biological parents."

"Like figure skating?"

"That's one of them. Buying Bitcoin is another."

"I'm happy to hear that," she said. "But let's cut to the chase. You want to learn certain things from me, as do I from you."

"That would be our arrangement."

She studied him. "So is it true you made a lot of money investing in cryptocurrencies?"

"It is."

"Tell me more."

"I recognized the power of the blockchain at a very young age, putting all my allowance and birthday money into Bitcoin. My parents thought I was crazy at the time, but by the age of seventeen, I had accumulated enough that I could live on my own."

"That was incredible foresight to have at such a young age."

"Those early life experiences informed my actions, and I swore that I would never end up poor and addicted to drugs like my biological parents. I wanted to control my own destiny. Be my own boss."

"Impressive."

"So you want to learn my secrets about getting rich?"

"Not necessarily rich, although that wouldn't be bad. I just want to have enough money for me and my son to live on once my husband is out of the picture."

"I see," he said, sipping his coffee. "I'm afraid it will take a significant sum of money for that to happen."

"Would one hundred thousand dollars be a good starting point?"

He whistled. "Does your husband know you have that kind of money?"

She laughed. "God no. He would make me hand it over to him if he did."

"That's not cool."

"Tom's not a very nice person."

"If he's that bad, why do you stay with him?"

"Unfortunately, I can't get out of my marriage right now." She looked away.

"Why not?"

"Let's just say there are complications."

"Like what?"

"Like he knows everything I've done and has a video that could put me away for life if he released it. It's another reason why I need your help."

"And you haven't ever considered…the other option you're good at?"

"Only every waking moment." She sipped her coffee. "Unfortunately, he sent the video to a friend with the stipulation that if something should ever happen to him, they are to send it directly to the police."

"That's cold."

"Tell me about it."

"So all you need to do is find out who he sent it to, and then your problems go away?"

"I suppose."

"I might be able to help you with that."

"Really?"

"Sure. Did you ever think that he may have hidden those videos on his computer before sending them off? They'd be very easy to find, assuming your husband's not too computer savvy."

"Oh, he's definitely not, unless it has to do with tax software," she said. "Are you good with computers?"

"Not to brag, but I'm a whiz."

She smiled. "You're quite the Renaissance man, Callum."

"I was somewhat of a prodigy, despite my unfortunate childhood," he said. "Aside from what you can teach me."

"Yes, aside from that."

"So if your husband emailed that video, it would be fairly easy to learn who he sent it to, even if he deleted it. I can help you with that."

"You would do that for me?"

"Of course, as long as you do certain things for me."

She waited a beat. "Like teach you all about murder?"

"I know it sounds crazy, but I've always had a fascination with the subject."

"When did that start?"

"I don't know," he said, tapping his cheek with his forefinger. "You remember that woman figure skater who hired those thugs to beat up her competitor?"

"Tonya Harding. I remember it well."

"I watched the movie, and it really hit home with me. In individual competitions like figure skating, the desire to win was so great that it's like a drug. I used to fantasize all the time about killing my competitors."

"Look, Callum, I don't do this to win skating competitions," she whispered.

He sat back and held up his hands. "Oh, I believe you."

"In my case, I do it because the person hurt others and doesn't deserve to live."

"Like my father?"

"If you weren't in that apartment that day, I wouldn't have taken his life."

"Do you consider what you did a good thing?"

"Of course. And I'd do it again in a heartbeat if it would help save another kid like you."

"From the bottom of my heart, I appreciate what you did."

"I have a five-year-old son to raise, and I'd want someone to do the same for him if he was ever in trouble."

"Of course you would."

"Now do you understand why I did it?"

"You see yourself as someone who is making the world a better place."

"Sure, when you put it that way."

"Let me ask you this, Gwynn. Do you enjoy doing it?"

"That's a difficult question to answer," she said, knowing in her heart that she did. "Every instance is completely different."

"But you must like doing it."

"Only because it delivers instant justice." She paused for a few seconds. "What about you, Callum? Do you think about it?"

"All the time."

"That can't be healthy."

He shrugged. "That makes two of us."

"Do you consider this a means to an end? Or a way to accomplish some other objective?"

"I don't really know," he said. "I wish I could say I shared your worldview of justice."

"But you're not sure how you feel?"

"I'm a young dude. I'm not sure how I feel about many things in life."

"At least you're being honest."

"Being honest with someone like you is always the best strategy."

"Someone like me?"

He leaned over and whispered, "Someone who has killed lots of people."

"Allegedly."

Callum broke out laughing.

"What's so funny?"

"That's precious."

Gwynn took offense but hoped to change the subject. "What crypto do you think I should invest in first?"

"We have a lot to cover before we start discussing an investment strategy that's right for you." Callum studied her, biting his lower lip. "So when the time comes, could I be the one who…makes your husband disappear?"

"We have a lot to cover before we start discussing a strategy that's right for you."

"Touché," he said, reaching for his laptop. He clicked it on and then turned his computer toward her. "I've identified some great cryptocurrencies that I expect to explode in the next bull cycle."

"Music to my ears," she said, scooting over so she could see the screen. Now it was her turn to be the student.

Chapter Nineteen

GWYNN

Five days had passed since Gwynn had helped Ivy get her fix, and not a word from the girl. She wondered if Ivy had made it to rehab in one piece. Or even if she was still alive. Most rehab centers didn't allow calls out during the first few weeks of a client's stay, so the possibility existed that she had checked herself in. That didn't stop Gwynn from texting the girl every day and checking up on her.

A stack of new intake cases sat piled on her desk. She glanced at her computer screen, seeing three windows open in the event Denise walked in. Otherwise, she'd been obsessed with watching the cryptos she'd purchased on Callum's advice. Every few minutes, she checked on them, watching as her tokens dropped dramatically in value. Two hours later, she deeply regretted her decision. Her one hundred thousand dollars had been reduced to sixty-seven in less than a week. Callum had warned her that these were volatile assets, but she had no idea how volatile until now. In some strange way, it reminded her of her own messy life. She cursed herself for being so stupid and allowing her nest egg to get plundered. She'd texted Callum numerous times, complaining about her losses, but he'd texted back every time, advising her to be patient. She couldn't blame him for the whimsical nature of the market. He had warned her that she'd be in for a wild ride, and she had willingly taken the risk. Just like she took the risk every time she killed someone. "Hold tight," he kept texting back, "because you don't lose anything until you sell."

She couldn't bear to return home tonight. It was not because Tom had been mean to her, but quite the opposite; he'd been super nice as of late, acting like a loving and devoted husband, showering her with gifts and complimenting her at every turn. Sadly, she didn't believe this to be an act. He really did love her in his own sick and perverted way. Gwynn at times wondered if he had a personality disorder, she being someone who suffered from a similar malady herself. This benevolent version of Tom made her miss the old Tom from their days at Brooks. The kind and caring Tom, who let her cry on his shoulder. The Tom she would converse with for hours on end. She'd much rather have the asshole version to fuel her rage and help her forget about the old Tom. Dealing with his unpredictable nature was the hardest part of being married to him. Had he always been this way, even back in college? If so, he'd hidden it well.

Her phone rang, a welcome interruption from the sad state she found herself in. She glanced down at the familiar number. Why was *he* calling? She answered, not sure what to expect.

"It's me, Gwynn."

"How have you been, Dr. Kaufman?"

"I've been better."

"Oh? What happened?"

He sighed. "My mother recently passed away."

"I'm sorry for your loss." This was the first time he had opened up about his personal life.

"Thank you. You obviously know how difficult it is to lose a parent."

"I do."

"How has the loss of your father affected you?"

She stood and closed her office door. "In some ways, it's been difficult. In other ways, a blessing. No one should have to live their final years like he did, even a man as…complex as my father."

He paused. "My mother had been quite healthy before her death. It happened so fast."

"How did she die?"

"She had a massive stroke. She lived for a few more hours before she passed away."

"Did she suffer?"

"No, and that's a good thing."

"Did you at least get to say goodbye to her?"

"I did, although I'm not sure she heard me. She was unconscious the entire time I sat with her."

"I'm sure she sensed that you were close by."

"I certainly hope you're right."

"I'm sorry for your loss, Dr. Kaufman, but why are you calling me?"

"My mother is not the only person I lost this year."

She didn't know how to respond to this.

"I'd love for you to come back to therapy, Gwynn. I won't even charge you if that's an issue."

"It's not," she said, "but things are complicated in my life right now."

"I realize that, which is why you need me more than ever. We need each other."

"Your mother passed away, and all of a sudden, you need me? Surely, I'm not the only person in your life you can turn to."

"You have to admit, we had a good working relationship. We knew each other better than most married couples do."

"That's not true. You know almost everything about me, but I know hardly anything about you."

"Is that what you want? To know more about me?"

She wasn't sure if she did.

"I suppose I could tell you more about myself if that's a dealbreaker."

She considered this. "Yes, I would like that."

"Consider it done, then. I will be more forthcoming about myself in future sessions."

"Are you really sure you want to see me again, knowing all the…things I've done?"

"It wasn't until I saw you at that awards banquet that it finally hit home."

"You were there?" she said, trying to act surprised.

"Don't play coy with me, Gwynn. You know very well that I was."

"Then why didn't you come over and say hello? Congratulate me on winning my award?"

"Knowing you like I do, you would have been embarrassed had I done so, especially considering the people seated around you."

He was right about that. "So why do you want me back in therapy so badly?"

"It was the speech that young man gave, thanking you for saving his life when he was a young boy. Then again, you and I are the only ones who know the truth about what happened that day."

She recalled what Callum had whispered to her while up on that stage.

"He might not even be alive today if it weren't for you."

"It's not that easy for me to sneak away now that Tom's been…"

"I know that Tom has not been treating you well."

"He's been treating me horribly, if you want to know the truth. It's why I would love nothing more than to see you again and talk through my issues."

"Think about it, then. You know how to reach me."

"If I can convince Tom to let me return to therapy, I just might."

"If you do manage to persuade him, we need to be completely honest with each other this time. No more secrets."

"I agree," she said. "Let me see what I can do."

Gwynn hung up, pleasantly surprised that Kaufman had called her. So he did want to see her. In some ways, she'd intuited it all along, but could never be sure. It meant he cared for her and not just as a patient. Her absence from his life had left an emotional void that she'd be more than happy to fill, assuming she could convince Tom to let her resume therapy. After all these years vying for Kaufman's attention, she believed she finally had it.

Ten minutes later, Denise barged into her office while she was checking on her portfolio. She closed the window and pretended to listen to the woman's long-winded lecture about efficiency in the workplace. Gwynn switched screens until she arrived at the intake case she'd been procrastinating on all morning. Her motivation had been sucked out of her by this dragon lady. She nodded every now and then as if paying attention, before Denise finally turned on her heel and stormed out. Rather than return to work, she typed Tift's name in the search engine, and a story from *Variety* popped up.

> *Tift Ainsley, star of Bolton City Blues and The Last Gorgeous Assassin, has gotten her own show on Netflix, Variety has learned.*
>
> *The highly secretive project, which wrapped up filming last month, is a scripted crime series with multiple episodes, numerous sources tell Variety, describing the project as focusing on a married LA therapist who has a secret life as a vigilante killing the worst elements of society. The first episode is to air sometime next month.*
>
> *Netflix declined to comment on the project.*
>
> *News of Ainsley's deal comes after word leaked out that Ainsley wrote, acted in, and produced each episode, all new titles for the Golden Globe–nominated actress.*
>
> *While the full scope of the series is tightly under wraps, an insider tells Variety that Garth Fuller will appear in the series as Detective Packwood.*

The news of Tift's show excited her, even if Tift had hijacked all the credit for herself. She wondered if Tift had changed enough of the story to hide her own culpability in these murders. It helped that they'd moved the location from Maine to the West Coast. By the time Hollywood twisted her story into a pretzel, no one would ever make the connection between her and all the murders she'd committed in Maine and beyond. Hopefully, there'd be more checks in the mail, too. Next time, she wouldn't be as careless and invest them in something as risky as crypto. She'd put them in mutual funds and bonds. Boring but safe. Her and Jack's future depended on it.

She thought again of Callum and couldn't help but feel that they were kindred spirits of sorts. Had she created this monster when she'd injected his father with that lethal dose of heroin?

A knock on the door and Denise barged in again, not even waiting for her to answer. She wanted to know the details of a specific intake case that had happened three weeks ago. Gwynn said she'd get the information to her as soon as possible. Rather than return to her office, Denise stood in the doorway, a look of concern on her face.

"I'm sorry to say, Gwynn, but this situation doesn't seem to be working out."

"What situation is that?"

"Our working relationship."

"Sorry to hear that, Denise. Does that mean you'll be handing in your resignation?" She regretted the snarky comment as soon as it came out of her mouth.

"Your lack of respect is insulting."

"Come on, I was only joking with you."

"You think all this is a joke? I take working with these children seriously."

"As do I," she said.

"It doesn't seem that way to me."

"What's your problem? You've been purposefully going out of your way to harass me and make my life miserable."

"I've done everything possible to accommodate you."

"So not true. Everyone in this office knows you want me out of your hair."

"Look, Gwynn, we have policies and rules in place that—"

"Oh, don't give me that bullshit about policies and rules. It's just you and me here, Denise."

The expression on the woman's face hardened.

"Why don't you just admit that you'd love for me to be gone. No sense staying where I'm not wanted, especially since you despise me."

Denise walked over to her desk and placed her fists down on the surface. "Okay, Gwynn. I'd rather you not be here. There, I've said it. I would be more than happy if you handed in your resignation and let me run this place the way I see fit."

"See. That wasn't so hard for you to admit, was it?"

"You're exactly the kind of person who has always stood in my way."

"Bravo for finally spitting out the truth," Gwynn said, clapping sarcastically.

"I should just fire you right now."

"Go for it. Just be forewarned: I still have some pull around here and can make life difficult for you if I choose."

Denise leaned over the desk, tall and solidly built. Gwynn stood to confront her, refusing to back down. She leaned over the desk and placed her face inches from her boss's.

"Do you really want to mess with me?" Gwynn said.

The woman seemed taken aback by such brazenness. "Excuse me?"

"I said: Do you really want to mess with me? It's a simple question."

Denise opened her mouth, but nothing came out.

"I'm fairly sure that you've been able to bully your way everywhere you've worked, but you don't scare me. And you want to know why?"

Denise's expression cracked, and she now seemed unsure of herself.

"Because I know exactly who I am and what I can do to people who try to take advantage of my good nature. So you'd better watch who you screw with, lady."

"Are you threatening me?"

"Yes, I believe I just did." Gwynn smiled. "And it's your word against mine if you choose to register a complaint with HR."

"You can't intimidate me."

"Oh, I'm not intimidating you, Denise. I'm threatening you. There's a big difference."

"This is not going to end well for you."

"Maybe not. But I can assure you that it will end much worse for you if you keep pushing me like you've been doing."

Denise stood to her full height and studied her. Gwynn knew that no one had ever spoken to her in such a direct and forceful way. She just didn't care about this job any longer, which meant she had nothing to lose by telling her boss off. Had it not been for the kids here at The Loft, she would have left much earlier.

Denise turned and walked out of her office. Once alone, Gwynn called her lawyer.

"Susan, I want to file a harassment suit against my boss."

"Harassment? Are you sure about this, Gwynn?"

"Absolutely. It's much better than the alternative."

"And what's the alternative?"

She imagined pushing Denise's lifeless body into that quarry. "Trust me, you don't want to know."

Chapter Twenty

DETECTIVE PETERS

Peters finished his third vodka tonic at J's Oyster by the time the booze had wormed into his brain. The dying light behind him fell over the bay. It had been over a week since he'd broken it off with Annabelle, and it felt like a giant weight had been lifted off his shoulders. Since meeting up with Gwynn, he'd come to the realization that all other relationships were meaningless. For that reason, and because Gwynn had admitted that she still loved him, he'd made the decision not to date anyone else, even if at times he found this vow difficult to keep. Attracting women had never been easier now that he had achieved a modicum of fame in town. Yet none of that mattered without the right woman by his side.

The bartender set down his fourth cocktail by the time Annabelle appeared on the flatscreen above the bar. She started in on a story about the sad lives of the girls living on the Bayside streets. He got off his stool and lumbered over to one of the tables by the window, carrying his drink in hand while staring at the fishing boats out in the harbor. Cutting out of work early was one of the benefits of his new status in the department. Why bust his ass when he knew all this time who was killing these girls. All he had to do now was find a mark to take the fall.

He'd been feeling lonely as of late, and stopping off for a few pops every evening hadn't alleviated the problem. He thought briefly that he might be an alcoholic, but just as quickly dismissed the notion. Gwynn's absence from his life was what had caused him to drink more than usual. Once he had her back in his life, he wouldn't ever need to drink again.

Swirling his cocktail in hand, he reminded himself to keep an even pace. He drank to hide the fact that the woman he loved was married to someone else, and that he couldn't have her until certain conditions were met. He drank because he knew that his reputation had been built on a lie and that he'd done nothing special to solve the Muddy River case. Knowing all this had caused his mind to turn on itself in the worst possible way, to the point where he couldn't even look at himself in the mirror without experiencing a wave of disgust.

Since kissing Gwynn at that banquet, he'd done some regrettable things. Last night, for example, he'd waited outside Tom's office until he left at six. It was the third time in the last two weeks he'd waited for him, and each time he stalked Tom, he felt closer to confronting him. It wouldn't take much to kick the guy's ass. Not only was Tom fat and out of shape, but he sat behind a desk all day. It was a good thing he hadn't done anything yet. Confronting Tom had the potential to destroy any hope he might have of rebuilding his relationship with Gwynn, and that had been the only thing holding him back. Come morning, nursing a hangover, he'd curse himself for being so reckless. Had he actually squared up to Tom and kicked his ass—or worse—he ran the risk of alienating Gwynn.

For that reason, and because Nguyen had woken from her coma, he needed to find those videos, and the person Tom sent them to—and fast. But he had no idea where to start looking.

He staggered over to the bar where a patron paid for his drink. After thanking the guy, he headed back to his seat. He could barely speak to anyone these days without wanting to punch them in the throat. Most people pissed him off, which made going out in public a challenge. He went out to bars because he was lonely, but then when he got there, he always wanted to drink by himself. Fame hadn't solved his problems, but instead magnified them and made his shortcomings seem even greater. So he sat stewing, worrying about everything, his ego getting pummeled into submission by his poisonous thoughts.

His phone chirped, and he saw that he had a few text messages. The first one was from his bookie, reminding him that he still owed him money. The second came from the studio in Manhattan. They had decided not to produce the true crime show based on the Muddy River Killer. Dejected about this news, he shut off his phone and slammed it down on the table. How many things could go wrong tonight? At this rate, his bank account would be empty by year's end.

Later that evening, he glanced up from his glass and, to his surprise, saw Tom sitting on one of the stools facing the bar. He'd recognize that jerk anywhere. He couldn't believe that Tom had ended up at the same gin joint as him, especially after he'd been stalking him like a Bengal tiger the last few weeks. The thought of Tom in the same establishment with him made him furious. The drunk devil on his left shoulder challenged him to go over and kick the guy's ass. The drunk angel on his right shoulder warned him that he'd regret it come morning. He glanced at his watch and saw that it was just past eight. Switching from vodka to beer had dulled his reflexes and altered his judgement. Tom's presence felt like a slap in the face, as if the man was daring him to come over and challenge him to a fight. He pictured Tom forcing himself on Gwynn in the bedroom, and the image made him hate the guy even more.

His pint glass sat empty in front of him, but he didn't care to go back to his condo. Surprisingly, he missed his ratty old apartment on St. John Street and the pleasant memories he'd made there with Gwynn. The new place, while nice, constantly reminded him of his failures as a cop, as well as the reputation he'd attained by fraud. Sadly, he began to loathe his waterfront condo, mostly because he hated himself. It was part of the reason he'd been staying out late most nights. That and the fact that he owed his bookie money and could barely keep up on his steep mortgage payments.

He stood and nearly tripped over the leg of the table. The pint glass slipped out of his hand and crashed along the floor. A few people sitting nearby turned and laughed, and he grumbled for them to mind their own business. He shuffled over to the bar until he found himself standing next to his nemesis.

"Well, look who it is," he said, sidling up to Tom and putting his hand on his shoulder.

"Do I know you?" Tom said, although his expression said otherwise.

"Fucking piece of shit. You know very well who I am."

"I think you'd better lay off the booze, pal. You're two sheets to the wind."

"Fuck you."

Tom turned to his friend. "Can you believe the lowlifes they let in this place?"

Peters grabbed Tom by the collar and pushed him off his stool. Something inside him snapped, and all he wanted to do was kill the bastard. He shoved him toward the far wall, against the advice of the bartender and waitress standing nearby. But then Tom stepped aside and threw him to the floor. The man's strength surprised him, and he struggled to his feet. His mind said to fight back, but his body didn't move. Tom warned him to stay down, but he couldn't possibly suffer another humiliating defeat. He stood, drunkenly, and put his fists up to his face. Everything in his vision started spinning as Tom's knuckles came smashing into his nose. He fell back against the floor, his nose exploding in pain. Tom's massive frame collapsed on top of him, and he landed punch after punch. The last thing Peters saw before passing out was Annabelle's smiling face on the screen above the bar, announcing the teaser story for the eleven o'clock news.

* * *

Pain radiated over the surface of his face as soon as the first rays of sunlight flittered into his bedroom. His phone buzzed, loud and obnoxious, like someone sending an electric shock through his brain. He sat up and groaned, ribbons of torment coursing through his skull. What the hell had he done last night? Had he dreamed that he'd confronted Gwynn's husband and challenged him to a fight? He felt his swollen and scabbed face and knew it was no dream. Grabbing his phone, he headed to the bathroom and stared at himself in the mirror. He resembled a slightly better-looking version of the Elephant Man. His left eye, partially closed, shined black and blue.

His upper lip was split and distended. How drunk had he gotten last night? And did Tom really do this to him? Fat and ugly Tom?

While taking a piss, he opened his phone and read the message from his boss. Another girl had been discovered down by the Presumpscot River, this time almost directly across from the Hannaford supermarket. He glanced outside the tiny bathroom window and saw rain pebbling the surface of the bay. He wanted nothing more than to fall back into bed and sleep for days, but he knew he couldn't now that there was another body out there to investigate.

He stepped out of his boxers and into the tiled glass shower. The hot water felt as if someone was firing a pellet gun at his body. Would Tom tell Gwynn what he did last night? Of course, he'd tell her. And Tom would boast about kicking his ass, warning Gwynn that he'd do the same to her if she ever stepped out of line. Would Gwynn hate him because of what he did? Or tried to do? She absolutely should because he hated himself. Maybe she'd be in a forgiving mood, knowing that everything he did—from killing girls to challenging Tom to a bar fight—he'd done because he loved her.

What would he tell the other cops when they saw his bruised and battered face? He could say he took a spill down the stairs, even though everyone would know the truth: that someone had kicked his ass. Word got around fast in Portland, and those nosy bastards didn't need to know every detail about his personal life.

He wanted to cry now because of how badly he'd screwed up. He punched the tiles beneath the shower head and, for a second, thought he might have broken his hand—and two of the imported mosaic tiles. But he didn't care. If Gwynn only knew how much he missed her, she'd understand the depth of his pain and what he'd done for her. For them. Sure, his actions have been extreme. But love pushed people to the brink. He'd lost his way—he'd killed—because of a woman. He'd gladly give up all the trappings of success so that they could be together.

He stepped out of the shower, examining his bloody knuckles. It wouldn't take long to drive over to where the girl's body had been found. He knew exactly what he would find and how she'd be positioned because he'd planned it that way. A familiar pattern had begun to emerge from these murders. Without even realizing it, he'd been copying the exact crimes of the Muddy River Killer, and he believed he knew why: women were attracted to men who resembled their fathers, even a father as monstrous as David Preston.

He grabbed a bag of frozen peas, pressed it against his nearly closed eye, and headed out.

Chapter Twenty-One

DETECTIVE PETERS

Everyone stood off to the side, ankle deep in the mud, allowing Peters enough space to view the body. He walked carefully with coffee cup in hand, glad he wore his L.L. Bean boots for traction. Thankfully, no one mentioned his bruised and battered face, but he could sense their curiosity as much as he could feel all eyes on him. The steady mist pelted his hood and rain jacket. From what he'd been told, a kayaker had been paddling along the bank of the river when he noticed a foot sticking out of the ferns. This was the third body to have been discovered along the river and beneath a canopy of ferns, a sure sign that the same killer had committed all three murders. He stepped back, feeling his stomach warble, trying to separate his official role as detective from his role as serial killer. A symmetrical pattern of ferns draped over the corpse. His eyes focused on the leaves, which glistened with beaded raindrops.

He'd done a fair bit of research on ferns and learned a few interesting things. To the indigenous Maori of New Zealand, the fern represented new life and new beginnings. The Japanese believed it represented family and hope for future generations. To the Victorians, it symbolized humility and sincerity. In the Middle Ages, their seeds were thought to make one invisible. But what people didn't know back then, and what even he hadn't known, was that ferns didn't have seeds but were spread by spores.

He squatted down, feeling his intestines unraveling like an emptying water hose, and spread the wet leaves apart. The girl's face immediately came into view, and he remembered covering it with the plastic bag and watching as she died. Her eyes remained open, staring up at the canopy as if she was a botanist studying a rare plant. Her body had assumed a bluish tint to it. A small tuft of pubic hair rose from her pelvic area. A series of dots ran from her wrist to her elbow. Her jet-black hair was still tied up in a ponytail and placed purposefully over her left shoulder. Every muscle in his body felt the gravitational pull of dehydration, and the coffee only exacerbated his thirst. He wanted to throw up, but somehow he managed to keep everything in.

Was his mind playing tricks on him? For a brief second, he thought he saw the girl's lips move, as if she was trying to tell him something. And then her eyes slowly turned toward him and seemed to regard him with curiosity. He wanted to tell the girl that she shouldn't judge him harshly for killing her, and that she should be thanking him for putting her out of her misery. But then he snapped out of his haze and realized he'd been hallucinating. Was he losing his mind? Had he really believed this dead girl was communicating with him? He couldn't go on like this; his sanity slowly slipping away.

The river flowed below, cold and dark, and moving at a steady pace. He released the ferns, and the girl slipped back into the landscape, except for her bare foot. It took him a second to notice the tattoo of a dream catcher on her ankle. Why hadn't he noticed that before? Was the girl Native American? An ocean wave made out of thin sterling silver encircled her long toe. He leaned over and examined the ring. Did it symbolize something deeper? He slipped it off and let it rest in the palm of his hand. It felt weightless and flimsy. Instead of putting it back on the girl's toe, he squeezed it in his hand, which he kept hidden out of sight.

He turned and made his way up the bank of the river, conscious of everyone staring at him. A thick wedge of trees stood between him and the parking lot. He stepped carefully over the roots and branches, not wanting to trip and spill his coffee. The steady mist made him keenly aware of the cuts and bruises over his face. When he reached the clearing, he saw the news crews waiting to question him. Lately, he viewed these people more as parasites than news reporters. The first reporter he saw was Annabelle, and the sight of her made him cringe. Annabelle held the microphone in a way that made it look like she wanted to hit him over the head with it. And she probably would have, assuming she could have gotten away with clocking him. The last thing he'd expected this morning was an encounter with his ex-girlfriend—no, his *scorned* ex-girlfriend.

"Oh my god, Mike, I swear I didn't hire someone to kick your ass," she said, reveling in his misery. "But I'm glad they did."

"I fell down some stairs, okay."

"Right. We'll run with that for now."

"Can we keep this professional, Annabelle?"

"You didn't care about professionalism when you were screwing my brains out," she said, not caring who heard this conversation.

"Control yourself. We have jobs to do."

"I know you better than you know yourself, Mike," she whispered, leaning into him. "I'm going to find out what happened to you and then tell the world who worked you over."

"Why would you do that?" The thought of that beatdown broadcast over the airwaves worried him, especially knowing that Gwynn might see it.

"That's nothing compared to how I'm going to screw you over. I bet no one knows that you stopped off at Howie's Pub for a few drinks before you shot that motorist."

"That motorist had a rap sheet a mile long."

"All the same, he didn't deserve to die at the hands of a drunken cop."

"I wasn't drunk." Admittedly, he did have a good buzz on that night.

"Good luck disproving it."

"Is it any wonder you can't hold onto a man?" He knew it was a cruel thing to say, but it came out of his mouth too late.

Her face compressed like a dying star. "You're a real shit, Peters."

"Hey, you can only push a guy so far."

"Trust me, I haven't even started pushing you," she said. "I'm going to be your worst nightmare from now on." She turned and waved for her cameraman to follow her back to the van.

As Peters shook his head and watched her leave, his phone dinged. A text message from Officer Romano.

Holy shit, Mike! Did you hear the news? Nguyen has started talking?

This day couldn't end soon enough.

Chapter Twenty-Two

Gwynn glanced at the alarm clock, unable to sleep. Beside her, Tom snored, his noxious breath defiling her nostrils. She hated weekends the most since getting back together with him. Two full days at his beck and call, pretending she loved him. Usually, he slept in late on the weekends, but the last few Friday evenings, he'd staggered home well after midnight, drunk and clamorous, often waking her up in the middle of the night to utter some boozy gibberish. It pissed her off when she thought about it, knowing he'd rather be out with the boys than home with his family. But after realizing how happy she was when he was gone, she hoped he would go out every night and leave her be. Last night she'd pretended to be asleep when he lumbered noisily into the bedroom, afraid Tom might make another one of his perverted demands. But thankfully, he hadn't. He'd nearly toppled to the floor while taking off his pants, laughing as he collapsed into bed, sending ripples across the mattress like a stone tossed into a pond.

Such a different person from who he was back in college. She remembered going over to his dorm one night and talking to him for hours on end, the two of them lying across his bed and eating Doritos and Skittles while Thom Yorke sang about what a creep he was. He had posters plastered all over the walls of the bands he loved: Pearl Jam, Nickelback, The Pixies, and Soundgarden. Sometime later, they fell asleep in each other's arms, the song 'More Than Words' playing over the speakers. Tom had been a gentleman the entire night.

After lifting the blanket, she slipped out from under the covers and tiptoed across the hardwood floor, hoping not to wake him. Maybe, hungover, he'd sleep until noon and give her some much-needed peace and quiet. She grabbed her robe off the door hook, noticing his clothes scattered over the floor. In addition to getting fat, he'd also turned into a slob, forcing her to constantly pick up after him. She had to clear his plates and silverware after every dinner, making sure they went straight into the dishwasher. She was also the one who took out the trash and rolled the bins to the end of the driveway for collection.

She checked in on Jack before heading downstairs, knowing he would wake up in an hour or so, unless that movie they'd watched last night had tired him out. The stillness of the house at this hour agreed with her, as did the morning sunlight filtering in through the blinds. She went outside and grabbed the newspaper, waving to a neighbor passing by before returning inside and brewing up a pot of coffee.

On the kitchen island sat her cell phone. It was the family phone that Tom continually monitored and made her keep with her twenty-four seven. She'd hidden her burner phone in the dropdown tiles above the washing machine. When she opened it, she saw a text message from Ivy.

Ivy: Thanks so much for helping me, Gwynn. I took your advice and am now going to outpatient rehab, which means I'm back with my family—for now. I might not be alive if it weren't for you.

This message made her happy, aside from the part about her moving back in with her family. It would only take one incident to cause her to spiral out of control, sending her back out into the streets and into the arms of prostitution and drug addiction. And if that happened, her chance at living a normal life would be significantly lower.

Before pouring herself a cup of coffee, she glanced briefly at her portfolio and saw that it was down another two percent. She promised herself that she'd stop obsessing over her holdings, yet every day she found herself checking on them. She was losing all the money she'd earned from that script, money she and Jack would one day need to live on once she freed herself from Tom.

She reminded herself to check her burner phone later in the day to see if Callum or Peters had left a message. But that could wait. No sense taking a risk with Tom sleeping soundly upstairs. She turned on the radio and lowered the volume. An Elton John song came on that she loved. 'Goodbye England's Rose', rewritten from 'Candle in the Wind' to honor Princess Diana. She sat enjoying the tune, comparing her own marriage to Princess Diane's, all the while trying to figure a way out of the mess she'd gotten herself into without ending up dead like Diane.

She recalled Callum saying that he could help her discover whom Tom had sent that video to. But how? Would he hack into Tom's computer and check out his emails? He obviously had advanced computer skills. She didn't know the password to Tom's laptop, which he kept upstairs in his locked study. Still, it gave her hope that Callum might figure something out before she went too far during their games and killed him. Despite the brief moments when she recalled their days at Brooks, killing Tom was all she could think about. It didn't even matter now that he was the father of their son. Tom fully understood what she was capable of. Yet every night he fell into bed with her, knowing fully well that he was sleeping next to a black mamba.

She heard the patter of footsteps on the stairs and saw Jack approaching, dressed in his firetruck pajamas. His hair stuck up at all angles, and crust had formed at the corners of his eyes. He climbed on the stool and rested his chin on his cupped palms. She thought of her other life while staring at Jack and couldn't believe she'd gotten away with it all.

"My wiggleworm has finally woken up. Are you hungry?"

"Uh-huh."

"What would you like for breakfast? I can make you pancakes if you like."

He shook his head. "Cereal. With milk."

"Okay. We have Cheerios or oatmeal," she said, moving to the pantry.

"Koko Krispers."

She shot him a look. "You know we don't have that, Jack. It's very bad for you."

"Daddy bought me some yesterday. He said if I was good, I could have Koko Krispers for breakfast."

"He did, did he?" She opened the pantry door and saw the familiar brown box sitting on the shelf. As a young girl, she'd craved the same sugary cereals, but her parents would never buy them for her.

"Wouldn't you rather have blueberry pancakes with maple syrup?"

"No, I want Koko Krispers."

She sighed, not wanting to get into a power struggle she knew she wouldn't win, especially since Tom had said Jack could have Koko Krispers. Best to go along for the time being and then retrain him once it was just the two of them. Now that her marriage had lost its natural checks and balances, Tom had morphed into an erratic dictator, sometimes cruel and other times benevolent. Whatever leverage she'd once had in their relationship no longer existed because of those stupid videos.

"Hurry, Mom. I'm hungry."

She grabbed the box of Koko Krispers off the shelf, filled the bowl with the brown pellets, and then poured milk into it. Jack reached out and snatched the bowl out of her hands and began to eat ravenously. She watched him, noticing how much he resembled his father. Without proper nurturing, he would develop into a testosterone-fueled cur. Too bad Jack couldn't have known his father back at Brooks when he was kinder and more caring. It was why she had to act as quickly as possible and get Callum to find out whom Tom had sent that video to.

The sound of Peters's voice startled her, and she realized it was coming from the radio. Jack crunched loudly, forcing her to turn up the volume. Another young girl had been found along the Presumpscot River. The police now believed it to be the work of a copycat. Her father came to mind, and all the terrible things he'd gotten away with over the years. Peters's gravelly voice transported her back to that woodsy cabin in the country, the two of them making love in front of the blazing fireplace, and on the same rug Tom had purchased for her.

For the last six months, the latest dead girl had been prostituting herself on the streets in exchange for drug money. Her family lived on the Penobscot Indian Reservation, and her mother said that she ran away from home over a year ago. She'd just turned seventeen at the time of her death. Gwynn leaned forward to hear more, but glanced up when she heard the sound of Tom coming down the stairs. Why had he gotten up so early?

Upon hearing his father's footsteps, Jack threw down his spoon and sprinted toward him. Tom smiled and caught his son in his arms, lifting him toward the ceiling. Jack giggled, and she couldn't help but feel envious that her son appeared to love his father more than he loved her. Maybe if she spoiled Jack like Tom did, he might feel differently about her. Instead, she'd been forced to play the role of evil mother until the time came when she could escape this domestic prison and raise him alone.

Tom, dressed in his powder blue Brooks College sweatshirt, hefted Jack in his arms and walked over to the kitchen island. He looked bloated as he leaned over and kissed her on the cheek. His eyes appeared as mere slits over his puffy face, and his wet hair spiked up from showering. He reached in his pocket and pulled out a shiny video game, laying it on the granite countertop: *Vigilante Justice*. The sight of it made Gwynn queasy.

"What's that, Dad?" Jack asked.

"Only the best video game ever."

"Really?"

"Yup. It's a game your old man used to kick play when he was a kid. I was in the store the other day and happened to come across it."

"Cool. Can we play it?"

"Maybe if you clean your room and get all your chores done."

"Awesome," Jack said.

"You also have to trace your letters."

"I will," the boy said, jumping off his stool and running up to his room.

Gwynn focused her gaze on the video game now resting on the countertop. She remembered Tom and his friends playing it for hours on end back in his dorm room at Brooks, one of the few things about him that bothered her. There were other offshoots of the game throughout the years as the technology improved and the characters became more realistic. At least five loathsome sequels, each of them progressively more violent and twisted than their predecessor. The game featured a first-person shooter making his way through an urban, crime-ridden neighborhood, which was populated by ex-cons looking to rob, rape, and kill people. Somewhat tame by today's standards, it definitely wasn't appropriate for a five-year-old boy. Players had the ability to switch between first-person and multi-person shooters.

"I know, I know, it's a bit graphic, but I'll explain to him the difference between real and make-believe."

"He's five years old, for god's sake."

"Kids play much worse games these days. Besides, it helps with their eye coordination and processing skills."

"Think about it, Tom, this game will put your son in the role of an active shooter walking through dangerous neighborhoods."

"Like mother, like son." He laughed. "Would you be a doll and pour me a cup of coffee."

Trying to remain calm, she got up and prepared his coffee the way he liked before setting it down in front of him.

"What? No love for your hubby this morning?"

"You don't deserve any love for buying him that stupid game."

"Come on, sweetie, don't be like that."

He wrapped his thick arms around her and kissed her on the lips, and it was all she could do to keep from gagging. His hot breath reeked of stale gin and whatever junk food he'd wolfed down last night.

"Would you mind making me some of your world-famous scrambled eggs?" he asked. "With that delicious maple sausage you bought last week?"

"You told me last week that you were going to start dieting and going to the gym."

"What's the rush? I'll start next week."

She grabbed the nonstick frying pan and heated up three pats of margarine. Grabbed the carton of eggs out of the refrigerator along with a package of shredded cheddar cheese and some fatty breakfast sausages. She cracked the four eggs and whisked them vigorously in a bowl along with some heavy cream and a pinch of pancake batter. Popped an English muffin in the toaster and thumbed down the lever. A John Mayer song played over the radio, reminding her of when Peters came over for their pizza 'interview'. She glanced back and saw Tom flipping through the pages of the newspaper. Turning back to the frying pan, she recalled the excitement she'd felt that day when Peters leaned over and kissed her on the lips, leaving her wanting for more. Now she wasn't sure how she felt about him. Did she really care about Peters? Or had she just gotten caught up in the thrill of the moment? Why was everything in her life so confusing?

"Hey," Tom said while she whisked the eggs a little too aggressively. "I ran into a friend of yours the other night."

"Really? Who was that?"

"That detective you were fucking behind my back. Remember him?"

She stopped whisking and held the fork up as if it were a bloody knife. Egg batter dripped into the bowl.

"I was out with some coworkers when that loser came over and started giving me shit."

She turned to face him. "What did *he* want?"

"First, he started calling me all these nasty names; then he tells me that the two of you are still in love." Tom sipped his coffee. "Can you imagine the balls on that guy?"

"He's obviously deluded."

"You sure about that?"

"Of course, I'm sure about it. I know how badly I screwed everything up between us." She put another pat of margarine in the pan before pouring in the egg mixture. "I love you more than anything, Tom."

"That's what I told him," he said. "But the guy didn't believe me."

"What did he do?"

"Challenged me to a fight."

"He what?" She turned and stared at him. How could Peters be so stupid, although she understood why. "I hope you were the bigger man and walked away."

"I would have, but he kept egging me on. And I couldn't back down and look like a pussy in front of my coworkers."

She turned to the stovetop and moved the eggs around in the pan before they burned, knowing Tom hated when his scrambled eggs turned brown. "I hope they kicked him out that place."

"Oh no, I had to teach your boyfriend a lesson he'll not soon forget."

"He's not my boyfriend," she said. "Did you fight him?"

"It wasn't much of a fight. Everyone at the bar saw the way he was harassing me. Let's just say it was self-defense."

She plated his sausages and eggs, adding enough salt and pepper to raise his blood pressure through the roof. The toast popped. She lifted it out and then spread a generous schmear of margarine over the nooks and crannies before setting the plate out in front of him.

"What happened after that?"

"They had to pull me off him."

She let his words sink in as the margarine dissolved into the toast. Hopefully, it would settle into his arteries and harden like cement. "Sounds like he deserved it."

"Oh, he deserved it alright. I really messed up that pretty boy's face."

She walked over and served him his breakfast.

"This looks awesome, hon. Thanks so much."

"You're welcome," she said, sitting down and resting her chin on her palm. "I have a big favor to ask you, Tom."

He didn't respond to this; he was too busy stuffing his face with scrambled eggs and sausage.

"You're such an amazing cook, Gwynn. I don't know how you do it."

She waited a beat to ask him. "I want to see Dr. Kaufman again."

"The way you get these eggs so moist and fluffy. It's amazing." He moaned, shaking his head while shoveling the food in his mouth. "And I love how you butter the English muffins. Cover all four corners."

"Glad you like it."

"Like it? I love it. I could pound this down every morning."

"Bet your cardiologist would love to hear that," she said.

"I've got the heart of a twenty-year-old," he said, thumping his chest.

"The issue is, my dissociative disorder's been acting up lately, and I've suffered from this problem since high school."

"Maybe your shrink is the one who screwed you up." He bit off a piece of his muffin. "Ever think of that?"

"No, Tom. He's the one who's helped me get through everything and be the person I am today. The great wife I am to you."

"Personally, I think shrinks are full of shit."

"Not him. He was the one who advised me to stay with you and not take up with that cop," she lied.

He stopped chewing and looked at her. "He said that?"

"Yes, and if only I'd listened to him from the get-go, I wouldn't have screwed things up as badly as I did."

"But then if you hadn't cheated on me, we wouldn't have started playing these fun little games of ours."

"That's true."

"God has His reasons for everything," he said, lips dotted with specks of egg. "It's just nice that you and I can now share our deepest, darkest secrets."

She felt like throwing up, especially when he brought God into the conversation.

"Personally, I think it's hot that you killed all those dirtbags."

"Yes, I know you do."

"And I've never once judged you for what you've done."

She took a deep breath and tried to maintain her composure. "So can I return to therapy?"

He took a bite out of his sausage. "Let me think about it."

She watched him eat, hoping he might gag on a sausage and choke to death.

"By the way, I told my mother that we'd be going over to her house next week for Easter. She and Trish are preparing an elaborate egg hunt for Jack."

"That sounds wonderful. Does she want me to bring anything over?" The thought of spending the entire day with Trish and her bossy mother-in-law filled her with dread.

"Not sure yet."

CHAPTER TWENTY-TWO

"Okay, but please give me enough time to go shopping if she does."

"Will do," he said. "Just to give you a heads-up, I'm spending a few days in Boston with some of the guys. I'll be driving home early Easter morning."

"Good. You've been working hard lately and deserve to have some downtime." She couldn't wait to be free from him, even if temporarily.

"When I come home that morning, we'll go to Easter service before we head over to my mother's house. I think going to church is good for Jack's moral development."

"No argument here. After all, my father was a minister."

"I don't think your father liked me very much." Tom glanced up at her.

"Of course he liked you," she said, knowing her father had always acted cool toward Tom.

"Doesn't really matter now that he's six feet under," Tom said. "Anyway, Jack needs to learn about these things."

"Maybe we should enroll him in Sunday school."

"Nah, he doesn't need all that churchy bullshit. I can teach him everything he needs to know about God." He forked another sausage into his mouth and chomped it in half. "Do you miss it sometimes?"

"Miss what? Going to church?"

"No, not church. The other thing." He sliced his hand across his throat.

She laughed. "I don't know what you mean."

"Offing dudes."

She found this question disconcerting. "No, not at all. I'm quite happy with my life right now."

"Hmmm."

She backhanded him on the arm. "What does hmmm mean?"

"I don't want you to completely lose your desire. I find it kind of sexy that you bumped off all those people, especially Sandra."

"Okay, Tom. I'll save a little of that badass for you." She laughed, believing him to be a truly disturbed individual. "The truth is, the urge never really left me."

"So I have my little murder bug back?"

"I never left. But remember, Tom, it's our little secret."

He rubbed his hands together. "Maybe we can play a little rough-and-tumble tonight after Jack goes to bed."

"Maybe." A tremble passed through her at the mere thought of being intimate with him.

"Cool," he said, pushing his empty plate away. "I'm going to grab Jack out of his room now so we can play our video game."

"Just make sure he traces his letters."

"Oh my god, Gwynn, will you chill out about those damn letters," he said, holding the video game aloft. "Who knows, maybe Jack will be as good as his old man someday at *Vigilante Justice*."

She turned the radio up as Tom went upstairs to get Jack. The first thing she heard was a reporter saying that Nguyen had started talking. This development worried her. Would Nguyen tell everyone what happened that night and that it had been her who chased her out into that street? Causing her to get hit by that car? Or that Peter's had offered her a sweet deal to help him solve the Muddy River Killer case? But with Nguyen's unreliable memory, who would ever believe her? Certainly not a defense attorney or jury of twelve people. Her credibility would be destroyed in a court of law.

Chapter Twenty-Three

DR. EZRA KAUFMAN

I'm expecting Gwynn to arrive any minute now. I can't believe I called and asked her if she would be willing to resume therapy. Hearing her voice that day made my heart leap, despite all the alarms going off in my head warning me otherwise. Loneliness does that to a person, even to a trained therapist who should know better.

And all of this comes amid the growing death toll from this copycat killer. Odds are, the person committing these murders is someone no one would ever suspect. Someone who is esteemed in the community and fits into the social fabric with ease.

I've spent the last hour tidying my office. It's a good thing I kept the lease for this place when it came up for renewal. I decided that I would keep it until the day came when Gwynn asked to resume therapy. Not once in all that time we were apart did I ever believe she wouldn't return. We need each other. And now that my mother is gone, she's all I have left in this world. I've worked with her since she was a teenager and feel an obligation to her.

I turn on the news each night, watching that detective answer the media's questions. I'm not sure what Gwynn sees in him, aside from his looks. There's something about Detective Peters that concerns me, although I'm not sure what it is. But she loves him, and he loves her, and he was willing to assume the mantle of celebrity in order to make sure her father faded quietly into the background. He just doesn't seem to possess the kind of keen intellectual mind that could solve such complex cases.

The deep-sea divers discovered Sandra's boot at the bottom of the ocean, attached to a section of nylon rope. I thought for sure that Gwynn would be revealed as the killer, believing that she had tripped up and left a trace of her DNA behind. But she did a good job covering her tracks. Instead, it only bolstered the case against Sandra's husband. Everyone now believes he went on the lam and is hiding out somewhere in the Alaskan backwoods. Only he's not. He's dead, his only crime having been to walk in on Gwynn after she'd killed his blackmailing wife.

And then there's Detective Nguyen. She recently woke from her coma and is reportedly talking. Will she open up and point the finger at Gwynn?

A knock on the door jars me out of my thoughts. Normally, the arrival of a patient wouldn't excite me, but today I feel like a schoolboy. I stand and straighten out my tie. My entire body trembles as I walk to the door. It's sometimes difficult to imagine that a woman so seemingly kind and generous, a devoted mother who has dedicated her life to helping abused children, would have it in her to kill.

I open the door and see her, the smile on my face growing. She looks beautiful in the most understated way.

"It's just nice to see you again, Gwynn."

"It's nice to see you, too."

"I suppose I'm becoming sentimental in my old age."

"Wow. That's the first time I've ever heard you say something like that."

"I'm not the same man I was a year ago," I say, welcoming her into my office. We walk to our appointed seats. "Being retired has given me time to reflect on my life. And my mother's passing has made me acutely aware of my own mortality."

"I'm sure a healthy guy like you has many more miles left on the meter."

"Maybe. Maybe not."

"So are these personal changes you've made a good thing?"

"I certainly believe so. My emotional rigidity has been one of the biggest roadblocks holding me back."

"It's good to recognize your shortcomings," she says, crossing her legs. "I have to admit, I'm very happy to be back here with you."

"I couldn't bear the thought of you starting over with a new therapist. We've been together since you were a young girl."

"True."

"My only rule now is that we be completely honest with each other. If we can't do that, then we're fooling ourselves and wasting time."

"I want us both to be an open book."

"Can I ask you something?"

"Of course."

"It's about these girls who are turning up along the Presumpscot River."

"What about them?"

I shift uncomfortably in my seat.

"Wait." She laughs again. "You seriously don't think that I had anything to do with their deaths?"

"No, but I felt I should ask since we're being completely honest with each other."

She pauses for a few seconds. "You know I would never do something that terrible."

I nod.

"The people I…dealt with deserved what they had coming to them. Like Callum Frye's father."

"Do you have any idea who might be committing these murders?"

"Oh no. I've been way too busy dealing with my own issues to worry about that."

"Yes, and we'll get to those issues in due time," I say, trying to choose my words carefully. "Have you been able to keep your impulses in check since we last met?"

She stares down at her hands for an uncomfortably long time. "I won't lie to you. I think all the time about getting rid of my husband."

"Considering the way he's been treating you lately, I can't say that I blame you."

"He plays these mind games with me. At times it gets so twisted that I sometimes feel like I'm losing my sanity."

"Things are that bad?"

"Worse than you know. I'm a prisoner in my own home and have no idea how I can continue on like this."

"So the answer to my original question is no?"

She looks up at me. "What was your original question?"

"Have you acted on your impulses since the last time we met?"

She looks away and starts to tear up. I pass her a box of tissues, and she takes one, blowing her nose into it. All my nerve endings stand at attention in anticipation of her answer.

"You go first," she says.

"What would you like me to tell you?"

"I'd like for you to tell me something about yourself, Dr. Kaufman. Something deeply personal that you've never told anyone before."

"This is not how therapy works, Gwynn."

"I thought this was our new arrangement going forward. Mutual transparency."

I pause for a moment.

"You think this is easy for me?" she says. "I thought we needed to trust each other."

"We do," I say, working up the courage to say it. "Okay, here it is." I hesitate for a few seconds. "I love you."

"You love me?" She looks up and laughs, which hurts my feelings. "You're in love with me?"

"No, I said I love you. There's a big difference."

"Explain, please."

"I don't have any children of my own. My brother died at a young age, and I never made any close friends. My mother died recently. I suppose you're the closest thing to a friend I have, as unprofessional as that may sound."

"I don't know what to say."

"You don't need to say anything. I wouldn't even have told you had you not pressed me."

CHAPTER TWENTY-THREE

"You love me despite all the questionable choices I've made in my life?"

"I've always believed there was context for the things you've done. And I know you have a kind and generous heart."

"You seem more convinced of that than I am."

"Now it's your turn."

She sits quietly for a while before saying, "My father did not die of natural causes."

"You…"

"Yes. I grew up only knowing the loving version of my father, not the evil monster he was in his other life. And he was suffering badly those last few weeks."

"How did you do it?"

"His caretaker had fallen asleep out in the living room. I placed a pillow over his face, and no one knew any better the next morning when he failed to wake up."

"I see."

"You don't blame me for doing it?"

"No," I say.

"Let me ask you this, Dr. Kaufman. Is there anything I could do that would cause you to turn against me?"

"If I ever believed that you were hurting innocent people, I'd turn you in immediately."

"I'll do anything to protect my son, if that means killing Tom or anyone else who threatens to harm him."

I try not to dwell on that inconvenient fact. "Tell me more about Tom."

"He controls every aspect of my life, from how many hours I work to where I can go in town and whom I can see. He decides what we're having for dinner to how we raise Jack. In the bedroom, he's turned our relationship on its head."

"How so?"

"He demands that I do certain…things to him."

"What kinds of things?"

"Domination and S&M," she says. "Who knew when I met him that he enjoyed being on the receiving end of pain?"

"You please your husband by hurting him?"

"Yes. He forces me to reenact all the murders I've committed on him in the bedroom."

"That's so disturbing."

She laughs. "You had to go to Harvard to realize this?"

"What in particular does he make you do?"

"Sometimes, before we make love, he makes me squeeze a plastic bag over his head until he passes out."

"And he's been keeping these fantasies from you for all these years?"

"Obviously, or I never would have married him. Back in college, he was a completely different guy, kind and caring, and everyone's best friend."

"I'm sorry, Gwynn."

"It's not your fault. Besides, I deserve all the bad things coming to me," she says. "And Tom had warned me that if I don't perform the way he wants, he'll take Jack from me and make our son live with his mother or sister."

I shake my head.

"If it weren't for Jack, I would have killed Tom by now. Or myself."

"You can always call me if you need to talk."

She stares down at her shoes. "That night you saw me at the banquet, I ended up with Peters down in the basement."

"You two are still in love?"

"I'm not sure. I've been having thoughts about someone else."

"That's normal, especially for someone who is being manipulated and controlled the way you are."

"I've been thinking about the young man who introduced me at that banquet."

"You mean the boy you rescued all those years ago from his drug-addicted parents?"

"He's a man now," she says, as if trying to justify it. "It's pathetic, I know, that I'm thinking about someone almost young enough to be my son, but since we're being honest."

I don't respond to this, waiting for her to continue.

"We met for coffee. Turns out he was once a talented figure skater. He's also rich from having invested in cryptocurrencies. In fact, he's helped me invest in them for when I'm no longer with Tom."

"And Tom doesn't know about this?"

"He can never find out about it, or else he'll steal all my hard-earned money."

"The money you've been saving from your job at The Loft?"

"No. He made me step down as director and take a lesser-paying position."

"Then where did you get the money?"

"I wrote a bunch of stories for my college roommate out in Hollywood, having no expectation that anything would come of them. She called me out of the blue the other day and told me that the producers loved my work so much that they started filming the episodes."

"That's amazing, Gwynn. What's it about?"

She laughs. "A serial-killing housewife. Write what you know, isn't that what they say?"

"But aren't you worried that people will put two and two together?"

"Fortunately for me, Tift stole the credit for my idea. Not only that, but they moved the show to LA. She's not only starring in it, but acting as one of the producers."

"That must have been quite upsetting to you."

"At first, I felt betrayed that she would do such a terrible thing to one of her closest friends, but then I realized how lucky I was that she did. I can now write in anonymity, and at the same time make more money if the show becomes successful."

"And that's what you used to buy your cryptocurrencies?"

"Yes, but my hundred thousand dollar investment is now down to fifty-one thousand."

"Be careful. You don't want Tom finding out about your secret stash."

"Oh, I am. I have to beg him for enough money to buy toothpaste and toilet paper."

I look up at the clock and realize that our time is up. She's given me a lot to chew on as she stands to leave. I walk her to the door. Instead of saying goodbye, this time I reach out for a hug.

"Thanks for taking me back," she says, hugging me.

"Thank you for coming back," I say. "Take care of yourself, Gwynn."

"I'll try. I just can't wait for the day when Jack and I can finally be free."

And with that, she walks out of my office. But this time I know she'll be back.

Chapter Twenty-Four

GWYNN

"What the hell is this?" Denise said as she walked into Gwynn's office clutching a piece of paper.

"Did you not read it? I feel like I'm being harassed at work. So I took legal action to protect myself."

"You're kidding, right?"

"Oh, but I'm not. And if you read the document closely, you'll see that the board of directors has mandated that you're to communicate with me only in writing until this matter is resolved."

"This is bullshit, and you know it. You'll never get away with this."

"I'm not getting away with anything. You've been harassing me at work, and I'm merely exercising my legal rights."

Denise balled up the paper in her hands. "You have no idea who you're dealing with."

"I'd like you to leave my office so I can get back to work."

"I severely underestimated you."

"Yes, you did, and that's your fault."

"It sure is, but I won't make that mistake again."

"Any correspondence you care to have with me from here on out should be done in writing. And I will be relaying all of our conversations to the board of directors, including this one."

"I should have fired you when I had the chance."

"Yes, you should have. Such a shame you missed your opportunity."

"There's something strange about you, Gwynn. It's like you're hiding something about yourself from everyone, but I'll make it my mission to find out what it is."

"Good luck with that."

Denise tossed the balled paper onto Gwynn's desk and stormed out of her office. Her words echoed in Gwynn's head. Had she sensed something dark about her? She shrugged it off. At least for now, she felt as if she could do whatever she wanted until this legal matter got resolved. And by the time it did, Tift's television show would be up and running, and it wouldn't matter whether she got fired or not.

Still, she couldn't figure out what to do if Nguyen started talking about her injuries and how she got them. She'd have to deal with that problem when it came up. Until that happened, she had much more to get done.

Rather than return to work, she picked up the newspaper and read about the most recent girl who'd been discovered down by the river. Peters was quoted as saying he believed this to be the work of a copycat killer. It pained her to think that her father had started all this mayhem, paving the way for an admirer to follow in his footsteps. She folded up the newspaper and put it away, not wanting to read any more about this depressing development.

It felt more relaxed now that she'd called off the hounds. She sipped her coffee and checked on her portfolio, pleasantly surprised to see that it had gone up overnight. Maybe if she held out long enough, she could recoup her losses and cash out. Then invest the money in a reputable mutual fund and make solid gains year after year. She still needed to make good on her deal with Callum, but she doubted he'd ever follow through on it. Very few people had the stomach to actually kill another human being, like she had done.

Her computer dinged, and she answered it, seeing Ivy's face filling the screen.

"Hey, Ivy. You look amazing," she said.

"Everything's going pretty well right now. My mom finally kicked my dad out, so things at home are pretty chill at the moment."

"That's great. Why'd she kick him out?"

"She found out he was cheating again, and she swore this time she'd never take him back. Then again, she's said that before."

"Hopefully, she means it this time."

"We'll see."

"What else have you been up to?"

"I've been attending the alternative high school in town and going to my rehab sessions. I feel much happier now, thanks to you."

"That's great. Maybe I can take you out to lunch sometime?"

"That'd be cool, although I'm really busy at the moment."

"Whenever you're ready, make sure and call me. For now, you need to focus on your classes and going to rehab."

"Gotta run. Class starts in a few minutes."

"Okay, take care."

"You, too."

"I love you, Ivy," she said, waving goodbye before the screen went black.

The news of Ivy's recovery made her happy beyond words. Combined with getting Denise off her back, as well as her portfolio starting to move in the right direction, this was the best day she'd had in a while. She switched screens and started to work on one of her cases. Fifty minutes later, she heard a knock on the door. When she looked up, she saw Callum standing there with a bouquet of roses in hand. The sight of him caused her to blush.

"What are you doing here?" she said, secretly excited to see him.

"These are for you."

"They're beautiful." She leaned over and breathed in their fragrance. "You didn't need to do this."

"I know, but it's been a little while since we last talked."

"Come in and shut the door behind you," she said, nervous that people might see him. "What do you want?"

"Wow." He laughed. "I thought you'd be more happy to see me."

"I am, just not here at my place of work."

"What better place to catch up, seeing as your husband keeps you on such a tight leash."

"Why are you here?"

"We had a deal, the last time I checked."

"We did, but it's not like you've done me any favors with these cryptocurrencies you told me to buy."

"Relax. They've rebounded nicely today."

"I'm still out forty grand."

"Those cryptocurrencies are going to make you a lot of money someday. Just sit back and HODL."

"HODL?"

"It's a term we use in the crypto community. It means to hold your digital assets for the long term."

"My initial investment has been cut in half. How am I supposed to support myself and my son once we're on our own?"

"You mean once Tom's out of the picture?" he said.

She glanced around nervously. "I mean once we're...separated and divorced."

"Separated and divorced. Right," he said, sitting back and smiling. "Maybe I'll be the one who separates him from you."

"Maybe. First, we have to find out who Tom sent those videos to."

"That'll be easy enough."

"And you can't come around here anymore if we're to work together. People will start making assumptions."

He held up his hands in mock protest. "Fine, I'll never show my face in this building again."

"Not like you don't know your way around this place."

"I remember living here like it was yesterday. It's why having enough money to support myself is so important. "

"Can you come over to my house next Thursday morning? Tom's going down to Boston to party with his friends, and he won't be arriving home until Easter morning."

"Perfect."

"We'll meet in the parking lot of the supermarket in town. Then I'll drive you over to my place."

CHAPTER TWENTY-FOUR

"Don't want the neighbors to see me?"

"Something like that."

"I get it. I'm a handsome dude."

"Humble too." She rolled her eyes, shooing him away with a file folder. "I just hope no one saw you come up here."

"Don't worry. No one saw me," he said, heading for the door. "And whatever you do, Gwynn, don't sell your crypto. Keep HODLing."

"Okay," she said, pointing for him to leave, "I'll keep holding."

"HODLing."

"HODLing. Got it."

"Remember what I said about volatility?"

"Yeah, yeah. It's the price of performance."

"Exactly. See ya soon, teach."

He strolled out of her office. After he left, she sat quietly, staring at the bouquet of flowers he'd brought for her. Inhaling their sweetness, she recalled a line from an English class she'd taken at Brooks and taught by her favorite professor. They were studying D. H. Lawrence's *Sons and Lovers,* and Tom, Sandra, and Tift were in the same class. "She touched the big, pallid flowers on their petals, then shivered. They seemed to be stretching in the moonlight. Then she drank a deep draught of the scent. It almost made her dizzy."

She felt slightly intoxicated on account of Callum's visit. And now hopeful. Maybe he could help her track down those videos and finally free herself from the nightmare she'd been trapped in for far too long. Would Callum be the one to liberate her? Something about him lifted her spirits and made her heart swoon, although she was reluctant to admit this even to herself.

It made her wonder: was she having second thoughts about her relationship with Peters?

Chapter Twenty-Five

GWYNN

She received a call just after lunch from the principal at Jack's school, informing her that Jack had been sent to the office. She needed to go over there right away and find out what happened. Jack had never gotten into trouble at school before. Considering all the violent video games he'd been playing with Tom, she had a good idea why. After gathering up her bag, she headed out, relieved that she didn't have to check in with her boss before leaving. Not until the board figured out what to do with the two of them.

* * *

"I don't see why they made such a big deal over this," Tom said at the dinner table. Jack had been relegated to his room as punishment for his behavior at school.

"He was walking around the schoolyard during recess, pretending to shoot other students. How do you expect him to act when you two are playing those violent video games every night?"

"Playing cops and robbers is what boys do."

"He ordered the kids to lie down and play dead. Is that how you want your son to behave?"

"It's so stupid," he said, waving his hand in the air. "I played those games all the time as a kid, and look how I turned out?"

Did he really say that? "Now I have to stay home from work tomorrow because of his suspension. Maybe you should be the one who stays home with him."

"Yeah, well, that's not going to happen," he said, spooning scalloped potatoes onto his plate.

"Then I suggest you stop playing those games with him unless you want your son to become a violent criminal."

"Hey, he doesn't get that violent gene from me."

She gripped the butter knife under the table, wanting more than anything to stab him in the neck for saying such a terrible thing. "That was not cool, Tom."

"What? Are you saying it's not true?"

"Why do you stay with me, then? It says as much about you as it does me."

"I didn't sign up for murder when I married you. You misled me about who you really were."

"What about you? I had no idea that you were into sadomasochism and kinky sex when we started dating."

"At least I'm not a serial killer," he said so calmly that it took a few seconds for his words to sink in.

"No, but you get your rocks off being married to one."

"What would you rather I do? Turn you in to the cops?"

"You get a perverse pleasure out of the things I've done and beg me to reenact them in the bedroom. And you don't think that's a little strange?"

"Hey, you marry a lemon, you make lemonade."

"What we do is weird, Tom. Most men are not like you in that regard."

"Of course they're not, which is why it's so much fun. But don't act so holier-than-thou. You must have known that I liked it a little rough back in college."

She laughed. "How in the world would I have known that? I always thought you were the cool guy who read poetry and played guitar."

"You really have no idea?" he said, putting his fork down on the table and staring at her.

"No, I really don't. So why don't you enlighten me?"

"Man, this is awkward."

"What's awkward?"

"She never told you?"

"Who never told me what?"

"Tift?"

"What about Tift?"

"Look, I always thought you knew about it but were too embarrassed to say anything."

"You're driving me crazy, Tom. Know about what?" She felt a savage impulse rising through her.

"Tift and I started messing around after you dumped me back at Brooks. She actually liked doing some of the things I asked her to do. Of course, it was nothing like what we've been doing, but we played a little rough at times."

His words cut through her like a jagged edge. She stood, barely able to breathe. Was Tom teasing her, or did this really happen? But why would Tift fool around with Tom? Tift always complained how much she hated him. Maybe that was the reason. Then again, she had no right to complain. She'd broken it off with Tom and had no right to determine whom he could or could not see. But having sex with Sandra and now Tift? How many of her classmates had he slept with? She found it reprehensible that Tift would sleep with Tom and not tell her about it. Yet she knew Tift wouldn't say anything for fear of alienating her, especially now with this new TV show set to premiere.

"Did Tift do all the crazy things that I do to you?"

"Nowhere near as kinky," he said, pushing his empty plate away. "It was more playful than what we do, but still fun."

"She was my best friend, Tom. I wish one of you had at least told me about it."

"Does it piss you off that she didn't?" He stared at her, enjoying this give-and-take. "Or that your best friend and I hooked up for some rough-and-tumble rolls in the hay?"

"No, it just makes me sad."

"Good. Serves you right for playing with my emotions all those years and claiming to be my best friend."

"I was your best friend. And you were mine."

"And that was the problem. I always wanted to be more than just friends with you." He stood angrily, pushing his chair back. "You took advantage of my good nature back at Brooks. You thought I was this sensitive, ponytailed dork who wanted to hug trees, read poetry, and play guitar solos in his dorm room all day, when what I really wanted was to be your boyfriend." He turned and walked away from her.

"Get back here, Tom. Where are you going?"

"Out. Maybe grab a beer somewhere. Anywhere but here with you."

"But you said you'd have a talk with Jack about his behavior."

"You're his mother, you talk to him. And I want this kitchen cleaned up by the time I get back. What have you been doing since you got home?"

"Tom?"

"What?" he said, reaching for the door handle.

She felt ribbons of rage passing through her. "What do you think about investing in cryptocurrencies for our retirement account?"

"Cryptocurrencies?" His face soured.

"Yes."

"You mean like Bitcoin?"

"That's exactly what I mean," she said, messing with his head.

"It's garbage. Besides, it's none of your business what I do with our money. Your job is to cook, clean, and take care of my needs in the bedroom." He left, slamming the door shut behind him.

She pulled out her burner phone and texted Callum, telling him that they needed to find those videos as soon as possible. She couldn't possibly deal with her husband for much longer, or she would die. If for no other reason, she needed to end her marriage for Jack's sake. His dad's cancerous behavior would eventually rub off on the boy, and she could never let that happen.

* * *

She thought she'd be happy to have some peace and quiet to herself, but with Tom out having a beer, and Jack upstairs in his room, she felt more alone than ever. She wondered if it was a sign of weakness to feel this way, like one of those mousy housewives who kept returning to their abusive husbands because they were too weak to live on their own. And although Tom emotionally abused her and made her physically abuse him in return, at least his attention was focused solely on her. In his own sick and perverted way, he really did love her. Was this his way of making sure she never left him?

And yet she took solace in being part of a family, being a mother and wife, regardless of how dysfunctional everything seemed. How would she deal with it when it all came apart? She'd have to reinvent herself. Retrain Jack. Become more confident and sure of herself and her skills. And stop killing people.

Had her and Tom's relationship back in college been a lie? Maybe the old maxim was true: a man could never be in a platonic relationship with a woman. Gwynn wondered if she'd been a dick tease back then and not even realized it, like a lot of the girls she'd known at Brooks? Had she toyed with Tom and led him on?

Jack called out for her, and she ran upstairs. He wanted something to eat. His collection of toys sat along the floor, scattered and random. He'd need to clean them up before he went to bed for the night. She bolted downstairs and got him some chocolate chip cookies and a glass of milk, and then carried the tray back up to him. He sat at his little round table, on the other side of the room, his hands supporting his chubby cheeks, still angry at her for having to be upstairs all night. She set the plate of cookies on the table and stared down at him.

"Do you understand what you did wrong, Jack?"

"Yeah. I can't play at school anymore."

"You can play, you just can't pretend to shoot people."

He gazed out the window.

CHAPTER TWENTY-FIVE

"Do you know why?"

He shrugged.

"Because it scares the other students and teachers."

"Daddy says it's just a game and all make-believe."

"True, but not everyone thinks like you and Daddy. Guns scare people."

"But I wasn't really shooting guns." He threw up his arms in frustration. "We were just playing with sticks."

"I understand. It's just that games like that are not appropriate during school hours. Okay?"

"Okay."

He grabbed a cookie and took a bite out of it. Staring at him, she realized she loved him more than anything in this world and needed to save him from Tom before it was too late. On the surface, the notion seemed comical. She wanted to protect Jack from his perverse father when it was she, his mother, who had killed a total of eight people. A daughter who smothered her own father to death with a pillow. Burned her mother alive. Yet she would step in front of a bullet to save the ones she loved. If it weren't for all the horrible, abusive adults in the world, she wouldn't need to kill. She might have turned out normal like everyone else.

Sunday was Easter, and Tom wanted them to go to church and then spend the rest of the day at his mother's house. It was the last place in the world she wanted to be, but what other choice did she have?

Her own father loved Easter Sunday the most, claiming it the holiest of holy days. After the service, her mother would roast a turkey with carrots and potatoes, and then they would celebrate the resurrection of Jesus with a big meal. Her parents didn't believe in egg hunts and candy-filled baskets delivered by an oversized, pink bunny. Her father thought it akin to worshipping false idols. But Tom and his family made a big show of holidays, and she'd reluctantly come to love these traditions. In fact, she'd grown fond of seeing Jack dash around the yard, searching for the brightly colored eggs that Tom's mother and sister took hours hiding. And Jack would squeal with delight whenever he found one, running back to her to display his prized possession.

She closed Jack's door and returned downstairs. Turned on the television and watched as Annabelle welcomed her audience to the six o'clock news. The first story was about the three dead girls found along the Presumpscot River and the city's response to it. The scene shifted from Annabelle to a clip of the mayor standing on the steps of city hall with Portland's police chief. The three murders had gripped the city, causing fear and panic among the residents, and especially the young girls living in the Bayside neighborhood. A few of the homeless people were interviewed, describing the mood as tense and scary.

The next story was a tearjerker about Nguyen's ongoing recovery. Her family stood in front of the camera and answered questions about her. They said she was talking and asking for the foods she grew up eating, and asking about what happened to her. It was a good sign, according to the doctors, but still too early to determine if she'd return to full health.

The final story surprised her even more. It was about Peters and the confrontation he'd gotten into at that bar. A witness to the scene claimed that Peters had been stumbling around drunk that night and had started a fight with another patron, but ended up on the losing end of the scuffle. There was a clip of Peters emerging from the woods, his face battered and bruised, one eye black-and-blue from Tom's fists. It embarrassed her to think that he'd fought for her honor and lost. Was that an omen for their relationship going forward? And getting his ass kicked by Tom must have really shattered his fragile ego. It was another bad sign for their relationship going forward.

She obviously didn't know Peters as well as she thought she did. Why was he stumbling around drunk that night and getting into fistfights he couldn't win? What if he continued on like this and, in a moment of weakness, told someone about what she had done? She needed to get in touch with him and have a serious talk. Lay down the law. And it was not like she could break up with him and go on living happily ever after. He knew too much about all that she had done. But what if she did decide to break up with him? What then? Would she need to kill him? She'd almost killed him once down at that cove when, by trickery, he'd learned about all the murders she'd committed. Could she do it again?

She shut off the TV and thought about those poor girls dying at the hands of this copycat killer. For whatever reason, she felt guilty about it, as if she were the one responsible on account of her father's sins. Did Peters have the smarts to solve these cases? Maybe she should help him. For who better to catch a serial killer than an actual serial killer? But how could she do that while living under Tom's oppressive regime? Something had to break. For whatever reason, she felt Callum held the key to unlocking everything.

Chapter Twenty-Six

DETECTIVE PETERS

Instead of going out after work, Peters headed straight home and collapsed on his sofa. He swore he wouldn't drink tonight, especially after the humiliating beatdown he'd taken at the hands of Gwynn's husband. Had he been sober, he knew he would have kicked Tom's ass. The beating stuck in his craw, a memory he would not soon forget. Once he and Gwynn found that video, he vowed to get payback and watch with pleasure as the life drained out of her cocky husband. The last thing Tom would see before he sucked in his last breath was him smiling down at him. And he knew he had it in him to kill Tom because he'd done it three times up to this point.

He settled down on the sofa and turned on the news. Six cans of Champ Lager sat cooling in the fridge, calling out his name, but he vowed not to touch a drop this evening. Annabelle's wrinkle-free visage appeared onscreen. Since breaking up with her, he found it easier to watch her segments. Besides, he needed to keep an eye on her in the event she started spreading unfounded rumors about him.

The top story was about the copycat killer. The mayor and police chief stood at the podium in front of City Hall, trying to allay people's fears. Then the next story came on, and it caused him to throw a sofa pillow across the room. A woman at the pub that night claimed he was drunk and tried to pick a fight with another patron. He couldn't argue with the woman's account, seeing as how he couldn't remember much about what happened. Not even what he'd said or how he had gotten home. Now he feared showing his face in public, having made such an ass of himself.

The cracks in his reputation were starting to show. He jumped off the sofa, pacing the room as if ready to pounce. What would be the next ball to drop? Nguyen speaking to the cops and ratting him out? Annabelle revisiting that civilian shooting? He doubted she'd find anything. And he'd only had a couple of beers and a shot of whiskey while watching the Sox game. His drinking had nothing to do with the shooting that left that scumbag dead. Yes, he'd purposely killed the gangbanger and would do it again. The world was a better place without him.

He gazed out at the bay and thought about calling Gwynn, even apologizing for his reckless behavior that night, but he decided against it. What would he say? That he'd had too much to drink when he saw Tom at the bar and lost his cool?

The anger inside him continued to build. *The hell with it*, he thought as he headed toward the kitchen. He snatched a can of beer out of the fridge and cracked it open. The first one went down with ease. He'd drink alone tonight and never leave his condo. Lately, this place had been starting to feel like a high-end prison. The pit in his stomach grew the more he drank, and he wished he could take out his frustrations on someone or something. Were it not for that video of him and Gwynn in Bruno's parking lot, he'd track down that fat fuck and beat the shit out of him.

Maybe he could find another girl to kill and take out his frustrations on her. But he knew not to kill while drinking. One mistake could be his downfall. And killing those girls had to be done methodically and with a distinct purpose. More importantly, he had to start searching for someone to pin these murders on,

Annabelle said something that caught his attention. He sprinted back into the living room and turned toward the flatscreen. Just the sight of his ex's smooth face irritated him, and he wondered what he ever saw in her. It took him a second to realize that she'd been reporting on Janet Nguyen. The clip segued to a young reporter standing in front of Maine Medical and talking about Nguyen's condition. The reporter lifted her mic and began to interview Nguyen's brother, Jimmy. A bespectacled doctor appeared onscreen, claiming that Nguyen's recovery was encouraging but that she wasn't out of the woods just yet. Although her talking was a positive sign, it didn't necessarily mean that she would someday recover her memory in full. It might take years of hard physical therapy before that happened. Or it might not happen at all, leaving her with a lifelong impairment. Just the fact that she had woken from that coma had given everyone hope.

Peters gulped down his beer and went out to the kitchen for another. At this pace, he knew that the six-pack—now reduced to a five-pack—wouldn't last long. It felt like his life was falling apart. He needed something good to happen. Maybe another lucky break like he'd gotten in the Muddy River Killer case. But how many lucky breaks could a guy expect in one lifetime?

Solving these cases would go a long way toward firming up his reputation in the department and shutting Annabelle up. No one in town would give a damn if the great detective had a few unsavory chinks in his armor, especially if he'd been responsible for catching two high-profile serial killers.

He strode into his bedroom and opened the top drawer, pulling out the manila envelope. He overturned it and emptied the contents onto his bed. Then he stood back and stared at all the personal possessions he'd taken off the dead girls' bodies. If he couldn't solve these cases himself, then he could at least find someone who might fit the bill. It didn't bother him in the least that he'd be setting up an innocent person for these murders, because the guy he eventually pinned them on, like he'd done with Vinny Lazzara, would be no altar boy. He'd make sure of it.

After chugging down two more beers, he thought about leaving his condo and hitting up the King's Head Pub downstairs. At this hour, the bar would be filled with an assortment of hipsters and young couples, and it quickly dissuaded him of the notion. The alternative was sitting in his condo all night, watching TV, and wallowing in self-pity. He couldn't possibly go to bed now, knowing he'd get no sleep. Had he ruined his relationship with Gwynn because of his reckless and drunken behavior? Would she ever forgive him for his temporary bout of insanity? Or maybe, by some long shot, she might appreciate the fact that he stood up for her honor—and got his ass kicked in the process.

Reluctantly, he pulled another beer out of the fridge and collapsed on the sofa, resigned to the fact that he'd be here all night. Grabbing the remote, he put on one of those silly sitcoms, hoping it might put him in a better mood. But it didn't. The canned laughter made everything worse, reminding him of the absurdity of his life. He just couldn't stop thinking about Gwynn. He'd fought her husband—and lost. He'd killed three girls to get her back in his life. If someone had told him years ago that he'd go to such extremes for the love of a woman, he would have told them they were crazy. Not anymore.

Chapter Twenty-Seven

GWYNN

Two can play at this game, Gwynn thought after watching Jack climb onto his school bus. She turned on her burner phone and opened the tracking app she'd ordered, using the new bank account she'd opened without Tom's knowledge. The overnight package had arrived at her office a day ago. She remembered taking it out and admiring it. Earlier this morning, before the sun came up, she'd snuck outside and attached the magnetic device to the bottom of Tom's car, similar to the one he'd attached to hers. She even knew where he put it because he bragged so openly about keeping tabs on her. If she removed it, he would know immediately what she had done. But she doubted he would suspect that she'd do the same to him.

The app informed her that Tom's car was currently in Wells, Maine, and heading south toward Boston. Perfect. She walked over to her SUV, got in, and drove to the local supermarket to pick up Callum. Tom would never suspect anything when he pulled out his phone and monitored her movements. She went to Hannaford at least three times a week to shop for groceries. Just this morning, the big spender had even given her two hundred dollars, acting as if he was doing her a huge favor.

She parked in the back lot and waited, watching people come and go from the store's front entrance. Ten minutes later, Callum's Jeep pulled up next to hers. It was the strangest shade of green she'd ever seen, and it made her glad he hadn't parked on her street for all the neighbors to see. They sat like this for a few minutes until she turned and made eye contact with him. Once she nodded, he jumped out and slipped inside next to her. Then she took off, eager to get back home.

"Duck," she instructed him as she turned onto her street.

"Is this really necessary?"

"You don't know how nosy my neighbors can be."

He slid down.

"Your Jeep's color is quite unique. What's it called?"

"British Racing Green. I had to special order it and wait six months for it to arrive."

"Must be nice to have money."

"You can have it too if you stay the course and HODL like I told you."

"Is the market down today?"

"Quite the contrary. It's up four percent."

"About time," she said, cruising down the street. "My portfolio has a long way to go before it's back to where I started."

"Remember what I said; Volatility is the nature of the beast."

"I know, you say it so much it's branded in my brain."

"So you have been paying attention."

"Volatility is the story of my life, don't you know? How do you think I've gotten away with everything up to this point?"

She turned into her driveway and pressed the remote over the visor, and the garage door went up. She parked inside and closed the door, reminded of the time when she'd done the same thing at William Clayborn's house. She imagined his body lying at the bottom of that quarry, next to Townsend, both men still attached to their kettle bells and keeping each other company. It reminded her of the old lawyer joke: What do you call five thousand dead lawyers at the bottom of a quarry? A good start.

Now that they were safely inside the garage, she instructed Callum to get out. They went inside the house and headed upstairs to Tom's study. She turned the handle, surprised to remember that he kept his office locked.

"Son of a bitch," she said.

"Do you have a paper clip?" Callum asked, taking out a Steelman tool set from his key ring.

She fled downstairs and found a paper clip, returned upstairs, and handed it to him. He straightened it out and then inserted one of the hex keys into the bottom part of the lock. He rotated it so that the key would turn in order to place tension on the lock. While maintaining the tension, he slowly wiggled the paper clip into the top part of the lock, moving it in an up-and-down motion. He lowered his ear to the knob, listening to the series of clicks as the pins in the lock rose. Once all the pins rose, the hex key turned, and he unlocked the door.

"Easy peasy."

"You're quite the criminal mastermind."

"Let's just say I'm resourceful."

They walked into Tom's office, and she realized it had been a long time since she'd been inside it. Callum moved straight for Tom's computer, sitting down in front of the screen. She couldn't help but be impressed with his confidence and swagger, and wished she was more like him in that regard.

"Is there a password to get in?" she asked.

"There is, but it won't be a problem. This computer's old as hell."

"You know how to hack it?"

Callum laughed as he typed away. "This is child's play. You simply hold the keys 'CMD+R' together until the logo appears on the screen. It opens the recovery mode of your Mac. Just open the window with the header macOS utilities. See there on the upper part of the screen?"

"What am I looking at?"

"The bar with the menu points. Where it says macOS Utilities File Edit Utilities Window."

"Okay."

"You click on Utilities and select Terminal to open the Mac Shell Terminal."

"Save your breath. I'm not going to remember any of this."

"You never know when you might need to hack into someone's computer," he said, typing away. "You click in the terminal and type reset password. That will prompt a new window with the header Reset password. From here, I can see all user accounts with their names and profile pictures. On this computer, there is only one user, making it easy. I'll put in a new password and confirm it by clicking save. Then I'll do it again and change it back to the original. All I need to do now is hit restart and log in with the new password, which also happens to be the old one. See. Now we're in."

"How did you learn to do all this?"

"Keeping abreast of software is one of my hobbies. Of course, this software is ancient."

"Let's see what this husband of mine has saved in his hard drive."

Gwynn stood just above him, staring down at the computer screen. Suddenly, a photo popped up of a woman in high-heeled leather boots standing atop a naked man with some kind of weird gag in his mouth. One of her six-inch heels was pressed into his roped-off testicles. She looked away, not wanting to see any more of her husband's photos.

"Please get those off the screen," she said, embarrassed.

"It appears that he's saved a lot of photos like these."

"Seriously, I don't want to know."

"Seems your husband has quite a rich fantasy life." Callum laughed.

"It's not exactly a fantasy."

He turned to her. "You mean he does this stuff with you?"

"Not exactly that, but similar."

"I'm sorry for laughing, Gwynn. I had no idea."

"How could you?" She pointed at the screen. "Can we just find what we're looking for?"

"Of course." He resumed typing. "If he's hidden that video on this computer, he's done a good job hiding it."

"Maybe he doesn't keep it on his computer. Maybe we should check his emails instead." She looked down and realized her hand was resting on his shoulder.

"Good idea. Even if he's deleted it, it's most likely still in the system."

She pulled up a chair and sat next to him. Their shoulders touched as he typed away, totally beyond her comprehension. She occasionally looked over and studied his face. A strange sensation came over her while staring at it. How long had she been without genuine affection? Did it take sitting next to an attractive man—although a much younger man—to bring up all these conflicted feelings? It felt so silly and juvenile, like when she was a teenager with a schoolgirl crush on one of the dumb boys in her class. But considering the sad circumstances of her life, she took comfort in this brief moment of intimacy. Callum was rich and smart, and he shared her affinity for killing. And Peters had screwed things up so badly the other night that she began to question her feelings for him. In no way did she want to end up in a relationship with a violent, insecure drunk who engaged in public brawls—with her husband, of all people.

A minute passed in silence, other than the sound of Callum's fingertips tapping on the keyboard. She closed her eyes for a few seconds and pictured him skating across a fresh sheet of ice and then performing a triple lutz. After his routine, she saw him bowing to the crowd while holding aloft a bouquet of red roses, dressed in a skintight, black sequin outfit that only enhanced his physique. His blue eyes sparkled in the proscenium of lights as the dramatic music played over the speakers. Snatched out of her daydream, she turned and studied him. The extreme concentration he displayed must have been the same he used when skating. Or studying the cryptocurrency market.

She pinched the skin over her forearm. Why was she feeling so needy right now? Worse, why was she thinking about undressing Frye and jumping his bones in this very room? To spite Tom? Or to sate her own sexual needs? Anyway, she thought it a silly fantasy. It brought her back to the day when she sat in that grimy apartment while he ran around in his soiled diaper, his father lying unconscious on the couch, slowly dying from the heroin she'd injected into his vein.

"How's it going?"

"Shhhh."

She laughed. "Did you just shush me?"

"Do you want me to find this video or not?"

"Sorry. Carry on."

While waiting, she recalled that night when she'd slipped into her father's room at night and pressed a pillow over his face until he stopped breathing. Surprisingly, he didn't put up a fight. It was almost like he'd been waiting to die, hoping to finally be put out of his misery. It occurred to her that she'd killed both of her biological mother and father: Kaufman would probably have a field day with that.

Callum pointed at the screen. "There it is."

She snapped back to the moment and turned to him. "You found it?"

"Yup. I recovered his emails and identified the video."

"Who did he send it to?"

"Two different videos to two different people," he said, staring intently at the screen. "One I might have expected. The other, not so much."

"Tell me," she said, excited that her long nightmare might finally be over.

"He sent two videos to his mother."

"His mother? The woman barely knows how to turn on a computer."

"She's obviously someone he trusts. He probably thought that no one would suspect her of being the recipient of his emails."

"Who's the other person?"

"This one really surprised me."

"Are you going to tell me or not?"

"Tift Ainsley." He turned to her. "Why would your husband send a video to a famous movie star?"

She couldn't believe her ears. Why did everything come back to Tift?

"Tift was my roommate back in college. The three of us went to Brooks College together."

"You and Tift Ainsley went to Brooks College? Wow. Are you still friends with her?"

She nodded, hoping to change the subject.

"Do you mind if I watch the videos before I delete them from Tom's hard drive?"

"Won't Tom know they're gone?"

"I doubt it. And even if he does find out they're missing, what's he going to do about it?"

"Sure. Let's see what's on them."

Callum clicked on the first video. Gwynn leaned in and saw herself, Peters, and Nguyen standing in the parking lot behind Bruno's Restaurant. She saw herself sneaking up behind Nguyen, and then the detective surprising her with that flying back kick to the head before sprinting toward Forest Avenue. Peters picked up the gun and gave chase while she staggered to her feet. She jumped in Nguyen's idling car and pursued her. Tom, still filming, followed her out of the lot, stopping once to capture Peters doubled over in exhaustion. Then he gunned it out of the parking lot until he turned left onto the deserted street. The camera shook violently as it captured Nguyen running down the sidewalk, occasionally looking over her shoulder to see if she was being followed. Gwynn's car veered to the opposite side of the road and parked on the wrong side of the street. She watched herself jump out the driver's side and sprint down the sidewalk in pursuit of Nguyen. The boxcar pulled out of the liquor store's driveway, forcing Nguyen to bolt out into the road to avoid getting trapped. But not before that car came speeding from the opposite direction and sent her flying through the air. Without warning, the video went black.

"Holy shit. That was you chasing that cop?"

"I didn't mean for her to get struck by a car."

"And I suppose you were going to shake hands with her and apologize for being such a rude person?"

"She's still alive, isn't she?"

"Barely. I think I'd rather be dead than in a coma."

She looked away. "For your information, she recently woke from her coma and is now speaking."

"Bad news for you, then, if she recovers her memory."

"Hopefully, she never will," she said.

"Were you planning to kill her?"

"I honestly don't know what I would have done had I caught up to her."

"I'm pretty sure we both know what would have happened."

"The woman knew too much about what I had done."

"Did she learn that you'd killed all those people and was going to turn you in?"

"She didn't have any hard evidence, but she suspected as much. It would have been hard for me to explain certain things if she went to her superiors with what she knew."

"And because she didn't die, I'm assuming you live in constant fear that she might one day recover her memory and spill the beans?"

She scratched the back of her neck. "Something like that."

"Damn, girl. You're more gangster than I thought." He reached out and put his hand over hers.

His touch felt light and yet firm at the same time. The physical intimacy felt so nice that she closed her eyes and savored it to the fullest. She had to remind herself that he was sixteen years her junior. Besides, she'd saved him from a hellish future when he was a little boy, neglected and abused, and running around in soiled diapers. So why in the world would he be attracted to her, a married woman many years older than him?

"Now for the next one." He turned toward the computer and clicked on the second video. "This one's only twenty-two seconds long."

He hit play, and she saw Tift lying semi-naked in bed, her arms covering her breasts. The video was taken at Brooks College, in their old dorm room. The person taking the video said something off-camera. He said it again, this time louder, and Gwynn instantly recognized the sound of Tom's voice. Then Tift rapped from an old Jay Z song, singing along to the racist lyrics. Gwynn knew immediately what this video meant for her career if it went public. The screen suddenly went black.

"Oh my god," she said, laughing. "Do you know what would happen if this video got out?"

"I think I can guess, being of mixed race myself."

"Forget the sex part of it. Saying the N word in those lyrics would get her blacklisted in Hollywood, even if she was only repeating the words from a popular rap song," she said, not bothering to hide her glee.

"Tough luck being a white person who digs rap music. You can only sing those lyrics in the shower."

She stared ahead, lost in thought, knowing that those big paychecks could come to an end if Tift's new cable show got canceled.

"This video can never see the light of day."

"Not if you're Tift Ainsley," he said.

"Would you please send that video to my email address before you delete it?"

"I'm afraid to ask what you're going to do with it."

"Best not to, then."

"There's something else on here," Callum said.

"More stuff?"

"Your mother-in-law wrote back to Tom saying he should leave you."

"No surprise there. My dragon-in-law hates me."

"You two don't get along?"

Gwynn laughed. "Hardly. She's always resented me for breaking up with Tom back in college."

"But then you got your revenge by marrying him."

"And dumping him again. Then getting back together with him, although that wasn't by choice."

"Sounds like she wasn't that far off the mark about you."

"No, she wasn't. If it weren't for that drunken pact we made on the eve of our college graduation, I would never have been in this situation to begin with."

"What drunken pact?"

"That if we hadn't married anyone by the age of thirty, Tom and I would marry each other."

"And you actually went through with that crazy plan?" He clapped his hands in amusement.

"Yup. He moved back to Portland and took a job at one of the local CPA firms. We ran into each other one night at Gritty's Pub, and he was looking fine. We had too many beers, and one thing led to another."

"I understand the booty-call part of the story, but marrying that jackass?"

"Believe it or not, Tom wasn't always the inconsiderate jerk he is today. What we had back in college was nice, even though I don't think I ever loved him the way I had hoped to love someone. I was dealing with a lot of personal issues, and marrying Tom just seemed like the right thing to do at that time."

"You two obviously weren't meant for each other."

"No, we weren't. Then again, I often wonder why anyone would want to be with someone like me."

"Don't be so hard on yourself, Gwynn. I think you're lovely."

"You're just saying that because I saved your life."

"Well, there is that, but I genuinely mean it. You're a special lady."

"I am?"

"At least I think so."

She stared into his eyes, not quite believing how attracted she was to him right now. She steeled herself to be strong and not do anything she might regret. She'd aligned herself with Peters, regardless of how badly he'd screwed up with Tom the other night. But it had been so long since she'd been touched that her body virtually screamed for affection. *Get up and leave*, she told herself. But she couldn't even heed her own advice. And yet she didn't want to lead him on, knowing they had no future together. But then he leaned over and tucked a strand of hair over her ear. She gazed at his chiseled face, which was now inching closer to her own. Even his breath smelled sweet and minty. Those beautiful blue eyes locked onto her own, and desire consumed her. His caramel-colored skin seemed so exotic that she wanted to lose herself in it. Despite her better judgment, she leaned forward and kissed him. And not just a peck but a full-on passionate kiss on the lips.

They stood kissing and made their way to her bedroom. Once inside, they tore off each other's clothes, tossing them haphazardly along the floor. His hands roamed her body, and his lips caressed and licked her neck. She knew this was wrong, but she couldn't rein herself in and stop this disaster from happening. Tumbling back onto the bed, she gazed up into Callum's eyes. Every part of her told her to run away, which made the sexual encounter that much more thrilling. That and the fact that she would be making love to a guy sixteen years her junior, in the same bed where she and Tom slept every night. The son of the man she had killed. And what about Peters, her partner in crime and secret lover? What would he think if he knew what she was doing? What would Tom think? Good thing neither of them would ever find out.

Chapter Twenty-Eight

GWYNN

Two hours had passed since they first started making love. She lay on her back, exhausted, gasping for breath, sweat oozing out of every pore on her body. Callum stared up at the ceiling, his hands interlocked over his smooth chest. She'd never in her life experienced anything like that. Her body felt drained of every life-sustaining fluid, and her knees felt weak and spindly, as if just the act of standing would cause her to collapse. She turned toward him and rested her arm on his washboard midsection, not quite believing he was able to perform three successive times in a row. Then again, he was twenty-two and blessed with youth and vigor.

"That was incredible, Callum, but we can never do this again."

"I'm cool with that."

"You are?" She laughed; he'd just hurt her feelings. "What kind of thing is that to say to the woman who you just made love to?"

"You were amazing, Gwynn, but I was hoping there wouldn't be any strings attached between us."

She shook her head, unable to believe he'd just said that, even if that was what she also wanted.

Callum turned to her. "I didn't hurt your feelings. Did I?"

"You absolutely did not hurt my feelings. I'm a married woman, remember?"

"Yeah, and we both know how much that means to you."

"True, but a vow is still a vow."

He laughed. "That didn't stop you from hooking up with that hunky detective."

"How did you know about that?"

"I got eyes in the back of my head, girl. You think I didn't notice the two of you sneaking downstairs together at that awards ceremony?"

"You're mistaken." She crossed her arms over her sweaty breasts.

"Like the mistake I saw on that video? Where that cop got smashed into by that speeding car?"

"Okay, I get it. There'll be no strings attached between us." She felt stupid for expecting him to desire her more than he did. Clearly, this romp had been just sex for him.

He leaned over and kissed her. "Don't get hurt feelings, babe. You can't expect me to get tied down at my age, can you?"

"No, I just expected you to enjoy what we did."

"I did enjoy it. Very much so. That doesn't mean I'm ready to settle down with the house and white picket fence."

Gwynn rolled her eyes. "I wasn't asking you to settle down. Or get a white picket fence."

He kissed her again. "Can you forgive old Callum?"

"I'm so tired I can barely think right now. But I do know it's time for you to go."

"Kicking me to the curb already?"

"Yes. I have to head back to work."

"What will you do about Tom's mother? She might know the things you and your detective boyfriend have done. And even if you destroy her hard drive, she could rat you out to the police if you're not careful."

"You're making it sound like I have no other options."

"Not if you want to free yourself from Tom and his family and be with your detective boyfriend."

"What are you suggesting?"

"I think you know what I'm suggesting." He knifed his hand across his throat. "Maybe I can help you with that."

"With Tom's mother?"

"Sure. And with Tom, too. It will take a lot of thought and planning, but I'm game for it. And you know you can trust me."

"Do I?"

Callum smiled. "Of course."

"You really want to help me?"

"I do. And I know I'll be good at it because I have the best teacher in the biz, and also because I'm meticulous about everything I do."

"Why do you want to help me so much, Callum?"

"I owe you my life. You rescued me from a shitty childhood and helped me be the amazing person I am today."

"But you didn't have to blackmail me to get what you wanted."

He laughed. "Do you really think you would have agreed to teach me how to kill if I hadn't?"

She realized he was right.

"The one good thing to come out of all this is that now we can be brutally honest with each other," Callum said.

"Yes, I suppose that's true."

"So it's okay to admit that you want Tom and his mother out of the picture."

"I very much want that, otherwise I'll never be free from them."

"'A slave is one who waits for someone to come and free him.'"

"Wow. Did you just make that up?"

"It's from Ezra Pound."

She laughed, impressed at his literary knowledge.

"I didn't need to go to some expensive college to educate myself." Was that a subtle dig at her Brooks education?

"So that's what you think I'm doing? Taking the initiative to free myself from slavery?"

"Of course. That way, you can finally be your authentic self."

"Then I guess that's what I'm doing," she said. "Does it bother you that I'm with that cop?"

"Not at all. I have no desire to interfere in your life once we finish what we started."

She got out of the bed. "Get dressed, playboy. I need to drive you back to your Jeep."

"Promise to share your plan with me as soon as you make one?"

She kissed him on the lips one last time. "Don't worry, Callum. You'll be the first to know."

Chapter Twenty-Nine

Gwynn walked to the copier room and waited off to the side while Denise finished using it. She hadn't felt this good in over a year. An amazing morning of sex will do that to a girl. Denise grabbed her papers out of the bin, shot her a nasty look, and then stormed past her without a word. Her boss's hostility amused her. Ever since she filed that harassment claim, she'd gained temporary immunity from Denise, making it almost impossible for the woman to fire her. She could do virtually anything short of murder as long as she got her work done in a timely manner.

What bothered her most, however, was Denise's words the other day. Had she really sensed something dark about her? Gwynn wondered if she wore her darkness like an aura for all to see.

The memory of having sex with Callum kept replaying in her head. His long hands caressing her body. His gentleness, as well as aggressiveness, when called for. For a man of such a young age, he appeared to be confident and skilled in bed. And while she didn't love him, not by a long shot, she couldn't stop thinking about him. She didn't even know how to define such an attraction other than to call it lust. Callum had opened up a whole new side of herself that she hadn't even known existed.

On top of that, she felt like a massive weight had been lifted off her shoulders, especially after learning that Tom had sent that video to his mother. Now she could see the light at the end of the tunnel. No need to rush things along and possibly screw up. She could take her time and plan for the endgame. She'd continue to play the role of obedient wife for a bit longer, satisfied in the knowledge that her misery would soon be over.

She returned to her office, warm copies in hand. Maybe she'd take a walk around the campus today. Or go out and have coffee somewhere. Sushi at Benkay sounded nice. Either that or head home and start planning Tom's demise.

It occurred to her that she needed to make a decision about Peters. For the moment, she decided not to tell him about what they'd discovered on Tom's computer. Her brief fling with Callum now made her question everything about her former life, especially her relationship with Peters. Had it been a mistake to get involved with that corrupt, drunken cop? She knew without a doubt that she'd never made love so passionately as she did with Callum. Distance made the heart grow fonder, but with Peters, the opposite seemed true.

She sipped her coffee and sat back in the chair, feeling little urgency to get anything done today, knowing that Denise couldn't discipline her. She switched on the computer and saw that her portfolio had risen by thirty percent overnight. Now that was a nice surprise. Maybe this crypto investment might turn out to be a good thing. It was like the swings of her mood; up one day and down the next.

Speaking of her mood, it changed almost immediately when she saw who was now texting her. She read it and learned that Ivy had run away from home again and was now living on the streets. Gwynn called the girl, surprised when she answered after the first ring. Ivy sobbed and sniffed back her tears.

"What happened, Ivy?"

"My father came home drunk."

"I thought your mother kicked him out of the house."

"Stupid bitch let him move back in."

"What did he do?"

She hyperventilated into the receiver, telling Gwynn all she needed to know.

"I fought him off the best I could."

Gwynn balled her hand into a fist.

"He apologized afterward, but I spit in his face. When I tried to leave, he smacked me upside the head and warned me not to tell anyone."

Gwynn felt her blood pressure rising. She briefly fantasized about killing George Fields and dumping his body in the quarry near her cabin.

"He told me to keep my mouth shut. Said if I went running to the cops, he would kill my brother and my mom. That's when I took off."

"Where are you now?"

"I don't want your help anymore, Gwynn. You can't do anything for a loser like me."

"You're not a loser, Ivy."

"I am. I don't deserve to live."

"Please don't give up now, I'm begging you."

"The street is where I belong and where I'll die."

The line went dead. Gwynn held the phone up in shock, not sure what to do about this latest development. She left the office and made her way to her car, climbed inside, and sped over to the Bayside neighborhood. She cruised the streets, circling around and around, asking people if they knew where Ivy had gone, but no one seemed to know or care. Later that afternoon, dejected and despairing, she headed home. Jack's bus would be pulling up in front of her house at any minute.

She sat quietly behind the wheel, trying to control her emotions. The urge to kill Ivy's father resonated inside her more than ever. She vowed that he would pay for what he'd done to his daughter, and what he might do to her in the future. She knew where he worked and where to find him after he got off his shift at the bean plant. Knew that he stopped at certain pubs each night before heading home. This time she would wait for him. Then she'd make him pay for all the pain and misery he'd caused his beautiful girl.

* * *

Tom had been texting all day, a problem she had to overcome if she hoped to act swiftly in regards to Ivy's father. She'd already called Callum and told him what she planned on doing, and he'd agreed to help. She needed only to find someone trustworthy to babysit Jack this Saturday night—and keep an eye on her phone. Because if Tom texted her, she'd need someone to be home and answer it, seeing as how his app would be tracking her every movement. Also, she had to temporarily remove the tracking device from beneath her car.

Then an idea came to her. She knew who she could trust, assuming he would agree to do it. Had it been last year, he never would have considered coming over and babysitting. Nor would she have asked. But everything had changed between them since that time. They'd grown closer. More mutually dependent on each other. And he'd do it because he loved her. He'd told her so. Gwynn wondered if he'd ever met Jack before, and didn't think so. Could he handle a child? He'd never had a wife or child of his own. It shouldn't matter: Jack would be sound asleep by the time he came over. And asleep when she came home.

She checked her calendar. Tom was due home Easter morning. After hanging out with his college buddies for two nights of drunken revelry, he'd be way too tired to question her about her activities. Still, she needed to be home well before that. Ivy's father worked at the baked bean plant from Saturday to Wednesday, starting his shift at twelve p.m. on Saturday afternoon. Gwynn needed everything to appear as normal as possible until she set out. No one could ever know she left home.

Chapter Thirty

GWYNN

Callum sat next to her in the SUV, the two of them watching the parking lot of the baked bean plant. Located just off the Veterans' Memorial Bridge, the antiquated structure was scheduled to be demolished next year and replaced with something modern and beautiful, befitting the city's changing image as a gritty port town.

Before she left the house, she had crawled underneath her SUV and removed the magnetic tracking device that Tom had attached to it. Then she rested it on the kitchen counter, happy in the knowledge that Tom would never know she'd left home.

She turned and smiled at Callum, happy that he'd decided to join her. An act of this magnitude could not be taken lightly—or be performed alone.

The bean plant sat on a jetty overlooking the bay, smoke billowing from the tall brick stack, perfuming the air with the stench of brown sugar, pork fat, and molasses. She drove mindlessly past it every day, going to and from work, never giving the eyesore a second look. Soon, it would be demolished and turned into a college campus. It reminded her of the bean suppers her father would put on at the church, the third Saturday of every month. Piles and piles of food would be served to the public for cheap money. Even as a young girl, she would work behind the counter serving people creamy casseroles, burgers, and hot dogs, and ladling baked beans onto paper plates.

"How did you know he worked here?" Callum asked.

"I've had many dealings with him when I ran The Loft. Sadly, I know most everything about him."

"Sounds like you've been thinking about killing the dude for a long time."

"Oh, I have. This creep should have been dealt with years ago for the way he treated his daughter."

"How did he get away with it for so long?"

"Slipped through the cracks, like a lot of other scumbags in the system. But he won't get away with it this time."

"How are you going to do it?"

She took out a roll of nylon rope and held it up.

"Smart choice. That way, there's no blood."

"A rope like this has many uses."

"Like what?"

"Say in the instance where you have to get rid of a body. Tie it down. Drag it over a cliff." She snapped the rope in her hands, reminded of what Tom made her do in the bedroom. "Or wrap it around the bastard's throat and squeeze the life out of him."

"Good to know."

"There he is," she said, pointing toward a burly man wearing a red flannel shirt and UMaine baseball cap. He strode toward his pickup truck, one person among many getting off their shift.

"Do you think he'll go somewhere after work?"

"According to his daughter, he goes out drinking most every night."

"Shall we follow him?"

"That we shall."

"Then what, teach?"

"Then we assess the situation and see what our next move will be."

"Perfect."

"Sometimes the best-thought-out plans don't go as expected. That's why you need to think on your feet when doing this sort of thing."

"Maybe I should take notes." He laughed.

"Another rule: never put anything in writing."

"Point taken."

The battered old truck rambled out of the parking lot. Gwynn followed his slow circuitous route. It was not long before he parked on a side street just off Washington Avenue and headed toward the busy intersection. Before hitting the crosswalk, he strolled into a parking lot and disappeared into a well-known dive bar called Howie's Pub. It had been in business for many years, proudly serving the blue-collar workers of Portland. The front entrance sat like a sentinel just above the on- and off-ramps to 295.

"I'm going to get out and see if his passenger door is unlocked. If it is, I'll slip in the back seat and wait for him."

"Catch him by surprise. I like the way you roll."

"Watch and learn," she said. "If he drives away, make sure to follow us. I might need to finish him elsewhere."

"You got it, teach."

"And please stop calling me teach."

Hearing him laugh, she slipped out of the car, pulling a wool cap over her head before making her way to his truck. She couldn't believe the adrenaline coursing through her. This time she felt no remorse for what she was about to do. George Fields deserved to die. She only hoped it wasn't too late to save his precious daughter. She made her way along the sidewalk and headed toward his battered Silverado.

How many times had she sat across from Fields and his obese wife, the two of them promising to do a better job raising their kids. Always the next time. And the time after that. She pictured him coming home drunk every night and slipping into his daughter's room to do bad things. Unthinkable ones. Over and over throughout the years, exacerbating Ivy's physical and mental scars. She gripped the rope in her pocket as a pedestrian approached on the sidewalk.

Once the pedestrian passed, she reached for the passenger-door handle and pulled. To her relief, it opened. After a quick glance around, she slipped inside, gently closing the door behind her. The interior reeked of dirty socks and molasses, and it nearly made her sick. She slithered between the bucket seats until she fell into the back. Fast food wrappers and trash piled high beneath her. She had a feeling she'd be waiting a long time, so she collapsed to the floor and tried to make herself as comfortable as possible. Despite it being April, she estimated the temperature to be just above freezing. She tightened the jacket around her and pulled the wool cap down over her forehead. In her pocket sat the one-eighth-inch strip of nylon rope, three feet in length and perfect for what she planned on doing. God knows, she'd had enough practice with Tom these past few months.

Lying there, bristling with rage, she could barely wait to wrap the rope around his neck and end his miserable life. Nothing would please her more. It would once and for all put an end to all the pain and suffering he'd caused his family.

Her mind switched gears, and she thought of Jack, up in his room and sound asleep. She'd hate for him to shuffle downstairs and come face-to-face with his unfamiliar babysitter.

* * *

Sometime later, Gwynn opened her eyes upon hearing the door open. A rush of cold air whipped into the cabin as Fields climbed inside. The godawful smell of stale beer and baked beans singed her nostrils. Simultaneously, he started the engine and lowered his window. Music played over the radio. He clicked open a Bic and lit a cigarette, the smoke irritating her eyes. She debated jumping up and attacking him, but decided against it. For all she knew, a group of people might be standing alongside the truck. Even worse, he might inadvertently lift the cigarette to his lips while she went to strangle him, causing his hand to get stuck between the rope and his neck.

Before she knew it, he pulled the truck out onto the road. This could turn out badly if he got stopped by a cop. The what-ifs reverberated in her brain and made her question whether this had been the right decision.

The Silverado's engine rumbled in her ears, rattling through her bones. It did, however, provide her with enough cover to sit up and get more comfortable. A country song by Waylon Jennings played over the speakers. Fields turned up the volume and sang along to it, his voice low and raspy.

The truck swerved slightly across the road. She lifted her head and glanced through the back window and saw the lights of the SUV trailing behind. Ashes from his cigarette flew back in her face and nicked her skin. It took a few seconds to realize that he was cruising down lower Congress Street. He turned left near the intersection and drove into the lot of the Pizza Villa. Glancing at her watch, she registered the time to be twenty minutes past eleven. One other car sat in the lot. He pulled up a bit too aggressively, and the front tires bounced off the granite barrier protecting the building. Then he sat, finishing the rest of his cigarette as Garth Brooks sang about friends in low places.

She needed to do it now if it was to happen. No way she could stay in this freezing truck much longer, especially if he decided to have a few more drinks inside the Villa. Her fingers felt numb from the cold, limiting her mobility.

Gripping the ends of the rope, she lurched over the headrest and looped it around his throat. Then she fell back, placing the soles of her sneakers against the back of his car seat. 'Goodbye Earl' by the Dixie Chicks began to play over the speakers. His head snapped back, and he yelped, his grimy hands reaching instinctively for his neck. Gwynn pulled, using every ounce of her energy to push her feet deeper into the front seat. But something didn't seem right. Despite her Herculean efforts, he'd managed to slip his fingers between the rope and his throat. She couldn't believe he had the strength to put up such a fight, especially after all the alcohol he'd consumed this evening.

Her arms and shoulders throbbed in pain as the Dixie Chicks sang about Wanda and Earl. She pulled back even harder, but to no avail. His left hand continued to slither beneath the rope until he'd freed himself. Turning, he stared at her in disbelief, a feral look over his jowly face.

"What the fu… You!" he growled.

"Die, you fucking bastard," she shouted.

She let go of the rope, and he flung it away, no worse for the wear. They stared at each other for a split second before he climbed between the seats. Falling back, she felt his hand grab her ankle. He grunted like a wild boar, pulling her toward him. Could Callum see this struggle? She kicked him in the head, but it only made him angrier. He glared at her, his face beet red and his chapped lips snarling.

"You're going to pay for this, you uppity bitch."

He slithered through the seats until his head hovered over her crotch. His free hand clawed at her face as she reached behind her for something to fend him off. But she only felt fast-food wrappers and trash. Would her string of good luck finally end here? She thought of Jack as she desperately continued to reach into the pile. Then her fingers found a plastic handle with grooves in it. Her hand moved over it until she felt the steel neck and pointy Phillips head. His hand cupped around her throat and squeezed as he brought his other hand up so that both thumbs pressed against her airway. So this was how it felt to die, she thought as she lifted the screwdriver out of the trash. Struggling to breathe, she reached back with her right hand and thrust the tip through his cheek. His mouth opened, and she could see the steel shank slide between his upper and lower molars. He screamed in agony as blood poured out of his mouth and down his lips, but he didn't let up. She yanked out the screwdriver, reached back, and plunged it in his neck.

"The first one was for Ivy," she said, watching his eyes go slack. "This one's for me."

His right hand loosened around her throat as she pulled the blade out of his neck. He lay there, gurgling, trying to staunch the wound with his hand. She looked down and realized she was covered in blood. Her only other messy murder had been that Frenchman down by the Seine, and in both instances, she'd needed to think quick on her feet. Now she had a body and a truck to dispose of. And yet Fields hadn't drawn his last breath. He twitched and hung on for dear life, trying to push himself up onto the seat, clutching his neck where the blood was still gushing out. Gripping the screwdriver, she reared back and drove the Phillips head into his temple. It made a weird squishing noise as it tore through his flesh and entered his brain. His entire body convulsed and shuddered. After a minute passed, a deathly stillness set in. She left the screwdriver in his temple and took a few deep breaths.

A patron staggered out the back door of the Villa. She remained still as he made his way to his car, having no idea that she'd just killed a man. Good, she thought, watching as he drove off.

Knowing she couldn't reposition Fields's body on her own, she jumped out of the truck and waved for Callum to come over. He bounded out of the SUV and sprinted toward her, staring through the door at the blood-soaked mess she'd left behind.

"Holy shit," he said, surveying the scene.

"Why didn't you come over and help me?"

"I thought you had everything under control."

"Well, I didn't."

"I can see that now."

"Don't just stand there. Help me get him in the back seat."

He moved to the driver's side door, lifted the man's legs up, and heaved them toward the back. Gwynn grabbed one of his belt loops and pushed his upper torso toward her until he was facedown on the floor.

"Go back to the SUV and get that small tarp I put in the back."

"What are we gonna do with him?"

"Just do it, Callum. Then go back to my vehicle and follow me. We're going for a ride."

He continued to stare at the body. "This is so cool."

"It won't be cool if the police show up and find his body in this truck."

"Nah. That wouldn't be cool at all."

Callum sprinted back and retrieved the blue tarp. Together, they covered Fields with it. Then she hopped in the driver's seat and took off, praying she wouldn't get pulled over. She'd been lucky thus far. But one day her luck was going to run out if she kept being careless.

A quick glance at the truck's inspection sticker told her that it had expired months ago. She only hoped she could make it to her destination without getting pulled over.

Chapter Thirty-One

GWYNN

An hour and forty minutes later, she turned onto the dirt road leading to her camp. She drove until she arrived at the quarry, the headlights cutting through the pitch-blackness of night. The stench of death permeated her nostrils to the point where she had to drive with the window partially open, allowing the brisk air to keep her focused.

She parked at the precipice, the headlights illuminating the granite walls on the far side of the quarry. A few seconds later, Callum pulled up and parked alongside her. He emerged from the car, leaving the engine running, and made his way over to the driver's side door. She stared at him, noticing the big smile over his face. A coyote howled off in the distance. Then an owl hooted. She looked up and saw the sky dotted with billions of stars, and it made her feel small and insignificant.

"That was a long-ass haul."

"Try doing it with a dead body in your backseat. And an inspection sticker that had expired two months ago."

"You're an Original G, girl.

"This Original G is lucky she didn't get pulled over by the cops," she said, getting out and walking around the back of the truck. Callum followed behind her. "Check that out. A busted taillight on top of everything else."

"And there's blood all over your clothes."

She looked down at herself. "I'm so stupid. I should have changed before coming here."

"I can't believe you pulled that off, Gwynn. That took a lot of balls."

"Big time miscalculation. I should have never tried to kill him in his truck."

"A screwdriver through the temple. Damn, girl, that's badass," he said, shaking his head. "I had no idea you were fighting for your life back in that parking lot, or I would have come over and helped you."

"Lucky I found that screwdriver in the backseat. If I hadn't, he would have finished me off."

"Nah, you would have figured something out. You're a warrior."

"Lesson number one: always bring a knife to a rope fight."

"Duly noted, teach," he said. "What now?"

She ignored him and began to strip off her clothes until she was standing only in her bra and panties. The frigid air made her skin pimple and her teeth chatter. She balled up her clothes and threw them in the back seat of the truck. Callum watched in disbelief, his eyes caressing her near-naked body.

"Do me a favor," she said. "Roll down that window. Then shift the truck into neutral."

"For real?"

"Yes. I'm going back in the SUV to warm up."

"You're going to ride all the way back to town dressed like that?"

"Don't worry about me. After you shift the truck into neutral, push it over the edge."

She scampered back to her vehicle and sat in the passenger seat, turning all the heating vents toward her. Callum opened Field's door and lowered the window. Then he shut it, went around the back, and shoved his shoulder into the dented tailgate. The truck slowly inched forward until it reached the cliff, tilted some, before finally going over the edge. Callum ran over and watched as it plummeted to the bottom. She rolled her window down and heard the splash, followed by the sucking noise as the water rushed inside the cabin and dragged it down to the watery depths. George Fields would soon be keeping company with Sam Townsend and William Clayborn.

Callum raised his arms in triumph, jumping up and down, and whooping it up. It was the most excited she'd ever seen him in the short time they'd known each other. He ran over to the driver's side of her SUV and jumped behind the wheel.

"That was amazing."

"Look, Callum. What we did tonight is not to be taken lightly."

"Believe me, I know."

"What we did was for a specific reason, even if I did manage to screw things up."

"I realize that," he said. "And you didn't screw up, Gwynn. You succeeded far beyond my wildest dreams."

"Thanks, but I did screw up."

"You got rid of a scumbag child molester and did the world a solid?"

"I don't do this for shits and grins. This is serious business for me."

"I get it. You kill assholes."

"Not just assholes. The worst of the worst."

"Yeah, dirtbags who don't deserve to live."

"People who hurt others, especially children, and then end up slipping through the system time and time again."

"Like my father?"

"Exactly like your father."

"And all the judges and social workers who refuse to do anything about it."

"If you're going to do this kind of thing, you need to think long and hard about why you're doing it. If it's for cheap thrills, then you and I should go our separate ways right now."

"I would never disrespect you like that, Gwynn. Nor do I take this matter lightly."

"Good. I don't want you to get the wrong impression about me or what I do."

"Trust me, I don't. And remember that I was once a victim of one of these dirtbags."

"I'd be a bad teacher if I didn't tell you all of this upfront."

"No, you're an amazing teacher. You could teach a master class on this subject."

"I'd be totally misunderstood by the public if I got caught. People would just look at the bad things I'd done, not all the good."

"But they'll never catch you, not if I have anything to say about it. Besides, I'm an accessory now."

She leaned over and kissed him, feeling aroused by what they'd just done. "Sorry, I don't mean to lead you on when I kiss you, especially now that there are no strings attached between us."

He laughed. "You're kissing me wearing only panties and a bra, and you don't want to lead me on? Talk about a mixed message."

"To do what we've just done, you must be smart and disciplined, and be prepared to do anything possible to get the job done," she said, caressing his cheek. "The same goes when making love."

"Seems to me it's you who needs to control herself."

She smiled. "You don't like being with me?"

"Never said I didn't."

"Just no strings attached, right?"

"Bingo."

"What do you say we go celebrate our success?"

"What do you have in mind?"

"I think you know what I have in mind."

"You want to get it on right here? Next to this big-ass quarry?"

She looked out over it, remembering the day she'd pleasured Peters on that same rim, and the frightened look on his face as she spun him around so that his heels stuck over the precipice. That memory triggered another memory, her as a frightened teenage girl, staring up and into that perverted teacher's eyes as he pulled down his shorts. Right before she pushed him to his death.

"Drive back onto the dirt road. I'll show you where to go."

He followed her instructions and drove off, and she felt a momentary sense of relief at having pulled off another successful murder. Her body hummed with energy, like a vessel filled to the brim with life-sustaining ambrosia. The need for human affection consumed her to the point where she couldn't wait to go inside that camp and jump into bed with him. Sitting half-naked and watching him drive, she felt a tingling sensation between her legs. Suddenly, it was not just him she was worried about. Could she ever return to Peters's after sleeping with Callum? Would she ever be able to live without Callum and the crazy, sensual pleasures he gave her? She wasn't in love with him. Not by a long shot. But she just couldn't stop thinking about his body pressed up against hers.

* * *

They began kissing and pawing at each other before they even made their way inside the camp. In a matter of minutes, they were wrestling naked on top of the sheepskin rug. Callum performed even more amazingly this time, forceful and generous at the same time. She'd never experienced orgasm after orgasm in rapid-fire succession as she did now. It felt as if her mind and body were two separate entities, blissfully connected in space and time, yet also disentangled from the kind of love she had been desperately searching for her entire life.

As Callum mounted her, she recalled plunging that screwdriver through Fields's neck. By two in the morning, she felt exhausted and worn out, her body trembling from the aftereffects of their vigorous lovemaking. Callum lay next to her on his back. He appeared asleep, but she knew he wasn't. She studied his handsome profile, gazing down at his long, lean body. She loved the caramel hue of his skin and the way his muscles rippled when he moved. What would Peters think if he knew what she was doing right now? In this cabin? Would he want to kill Callum? Would he despise her and never want to see her again? The thought of losing him didn't bother her one bit.

For the first time in a while, she felt confused. The last time she felt this way had been in college, when she and Tom were playing their cat-and-mouse game of romance. Could her love for Callum develop, given enough time? That scenario seemed as unlikely as remaining married to Tom. And it occurred to her that her choice in men throughout her life had been questionable at best.

"Get up," she said, slapping his stomach.

Callum's eyelids opened, and he looked over at her.

"We have to drive back to Portland."

"Now?"

"Yes, now."

"Why?"

"I need to get home before my husband does. It's Easter Sunday and past midnight. My babysitter's on overtime."

Callum yawned. "Is this your camp?"

"Mine and Tom's."

"It's an amazing place. I might need to get one of these for myself."

"Come on, Elon Musk. Get dressed so we can get out of here."

She put on her bra and underwear. Scurried upstairs and put on some spare clothes she kept in one of the closets. Staring in the mirror, she noticed tiny specks of dried blood over her face. She went into the bathroom and washed them away with a wet handcloth. Why hadn't Callum told her about the dried blood before they made love? Did the sight of blood turn him on? She checked the cabin one last time before she departed, making sure everything was exactly the way she'd left it. Tom noticed every little detail these days, looking for any reason to punish her. But now that she knew whom he sent that video to, his day was coming. It wouldn't be long before she ditched him and returned to being herself again. She could see the glorious light at the end of the tunnel, and she pictured herself sprinting headfirst toward it. Embracing her and Jack's newfound freedom. Whether that be here in Maine or out in Los Angeles, she didn't quite know yet.

She glanced at her crypto portfolio and saw that it had risen seven percent today. Things were looking up.

Chapter Thirty-Two

DR. EZRA KAUFMAN

When she called and asked me to babysit her son, what was I going to say? I couldn't deny her request, especially after admitting in therapy that I loved her. When you love someone, it must go beyond words. It must translate into action. Besides, I figured she must have had a good reason for asking me. Maybe she needed a quiet night out with the girls while Tom was away. She deserves at least that.

When I first entered her house, I realized that I'd never been inside it before. Yes, I'd seen it from the outside a few times. Modern suburbia is not my style, but her house is tastefully decorated, although from the outside one could hardly discern one home from the next. It has the bland interior that the younger generation finds palatable these days. It makes me appreciate my old Victorian with its custom molding and grand stairway. Its wide porch and impressive turret. Gwynn seemed so happy to see me that she gave me a big hug. She took me up to Jack's room and showed him to me while he slept. Afterward, she gave me a detailed set of instructions in case something happened. Then she pecked me on the cheek and left, giving me no details about where she was going or when she would return.

What am I to do? I don't watch television. And I didn't bring along any of my books or psychiatry journals. I saunter around the house, thinking about the precarious position I've put myself in. I climb the stairs and peek my head into all the bedrooms, checking every once in a while to see if Jack is okay. I study all the pictures hanging on the wall of the Denning family in better times, if indeed those times were better. I go into Jack's room and study his angelic face, thinking he looks a lot like his father, thick and brawny, but much cuter. I tiptoe out and gently shut the door behind me.

I enter Gwynn's and Tom's bedroom and walk around, letting my imagination get the best of me, but there's not much to see here except a plastic bag and hairbrush sitting on the dresser. I head back downstairs and settle onto the sofa. It's amazing how uncomfortable I feel when out of my element. I think about everything that's been happening as of late, especially what she might be doing.

As I'm sitting here contemplating all this, her phone rings. She gave me specific instructions about what to do if it's Tom. I glance down at the phone and see the text message he's sent. He says he's going to be home tomorrow before noon, and he expects me—Gwynn—to be ready for him. Then he explains in graphic detail what he wants her to do to him before they go over to his mother's house for Easter dinner. I had no idea how bad it was, yet I type a message back like some erotic pen pal.

Is this how monsters are created? When given the chance, and without having to suffer the consequences of their depraved actions, do humans abandon all morals and take the low road? Or are humans essentially decent creatures who sometimes stray from the light?

He keeps texting me, and I reply back each and every time. Gwynn obviously knew that I would see these texts, which means she trusts me. But of course she trusts me if she's asked me to babysit her only son, the person she values most in this world. He's the entire reason she keeps on going.

So what does this say about Tom? It tells me that he manifests abnormal sexual and social desires. Has he been hiding these obsessions his entire life? Like Gwynn with her own secrets? And whose secret is worse? Despite my bias, I have to say that Tom wins on that count. He humiliates and degrades her through his aberrant sexual needs, acquired, no doubt, through many hours of watching hardcore pornography. It's misogyny turned on its head: he degrades Gwynn by making her abuse him, and then forces her to reenact the murders she's committed on him. Frankly, I've never seen or heard anything quite like it.

There's one last text from Tom. He wants her to pick up some Easter eggs before they head over to his mother's house Sunday morning. I type back that it will be done, hoping my texts resemble the words Gwynn might say. I text back each time, on Gwynn's instructions, and tell Tom that I love him. Or that Gwynn loves him. Of course, he never reciprocates. Whether he loves Gwynn or not is beside the point. Their marriage is about power. Control.

Then his texts stop. It's almost eleven at night. I turn on the news to keep my mind off those terrible demands he made. There's no breaking stories about the three dead girls found along the river. First, the mayor speaks on the issue, and then that cagey detective who interviewed me last year. His face is battered and bruised, the result of some pub brawl he was involved in the other night. He was fined for what happened and had the incident put on his record, but because of the necessity of solving these murders, his superiors allowed him to continue working on these cases.

It's the next story that surprises me. Detective Nguyen has started talking about the night she was injured, but she can't remember much about what happened. There's a brief recap of her history on the police force and her tragic accident, but other than that, there's no further explanation about her progress. This could be bad for Gwynn. If she hasn't already heard about it, I'll be forced to tell her. She never told me when she'd be arriving home, although I hope it's soon. Then again, I have nowhere else to be.

Halfway through the weather report, I hear steps on the stairs. When I turn around, I'm shocked to see her son walking toward me and rubbing his eyes. For a brief second, I panic. What will he do when he sees me? Will he start to cry uncontrollably and scream? Will he tell his father? I have no choice but to deal with him.

"Mommy," he says, dressed in his footie pajamas decorated with racing cars.

"Your mother's not here," I say, standing to greet him.

He squints his sand-dusted eyes and looks up at me. "Who are you?"

"Your babysitter."

"Oh." He looks around. "Where's Kelly?"

"Kelly couldn't be here tonight."

He looks around again. "I'm thirsty."

"Would you like me to get you a glass of water?"

"Uh-huh." He nods, not at all frightened of this strange man standing over him.

I go into the kitchen and pour him a glass of water. Then I return to his side and hand it to him. He takes a few sips and then hands it back to me.

"Can I stay up with you?"

"I don't think that's a good idea, Jack. The Easter Bunny is due to arrive at any moment now."

"Oh yeah." He runs over to his empty basket and peers inside, turning to me with a disappointed look.

"He's waiting for you to fall asleep," I say. "Would you like me to walk you back up to your room?"

He nods, and together we walk up the stairs. I follow behind him, this little creature so innocent and vulnerable. It's sometimes hard to believe that I was just like him at one time. He goes into his room, the night-light by his bed illuminating his profile. He climbs under the covers and disappears under the race car-themed blanket.

"Aren't you coming over to tuck me in?" he says, peeking his head out from under the blanket.

"If you want."

"Yes, please."

I walk over and tuck the blanket under his chin, not really having any idea what I'm doing. He stares up at me with those big blue eyes, as if trying to figure out who I am and why I'm here.

"Will you sit with me until I fall asleep?"

"Of course."

"Hug?"

He sits up and holds out his stubby arms, and I embrace him. After releasing my grip, he lowers himself to the mattress and pulls out his teddy bear, his pink cheek resting against it. His eyes remain open for a few seconds, but then they start to close. My own eyelids feel the same way. After a few minutes pass, I slip out of his room and head back downstairs. Sitting on the sofa, I start to nod off. Hopefully, Gwynn will be home soon to relieve me.

* * *

I lift my head when I hear someone keying the front door. Looking around, I see that I had fallen asleep on the leather recliner. This can't be good. Is Jack still asleep in his room? God forbid something happened to him because of my carelessness.

The door opens, and the morning light rushes in. Gwynn walks inside and sees me. Smiling, she rushes over and sits next to me. Her face glows with contentment, making me wonder what she's done to cause this. She leans over and gives me a big hug, and I wonder how I will tell her about Nguyen.

"Did you have a good night?" I ask.

"I did. How was Jack?"

"He woke up and came downstairs. There was nothing I could do."

"Oh. How did he react when he saw you?"

"He was half asleep and wanted a drink of water. He asked who I was, and I told him I was the babysitter. It didn't seem to faze him."

"That's a relief."

"What will you do if he tells Tom?"

"I'll just say he was having a bad dream."

"After he finished his glass of water, he asked if I'd walk him upstairs to his room."

"Oh my God. That's so cute."

"He's an adorable little boy."

"Can you see now why I'd do anything to protect him?"

"Yes," I say. "He asked me to give him a hug goodnight."

"And did you?"

"I did."

"I can't thank you enough, Dr. Kaufman."

I shrug self-consciously. "There's something else you should know."

"What's that?"

"Tom texted a list of things you're to do to him before you go over to his mother's house for Easter dinner."

"Okay."

"It's quite a detailed list."

"What did he want?"

I pick up the phone and show her what he texted.

"No worries. I can handle Tom."

"I'm sorry you have to do these things."

"I'm sorry you had to read it."

"At least I'm aware of how badly he's treating you."

"You're a good man, Dr. Kaufman. Don't worry about me, I'll be fine."

"There's something else you should know."

"More?"

"Yes," I say. "Detective Nguyen has started speaking about the night she got injured."

"Did she remember anything specific?"

"No, but she's suspicious."

Gwynn stares at me for a few seconds before breaking out into a fit of laughter. "Rather ironic, wouldn't you say?"

"How so?"

"Her coming back to life so close to Easter Sunday?"

"I never thought about it like that, but yes," I say. "So what will you do now?"

"I'll figure something out. I always do."

Exhausted, I stand to leave. She walks me to the door. Although I've never babysat before, and will be in no rush to do it again, I feel closer to Gwynn than ever. I've met her son and spoken to him. I've seen with my own eyes what her husband instructs her to do behind closed doors. If she ever asks me to babysit Jack again, I will. As stupid as it sounds, that hug from the boy was possibly one of the best moments of my life. It brought me back to my childhood when my mother tucked me in at bedtime, and me feel safe and loved. It almost made me wish I had a son or daughter of my own, or a grandchild, but that time has come and gone. Good thing Jack didn't see the tear rolling down my cheek when I embraced him. Now I know how she feels because I, too, would kill to protect a child like that.

Chapter Thirty-Three

GWYNN

Gwynn smiled as the minister delivered his sermon about the resurrection of Christ. Easter Sunday: the most important day in the Christian calendar. Sunlight streamed in through the stained-glass windows, giving the inside of the church an ethereal glow. She glanced over and saw Tom standing at the end of the pew, dressed impeccably in his pinstripe blue suit and looking like the requisite family man, and this despite his weekend of drunken revelry. The suit managed to hide the collection of welts and bruises she'd given him this morning, like ribbons awarded during battlefield heroics. She stared down at her son standing between them, dressed in his shirt and bowtie. For the first time ever, she thought he looked like a little man.

Last night, she'd killed George Fields, a man who had abused his two kids and continually cheated justice. Last night she'd cheated on both her husband and her secret lover. On the surface, her actions looked sinful, but there was a reason for everything she did.

Tom came home from his weekend out with the boys and immediately took her up to the bedroom, despite Jack playing with his toys downstairs. She did what he asked, knowing that her days of pleasuring him with pain were coming to an end. She had absolutely no desire to kill him. Oh, she wanted him dead when the time came, but not just yet. And not like that. Besides, she couldn't kill him without legal consequences. His death had to be meticulously planned and thought out. Maybe even made to look like an accident. More than anything, she wanted him to know why she was killing him, especially when the time came for him to take his last breath. She wanted him to weep and beg for his life. Only then would she be able to put him out of his misery.

Her mind wandered during the church service, and she snapped out of her daydream to catch the pastor making eye contact with her, as if he'd caught her doing something naughty. The same thing happened when she was a little girl, while listening to her father's long but powerfully delivered sermons. Christ's death and resurrection had always fascinated her, especially at a young age. The thought of Jesus meticulously folding his robes and then walking out of that tomb seemed so cool at the time. Her father used to joke that Christ took one for the team, and she never quite understood what he meant until she was older. As a child, it almost appeared that Christ took great satisfaction at having those metal spikes hammered through His wrists, then hung on the cross between two garrulous thieves. Back then, it was the most excruciating way to die. Jesus willingly went to his death with the understanding that he would rise up in three days. She always believed that knowing with certainty that there was life after death made the prospect of dying that much easier. But then again, that was the whole point of faith. Christ hadn't wanted his death avenged. At least not in the way she would have avenged it. He wanted His enemies and tormentors to turn their souls over to God and ask for forgiveness. Appreciate that He had died to wash away their sins. Had it been her sentenced to death, she would have avenged all those who wronged her. And she would have done it with glee.

She stared at the windows along the far wall, admiring the colors of the stained glass, made even more beautiful by the sunlight filtering through them. Jack shifted and squirmed next to her, behaving far better than she'd expected. She thought of George Fields at the bottom of that quarry, and the poor homeless girls who had been killed and left for dead next to the river. Not even Nguyen's metaphorical resurrection from that coma could upset her today, especially when she'd heard that Nguyen was talking about the night she was injured. Fortunately, she couldn't remember anything in detail. She recalled the smug look on Tom's face when he heard the news while driving to church.

The sermon ran longer than usual today. Jack tugged at her dress midway through the service and whispered that he needed to use the bathroom. His request actually gave her an excuse to take a break from the pastor's long-winded sermon. She grabbed Jack's hand and stood. Tom scooted his legs in so they could pass, eyeing her suspiciously when she whispered that Jack needed to use the restroom.

They walked down the aisle and turned until they left the nave, making their way down the oak-paneled hallway. Jack seemed quiet this morning, and she wondered if he was okay. Did he sense the weird dynamic growing between her and Tom? They made their way downstairs and headed to the restroom. She stopped and let go of his hand when they reached the men's room. Instead of going inside, he stood staring up at her.

"Are you okay, Jack?"

He rubbed his nose with the back of his hand.

"What's wrong?"

"Where did you go last night?"

She squatted so they were eye to eye. "I had a quick errand to run. It's best not to tell Daddy about it. Okay?"

"Why?"

"Because I had to run out and get him some of those special candies he likes. The Easter Bunny only gives baskets to good boys and girls."

"Is that why you and Daddy don't get Easter baskets?"

"Yup."

He seemed to think it over, squirming because he needed to relieve himself.

"Go to the bathroom, Jack," she said, laughing at his discomfort.

"Who was that man last night?"

This surprised her that Jack remembered Kaufman. "You promise not to tell anyone?"

"Promise."

"He works for the Easter Bunny."

"He does?" His eyes widened.

"Yes. He was keeping an eye on you to make sure you were being a good little wiggleworm." She nodded. "Now go to the bathroom before you have an accident."

Jack came out a few minutes later, rubbing his wet hands together. She thought about Ivy and prayed the girl was okay. If she could somehow find her, she could tell her that it was safe to go home now that her father could no longer hurt her. But how could she tell the girl this without incriminating herself?

They walked back upstairs and down the center aisle. Tom stepped out of the pew to let them enter. She sat back down and tried to pay attention to the service, but to no avail. Her mind started to wander, restless and unceasing. Could anything go right? Killing and telling lies had a lot in common: once you did it, you had to keep doing it to cover your tracks.

She glanced over at Tom, and their eyes met. He smiled at her, and she smiled back before turning to the altar.

Her marriage would soon come to an explosive and violent end. Then she'd be free from that wolf sitting two seats over from her and dressed in nice clothes. She wanted him out of her life so bad it hurt. But then what? Her job sucked, and her boss wanted her gone. She thought she loved Peters, yet she couldn't stop thinking about Callum Frye. So what did she feel for him? Was her attraction to him the byproduct of the murder she'd committed? Their shared interests? Or was it the real deal?

The only good thing she had going for her was her writing. Oh, and that TV show she'd penned but had not gotten any credit for. And her growing crypto portfolio, which made her feel confident that she could provide for her and Jack once they were on their own. But she couldn't start her life anew until Tom was out of the picture. Tift had stolen her story, holding her creative life in the palm of her hand. Then she remembered that video on Tom's computer and those racist rap lyrics her friend had sung along to, and she knew she had the upper hand in their relationship. And soon in her marriage, too. And maybe one day she could assert control over those voices in her head and finally stop killing.

The organ started to play, signaling the end of the service. Gwynn closed her eyes and bowed her head, praying that Ivy was alive and well, and would emerge from the ashes of her nightmarish existence in one piece.

Chapter Thirty-Four

GWYNN

They stood in the backyard of her mother-in-law's house, watching as Jack ran around searching for hidden Easter eggs. To Gwynn's right stood Trish, Tom's older sister, who hated her. To her right stood Tom, and next to her, Susan, his cheerless mother. Seventy-two and with a patrician temperament, she held ridiculously high standards when it came to her children. Gwynn knew that her mother-in-law thought Tom could have done much better in marriage. At least Susan loved Jack and doted on him whenever he came to visit. Tom's father had passed away five years ago from a heart attack, making Susan her son's only living grandparent.

Jack turned and waved his arm for them to come over. Tom and his mother walked across the yard, leaving her standing next to Trish. Two years older than Tom, Trish had yet to meet anyone special in her life. Susan had been sorely disappointed when her daughter announced, at the age of twenty-four, that she was attracted to women. But in the past few years, Susan had come to a begrudging acceptance of the situation. The last thing Gwynn wanted to do now was engage in small talk with her sister-in-law.

"I know we've had our differences, Gwynn, but I'm happy you're back with Tom."

"So am I."

"Despite what you might think, he does love you."

Gwynn turned and laughed. "He really does, doesn't he?"

"Yes, and you should be grateful that he took you back. He's an amazing father and a wonderful man. A great provider, too."

She stared at Trish, trying not to laugh. "I realize now that I'd be lost without him."

"Can I ask you something?"

Gwynn nodded.

"Why did you cheat on him?"

"Not that it's any of your business, but we were separated at the time and contemplating divorce."

"But you were still married to him."

"True, but I realized I'd made a big mistake by engaging in that affair. Taking responsibility for my actions made me a better person, and made me see how much I loved Tom."

"Jack is much better off with his parents together."

"I couldn't agree more," she said, wanting to escape from this overbearing busybody. At least Trish didn't know the details about Nguyen's 'accident' and all the murders she'd committed.

"We might not ever be best friends, Gwynn, but we can at least be civil to each other."

"I would like that, Trish. Maybe someday we can even be friends."

"Maybe."

"That would be wonderful if it happened."

"I don't want this to come off the wrong way," Trish said, leaning into her, "but if you ever hurt my brother again, you'll have me to deal with."

She nodded, not wanting to get into an argument on Easter Sunday, of all days.

"My mother and brother mean everything to me. And of course Jack does, too."

Gwynn turned and saw Jack running over with his basket in hand, a big smile on his face, and his basket brimming with brightly colored Easter eggs. She knelt down and examined his booty, congratulating him on his stash. Then they all went inside to get ready for dinner.

"Gwynn," Susan said once they walked through the door, "would you mind helping me out in the kitchen?"

"Of course. What would you like me to do?"

"Come in, dear, and I'll tell you what I need from you."

Gwynn walked nervously into the kitchen and watched as Susan tied a white apron around her waist. The kitchen was neat and tidy, and everything in its proper place. Susan slipped on two oven mitts and looked over at her as if expecting her to do something. Not knowing what to do, she waited for her cue, but Susan didn't give her any instructions. Instead, her mother-in-law took the ham out of the oven and placed it on the kitchen island. Smoke curled off the honey-glazed flesh, and it smelled heavenly. She removed the gloves and picked up the knife that had been lying on the counter.

"Come over here, Gwynn. I'd like for you to carve it."

Gwynn walked over and reached for the knife. Instead of extending the handle, Susan reversed the utensil and pointed the blade at her. The blade inched close to her stomach until the tip pressed lightly against her shirt. One push and it would break through to the skin.

"I know everything you did."

Gwynn stared down at the blade. "I have no idea what you're talking about."

"Oh, I think you do." She pushed the blade a bit harder. "That cop you chased? And you cheating on my son? Does that jog your memory?"

It surprised Gwynn that her mother-in-law would come right out and admit this. "Not that it concerns you, Susan, but Tom and I have worked out all our problems and are quite happy now."

"Tom told me all about that Asian cop you were arguing with. She was your boyfriend's partner on the PD."

She hadn't expected to hear that.

"You thought she was sleeping with your boyfriend."

Hearing this relieved her; Susan didn't know the whole story. "I didn't try to kill her, Susan. I only wanted to talk to her about what was going on between the two of them."

"It's a good thing Trish doesn't know about this, or you'd be in prison now. Fortunately for you, I told my son I'd honor his wish to remain silent, but that's only for the time being. I'm doing it because he begged me not to turn you in, for Jack's sake, but god forbid something should ever happen to my son."

"Do you really think I'm that much of a monster?"

"You're the sole reason she went into that coma," Susan said. "Bet the police would love to get their hands on that video."

"Have you heard the news, Susan? Detective Nguyen woke from her coma and is now speaking."

"Not good news for you, then?"

"Doesn't affect me at all because I didn't do anything wrong."

"I've sensed that something was off about you for a long time, Gwynn, but as much as I tried, I couldn't convince my son not to marry you."

"Good, because Tom and I love each other. We always have."

She laughed. "He certainly does love you, but for the life of me, I don't know why. You're a snake in the grass."

"You're wrong, Susan. Tom and Jack mean the world to me."

"I swear to god, Gwynn, if you ever hurt either one of them again, I *will* kill you." She pushed the blade so Gwynn had to suck in her stomach.

"Kill me?" She laughed. "Now that's rather harsh, don't you think?"

"I'm seventy-two years old and have had a good life. I will do everything in my power to protect my family."

"As would I."

"When Tom told me that you cheated on him, and that you'd chased that Asian cop out into the street, I wanted to strangle you with my bare hands." She flipped the knife around so that the walnut handle faced her. "Now start cutting."

Gwynn took the handle and long fork, and instead of cutting the ham, she stuck the tip of the blade into Susan's stomach.

Susan stared at her. "So now you're going to use it on me?"

"If you're anything like your son, you'd probably enjoy it."

Susan cocked her eyebrows. "What's that supposed to mean?"

"I think you know what it means?"

"I'd let you kill me right now if it meant that you'd rot in prison for the rest of your life."

"Unfortunately, Susan, you don't get to decide my future," Gwynn said, pushing it in a little further and causing the woman to gasp.

"I suggest you not mention to Tom what I told you," Susan said, glancing down at the knife. "He's finally happy for the first time in his life, and I want him to stay that way."

"Oh, he's happy all right," Gwynn said, taking back the knife to carve the ham. "Have you any idea the things he does to me in the bedroom?"

"What you two do in the privacy of your own home is none of my business."

"Oh no, I think it most certainly is your business, seeing as how you raised that pig."

"Stop talking about him like that. I don't want to hear it."

"Oh, you're going to hear it." She stopped carving and looked up at her mother-in-law. "Did you know he makes me choke him while we're having sex? He says it's the only thing that turns him on."

Susan's eyes lit up. "Why are you spewing such lies?"

"It's true, Susan. I would never lie about something like that. Go ask him yourself if you don't believe me."

"You're a despicable woman."

"Sometimes he makes me wrap a plastic bag over his head until he passes out. Or beat him over the ass with a hairbrush. It really helps him get his rocks off."

Susan turned to walk away.

Gwynn grabbed the woman by the elbow and spun her around. "No, you're going to hear what I have to say about your wonderful son. He's a controlling narcissist who gets off on pain and suffering, both giving and receiving it. He's actually been like this for many years now, but he obviously wouldn't ever tell his mommy about the sick desires he's been hiding from everyone. Then again, you probably always suspected this about him."

CHAPTER THIRTY-FOUR

"Why are you telling me this? I'm his mother, for god's sake."

"Did you know that he did the same thing to my college roommate back at Brooks?"

Susan stared at her as if unable to speak.

"Maybe Tom enjoyed all those spankings you gave him when he was a little boy."

"Go to hell."

Susan snatched her arm back and walked over to the stove. She stirred something in the pan before putting the mashed potatoes and peas into their respective bowls. Gwynn resumed cutting the ham into paper-thin slices, knowing that Susan would never mention this to Tom. Once they had enough plated for dinner, Susan carried the tray out to the dining room table. Gwynn peeked briefly into the living room and watched as Tom and Jack played a video game. They laughed and appeared to be having a good time. Trish watched them from the opposite couch, cheering Jack on. On the surface, they looked like the perfect family. Underneath it all, she knew they were anything but.

Without speaking, she and Susan carried out the remaining plates and trays to the dining room. Once the table was set, Susan made her way into the living room and called the three of them to the table. Tom asked for a few more minutes so they could finish the game, and Susan returned to the dining room, sitting across from her and spreading a napkin priggishly over her lap. They sat like this for a few uncomfortable minutes before Gwynn walked over to the living room. On her way there, she saw a door in the hallway. She opened it, flicked on the light switch, and saw a steep set of stairs leading down to the basement. Susan's cat came sprinting up the stairs and bolted out of the doorway. An idea came to her as she closed the door and returned to the living room.

"The food your mother spent all day cooking is getting cold, people," Gwynn announced.

Tom turned, looked at her, and then shut off the video game. He grabbed Jack in his arms and carried the giggling boy to the dining room, eyeing her as he passed. Trish followed behind them, and she followed her sister-in-law.

Once in the dining room, they all settled into their respective seats.

"It's so good to be with the ones I love on the holiest of days," Susan said, looking around the table until her eyes settled on Gwynn. "Before we eat, I think it's appropriate that we say Grace. Would you mind doing the honors, Gwynn?"

"Of course."

Gwynn stared at Susan before saying a prayer. But in her head, she prayed for Susan to have a quick and painless death. In a weird sort of way, she respected her mother-in-law's fierce loyalty to her kids. After all, Susan was a mother bear like her, protecting her cubs at all costs. She, too, would protect Jack with everything in her arsenal. At least they had that in common. When she finished saying Grace, they passed around the trays of food and began to eat.

Chapter Thirty-Five

DETECTIVE PETERS

Easter Sunday, and Peters was more miserable than ever. Even more miserable than before he'd gained fame by solving that age-old serial-killing case. At least he'd had Gwynn back when he'd 'identified' the Muddy River Killer. Now she barely answered his calls. And what was going on with that handsome young guy he'd seen her with the other night? Peters knew it had been a mistake to follow her in his car. Yet he couldn't help himself. He wanted to know why Gwynn and Callum Frye drove over to that baked bean plant so late at night, on the eve of Easter Sunday. He'd watched them for thirty minutes but didn't see anything untoward. They merely sat in her SUV, talking. Maybe they were just friends. After all, she did bail the kid out sixteen years ago after murdering his drug-addicted father.

The shift workers started filing out of the plant, and Peters knew he had to get out of there before he got stuck in the outgoing traffic. What if Gwynn saw him? How would he explain that away? If she caught him spying on her, she wouldn't want anything to do with him. He found it frustrating that his hands were tied and he couldn't do anything about it.

The other day he'd bought a GPS tracking device from one of the big box stores, planning to attach it to Gwynn's SUV as soon as possible. Now that she was involved with Frye, he needed to keep a closer eye on her.

He arrived at Dimillo's and followed the host into the dining room, walking past families and couples enjoying the holiday. The host sat him by the window, providing him with a stellar view of the bay. Boats bobbed in the harbor, and the sun reflected magnificently off the water. He thought a nice meal and a great view would cheer him up on the holiday, but for some reason, it made him feel worse.

He remembered being a young boy and waking excitedly on Easter Sunday to discover his basket filled with chocolate eggs and marshmallow Peeps. Then going to Easter Mass with his family, dressed in his Sunday best, impatient for the service to finish so he could go home and eat more candy. They didn't go to church often, but always on Christmas and Easter, and he'd spent much of the services checking out the cute girls in their holiday dresses. When they arrived home, they ate a baked ham dinner with peas and honey-glazed carrots, and then enjoyed hot cross buns for dessert. He wished his life were that simple now. But after killing four people, he knew his life would never be that innocent again.

He ordered the lobster Benedict with home fries and a coffee instead of his usual Bloody Mary, knowing he had to stay sober today. The Sunday paper sat like a granite block in front of him, the pages filled with tragedy and despair. The waitress brought over his coffee, and he added generous amounts of cream and sugar before stirring it. Then he unfolded the paper and perused the headlines.

The top story detailed the lives of the three dead girls found along the Presumpscot River. He skipped down to the news about Nguyen, not quite believing that his partner had woken from that coma and started talking to her family about what caused her injuries. When he first heard about it, he became worried. But not anymore. Her brain trauma was more significant than anyone realized and, even in the worst scenario, had rendered her an unreliable witness, even assuming she managed to remember the events of that night. The only concern he had right now was that video Tom made corroborating her story. But he doubted that would ever come to light. Gwynn would take care of things on Tom's end.

Bitterness consumed him as he stared out the window, wallowing in his despair. Families seated nearby laughed and talked, adding to his loneliness.

He wanted a Bloody Mary so bad it hurt, but he needed to stay sober for later. Couples around him kissed and snuggled against each other. If he hadn't already ordered breakfast, he'd have gotten up and left.

After taking out his phone, he examined the unanswered texts he'd sent to Gwynn. Why was she ignoring him, especially after that passionate kiss they'd shared at the awards banquet? Even as they kissed, he'd sensed that something was off. Had she been jealous? He cursed himself for ever taking up with Annabelle.

But the worst mistake had been to approach Tom at that bar after a hard night of drinking. He still couldn't forgive himself for that unforced error. What were the odds that Tom would come into the very same bar that he'd been drinking in? Had he been sober, he never would have challenged Tom to a fight. He would have slipped out quietly without incident. His ego, now bruised from that humiliating defeat, wanted to teach Tom a lesson he would not soon forget. Not on his worst day would he ever lose a fight to that lard.

His waitress delivered his brunch, and he ate quietly, barely able to taste the fresh chunks of lobster in his Benedict. As he chewed, he stared out at the bay, imagining Gwynn ambushing Sandra while she took her morning swim. His thoughts shifted, and he recalled how she'd pleasured him on that cliff. Now two bodies lay at the bottom of that quarry. Would Tom end up there, as well? And whoever else he'd sent that video to? Would he end up there?

His appetite ruined, he pushed his half-eaten plate away and stood to leave, leaving a big tip for the waitress. On the holiest of Christian days, he had much to accomplish if he hoped to get back in Gwynn's good graces. He jumped in his car and headed over to the Bayside, eager to find another girl to add to his tally. Although it was still early, he texted Gwynn on her burner phone, not expecting to get a response, knowing she'd be spending the day with Tom and his family. That he couldn't talk to her ate away at him. Or hold her in his arms and tell her how much he loved her. Sadly, he'd come to the conclusion that he had nothing to live for without Gwynn. What a sad and pathetic thought. Why would Gwynn ever want to be with a loser like him?

The Old Port appeared quiet this morning, populated by the zombies wandering about. The only sign of life were the congregants filing up the steep stairs of the First Parish Church. It was a beautiful stone structure, elevated above Congress Street, and Peters could see himself someday attending church there with Gwynn on his arm while clutching Jack's hand. Even if he didn't believe in God, he liked to think of himself as a man of faith. It was why he needed to make something happen before Gwynn lost interest in him. Before he lost her for good.

He crossed over Congress Street, the boundary separating the haves from the have-nots. The Bayside seemed unusually quiet this morning due to the holiday. He needed to find another victim before he changed his mind. The resentment building inside him made it easier to kill, and he didn't want to lose that edge.

Just then his phone dinged. Another message from his bookie looking for his money.

Chapter Thirty-Six

After cruising around for an hour, it both surprised and pleased him when he saw the girl sitting slumped on a brick wall, looking pale and sickly. He pulled over and lowered the passenger-side window.

"Hey, kid. You okay?"

She looked up at him, her eyes glazed over.

"I'm a cop," Peters said, showing her his badge.

She flipped him off and lowered her head.

"Maybe you can help me out. I'm investigating the deaths of those three girls who hung out down here," he shouted to her.

"Fuck off," she said, lifting herself off the wall.

"Help me out, and maybe I'll help you."

"How's a stupid cop like you gonna help me?" She shuffled toward his car.

"By catching this creep down here and making the streets safer for you kids."

"You wanna catch the real killer?" She leaned into his passenger window and gazed at him with faraway eyes. "Then arrest the drug dealers and pimps. They're the ones causing all the problems down here."

"If it were up to me, I'd toss them all in jail and throw away the key."

He pulled out two twenties.

She laughed. "Dude, I charge way more than that for a date."

"No, I'm not looking for a date. What I want is some information."

"Make up your mind."

"If I help you get a fix, will you tell me all you know about these three dead girls?"

"Hell no. I don't trust cops."

Peters pulled out two more twenties and held them out to her.

She snatched the bills out of his hand and stuffed them in her pocket.

"You might recognize me, kid. I'm the guy who solved the Muddy River Killer case."

"Nope. Never seen you before." She wiped her runny nose.

"Okay," he said, his ego dinged. "Did you know any of the girls who died?"

She glanced down the empty street, ignoring him.

"Tell me something about them. Anything. What they were like, where they hung out?"

"Maybe when I get my fix, I'll tell you everything I know."

"Hop in. I'll drive you to wherever you want to go," he said, watching as she walked around his car and settled in the passenger seat. "Where to?"

"Just up the street. I'll show you when we get there."

He cruised over to Grant Street and pulled over when she pointed out the house. She reached for the door handle, but he grabbed her wrist before she left.

"Better not take off on me, kid."

"Don't worry, cop, I'm not going anywhere."

"Because if you do, I'll find your sorry ass and toss you in jail. Then you'll really be sick."

She rolled her eyes. "I said I'd be back. Now let go of me." He released her wrist and watched as she took off toward the front door, disappearing inside.

Five minutes later, she came out and slipped back into the passenger seat. She asked him to find a safe place to shoot up, and he drove down the hill, turning into the weedy lot of an abandoned warehouse. After parking in the back, the girl took out a black rubber band and wrapped it around her emaciated bicep. Then she pulled out a spoon, lighter, and needle.

"Been living on the streets long?" he asked, excited about what he was about to do.

"What do you think?"

"Your parents must be worried about you."

She laughed. "My parents could give two shits about me."

"Is that why you ran away from home?"

"No, I ran away because my daddy wouldn't buy me a pony." She flexed her arm, tapping in search of a good vein.

"Don't be a wiseass. I just paid for your fix."

She continued to tap tap tap away.

"I'm sure your parents are concerned about you."

"You know what sucked about growing up in my house? Having to smell baked fucking beans all day."

Her words got his attention. "We used to have baked beans with hot dogs and brown bread every Saturday night."

"We had it almost every night. That disgusting brown bread, too. My father gets all that shit for free where he works."

"He works at the bean plant?"

"Lucky me."

He couldn't believe his ears. Then it dawned on him. This was the same girl Gwynn had been mentoring at The Loft. The girl he'd seen Gwynn talking to when he snuck into her office last year, hoping to surprise her with a bouquet of flowers and box of Haven's candies.

What a stroke of luck.

She settled on a vein, lit the flame, and placed it under the spoon. Then she sucked the liquid into the syringe. Once full, she plunged the needle into her vein. Her entire body went slack as soon as the drug wormed its way into her system.

"What's your name, kid?"

"Ivy."

Just as he expected. "I'm Mike."

She glanced over at him with a dazed smile. "Mike's a cool name."

"Not better than yours."

"I hate my name. Seriously, a poisonous weed?"

"It's very cinematic."

"What's your last name?"

"Peters."

"Very cool. A cop with two first names," Ivy said, closing her eyes.

Once she passed out, he got out of the car and went around to the passenger side. Adjusted her seat until it reclined. Taking the phone out of her hand, he punched in Gwynn's number, leaving a text message for her. He then programmed a second message set to send the following morning.

He studied the girl, unable to believe his good luck. She looked angelic as she lay next to him. He reached over and pinched her nose with one hand, and then covered her mouth with the other. She kicked some, but was too weak to put up much of a fight. He waited a few minutes until she stopped moving, checked her pulse, and when he didn't find one, removed his hand from her face. After sliding the pink ring out of her eyebrow, he stashed it in his pocket. Then he got back behind the wheel and took off.

Now he could pin these murders on someone wholly deserving of life in prison. And once Gwynn received the news of Ivy's death, it would only bring them closer together. She never needed to know that he'd killed these girls to win her affections. Only that he solved the murders and delivered the 'killer' to Gwynn on a silver platter. Once that happened, she would never leave him.

He wanted Ivy's body to be found quickly so that it accelerated his reunion with her, but he couldn't deposit her next to the river just yet, not during daylight hours when people were out and about. He got out of the car and carried her to the trunk, slipped her body inside the bag, and zipped it up.

Needing to kill some time, he drove over to the Forest Gardens and parked in front of the pub. Went inside and sat at the end of the bar, next to the window, so he could keep an eye on his car. Skip came over and poured him a draft beer. The guy was a legend who'd been working here for the last thirty years.

"How's it going, Mikey?"

"Better than I deserve."

"Tin roof for Portland's finest," Skip said, placing the beer down in front of him. Tin roof; on the house.

Peters ordered a cheeseburger with fries, anxious to get moving again. Now he knew why Gwynn and Frye had been at that baked bean plant. Gwynn had planned on killing Ivy's father. It hurt that she would do this without asking him for his help. It felt like a betrayal of sorts, as if she had been unfaithful to him. Killing those girls had started out as a means to an end—until he started enjoying it. But he knew he could stop killing once he and Gwynn were back together. Hopefully, she would stop too.

Once the sun set, he staggered out of the Forest Gardens and drove toward the river. The traffic along this stretch of road was light at this time of night. After finding a secluded spot to park, he put on some rubber gloves and then dragged the body bag all the way down the grassy hill. The river below bubbled and boiled. After taking out his flashlight, he slid her corpse out of the bag, removed all her clothes, and then positioned the dead girl beneath a grove of ferns. When he turned to leave, he saw a homeless man staggering out of the woods. The man looked surprised to see him. Had he witnessed him placing the girl's body under the ferns?

The guy stumbled backwards, falling on his hindquarters. Peters pointed the flashlight at the man's face.

"You killed her," the man said, hands over his eyes.

"Yes, I did," Peters said. "Isn't it crazy what we will do for love?"

"Hey, you're that famous cop. The one who solved the Muddy River case."

"That's me."

"Why'd you kill her?"

"I had no choice," he said, moving closer to the man.

"Don't hurt me, bro. I swear I won't say nothing."

He took a few more steps forward. "What's your name, pal?"

"Eddie Sutton."

"Well, Eddie, you have to understand the difficult situation I find myself in." He took two more steps until he was standing directly over him.

"Swear I'll say nothing. Swear, bro."

"I'm sorry, Eddie, but I just can't take that chance," he said, taking the gun out of his holster. "Believe me, I'll take no pleasure in killing a guy like you."

The man stared at him for a second before turning and crawling up the hill. Peters gave chase, striking him three times over the head. The man collapsed to the ground, groaning in agony. Blood began to dampen his hair and neck. After cracking him repeatedly in the skull, Peters went over and grabbed the plastic body bag he'd used on the girl. He spread it out on the ground and then slid the man's body into the bag. He found some river rocks and threw them in with the girl's clothes, and then zipped the bag shut. He dragged it into the river until it floated over the surface of the water. The current eventually sucked it toward the middle, and the bag disappeared beneath the rippling surface.

Confident that he'd covered all his bases, he headed to his car, knowing that Ivy's death would force Gwynn to ask for his help. He drove back to his condo, hoping his luck would finally change for the better. Once he framed the right person for these murders, his days of killing would be over.

Chapter Thirty-Seven

GWYNN

She and Tom sat side by side on their sofa, exhausted from the long day at his mother's house. The ten o'clock news came on, and five minutes into the segment, the news anchor reported on a missing man from the baked bean plant. Tom asked her to go get him a beer. She went over and grabbed a bottle out of the fridge, opened it, and then walked over and handed it to him. Tom seemed happy this evening, the magnanimous and kind version of her husband. He'd spent a booze-filled weekend in Boston hanging out with his college friends and then spent a solemn Easter Sunday with his family, all of which had put him in a good mood.

He rested his hand on her knee and told her how much he loved her. She snuggled up next to him, playing the role of loving wife to a tee, trying her best not to display any negative emotions as she watched Ivy's mother appear onscreen. Gwynn blamed the woman for enabling her abusive spouse, always caring more about her evil husband than her neglected kids. No one watching this report would ever know what bad parents they were. Or that their daughter ran away from home and took to the streets because of the emotional, physical, and sexual abuse her father had inflicted on her throughout the years.

"Look at her," Tom said, pointing at Ivy's mother. "What guy in his right mind would ever take her home?"

"Don't be cruel, especially when her husband has gone missing."

"He probably went on a bender after she nagged him to death. Hell, if I had to spend the rest of my life looking at that cow, I'd probably leave home too."

"It's still Easter, Tom. Try not to be so judgmental," she said, thinking about her other life. Being judgmental was the reason she killed people.

"Hope those two didn't pass on their genes."

She thought of poor Ivy and her brother. "That's why we need to make sure Jack is brought up properly."

Tom turned to her and smiled. "Wouldn't it be cool if he went to Brooks like we did? And met his future wife there?"

"He'll never get into Brooks if you don't make him trace his letters."

"You and your goddamn letters," he said, laughing. "The kid will probably be a ballplayer, anyway. You see how strong he is?"

"We both know that Brooks is academically challenging and a hard school to get into. It's important that Jack keeps up his studies."

"Then you stay on him about his letters, and I'll teach him how to play ball." He gave her a peck on the cheek. "Those years at Brooks were some of the best of my life. What I wouldn't give to go back in time."

"Me too. I miss watching Dirt Fish rocking out at the Rat. We all thought you guys were going to be famous one day," she said, trying to put him at ease.

"Yeah, that was so much fun. Are you upset that I became a CPA instead of a rock star?"

"Not at all. You're a hard worker and great provider to our family. I don't know what we'd do without you."

"Did I ever tell you what a great mother you are?"

"Only all the time."

"I've loved you from the moment I first laid eyes on you strolling across that campus," he said, the alcohol making him sentimental. "You are the most amazing woman I've ever known."

"You really do love me, Tom, don't you?"

"More than you'll ever know. And you love me too, right?"

"I've never loved anyone more."

"I hate to say I told you so." He kissed her, his breath hot and beery. "But I told you so."

"Yes, you did."

"Besides, it never would have worked out with you and that pretty-boy cop."

"You always did know what was in my best interest."

"Of course I did," he said, swigging his beer. "You might be surprised to hear this, Gwynn, but I think my mother and Trish are finally coming around on you."

"You think?"

"I could see it in the way they acted toward you today."

"I still can't believe that your mother asked me to help her out with Easter dinner. That's a first."

"I know my mother's been hard on you these past few years, but she's always been super protective of me and my sister."

"It's the reason you turned out to be the wonderful man you are today." Could she keep saying all this with a straight face?

"I want us to grow old together, babe."

"Not more than I do," she said, almost gagging at the thought of spending the rest of her life with him.

They sat quietly for a few minutes, his hand on her knee. Maybe she'd be able to appreciate this side of him if she could forget about his perverted demands. In many ways, it would have been better if he'd just be an asshole twenty-four-seven. And yet she often felt that she deserved such harsh treatment for the things she'd done, despite believing that all of it had been justified.

The strangest part about their marriage was that he seemed happy about the way things had turned out. Did he genuinely believe that they had a relationship built on love and mutual respect? As she sat staring at him, trying to act sweet, she could barely keep herself from breaking out into a fit of laughter. Could he really be that deluded? Did he not know that she couldn't wait to be free from him? She recalled the look on his stupid mother's face when she'd told her about the sex games her son liked to play.

"You look tired," he said.

"I am. It's been a long day."

"But a good one, right?"

"A wonderful day," she said, kissing his cheek. She studied him, still not believing all the weight he'd put on in the last year. He looked virtually unrecognizable from that lanky guitarist he'd been at Brooks.

"Go on upstairs and get ready for bed. I'm going to have one more beer before calling it a night."

"You sure? I can stay down here and keep you company if you like."

"No, you go on up. I'll snuggle next to you once I'm done."

She kissed his head and headed upstairs, relieved to be away from him. Oh, and she could hardly wait for him to 'snuggle' next to her and breathe stale beer onto her neck all night.

Before she went into her bedroom, she checked in on Jack. He was sound asleep, his pink cheek resting on his folded hands. On his night table sat his Easter basket loaded with goodies. He looked so adorable that she leaned down and kissed him on his warm forehead. He was the sole reason she soldiered on, and the only good thing to come out of her marriage to Tom. It was why she would be merciful and make sure he died quickly and without pain. She touched Jack's cheek with the back of her hand, and he squirmed under the blanket.

She left Jack's room and went into her bedroom, checking her phone to see if there were any messages. One popped up, a text message sent from Ivy's phone.

I'm tired of living like this, Gwynn, Ivy texted.

Call me, Ivy, she texted back.

I just can't go on like this anymore.

Please don't do anything rash. I can come get you.

Forget about me and live your own life. I'm not worth it.

A feeling of dread shot through her. Gwynn called the girl, hoping to hear her voice, but the call went straight to voicemail. She needed to convince Ivy that her father would no longer be a problem for her going forward.

But how could she do that now that she'd killed him?

As she slipped into her robe, she thought of all the creeps and perverts out there who might be doing bad things to her. She rubbed moisturizer on her hands and arms while studying her face in the bathroom mirror. It was a relief to know that Ivy's father was no longer around to hurt anyone.

She settled under the covers. Tomorrow, she would drive down to the Bayside and search for the girl. Whether Ivy would listen to her or not, she didn't know, especially considering the severity of the girl's drug habit. It was the least she could do for the poor kid. She hadn't killed George Fields only to fail Ivy now, when she needed her the most. Ivy deserved at least one more shot at life.

Chapter Thirty-Eight

GWYNN

Her alarm blared at six, waking her out of a deep slumber. Another few hours in bed would have been nice, but then she remembered that text from Ivy. She turned but didn't see Tom next to her. No wonder she'd slept so soundly. No snoring, farting, or bad breath polluting the air and keeping her up all night. Had he slept on the sofa?

Yawning, she made her way downstairs. Since their arrangement, Tom demanded that she be the first one up every morning. It was her job to set out their clothes and prepare breakfast. She couldn't stop yawning as she made her way down the steps, but she couldn't see Tom anywhere. Had he left for work already? On the coffee table sat six green bottles and an empty pizza box. It disgusted her to realize that he'd drunk five more beers and ordered a delivery pizza after she'd gone to bed.

Walking over, she saw him asleep on the sofa and decided not to wake him. He was still dressed in his Easter clothes and snoring loudly. At least he'd kicked off his dress shoes. On the table sat his iPad. She tiptoed around the sofa and turned it on, remembering his four-digit password, which was the day and year he met her. When the screen blinked to life, she clicked on the history icon and a long list of porn websites popped up, much of it of the S&M variety. The discovery of his digital trail repulsed her, although it shouldn't have been a surprise. She'd only have to endure his behavior a bit longer. Making him disappear would be her final act of justice.

Tom groaned, and she quickly put the tablet back where she found it. She gathered the bottles in hand and placed them in the recycling bin. Picked up the greasy pizza box, folded it in half, and stuffed it in the trash. Then she brewed some coffee, knowing that both she and Tom needed to go to work this morning.

"Why are you making such a racket?" Tom shouted, sitting up red-faced. His hair stuck out at odd angles, and his belly protruded from his unbuttoned shirt.

"You drank too much last night and never made it to bed."

"Don't you lecture me about my drinking."

"Okay, hon, but you need to get ready for work. Those tax returns won't file themselves."

Tom reached up and gripped his temples. "Never mention tax returns to me again when I'm hungover."

"I need to get breakfast on the table for you and Jack."

"Holy shit. My head is pounding."

"Why don't you call in sick?"

"I can't. I've got some big clients coming in today, and they only like to deal with me."

"Do you want me to make you some eggs?"

"Just coffee," he said, shuffling over to the kitchen island. "Why didn't you come downstairs and stop me from drinking so much?"

She almost started laughing. "You told me to go upstairs and wait for you. You said you'd be right up."

"Seriously, Gwynn? Are you that fucking stupid? You know, when I start to drink like that, you need to put your foot down and drag me up to bed."

"Yes, you're right. It's all my fault. I should have insisted you come upstairs with me."

"Don't be a smart ass."

"I'm not, Tom. But I was really tired from the long day at your mother's house."

"I can't believe how selfish you are."

"Me selfish?" she said, unable to control herself. "Last I checked, my head's not the one in a vice grip right now."

"Why are you being such a bitch?"

Gwynn turned and saw Jack standing by the sofa with his teddy bear tucked under his arm, staring at the two of them. Neither she nor Tom had heard him come down. He lifted the teddy bear up to his chin. Had he heard what his father just called her?

"What the hell do you want?" Tom turned and shouted at the boy.

"You shouldn't have called Mommy a bad name," Jack said.

Tom ignored him and turned back around. She poured a cup of coffee and placed it down in front of him.

Gwynn approached Jack. "Go on up to your room and get ready for school, honey. I'll fix you a bowl of your favorite cereal when you come down."

He turned, glared at his father for a few seconds, and headed back upstairs.

Gwynn walked over and put her face in Tom's.

"You upset Jack. I suggest you be a lot nicer to us from now on," she whispered.

"Or what?"

"You know what."

"You'd never do it. Not if you want to see him again."

She bit her tongue and turned to her coffee. Little did he know that she and Frye had discovered whom he sent that video to, and that Tom's mother had told her about it. She turned and headed toward the kitchen island, pouring Jack's cereal into a bowl, listening as the pellets pinged against the ceramic. Tom guzzled the rest of his coffee and went upstairs to shower. In his absence, she felt nothing but bliss. Soon, she'd get to experience that feeling permanently.

* * *

Freshly showered and dressed in his gray suit, Tom walked downstairs and headed toward the front door. She approached him with lunch bag in hand, noticing from his expression that he was still in a foul mood. His face looked red and puffy, and it would no doubt be a miserable day for him preparing tax returns, meeting with clients, all the while trying to fend off his lingering hangover. Knowing this made her happy.

"You sure you don't want to call in sick?"

"I told you, I have an important client coming in at nine," he said, snatching the brown bag out of her hand.

"Make sure you drink a lot of water. Do you have any aspirin at work?"

He frowned. "Of course I have aspirin. I'm not a moron."

"Did you take all your meds?"

"Yes, *mother.*"

"The next time you start to drink too much, Tom, I'm going to drag your butt upstairs and tuck you in myself."

"You better have something good for dinner, because I probably won't be eating any of your shitty sandwich for lunch." He held up the paper bag she'd prepared for him and dropped it to the floor.

"I'll make you one of your favorite dishes tonight. Stuffed shells."

"Oh, and I meant to tell you this the other day. The Chamber of Commerce emailed me while I was in Boston to say that they nominated me for one of their big awards."

"That's wonderful," she said, remembering how badly he'd wanted to win. "When's the ceremony?"

"Saturday night," he said. "It's about time they recognized my contributions to this town."

"Now they will. Tom Denning, the best CPA in Maine."

Tom grunted as he left the house. Watching him from behind, she couldn't get over the size of his ass. At this rate, he'd be three hundred pounds by the time he hit forty. She knew he'd been feeling self-conscious about his weight. He'd bought a couple new suits and had even taken out a gym membership last month, although he still hadn't gone as of yet. Even his mother had made an offhand comment about his girth at the Easter dinner table, which had bothered Tom more than he wanted to admit. He'd put off going to the doctor last month, afraid of getting a tongue-lashing for being so out-of-shape.

She closed the door and picked up the paper bag containing his lunch, reveling in her temporary freedom.

Jack would be down soon to catch his school bus, giving her a few minutes of quiet time to reflect on everything.

Later in the day, she would work on her newest script, but now she needed to head down to the Bayside and search for Ivy. It might be Ivy's last chance to save herself from a life of addiction and pain. If she could just get through to the girl, she knew Ivy would go on to lead a happy and healthy life. But she had to find her first. Then somehow convince her that her father would never bother her again.

Jack walked down the stairs, his tiny pack attached to his back. He looked so cute this morning that she wanted to pick him up and squeeze him. But he wore a grim expression that she'd never seen before. Soon, Jack would be free from his father's sway. Free from the violent video games they played together. And the fact that she'd caught her husband looking at S&M pornography last night didn't help matters. Tom had probably been looking at that trash since his days at Brooks.

Gwynn handed Jack his lunch box and then grabbed his hand, but he quickly snatched it away. He didn't say anything, but she knew he'd heard Tom call her a bitch. Maybe she'd have a talk with him later and explain why his dad had called her such a bad name. But what would she tell him? That his father had a drinking problem? A woman problem? That he was a glutton for food as well as pain? That he made her take part in sick, perverted sex games in the privacy of their bedroom? *Other than that, Jack, he's a really great dad. And husband.*

They walked in silence toward the bus stop. The sun shone brightly, and all the trees were in bloom. Birds sang and flew about. A squirrel stared at her from across the road. Amidst these signs of spring, Gwynn couldn't help but think about all the ways she might kill Tom. And his mother, too. Susan would be easy, as she already had a plan for her after seeing those steep stairs leading down to the basement. Tom would be the ultimate challenge. It would test her mettle more than all her other murders combined.

A neighbor passed with her dog on a leash, and the dog rushed up to Jack, wagging its tail and looking for affection. Jack squatted down and rubbed it behind the ears, laughing as the dog licked his face. Maybe that was what he needed: a dog. She'd asked Tom many times if they could get a puppy, but he'd always said no.

The bus turned the corner and barreled down the street. A few other children joined them at the stop and said hi to Jack, but he barely responded to them. The bus pulled up, its doors wheezing, and the older students climbed the stairs first. Jack followed behind, not even saying goodbye. Was he mad at her? For not standing up for herself? She stepped back and watched as he took a seat by the window. He gazed down at her with a strange expression as the bus inched forward. She waved goodbye, but he looked away. She badly wanted to tell her son that she was not that kind of woman, the kind that accepts the role of victim and lets people run all over her.

She went back inside the house, eager to spend some time alone before heading over to the Bayside. The house took on a different vibe when Tom and Jack were gone. She poured herself another cup of coffee and turned on the radio. Heard about the missing man from the baked bean plant and recalled the way she'd plunged that screwdriver into Fields' temple. Remembered watching as his truck plummeted off that cliff and into the quarry. Remembered how she and Callum made love in her cabin, which sent wave after wave of incomprehensible pleasure through her body. Was it the act of murder that fueled her lust? Or was it because she'd been deprived of intimacy and affection for so long now that just about anyone would have sufficed?

Her phone rang. Another message from Ivy. She read the text in a state of shock.

I read all your texts with the girl. Don't worry, she's at peace now. You'll find her body next to the river on Route 26. Behind the old tire place.

Gwynn sprinted out of the house and into her car, speeding to the location mentioned in the text. When she got there, she parked and sprinted down to the grassy embankment. Searched around until she located a dense cropping of ferns. Lifted them up until the sight of Ivy's body came into view. She fell to her knees, sobbing. The girl's eyes remained open, staring up at the canopy. Gwynn hyperventilated, struggling to breathe.

There was only one other person who could help her out of this mess, and she needed to call him immediately. She headed back to the car, grabbed her phone, and punched in Peters's number. He picked up after the third ring.

"Gwynn," he answered, "what's up?"

Chapter Thirty-Nine

DETECTIVE PETERS

Peters smiled after the call with Gwynn ended. Sipping his brew, he made his way out of the coffee shop until he reached Commercial Street. After surveying the busy waterfront, he inhaled the salty air. Sitting against the building were two panhandlers and a scruffy dog. Feeling generous, he dropped a dollar in their bucket and headed to his car.

His plan had worked. Of course, he couldn't deny the hand of Lady Luck in the matter. What were the odds he'd run into the very same girl who once lived at The Loft? The same girl Gwynn had been trying to rescue for the last two years? He didn't feel particularly bad about killing her, seeing as how she was a drug addict living on borrowed time. Gwynn had told him about Ivy's abusive childhood and dysfunctional home life. It had been filled with so much pain and misery that hardly anyone could have ever envisioned a happy life for her going forward, nor for any of the other girls he'd killed. Their deaths would serve a useful purpose.

Besides, a small part of him had enjoyed killing them. How had that happened? He never expected that. Was it the feeling of power he'd gotten from taking their lives? Or knowing that it would bring him and Gwynn closer together? Not to mention, he took a perverse pleasure in being able to get away with committing these crimes, as well as being the lead detective in the case.

He got in his car. Before taking off, he took Ivy's eyebrow ring out of his pocket and studied it. It resembled a miniature barbell, the type he once used to pump when he worked out at the gym. He felt a powerful connection to the girl just by holding it in his palm, and he remembered the day he'd stood in Gwynn's office and watched as the two of them embraced on that school playground. He put it back in his pocket, reminding himself to add it to his collection once he returned home. It would be another piece of evidence he would use to set up the mark.

He headed out to meet up with Gwynn.

* * *

He'd agreed to meet her in a parking lot a half mile from the crime scene. Once he arrived, he saw her SUV parked in front of the strip mall. Should he ask her about George Fields? No, he decided to keep that to himself—for now. Otherwise, she might accuse him of stalking her, and if that happened, she might end up pushing him further away. Maybe Gwynn had no choice in the matter *but* to kill Ivy's father. But then why ask Frye to help her when she could have asked him, her lover and partner in crime? He would have happily helped her out. Together, they were a force to be reckoned with. Apart, they were certain to mutually destruct.

He reached in his pocket and made sure the tracking device was still inside. Then he parked alongside her car, got out, and slipped in through her passenger side door. When she looked away, he placed the tracking device beneath the seat. She turned and immediately reached out for a hug, and he held her in his arms, waiting for her to compose herself. A few minutes later, she sniffed up her tears and sat back in the seat.

"What happened?" he said.

"Someone killed Ivy, the girl from The Loft." She wiped the tears away with a handkerchief. "They placed her body under some ferns down by the river."

"Take a deep breath now," he said, holding her shoulders. "First off, how did you even know she was there?"

"Ivy and I had been texting, and the killer sent me a message from her phone. Whoever did this obviously wanted me to find her."

"Are you sure it was Ivy?"

"Positive." She wiped her nose.

"I'm so sorry about this, Gwynn, but you did the right thing by calling me."

"I couldn't risk calling the police."

"No, calling me was the right thing to do," he said, knowing he was the police.

"She was such a sweet girl, and trying so hard to turn her life around."

"I remember you telling me about her."

"I'm going to kill whoever did this to her."

"Promise me you won't do anything stupid. Because I'll find the scumbag and put him away for life."

"Just like you found the last killer?"

He was taken aback by her sarcasm and wanted to wipe that look of scorn off her face. "That was not a nice thing to say, especially since I helped you and your father out of that mess he made."

She turned and stared out over the steering wheel. "You're right. That was uncalled for, and I'm sorry."

"I'm a damn good detective, Gwynn. I'll find the guy who did this to her. And to all the other girls he killed."

She continued staring out the window.

"I've missed you so much," he said. "I can't tell you how badly I've wanted to hold you in my arms."

"I've missed you, too," she said rather unconvincingly.

"There's not much we can do for Ivy now. At least she's in a better place and not suffering."

She didn't respond to this.

"Look, I need to get down to the crime scene and sort everything out."

"Promise me you'll keep my name out of this? Including how you found Ivy?"

"Of course," he said, reaching for the door handle. Before leaving, he leaned over and kissed her. "Go home and rest, and act like nothing has happened."

"How can I act like nothing has happened after what I just saw?"

"I know it's hard, Gwynn, but you have to try."

"I think I'll go into the office. Work might help me keep my mind off everything."

"Good idea. We have to be a team if we're going to catch this guy."

"Of course."

"I love you so much, Gwynn."

"Love you too."

He got out of her car and returned to his. Then he headed down to the crime scene to start the discovery process. Upon arriving, he lifted the vegetation and stared down at the dead girl's eyes. Seeing Ivy look so angelic brought a smile to his face. He thought, in some perverse sort of way, that Gwynn would be proud of him if she knew all that he'd done for her. After all, he'd learned from the master. There was a small part of him that took pride in knowing he'd gotten away with six murders. Why deny it? Gwynn never did. And look how much she'd doted on her father after learning about all the terrible things he'd done. It was a well-known fact that women desired men who resembled their father, and now he was just like hers.

He took out his cell phone and called the station, telling the officer at the desk what he'd just discovered. After hanging up, he waited for the evidence techs to arrive, pleased with himself for the way things had turned out. He didn't for one second regret becoming a serial killer, although he'd never anticipated that his life would turn out this way. It all started with him shooting that thug motorist years ago, and it now led to him killing four street girls and a homeless guy who happened to be in the wrong place at the wrong time. And he'd do it again if it helped him get Gwynn back in his life. Love, like murder, required discipline and hard work. Both required one to make the ultimate sacrifice.

Chapter Forty

Gwynn sobbed once Peters drove away. How had it come to this? She'd been too late to save Ivy's life. If only she'd killed Fields sooner, Ivy might still be alive today. She blamed herself for the girl's death. But mostly she blamed Ivy's parents.

It took over an hour before she composed herself. She vowed that these would be the last tears she would ever shed for the girl. Tears proved useless in fighting against the evils of this world. Only action got results. The courts and child welfare system had failed the girl. She'd failed her, too. After a period of mourning, she vowed to get her life back on track. Focus on saving her son and making sure he grew up to be a decent human being. Save money for the future. Keep writing and hope that this new career path might lead to greener pastures. Possibly move out to LA? Everything she did now was for Jack. Or was it? Had it all been for her? To sate her murderous and sexual desires? The thought filled her with sadness, and she quickly erased them from her mind.

Gwynn sped out of the parking lot and raced into town. The first person she vowed to kill was Tom's mother. Then Tom would be next. But tonight, when she arrived home, she would hug Jack and tell the boy how much she loved him. She only needed to be nice to Tom for a bit longer. Or until she figured out a way to make him disappear.

* * *

She called Callum and asked him to meet her at the coffee shop where they'd first met. It felt like a piece of her soul had been ripped away now that Ivy was gone. One of the truisms of social work was to never get too close to your clients because they'll inevitably break your heart. Yet she couldn't help getting involved when it came to the children in her care.

She drove over to the cafe and went inside, ordering an iced coffee at the counter. Her phone rang as she walked to her seat. She glanced at the screen and recognized Tift's number, debating whether to answer, especially after Tom had admitted to engaging in rough sex with Tift back at Brooks. But then she remembered the big check sent to her, and the ones that might come in the future, and she picked up.

"It's so good to hear your voice, Gwynny. How's everything going?"

"Couldn't be better." She looked toward the entrance but saw no sign of Callum. "You?"

"Amazing. Both the producer and director absolutely loved the way the first season turned out. I think we might have a hit on our hands."

"But the pilot hasn't even aired yet?"

"True, but they showed a rough cut to some focus groups, and they all raved about it. They especially loved the main character."

"The avenging housewife who kills bad people? Or do you mean to say they loved the actress who played her?"

Tift laughed. "Both, I guess."

"What in particular did they like?"

"They found themselves rooting for her, even though they knew that what she was doing was morally reprehensible."

"So they believed she was justified in killing all those people?"

"I suppose," she said. "I totally downplayed my role in order to get the audience to relate to her."

"What about—" She almost said Tom's name. "What about the character who plays Samantha's husband? What does he do for work?"

"The director decided to make him an attorney. He's handsome and makes oodles of money. And of course, he and his wife have been best friends since college, even though she never really loved him back then."

Gwynn felt a pang of guilt. "That wasn't in the script. The part about her not really loving him back at Brooks."

"Brooks?" Tift said, laughing. "I thought this was fictional?"

"It is," she said, realizing what an idiot she was for saying this out loud. "I was just using Brooks as inspiration."

"Sure, that's totally cool," Tift said. "We fudged the script a bit and added some extra details. I thought it would make the story far more compelling."

"Fair enough," she said, waving Callum over as soon as he entered the cafe. "In my script, Samantha and Hal have two kids."

"Two kids made the plot far too convoluted, so we cut it down to one."

We? "A daughter?"

"A six-year-old boy named Jett."

This plot development was hitting too close to home. "What does the wife do for work?"

"Do you really want me to ruin the show for you?"

"Ruin the show? I was the one who wrote these scripts, remember?" Gwynn said, trying to control her anger. "Now tell me what the wife does."

"Okay, girl, chillax," Tift said. "Samantha's a family therapist who counsels children and married couples."

"A therapist? The character I developed was a high school teacher."

"Way too dull. The director wanted to make the couple hipper and more psychologically interesting."

"What about the wife's psychiatrist in the script. He plays a central role."

"Cut it out. Too cliche, the director thought. And it had already been done so brilliantly in *The Sopranos*."

"You should have left the script the way I wrote it."

"The one rule about working here in LA is that scripts *always* get rewritten," she said. "Then rewritten again and again until it's the way the director wants it."

"Is that it? No other surprises?"

"Well, we do learn near the end of the first season that the husband is a bit of a perv."

Gwynn's head felt about to explode. "What do you mean?"

"He enjoys rough sex and sees a dominatrix on the q.t. His wife has actually known about his perverted behavior for quite some time, but for the sake of family unity, she ignores it. Maybe that's another reason why she kills dirtbags."

Gwynn wished she could reach through the phone and strangle her friend.

"Also, he had an affair with her best friend back in college."

Was this Tift's way of admitting her guilt? "You practically rewrote the entire thing."

"What are you complaining about? The focus group loved your story. So much so that the network is thinking about ordering up a second season based on their reactions. And if that happens, you get to write more episodes—and make more money."

"How much more?"

"Oodles."

She liked the sound of that. "Are there any more changes I should know about?"

"No. The focus groups really liked the subplot of a copycat serial killer stalking the streets of LA and killing young, troubled girls. Oh, and the sexual tension between Samantha and Detective Packwood added a nice touch."

"Great."

"Coincidentally, we do have a serial killer here in LA. Ten years now, and the creep still hasn't been caught. And many of the girls' bodies have been found up in the hills."

She couldn't stomach hearing about another serial killer right now. "What else did they like about my story?"

"They really loved that subplot where one of her victims survived an attack and went into a coma. That added a lot of suspense to the plot, wondering if she would wake up someday and rat her out."

She watched Callum walk over to her table. "Will I get any credit for what I wrote?"

"Gwynn, you know that's not possible. I can maybe add you on as one of the staff writers in the second season if you really want, but I'd advise against that. You can't get credit for creating a story that has already been credited to me."

"I'm still mad at you for doing that, Tift. You should have at least asked me before you stole my idea."

"How many times must I tell you? That show never would have been made had I not added my name to it."

"Whatever," Gwynn said, staring up at Callum. "I don't want my name associated with that dumb project, anyway."

"You're sore now. Please don't be that way."

"Trust me, I'm not the least bit sore."

"After this series finishes up, I promise you we'll find you your own project to work on."

She debated hanging up on Tift but decided against it, knowing she couldn't afford to lose those hefty paychecks coming her way. And the idea of her own show, and her own identity, appealed to her.

"I promise you, girl, the checks this time around will be much bigger."

"When will the pilot air?"

"Soon, but I'm not entirely sure. Will you be coming out for the premiere when it does?"

"I don't know right now," she said, wanting more than anything to attend.

"If you do come out, we can walk down the red carpet together in our most gorgeous dresses."

"Sounds good, but I can't commit to anything just yet."

"At least come out and spend some time with me. I really miss hanging out with you, Gwynny."

"Let me think about it."

"If you don't come, I'm going to have a serious talk with Tom and force him to let you come and see me. And I won't take no for an answer."

The thought of Tift talking to Tom terrified her. She pictured Tift and Tom lying naked in bed together back at Brooks, and Tift letting him do those nasty things to her. And then Tift uttering those racist rap lyrics that had the potential to destroy her career.

"Please don't say anything to Tom just yet. I promise I'll make an effort to come out and see you."

"Okay, but I better hear from you soon or I'll call Tom and ask him myself."

"You'll hear from me shortly, I promise."

Once the line went dead, Gwynn motioned for Callum to sit down. He looked handsome today, and she couldn't deny being a little obsessed with him lately, recalling their intense lovemaking in her cabin. She wondered if he had a girlfriend. Not to stereotype, but she had always assumed that most figure skaters were gay.

"Nice to see you," he said, sitting across from her with his coffee cup in hand. "Maybe not as exciting as the last time we met, but it's all good."

Gwynn wondered whether he meant the sex or the fact that he'd helped her kill Ivy's father.

"I need your help again," she leaned over and whispered. "And soon."

"You have someone in mind?"

"I do."

"Is that why you called me here?"

She nodded.

"Who is it you want me to—"

"My mother-in-law," she said before he could finish.

"Your mother-in-law?" He sat back and crossed his arms over his chest. "Wow."

"Wow is right," she said. "We know that Tom sent her that video."

"Yes, we do."

"She's the kind of woman who will do anything to make her son happy, including coexisting with her murderous daughter-in-law. She pretty much told me as much."

Callum whistled. "She came right out and said that?"

"In a roundabout way. She even held a carving knife to my stomach and threatened to kill me."

"She obviously had no idea who she was dealing with."

"Obviously not."

"That's cold," he said. "Talk about lacking in scruples."

"Are you referring to me or my mother-in-law?"

"Your mother-in-law, of course," he said as if she'd asked a dumb question. "You, at least, adhere to a code of ethics when it comes to that sort of thing."

"True."

"That mother-in-law of yours is a real whack job. So is her crazy son."

"As much as I despise the woman, I do respect her maternal instincts. Because I, like her, would do anything to protect my son."

"Even if he married a serial killer?"

She thought about this for a few seconds and it gave her pause.

"Just playing with you. I'm sure your son will grow up to be an amazing dude one day," Callum said.

"He better."

"And with his father out of the picture, it'll make things much easier for you going forward."

"I want to put an end to all this. I want to live my life and be normal like everyone else."

"I got news for you, Gwynn: you're far from normal."

"You think I don't know that?"

"Personally, I don't blame you for the things you've done. The system is broken and is screaming out for someone like you to fix it."

"What about you? Have you decided where you stand when it comes to this sort of thing?"

"Are we being completely honest with each other? Because I'd hate to disappoint you if I answered the wrong way."

"Honesty is the entire basis of our arrangement."

Callum sat back in his chair and laughed.

"What's so funny?" she said.

"That's obviously not true."

"It is true."

"The sole reason you kill people is *because* you judge them, or else you wouldn't do it. You're probably judging me as we speak."

"But what you and I have is different, Callum. Don't you think?"

"How is it different?"

"We share a mutual interest, and we like and trust each other."

"How can I trust you if I'm worried that what I say might piss you off? And then you'll want to kill me."

"Don't be silly." Gwynn sipped her coffee and considered this. "I suppose you'll just have to trust me. Just as I need to trust you."

"A Mexican standoff, of sorts?"

"Precisely. It's like believing in God: you just have to make that leap of faith."

"Okay, I'll take that leap with you," he said.

"Good. Now tell me how you really feel."

Callum eyed some patrons walking past their table. "I only know that after watching you in action, I'm all in."

"And that's it?"

"No," he said after sipping his coffee. "I realized that I enjoyed helping you and want to do it again. Is that being honest enough?"

"It is. Anything else you want to say?"

"I like knowing this about you. That you have this dark, secret side of you that no one else knows about. Kind of gives me a power trip."

"Oh, so now you're going to be like Tom?"

"No, I'd never power-trip you like he does."

"But now you're an accessory to murder, pal. This I know about you."

"True. I just like knowing you murdered all those pervs, and the cops don't."

"Is that why you had sex with me?" she said. "With dried blood all over my face?"

"I must admit, it did add to the thrill."

"Thrill or no thrill, you and I need to stop jumping into bed together."

"Hey, you're the one who's been initiating it—not that I'm complaining."

Callum had hurt her feelings again, but she didn't want him to see her become upset.

"Okay, I promise I'll keep my hands off you," she said.

Callum sipped his coffee. "So what's the plan?"

She leaned over the table. "I want you to take care of Susan."

His face lit up.

"That's assuming you still want to help me?"

"Of course I want to help you."

"But?"

"But I don't want to end up behind bars."

"You'd look cute in an orange jumpsuit," she said.

"I'm serious, Gwynn."

"You won't end up behind bars if you do exactly what I say."

He waited a beat. "Go on."

"I'll call you later, and we'll go over everything once I get a better handle on things."

He rubbed his hands together. "Can't wait."

"Keep your phone on. The call might come sooner than later."

"I promise I won't let you down."

She patted his hand. "I know you won't, lover boy. That's why I asked."

Chapter Forty-One

GWYNN

She returned to the office just after noon. Where once she used to love coming into work, now she dreaded it. Despite outwitting Denise with that sneaky legal maneuver, she'd noticed the mood at The Loft had gotten more tense in the last few weeks. Morale among the staff had plummeted, and she could sense that the children had picked up on this vibe, as their behaviors seemed to be getting more erratic as each day passed.

A stack of folders sat on her desk. She tried to erase the memory of seeing Ivy's body, but she was having a difficult time doing so. Instead, she remembered all the good times she'd spent with the girl and what a beautiful soul she'd been. Had Ivy been dealt a better hand in life, she was certain that the girl would have gone on to do amazing things. It at least comforted her to know that she was no longer suffering.

"Where have you been?" Denise said, standing in her doorway.

"Last I heard, you're not to have any contact with me until this matter is resolved."

"I've been trying to reach you all morning. The board set up a conflict resolution meeting for us today."

"A conflict resolution meeting?"

"Yes. The mediator and I have been waiting for you in the conference room for the last thirty minutes."

"Do we have to do it now?"

"If you want to keep your job."

Gwynn didn't really want to keep her job, but she also wasn't ready to quit just yet. She followed Denise to the conference room and saw a petite, older woman sitting there who looked like a librarian, her hair tied up in a bun. Denise sat across the table from her, avoiding eye contact and twiddling a pen in her fingers. Gwynn studied her boss and, for the first time, noticed how pretty she was. She wondered what the woman did in her spare time, whether she had a boyfriend or girlfriend, or any hobbies. Did she get good grades in college? They sat quietly for a few minutes while the mediator typed away on her keyboard. Was this silent treatment some sort of psychological ploy designed to bring them closer together?

"So glad the two of you could make it," the woman finally said, closing her laptop.

Denise pointed at Gwynn. "Did you record the fact that she was thirty minutes late? This is what I've had to deal with since I started working here as director."

"That's not true," Gwynn said. "I didn't know about this meeting."

"You were sent an email about it," Denise said.

"I obviously missed that."

"She comes and goes as she pleases, and seems to think she can do whatever she wants," Denise said to the mediator.

"Please," the woman said, holding her hands up. "Let's hold off on judging one another and work to a mutual agreement."

Gwynn wanted to tell the woman the real reasons she was late: that a former client had been murdered because she'd failed to act. That she and Callum, a former client of The Loft, had been planning the murder of her mother-in-law. And that she desperately wanted her husband out of her life. But she kept her mouth shut and played along. Every question the woman asked, she answered in the most appropriate way, as if she'd spent all night cramming for a human relations exam. Two hours later, she found herself shaking hands with Denise and agreeing to certain parameters. But she didn't care anymore about following the rules. She had enough rules to follow at home. As soon as she freed herself from Tom and his overbearing mother, she'd hand in her resignation and walk out the front door with her head held high.

Gwynn returned to her office, work being the last thing she wanted to do right now. She took out her phone and checked her crypto portfolio, pleasantly surprised to see that her investment had shot up to one hundred and fifteen thousand dollars. Callum's voice echoed in her head and repeated the familiar mantra: volatility is the price of performance, volatility is the price of performance, volatility is the price of performance. She thought of her impending freedom from Tom and his dragon-like mother, and thought about what she would do if she learned the identity of the psychopath who had murdered Ivy. There'd be no soul-searching or asking God for forgiveness when she killed that lowlife. She'd savor it Old Testament style and never lose a night's sleep.

Her phone chimed, reminding her that she had a therapy session with Kaufman in one hour. During the craziness of the day, she'd forgotten about that. It meant she would need to leave work early. Would she get in trouble for this? She didn't care one way or the other.

Gwynn powered down her computer and gathered up her stuff. She needed to focus all her energies on successfully carrying out her plan. Only then could she return to a normal life.

Volatility is the price of performance.

Killing is the price of freedom.

And more than anything, I want to be free again.

Chapter Forty-Two

I'm expecting Gwynn in thirty minutes, and once again I can't seem to settle my nerves. Will these butterflies ever go away? I'm a grown man, for god's sake, old enough to be her grandfather. Being with her is like the feeling a lion tamer must experience while inside the cage with an old friend, knowing that at any moment this friend could turn on you in the worst way.

Making me even more nervous is the news of this missing man from that bean plant. They reported that he disappeared into thin air. Surprisingly, no one yet has connected his disappearance with the disappearances of Sam Townsend and William Clayborn. It can't be a coincidence. Do I dare ask Gwynn about it? I'm not in a confrontational mood today, especially after reading about the most recent girl found dead along the Presumpscot River.

The other development I'm trying to wrap my head around is Detective Nguyen asking questions about the night she was injured. Fortunately for Gwynn, she hasn't said anything yet that might incriminate her. Will the details come back to her at some point? Will anyone even believe her if and when she tells the world what happened that night? That Gwynn chased her out into the street until she collided with that car?

The gentle knock on the door brings me back to the moment, stirring the butterflies in my stomach. I stand to let Gwynn in, and we greet each other warmly. She takes a seat across from me and folds her hands over her lap. Although prim and proper today, she looks as if she's been crying. I remain quiet and let her do most of the talking.

"More troubles at home?"

She grabs a tissue out of the box on my desk and blows her nose.

"That's the least of my problems right now."

"What's wrong?"

"That dead girl they found by the river is the same girl I've been trying to help for the last year."

I position my hands into a steeple over my desktop. "That's terrible news, Gwynn. I'm sorry to hear that."

She grabs another tissue and wipes at her eyes.

"And she was trying so hard to turn her life around. Then her father did the unthinkable, and she took to the streets again."

"You'd been in contact with her?"

"I helped her buy drugs recently. I wouldn't have done it, but she was sick and in desperate need of a fix. She promised me she would go to rehab if I helped her this one last time. And she did check herself in, and was doing quite well, until her father came back into the picture."

"Her death was not your fault. You did the best you could for the girl."

"But my best wasn't good enough. And I know Ivy would have gone on to do amazing things had that piece of shit not put his hands on her." She crosses her legs. "That fucker managed to slip through the cracks of justice time and time again."

"Listen to me, Gwynn. Don't do anything stupid."

She wipes away her tears and stares down at her hands.

"I know how badly you want to avenge the girl's death, but I'm beseeching you not to do it. Think of Jack. Do you really want Tom raising him by himself?"

She gazes vacantly over my head, and for a moment, I think she's having an episode.

"I know you have a lot on your plate right now, dealing with your troubled marriage and the stress of your job, but you must try and temper your worst impulses."

"I could care less about my job. I won't be there much longer, anyway."

"But you're so good with those children."

She looks away from me.

"How will you support you and your son once you're on your own?"

"You mean after my husband and I go our separate ways?" Gwynn glares at me. "Come on, Dr. Kaufman, don't act so surprised."

I adjust the glasses over my nose.

"Sorry for being so pissy, but I just had to sit through a two-hour mediation class at work where we talked about 'appreciation', 'facilitation', and 'reframing' our discussions about race and gender. I swear I was going to explode."

"I know how much that place means to you."

"It does mean a lot to me," she says. "My boss accused me of neglecting my duties and putting the kids' lives in jeopardy. Can you believe that? That woman is so power hungry that she'll stop at nothing to get rid of me."

"Why does she hate you so much?"

Gwynn shrugs. "I have no idea. Maybe she sees me as a threat, despite telling her that I have no desire to ever be director again."

"Is it possible she had a bad experience once and is projecting all her negative emotions onto you?"

She shrugs. "Maybe, but there's nothing I can do about that."

"No, there's not," I say. "What will you do if you lose your job?"

"Remember those stories I was writing?"

"I do. You said your friend out in Hollywood is interested in producing them."

"Tift Ainsley."

"That's the one."

"She loved what I sent to her. So much so that the pilot is to air soon."

"On television?"

"Yes. Netflix, in fact."

This stuns me. "That's wonderful news."

"Did I ever tell you what the story is about?"

I shake my head.

"A serial-killing housewife who falls in love with the detective investigating the murders she's committed."

"Sounds very familiar."

"Write what you know, isn't that what they say?" she says. "She sent me a check for one hundred thousand dollars, promising to send more if the show does well."

"That's amazing, Gwynn. Now you can add screenwriter to your list of accomplishments."

She laughs. "Yeah, my long list of accomplishments."

"I didn't mean it like that. You're a devoted mother and a dedicated advocate for children in crisis."

"Thanks," she says. "Things are looking up for me. Even my cryptocurrencies are doing well."

"I'm no financial advisor, but don't you think you'd be best served by investing in traditional assets?"

Gwynn leans over my desk. "Jack and I need a lot of money for when Tom is…out of the picture."

I stand and gaze down at my watch, and she gets the message. Before leaving, she hands me a check. I take it because there's no arguing with her about our financial arrangement. She's stubborn and proud, and I admire that about her; two traits that may also be her downfall one day.

She leaves my office.

The sun is shining, a good day for a walk around the West End. I depart my office and arrive home, put on my new sneakers, and set out for a stroll. It's about time I get blood pumping through these old veins of mine.

Chapter Forty-Three

GWYNN

As soon as she left Dr. Kaufman's office, she called Callum and told him to meet her on the Western Promenade. Then she drove directly over there.

"That was quick," Callum said as she sat next to him on the park bench.

"Sorry I couldn't fill you in on everything back at that coffee shop. I had to meet with my therapist before I could do anything else."

"You see a therapist?"

"Anything wrong with that?"

"Not at all. You just seem like someone who has their shit together."

She laughed. "I kill people, Callum. I wouldn't exactly call that having my shit together."

"Yeah, I suppose you're right."

"You wouldn't understand because you've never killed anyone."

"How do you know that?"

His response surprised her. "I just assumed as much, seeing as how you came to me asking for help."

He stared out at the scenic West End.

"So have you?"

"Maybe I have. Maybe I haven't."

She punched him in the arm. "I thought we were going to be completely honest with each other."

"Have I asked you every little detail about your life?"

"No."

"There you go, then."

"But this is important."

"I'm here now, willing to learn from you. Willing to help you get rid of your family members. Isn't that enough?"

She watched below as a plane landed on the JetPort runway.

"Not only that, but I'm helping you make a killing with those cryptos you bought."

"I'm up fifteen thousand dollars as of this morning. Not a bad return, I'll admit, but it's far from making a killing."

"Trust me, you'll one day thank me," he said. "Just be sure to lock in your profit before they crash down to earth."

"You never said anything about locking in my profit. All you ever said was that volatility was the price of performance."

"There's a lot more to learn about cryptos than simply knowing which ones to buy, and one of them is to sell when the time is right. Don't be greedy."

"How will I know when to sell?"

"You scratch my back, I scratch yours."

She turned to him. "The Portland Chamber of Commerce is holding their awards banquet Saturday night, and my husband has been nominated for their most prestigious award."

"He get nominated for biggest asshole of the year?"

She laughed. "He'd win that one hands down."

"So why do you need me?"

"You're going to take care of my mother-in-law while I attend the ceremony with him."

"But won't she be there?"

"She wouldn't miss seeing her son win his award for anything. That's where you come in. You make your way inside her house before the ceremony starts and take care of business."

"I break in?"

"You won't have to break in. She keeps a spare key in one of those fake rocks hidden in her backyard. It's easy to spot."

"Is there a security system I should know about?"

"No security system. She lives in an old community on the ocean. There hasn't been a break-in in that neighborhood in years."

"How should I do it?"

"There's a door in the hallway with a steep stairway leading down to the basement."

"I see where you're going with this. Give the old biddy a gentle nudge and make it look like an accident."

"Exactly."

"But what if she doesn't die right away?"

"That's where you'll need to be…creative."

"Hey, creativity is my middle name."

"The police will never ask questions about a broken neck from falling down the basement stairs. It happens all the time to old people."

"Where does she live?"

"Cape Elizabeth. You park in the Crescent Beach lot and then walk along the beach until you arrive at her house. That way, no ring cameras."

"Cool. I know that area well."

"You do?"

"Sure. I own a house not far from there."

This got her attention. "You're telling me you own a house in Cape Elizabeth? Near the water?"

"You seem surprised by this."

"It's such an expensive town—and so white."

"White don't bother me. And neither does expensive."

"Fair enough," she said. "The banquet should go until about nine or ten, which should give you plenty of time to get in and out of there. Until then, we shouldn't meet unless it's out of the public eye."

"What about the momma's boy?"

"One thing at a time," she said, caressing his cheek with the back of her hand, wishing she could keep sitting with him on this bench.

"You don't know how much I appreciate this opportunity."

"We're helping out each other, right?" she said, standing to leave.

"Tit for tat."

"Exactly. You got my back, and I got yours." Gwynn stood and walked away, glancing back at him one last time.

She jumped in her car, knowing she had forty-five minutes to kill before Tom arrived home. Yet for some reason, she couldn't force herself to drive away. She stared out the passenger window and watched as Callum continued to sit on the bench. Why hadn't he left? Was he waiting for someone else to show up? Sure, they'd jumped into the sack a few times for some harmless fun. He didn't owe her anything.

Ten minutes later, a tall blonde girl approached the bench and sat down next to him. She had on a pink Portland sweatshirt and matching yoga pants. Callum put his arm over the top of the bench, and the girl rested her head against his shoulder. He leaned over at one point and kissed her, wiping a few strands of hair over her ear. After sitting like this for a few minutes, they got up and walked hand in hand across the Western Promenade.

Gwynn realized she had a death grip on the steering wheel. She had half a mind to track this girl down and push her in front of the Downeaster. But the girl hadn't done anything wrong. Rather than stew about it, she headed home, trying to reconcile her hostility with the reality of what she had just seen.

Callum was not her boyfriend, and they had never been in a romantic relationship, not counting those two random times they fell into bed together. What they had was a mutually beneficial relationship. Friends with benefits. Just because she'd saved his life all those years ago didn't mean she got to dictate whom he could and could not see.

More importantly, she needed to focus on Tom this evening. But what version of Tom would she be dealing with when she got home? The kind and caring man he'd been at Brooks, or the controlling asshole who she married and knew how to push all her buttons?

She stepped on the gas and rocketed onto the highway, praying that she arrived home well before Jack's bus pulled up to their house.

Chapter Forty-Four

DR. EZRA KAUFMAN

I make my way across the Promenade, high above the city, admiring the amazing view. Behind me stands the massive campus that is Maine Medical. Further off on the horizon, I see Mount Washington, snowcapped and majestic, the jewel of the Whites. A plane takes off from the Jetport and disappears into the cottony clouds.

Then I see something that gets my attention. It's Gwynn sitting on a park bench next to the young man who introduced her at that Dirigo awards banquet. It is the same man she saved from a childhood of abuse and neglect. I'm far enough away so that she can't see me. The bench faces in the opposite direction, looking out over the scenic view. The young man stares ahead while Gwynn looks directly at him. I keep walking, trying not to be a busybody, although I can't take my eyes off the two of them.

I finish the three-mile loop and collapse in my leather armchair once I arrive home. It often takes me a while to recover these days, as age is starting to catch up to me. I turn on the news and am stunned to learn that the dead girl and the missing man from that baked bean plant are father and daughter. The news pundit theorizes that George Fields may have killed his daughter, as well as the three other girls, and fled town. Part of me wants to laugh at such a silly conjecture. The idea of George Fields murdering those girls and fleeing town is as absurd as the theory about William Clayborn murdering Sandra and Sam Townsend, and then going on the lam. Both men are most certainly dead, victims of my avenging angel.

Chapter Forty-Five

GWYNN

Gwynn parked in the driveway and realized that she had missed seeing Jack off his bus. His backpack sat on the stairs by the front door, and she kicked herself for being so careless. A wave of panic surged through her at not seeing him anywhere. Had someone kidnapped her son? She ran onto the street and searched around, calling out his name, but saw no sign of him. Her entire life revolved around Jack, and if she ever lost him, she'd lose all her motivation to live. Should she call the police? Or had he taken off on an adventure throughout the neighborhood? Her entire body began to tremble at the thought of a child molester luring the boy into his car. If something ever happened to him, she'd kill the bastard first and then kill herself.

Things were so different from how she grew up. Her father had encouraged her to walk amongst the homeless population while he ministered to them. No sane parent in this day and age would ever let their child roam so freely.

She sprinted behind the house toward the backyard and, to her relief, saw him on the swing set, his little legs kicking his body higher, laughing the higher he rose. For a brief second, she worried he would do a full loop. She wanted to run over and wrap her arms around her son and never let go, but she didn't want to worry him. A day would come when he'd be independent and on his own, and she knew she had to get used to this coming reality.

"Jack, it's me," she called out to him.

He shouted and waved, kicking his legs higher and higher. On the upswing, he jumped off the seat and flew through the air, crashing into the soft grass like a paratrooper landing behind enemy lines in Normandy. Once he stood, he ran over and wrapped his arms around her waist.

"I love you, Mama."

"I love you too, wiggleworm," she said, choking back the tears. She ran a hand through his thick hair, happy he was no longer mad at her. "Now go get your backpack and bring it inside."

Chapter Forty-Six

DETECTIVE PETERS

Peters found himself deluged with media requests when he returned to the station. Every news outlet in the city and beyond wanted to ask him about the latest girl that had been found along the banks of the river. Too bad they knew nothing about the homeless guy he'd killed, stuffed into a bag, and then submerged in the Presumpscot. Before he talked to the press, he needed to confer with the chief and get his perspective on things. All this would allow him to steer the narrative away from him. He knocked two times before entering the man's office, checking Gwynn's tracker app one last time before he sat down, and seeing her SUV parked near her therapist's office.

"We need to make this quick, Peters. I don't have much time," the chief said, glancing nervously at his watch.

"What's going on?"

"I'm due at a press conference in five minutes," he said, putting on his dress jacket. "What's your best guess? Do we have another serial killer on our hands?"

"No doubt in my mind now, Chief. Guy's definitely a copycat."

"That's what I thought," the Chief said, shaking his head. "What do you make of this girl's father going missing?"

"It's a tad unusual, but he's definitely not our guy."

"Why not? You believed that William Clayborn killed his wife and went on the lam."

"Clayborn was not only a skilled attorney but also a brilliant psychopath. Fields, on the other hand, is a drunken loser who abused his daughter and somehow managed to slip through the cracks of justice time and time again."

"There's no possibility he could be our guy?"

"For god's sake, Mark, he worked at the baked bean plant. No way a dunce like that possesses the smarts to pull off a series of high-profile murders like these. And where would he go? The guy barely has two nickels to rub together."

"Yeah, you're probably right."

"He might have been with his daughter when she was killed, in the wrong place at the wrong time."

"Then where's his body?"

Peters sat back and shrugged. "Good question?"

"Do you have any theories about who killed these girls? Because I have a press conference to give and these vultures need something to chew on."

"Tell them our guy is smart. Brilliant, actually. And he's sending us a message by playing this game of cat and mouse."

"What kind of message?"

"I'm not entirely sure yet, but it's one definitely connected to the Muddy River Killer case. He's relishing the notoriety of what he's done and wishes he could announce to the world about all the murders he's gotten away with," Peters said, knowing that much of what he'd just said was true. "He's bitter the way his life has turned out and is full of rage. Maybe he's been in a series of bad relationships and has been badly burned. Or maybe he just likes to kill young girls to gratify his own ego."

"Alright, time to face the music. Wish me luck."

"Break a leg, Chief."

"Don't get too comfortable, Peters, because your time is coming."

"Trust me, I know," he said. "I've solved a case like this once before, and I'll do it again."

"You'd better. These residents of this city can't take much more of this."

Peters returned to his cubicle and stared at the glowing computer screen, thinking about his next move. On the desk sat his phone opened to the tracking app inside Gwynn's SUV. He knew that her sessions with Kaufman lasted one hour. After that, she'd drive home to see Jack off his bus. As much as he loathed Tom, he knew that her husband posed no threat to them at the moment. Gwynn hated Tom as much as he did, and they were united in their belief that Tom needed to die—and the sooner the better.

It was Callum Frye he worried about the most. He was the same kid she'd rescued sixteen years ago from his drug-addicted father. Was that the reason she'd been standoffish toward him lately? Peters wondered if he'd done anything to make her feel this way? He'd certainly been acting paranoid as of late. And getting his ass kicked by Tom had been a big mistake, making him look like a chump in her eyes.

He searched the department website for any possible suspects, someone he could pin these murders on and make the charges stick. It would have to be just the right guy, someone with motive and time on their hands. Someone smart and successful, and not bound by a nine-to-five schedule. Everyone on his list had a long rap sheet, but the wrong kinds of crimes befitting the profile of an astute serial killer. The person he would arrest wouldn't be a run-of-the-mill criminal. It would be someone who had a flexible schedule and with enough skeletons in their closet to cause suspicion. He scanned through the list again, searching for possible candidates, but none appeared close to fitting the bill. For a brief moment, he thought about pinning these murders on Tom, but Gwynn would be furious if he did that. The stain of those brutal crimes would forever stigmatize her and her son, leaving them pariahs in the community. She'd probably move away if he did that and never speak to him again. Too bad, because it would be a brilliant way to make the jerk disappear. For that reason, Tom would have to disappear the old-fashioned way. Besides, they still had to find those incriminating videos.

After an hour, Peters saw her car represented as a red dot on his computer, driving away from Kaufman's office. But instead of returning to The Loft, she headed over to the Western Promenade. He shut down his laptop and sprinted outside, using the back door so the media wouldn't see him leaving. He jumped in his car, flashed his lights, and raced over to the West End, noticing on his phone that her car had stopped along the Western Promenade. She'd told him that she'd be heading back to work. So why had she lied?

Peters whipped through the narrow streets until he arrived at the hospital's entrance. It looked relatively calm at this hour; no ambulances parked in front of the ER. He cruised slowly past it until he arrived onto the Promenade. The sun shone brightly, and the trees were just starting to bloom. Off in the distance, the snow-capped White Mountains appeared. A cargo plane taxied along the Jetport below. Above him, a helicopter landed on Maine Medical's rooftop helipad, delivering an injured patient or lifesaving organ. As he drove past, he saw Gwynn walking toward a park bench. She sat down and stared out at the view. He circled around the block, passing the quaint old Tudors and brick mansions until he returned to the Promenade. This time, he noticed someone sitting next to Gwynn. After moving his car into a better position, he punched the steering wheel upon recognizing the guy. Trying to remain calm, he pulled up across the street and watched as the two of them started talking. Why was she meeting Frye here?

He turned and saw a familiar figure standing on the sidewalk, also watching them. It was hard not to miss the diminutive shrink wearing the bright yellow HOKA sneakers. Was he, too, spying on Gwynn? Maybe Gwynn had mentioned something in their therapy session that had caused him to be suspicious. Peters wanted nothing more than to run out there and throttle Frye, but then he got to thinking. Maybe their relationship was not romantic, but something else. Something more sinister and deadly, owing, in part, to what she had done for him those many years ago. He had no doubt now that Gwynn and Frye had murdered Ivy's father, and now he thought he knew why.

Then Gwynn turned and stared up at Frye, and something in her gaze gave him pause, especially when she reached up and caressed Frye's cheek. Peters felt his hands balling up into fists.

He wanted to kill Frye now more than ever. But how? He'd pored over Frye's website and read how he'd once been a competitive figure skater. Mixed race and Hollywood handsome. Tall with blue eyes. Self-taught, never having attended college. And super rich from investing in cryptocurrencies. Frye was everything he was not, and this pissed him off.

Then an idea occurred to him so Machiavellian that he wondered why he hadn't thought of it before. Who better to pin these murders on than a young, rich guy with lots of time and money on his hands? A guy who lived nearby and who took part in the murder of George Fields? It would be easy to set him up; Peters had all the girls' personal items in his dresser drawer. Assuming he could get inside Frye's residence, he could plant them somewhere without the guy knowing. Then get a search warrant and make the arrest. Or tell Gwynn his theory about who had killed all those girls. Such a plan would take time and much planning. Eventually, he would need to convince Gwynn that Frye was their killer. After what had happened to Fields, she would no doubt believe him. And if that happened, Peters wouldn't need to kill Frye. Gwynn would gladly do it herself. Then, after eliminating the competition, he and Gwynn could finally be together, and he would never have to worry about looking over his shoulder, wondering whether or not she would be coming for him.

Yes, this would be his plan going forward. He would set Frye up for the four girls' murders and then hope that Gwynn would kill him. He might not end up getting credit for solving these cases, but he'd get something much better in return.

Chapter Forty-Seven

GWYNN

Tom woke around eleven that morning, smiling and in a good mood. Once downstairs, he kissed Gwynn on the cheek and then twirled Jack through the air. Jack squealed with delight and pleaded with his father to do it again. Tom agreed to play with him after he went upstairs and changed out of his clothes and into something more comfortable.

Upon returning downstairs, Tom instructed Jack to go out in the backyard, and he'd pitch some balls to him. Jack grabbed his Whiffle ball and bat and dashed outside in anticipation of his father's arrival. But first, Tom walked over to the fridge and pulled out a beer. Come weekends, he usually didn't start drinking until after lunch, but today was cause for celebration. He'd convinced himself that he was going to win a big award tonight. After cracking open the first green bottle, he kissed Gwynn on the lips, his free hand reaching down to squeeze her ass. She smiled, the feel of his touch making her stomach turn.

"Are you going to play ball with me tonight?" he whispered.

"No, I'm going to take you over my knee and slap you as hard as I can."

"That's my badass wife."

"Maybe I'll use the bag on you tonight if you're a good boy," she said, feeling his fingernails digging into her skin.

"I like the sound of that."

"And who knows, I might really go all the way this time."

"Oh no, you love me way too much to do that."

"That's true," she said, kissing his unshaved cheek. "I could never go on living without you."

"Not if you know what's best for you," he said. "And the boy."

Tom released her and stood to his full height, his face beet red and puffy. Did he suspect that she was up to something? He lifted the bottle to his chapped lips and drained half of it in one gulp.

"Something seems different about you today," he said.

"Nothing different about me. I'm just happy the way everything has turned out."

He pointed at her. "You belong to me now, lady."

"And you to me. We're soul mates."

"I would hate for you to disappoint me again."

She laughed. "Like that's ever going to happen."

"Better not, buttercup." He pinched her chin a little too tightly. "You just need to be reminded of that from time to time."

"Trust me, you'll never need to remind me again." She kissed him on the lips. "You're the most amazing man in the world ."

"Lucky you, then, getting to sleep with the Citizen of the Year tonight."

"Hopefully, more than just sleeping." She winked at him. "That's assuming you win."

"Oh, I'll win alright," he said. "I win at everything I set my sights on."

"Can't argue that."

"I want you to wear something sexy tonight. Drive all my coworkers crazy."

"Sure, I'll pick out something nice."

"That skimpy red dress looks hot on you. Wear that."

She pointed at him. "Good choice."

"Go commando, too. I might need a quick thrill while I'm waiting to accept my award."

"Aye aye, Captain," she said, winking at him. "I have to get the steaks off the pan before they burn."

"Hurry up because I'm starving."

"Go play ball with Jack. I'll call you guys when lunch is ready."

He went to the fridge and grabbed another beer. Then he turned and headed outside to play ball with his son. The steaks sizzled loudly in the cast-iron pan. She turned down the heat, hoping they hadn't burned, adding some heavy cream, lots of salt, and margarine to the sweet potato casserole. On the counter sat a bowl filled with Mexican corn on the cob, slathered in mayo, crema, and crumbled cotija cheese. Ten minutes later, Tom came back inside, and she knew what he wanted. She darted to the fridge and grabbed him another beer, which he practically snatched out of her hand.

"I saw where that Asian cop woke from her coma and started talking."

"Yes, I heard about that too."

"That's bad news for you, my dear."

She stared at the Brooks College sweatshirt stretching over his belly.

"I'm the only one now who can alibi your sorry ass."

"I know, Tom, and I can't thank you enough for forgiving me and giving our marriage a second chance."

"Fucking whore," he said, pointing his finger at her. "If you ever again betray me like that, it'll be the last time." He turned and walked toward the sliding glass door, disappearing outside.

She heard the peal of her son's laughter before Tom closed the sliding glass door. Trying to maintain her composure, she plated the steaks and set them aside to rest. His words unsettled her, but she needed to remain calm and focused and not take his insults to heart. Maybe it would be best to just accept her shitty lot in life and stay married until Jack went off to college. By that time, she wouldn't care what Tom did to her. And Susan would be long gone by then. Could she ever convince herself that she loved Tom? No, that time had come and gone. She despised him and always would, despite the nostalgia she sometimes experienced over their college days.

She walked over to the sliding glass door and watched as her husband pitched the ball to their son. Jack swung, hitting the ball a long ways. From her vantage, Tom looked like a loving and dedicated father. He really did love Jack, although in the worst possible way. A loving father wouldn't blackmail his son's mother and treat her like shit. He wouldn't ask her to do sick things in the bedroom that killed a part of her soul and made a mockery of the institution of marriage. Tom's love for her was a barbed arrow, dipped in poison, and shot in one direction. Jack didn't know it yet, but the damaging effects of his father's behavior would last well into his adulthood if she didn't act soon.

Gwynn went to the stove and plated the food. The fragrance of seared meat and sweet potatoes overwhelmed her. She placed another large pad of margarine on Tom's steak just the way he liked it. On the side of his plate, she spooned some neon green Chimichurri sauce. The fats began to melt over the seared surface of the beef. A glass of milk for Jack. Sparkling water for her. And another cold beer for Tom. Satisfied that he would approve of this meal, she walked over to the sliding glass door and called them to the table. Tom snatched Jack in his arms, heaving him up over his shoulder, and carried the giggling boy into the house, both of them laughing. Tom's bloated face was dripping with sweat when he sat down, and he was breathing hard. Jack grabbed his milk, drank half of it in one gulp, leaving a white mustache over his upper lip. Gwynn reached for one of the steak knives and started to cut Jack's meat into tiny slivers.

"Why do you baby the kid so much?" Tom said, shaking his head. "He's perfectly capable of cutting his own meat."

"Do you want him to choke? Or handle a sharp knife?"

"Why not? You know how to do both of those things pretty well."

She glared at him. "Very funny, Tom."

He smiled while sawing off a thick chunk of steak.

"I'm just playing with you," Tom said.

Gwynn spooned some sweet potatoes onto her plate. "Don't ever joke about that."

"Sure, babe," Tom said, reaching for her hand. "I feel so lucky to have such a wonderful family by my side."

Gwynn placed the steak knife down and took his clammy hand in her own. "Hey there, mister," she said to Jack. "We need to say Grace before we start eating, and it's your turn tonight."

Tom folded his hands together as Jack recited Grace as fast as he could.

She felt like she was in some surreal play where they were all playing their roles to a tee, and her real character sat just offstage, waiting to do damage. Once Jack finished the prayer, they resumed eating. Tom stuck a fork into his steak, making an appreciative face once the beef hit his tongue. Everything inside her felt numb and broken, and her murderous past felt like it had never happened. Tom buttered a potato roll with a gob of margarine, always believing it was butter, never knowing that she'd switched them out. He dunked his roll into the bloody steak drippings and then stuffed the sopping mess into his mouth. As she ate, she thought of Ivy and what the poor girl must have experienced in her final moments.

She wanted revenge more than anything: revenge against the person who killed the girl and placed her body under those ferns. And revenge against Tom and his manipulative mother-in-law for punishing her so cruelly these past few years. She'd kill Susan with her bare hands if she could, and savor every second of it. But she'd never get away with it. It was why she needed Callum's help. And Peters help, too, although he would never know why.

"This steak is amazing, hon. What's the green stuff next to it?"

"Chimichurri sauce. It's a Mexican recipe."

"You've really upped your game in the kitchen."

"Thank you," she said, covering her mouth.

"The bedroom, too," he leaned over and whispered.

"You're the one who motivated me to do better."

"Can't argue that." He picked up an ear of corn using the cob holders and took a hearty bite out of it. "This maize is amazing."

"What's maize?" Jack asked, cocking his head.

"It's what they call corn in Mexico," Tom said. "Remember when I took you to the apple orchard, and we walked through that corn maze?"

"Yeah, that was fun."

"Kind of the same thing. Corn. Maize."

Jack giggled. "You're funny, Daddy."

"I know," Tom said, reaching for his beer. "Your dad is a-maize-ing."

Gwynn fought back her depression, wishing she were a million miles from this dinner table and her husband's stupid puns.

Chapter Forty-Eight

GWYNN

Tom seemed unusually excited for the remainder of the day, unable to sit still for more than a few minutes at a time. After playing ball with Jack, he went outside and mowed the lawn. Then he puttered around in the garage for a while. Sometime later, he came in and started in on some other mindless task. Winning that award tonight would be a huge deal for him, bolstering his name in Portland and adding to his professional resume. Too bad the people who nominated him didn't know the real Tom like she did. The Tom behind closed doors.

At times during the day, he reminded her of that fun-loving college boy she'd known back at Brooks. Briefly, it gave her second thoughts about her desire to kill him. But then she remembered all the nasty things he forced her do in the bedroom, as well as what he had on her, and she knew it was the right decision. The *only* decision.

She tried to keep herself busy. She mopped the floor, put away all the dishes, and scrubbed every household surface as if she were the modern-day version of Cinderella. She didn't mind doing household chores if she hadn't been *forced* to do them. Doing chores freed her mind up to consider all that was going on in her life. Like Ivy's death. And Callum's long-legged beau meeting him on that park bench. It shouldn't have bothered her as much as it did. So why did it? Gwynn knew she didn't love Callum—or at least she didn't think she did. Her attraction to him was purely sexual, a result of being lonely and stuck in a bad marriage. Oh, and their shared affinity for murder.

Around six o'clock, Tom gathered Jack up to take him to his friend's house for their sleepover. She rushed over and gave her son a big hug, telling Tom that she'd drive him, but he wouldn't hear of it. Before Jack left, she promised to spend more time with him tomorrow. He smelled distinctly of boy, which she loved about her little wiggleworm.

Tomorrow would bring fresh challenges to their household, assuming that Callum took care of Susan tonight. The news of her 'accidental' death would send shock waves through the family. She needed to be mentally prepared for this and act both sympathetic and somber. She would need to comfort Tom and Jack and provide them with the emotional support needed in order to deal with Susan's sudden passing, no matter how much it pained her to do so. Tom would be devastated when he received the news. But would he blame her for his mother's death? She would be with him when his mother tumbled down those stairs. There'd be no way he could point the finger at her.

Peering through the blinds, Gwynn waited until Tom drove off. Then she called Peters, knowing how happy he'd be to hear from her. She could tell the last time they'd met that he still loved her. If only she felt the same way about him. Because the more time passed, the more she realized that she didn't love him. He'd proved to be a disappointment in so many ways.

"Gwynn?"

"I really need to see you," she said, feeling guilty for using him for her own selfish needs.

"I want to see you, too. That's all I've ever wanted."

"I know I haven't been the best girlfriend as of late, but things have been complicated in my life, especially with Ivy's death and Tom's erratic behavior."

"I totally understand. And I know you're still mourning that girl."

"She's all I've been able to think about." She heard a pause on the other end of the line and realized she'd hurt his feelings.

"Don't worry, I'll find the piece of shit who did this to her."

"Can we meet tonight?" she said, staring out the window as Tom spoke to the father.

"Tonight?" The desperation in his voice came off as pathetic.

"Only if you're free."

"I'm always free for you."

"Thanks. I appreciate that."

"Where should we meet?"

"The Chamber of Commerce is having their awards banquet tonight. It's at Ocean Gateway, and Tom is up for a big award."

Another pause. "You want to meet me at Ocean Gateway? With Tom in attendance?"

"Yes. It will make it even more special when we meet down in the basement."

"Are you sure about this, Gwynn?"

"One hundred percent sure. My husband will be so happy after winning his award that he'll have no idea what we're up to."

"And you know for certain he's going to win?"

"The committee's already informed me that he will. They want to make sure he shows up for the ceremony."

"Okay," he said, "but I'm the last person in the world your husband wants to see right now."

"That's where you're wrong. Seeing you there will make his night."

"Why?"

"No offense, Peters, but getting into that fight with you is all he ever talks about." Had she gone too far? "Of course, we both know that you would have kicked his ass had you not been drinking so much."

"I would have, but I'll have another shot at him someday."

"You most certainly will."

"And I'll be with you long after that prick is dead and buried."

"That you will." His boasting sounded insecure and off-putting, but she had to boost his ego.

"Can I ask you something, Gwynn?"

"Of course."

A few seconds of silence. "Do you still love me?"

She laughed. "What kind of question is that?"

"It's just that I barely see you these days."

"And you know why that is, right?"

"I do, but I still need reassurances."

"Of course I still love you. Would I be calling otherwise?"

"No, I suppose not."

"I have to hang up before Tom comes back inside. Make sure you come over to our table and congratulate him on winning. I want you to act like the bigger man. Yes, he'll gloat a little, but inside you'll know the truth, especially when I'm kissing you down in that basement."

"That's going to be hard, swallowing my pride like that, but I'll do it for you."

"Thanks," she said. "There's a function room downstairs. I'll text you, and then we can meet there at some point during the ceremony."

"I can't wait to see you."

"I can't wait to see you, too." But she knew that she could wait, and she felt guilty about stringing him along.

"Once Tom's out of the picture, we can finally be together."

"It can't happen soon enough for me."

She ended the call, knowing she had to utilize every weapon in her arsenal to pull off her plan. Next, she called Kaufman, expecting to get his voicemail, but instead, he picked up after the second ring.

"Hello, Gwynn."

"I don't know how I can go through with this, Dr. Kaufman."

"Go through with what?"

"Tom's up for a big award tonight at Ocean Gateway, and I'm not sure I have the strength to accompany him."

"What award is this?"

"Chamber of Commerce is awarding him Citizen of the Year."

"I see," he said. "You have your medication. Take an extra dose like I've advised you to do when you get this way."

"Okay, but I'm also starting to experience that detached feeling, and I don't want to upset Tom during his proudest moment and then have to return home and face his wrath."

"Do those breathing exercises I taught you."

"I'll try, but I'm not even sure that will help."

"You can always call me if you want. I can keep my phone on just in case."

She paused for a few seconds. "Could I trouble you for a favor?"

"What's that?"

"Is there any way you can show up tonight? It would mean so much to me."

"You want me to go to the ceremony?"

"If it wouldn't be too much to ask. I know you've done so much for me already, but seeing you there in person would really help me make it through the evening."

She heard silence on the other end of the line.

"I'll even pay you for your time if you want."

"Don't be ridiculous," he said. "Okay, I'll go."

"Really? That's so sweet of you."

"Has Tom been treating you badly?"

"Worse than ever. He's been barking at me all day. And my mindset has not been right ever since they discovered Ivy's body down by the river."

"Okay, I'll see you tonight."

"Would you mind stopping by our table. Tom's always wanted to meet you."

"You want me to stop by?"

"If it's not too much of a problem. It will help knowing Tom knows who you are and approves of me seeing you."

"Sure, I'll stop by and give him my best."

"Thank you so much, Dr. Kaufman."

"You might not know this, Gwynn, but I won that award many years ago."

"Wow. You must tell me more about it in our next session," she said, quickly ending the call.

All the pieces seemed to be falling into place. For a moment, she debated calling Callum and going over the plan with him again, but she knew that it was a bad idea, especially over the phone. They'd talked over everything in detail. And Frye was smart and capable, and knew what needed to be done. Delegating tasks had been one of her strengths as director of The Loft.

Once Tom walked through the door, she ran up and hugged him, trying to appear as loving as possible. He held his arms out and gave her a beery kiss, confessing how much he loved her. How quickly Tom had returned to that kind and caring version of the sweet boy she'd befriended back at Brooks. His wholesome nature irritated her almost as much as his dark and twisted side. Funny how life had turned out. She vowed to never again settle for less than she deserved, happy to raise Jack by herself if need be, the two of them solely dependent on each other.

"You're sweating, Tom. You feel alright?" she said, placing the back of her hand against his forehead.

"I'm fine. Not in the shape I used to be."

"Take a few Tylenol, and you'll feel better."

"What I need to do is get back to the gym and lose a few pounds. And your cooking is so damn good that I end up eating way more than I should."

"Then it's salads and more protein for you, my love. And no more beer."

"Not likely."

Tom kissed her before heading upstairs to get ready for the ceremony. She could hear his footsteps creaking along the staircase, and she was glad to be rid of him.

She realized she had no choice but to trust Callum. He knew that she'd murdered his father, not that he could prove that. Was it possible a malnourished and abused child could recall such a horrific event? Callum had obviously watched his parents shoot up many times before. And though he was five at the time, he looked to be three. She had no idea why she was going over all this in her head, because it didn't matter now. She had no choice but to trust him.

She opened the dishwasher and put the plates and cups in the cabinet. While doing this, she heard Tom thudding down the steps. She turned and saw him standing halfway down the staircase, a white towel barely covering his potbelly. His skin looked white and pasty, splotches of pink just over his spare tire. A weird smile came over his face as he wagged his finger for her to come upstairs.

Pleasing him was the last thing she wanted to do right now. Her mood shifted as she placed the dish down on the counter and followed him up to the bedroom. Tom dropped the towel and stood waiting for her at the top of the stairs. Wrinkles of cream cheese jiggled around his buttocks and upper thighs. Small welts appeared over his back and butt from the last time she struck him. He dashed into the bedroom and jumped on the mattress. Before going inside, Gwynn took a deep breath, trying to summon up the strength to perform for him. Hopefully, she could stop doing this soon and return to a normal life.

Chapter Forty-Nine

DETECTIVE PETERS

Peters couldn't believe his good luck. Although he had no desire to shake Tom's hand and relive that beating at the bar, he yearned to see Gwynn again. The fact that she had called and invited him to Tom's award ceremony proved beyond a doubt that she still loved him. He couldn't wait to meet her downstairs at Ocean Gateway and reignite the chemistry they once shared.

But first, he had to get Frye out of his head. The kid had taken up space in there like a squatter. He remembered the way she'd looked at Frye while sitting on that park bench, caressing his cheek, and it emboldened him to act. Gwynn used to look at him in the same way before Tom walked into that cabin and ruined everything. Was he imagining all this? Maybe Gwynn's gaze had been maternal and his fears unjustified. All the same, he needed to learn more about Frye before he set the guy up for these four murders. Once he had Gwynn back in the fold, he knew they could reignite the spark they once shared. If not, he feared that one of them would need to die.

He typed Callum Frye's name into the search engine, hoping to learn more about the guy, and the results popped up. Most of the articles had to do with his figure skating accomplishments. Peters clicked on a few of them, but they provided him with no real details about his life. Thirty minutes later, he discovered an obscure story about Frye's childhood. He was taken from his parents at a young age and ended up living in a succession of foster homes before getting adopted by John and Edith Frye. Callum moved in with them when he was eleven.

Should he try and track down John and Edith Frye and ask about their adopted son? He had nothing to lose. An hour later, after a lot of digging, Peters found a phone number for the couple. He punched it in, expecting little in the way of useful information. After the third ring, someone picked up.

"This is Detective Peters with the Portland Police Department," he said. "Is this John Frye?"

"It is. What can I do for you?"

"I'm investigating the serial killings of these girls up here in Portland."

"Okay."

"Is Callum Frye your son?"

There was a noticeable pause. "Adopted son. My wife and I took him in when he was in sixth grade. Why? Is he in trouble?"

"No, I'm just trying to be thorough and track down every lead."

"How does that involve me and my family?"

"For whatever reason, Callum's name came up in my database. It could just be nothing."

"Callum's name came up in a murder investigation? Why?"

"Could be someone jotted down his license plate near where one of the girl's body was found. Look, Mr. Frye, I'm desperate at this point and reaching for straws."

"Okay."

"Have you and your wife talked to Callum lately?"

"My wife died last year," he said. "Should I be talking to you without a lawyer?"

"Oh, no, it's nothing like that. I'm sure your son had absolutely nothing to do with any of this. This is merely a formality."

"Okay."

"And I'm sorry about your wife."

"Thanks," he said, sounding nervous. "So what do you want to know?"

"Can you tell me about Callum?"

"I don't know much about him anymore. We haven't talked since he moved out."

"Any reason why?"

"You'll have to ask him. We did the best we could for him, but he never seemed to bond with us."

"He never thanked you for all the support you gave him during his figure skating career?"

"You know about that?"

"It's my job to know."

"Callum was a reserved child. Maybe being abandoned at a young age was to blame for his aloof nature. We didn't have the financial resources to help him with his skating, but we did what we could."

"Who paid for it?"

"The Maine Figure Skating Association picked up much of the tab."

"Did you know about Callum's childhood before you took him in?"

"Only that he lived in a few foster homes and then at The Loft for a few years. And that his biological parents were drug addicts."

"He lived at The Loft, you say?" This surprised him.

"Yes, but Callum didn't talk much about his time spent there. He was quiet and unassuming. I suppose it just didn't click between us, but he was always well-behaved and never gave us any problems. And he was very smart, the way he had us buy all those Bitcoins for him."

"So you have no idea why he stopped communicating with you?"

"No, but then again, it didn't really surprise me."

"Why not?"

"He used to tell me all the time that he couldn't wait to leave home and be on his own. And he made all that money from his Bitcoin investments."

"Made him a rich man."

"It did," the man said. "Anything else you need to know?"

"Did he ever repay you for raising him?"

"No, and we never expected him to. He earned all that money on his own."

"I think you answered all my questions, Mr. Frye. Thanks for your time."

Peters hung up and thought about everything he'd learned. Gwynn must have started at The Loft soon after Frye left. They could have just missed crossing paths with each other. Maybe Gwynn found out about his stay at The Loft and the two of them had bonded over it.

His interest piqued, he looked up The Loft's phone number and punched it in. On his first try, he got the girls' home. A woman transferred him to the boys' residence, and he asked the person who answered if anyone there knew a kid named Callum. The man told him to hold on a minute before handing the phone off to a woman. After explaining that he was a Portland detective investigating the serial killings in town, he asked if she remembered Callum Frye.

"Yes, I remember him. His name was Callum Barrios when he lived here. I'd say he was one of The Loft's biggest success stories."

"How so?"

"Did you know that he was a champion figure skater? I was the one who took him to all his skating lessons at the Portland Ice Arena. Callum was such a natural on ice."

"Yes, I heard he was good."

"For a while, we all thought he had a shot at the Olympics, but then he started having knee problems and his career came to a halt."

"What was Callum like?"

"Quiet. But he was very smart and a quick learner. His teachers said he tested off the charts."

He needed something that might help him better understand Frye. "Is there anything else that could help me?"

"It really devastated him when his best friend died. I remembered that it happened six months before he got adopted and moved out."

"How did he die?"

"Jayson was frail and sickly when he came to us. He passed away from a nut allergy on a camping trip. I remember it like it was yesterday."

"None of the staff were carrying EpiPens?"

"We were, but by the time we got to him, it was too late. Callum found him in the woods and came running back to us with the news."

"Didn't staff take precautions as far as the boy's meals were concerned?"

"Of course we did. We had a whole shelf dedicated to Jayson's dietary needs. Still, we couldn't completely prevent cross-contamination. Sometimes, even a trace of peanut dust would set him off, which is why we all were required to carry EpiPens."

"So how did he get a peanut allergy out in the woods?"

"I'm not really sure."

"How did Callum react to his friend's death?"

"He was distraught for weeks and wouldn't even talk to anyone or eat dinner. He and Jayson were extremely close."

"What was Jayson's last name?"

"Hooker."

"I hope you don't take this the wrong way, but is it possible that his death was intentional?"

"Intentional?" There was a long pause. "You mean like murder?"

"Yeah."

"No, no. That's crazy talk," she said. "Jayson was a popular resident here. All the other kids were very protective of him, especially Callum."

"One last question. Do you know anything about Jayson and Callum's family history?"

"I can't remember Callum's, but Jayson's father died of a heroin overdose. A social worker found Jayson alone in the apartment, badly abused and neglected. Jayson was frail and sickly in appearance, and looked much younger then his actual age."

This shocked him. "Thank you. That's all the information I need at the moment."

He paced the room, not believing what he had just learned. Had Frye killed Jayson and taken his life story as his own? Had he planned on blackmailing Gwynn all along? Jayson must have told him the story about what happened to his father that day, including the name of the social worker who had injected him with that lethal dose of heroin. Maybe Jayson harbored his own plan to avenge his father's death and talked about it with Frye. Or maybe Frye had researched the case and found out Gwynn's name on his own, and put two and two together.

What a manipulative, sick bastard. The perfect guy to become his next mark.

Now he had to find a way to present this information to Gwynn. Should he tell her that the boy she had saved from a tragic childhood had actually died from a peanut allergy on a camping trip, and that Frye had co-opted his life story? That he had possibly even killed him on that trip? The bigger question was this: why did he murder his best friend? Had Frye been a bad seed from birth?

Knowing all this excited him. In a few hours, he would see Gwynn. He couldn't wait to hold her in his arms again, knowing what he did about Callum Frye.

Chapter Fifty

GWYNN

Gwynn arrived at Ocean Gateway with Tom, and the two of them headed upstairs to the main function room. She hadn't been to an event here in ages. When she entered, she became quite taken with the view. Massive windows surrounded the oversized room, letting in the final throes of sunlight. She took in the glittering water and all the sailboats cruising in the bay, and it made her slightly giddy with excitement, knowing what would happen later this evening. A host escorted them to their table. As they walked down the aisle, Tom stopped and said hello to all his friends and coworkers. It impressed her that he knew so many people and was so well-liked in the business community. It gave her a newfound perspective into her husband's complicated psyche. She sometimes forgot that he'd been a popular student back at Brooks and that he was highly regarded in the firm he worked at. Of course, no one knew the real Tom like she did. The Tom who could be cruel and manipulative one minute, and then kind and loving the next.

She couldn't help but feel self-conscious when Tom introduced her to his colleagues as his better half. They stared at her in envy, almost not believing that a guy like Tom could land such a hot-looking wife, even though she never remotely viewed herself as hot. She always felt like a hideous monster, unattractive and beast-like. Gwynn shook everyone's hands, wondering what he told his office mates about her. Did he brag about her talents in the bedroom? Tell them what a great wife and mother she was? She doubted it, although she couldn't help but feel their gazes sweeping over her exposed cleavage and bare legs. Tom had chosen this outfit, which was a low-cut red sheath dress that fell to mid-thigh, accompanied by three-inch heels and no panties. She felt like a cheap whore.

The introductions to his coworkers continued until they reached their table. Place cards informed them where to sit. To her dismay, Gwynn noticed that she'd be sitting next to Tom's sister. She nodded to Trish and sat, placing her purse down on the table. The seat next to Tom belonged to his mother, but if everything went as planned, she wouldn't be showing up this evening to witness her son's crowning achievement. And that made Gwynn happy. Giddy, almost. She pictured Susan sprawled at the bottom of those basement stairs, bloodied and bruised, staring up at Callum's face as he ended her life. Hopefully, everything would go smoothly and without incident, and her death would appear to be an unfortunate accident.

She studied Tom as he spoke with a colleague about Schedule D forms and long-term capital gains. He actually looked handsome tonight despite his girth. Surprisingly, he sounded smart and sophisticated. And yet she would kill him in a heartbeat, assuming she could get away with it. Only the thought of her impending freedom kept her from slipping out of character. So she smiled on cue and made small talk with Trish. If Trish knew what her brother was really like, she might not adore him as much as she did. If Trish knew how much of an arrogant and misogynist jerk he was. Or the fact that he stayed married to an admitted serial killer because he loved his wife more than he loved himself.

A figure stood over her, waiting for Tom to finish his conversation. She continued to converse with Trish, swallowing her pride for the sake of expediency. Tom turned when he caught sight of the individual, standing out of his chair. Gwynn couldn't believe it when she saw Peters dressed in a blue suit and with his right hand extended.

"What are you doing here?" Tom said, a look of surprise over his face.

"Look, Tom, I wanted to come over here and apologize for what happened the last time we met."

"Okay," he said, ignoring Peters's hand.

"I was drinking that night and in a bad way. It should have never happened."

Gwynn smiled, taking a perverse joy in watching Peters beg her husband for his forgiveness. Why did this please her so much?

"Getting your heart ripped out will do that to a guy."

"Right." Peters paused to swallow his pride, taking his hand back. "It was no excuse for my actions, but there it is."

"As long as you know that you were wrong."

"Yeah, it was my bad."

"Anything else you want to say?" Tom said, glancing down at her.

"Nah, that's it."

"Then I guess we're done here. Unless you need to speak to someone else at this table."

"No, that's all I wanted to say."

"Okay, then. Have a nice day, Officer."

Gwynn thought this last line rather funny, but she didn't laugh. Nor did she acknowledge Peters or even look in his direction. Instead, she turned to Trish and continued their conversation about the ridiculously high food prices. But Peters's apology pleased her to no end. He did exactly as instructed, perfect and to a tee. Everything was going as planned. Gwynn glanced toward the back of the room and saw Peters slumped over the bar, waiting for his drink to arrive. It didn't surprise her that he looked so glum. It must have killed a part of his soul to ask for Tom's forgiveness.

Trish changed the subject and started to complain about her coworkers at the bank. This conversation would have driven Gwynn crazy if she hadn't been enjoying the moment so much. She thought about the punishment she'd inflicted on Tom this afternoon, which included a Bic lighter and a wire hairbrush pounded over the flesh of his back, and it made her eager to see his reaction when he learned about his mother's death.

"Hello, Gwynn," a familiar voice said.

She turned and saw Kaufman standing not much taller than her, sitting down.

"Dr. Kaufman, what are you doing here?"

"I thought I'd stop by and say hello," he said, turning to Tom.

"Tom, this is Dr. Kaufman," Gwynn said.

"So this is the world-famous Dr. Kaufman. I've been looking forward to meeting you, Doc," Tom said, shaking the man's hand.

"Congratulations on your nomination, Tom. I'll certainly be rooting for you."

"Thank you so much. And thanks for straightening out the ole ball and chain here," Tom said, nodding toward her. "She swears that you're the best shrink in town."

A pained look came over Kaufman's face. "I do what I can."

Tom's comment embarrassed her, and her eyes met Kaufman's just before he said goodbye. Tom turned and resumed his conversation with his colleague sitting next to him. Despite the insult thrown her way, Gwynn decided to wear it like a badge of honor. Tom's words echoed in her head and reminded her of the man she'd unwittingly married. The disrespect he had showed Kaufman and her only fueled her desire to be free from him.

After finishing his conversation, Tom turned to her and placed his hand on her leg underneath the table. The sensation of his touch made her stomach turn, and it was all she could do to remain calm and not slap it away. Slowly, he moved his hand up her inner thigh. He must have thought she enjoyed this when in reality, pleasing him was the last thing she wanted to do right now. She had to close her eyes so she wouldn't say anything she might regret. Compared to Callum, Tom's touch felt like sandpaper over a bad skin rash.

The hum of conversation filled the room as his hand slowly slid towards its intended target. But then a woman walked up to the podium, and Tom removed his hand from her thigh.

"Where the hell is Mom?" Tom asked his sister.

"I don't know. She said she would be here by now," Trish said, glancing at her watch.

"Why didn't you pick her up?"

"I offered to, but she wanted to drive here herself. Said she might head home early if she started to get tired."

Gwynn listened to this conversation, wondering if the deed had already been done. She conjured up images of Callum jumping out into the hallway and pushing Susan down those stairs. Would Susan survive the fall? Or would she require additional attention to reach the great beyond? Would Callum make her suffer before she died, or was he the kind of killer who preferred to end things quickly?

"I'm going to text her," Tom said, pulling out his phone.

"Maybe she got stuck in traffic," Trish said.

"Traffic in Portland? On a Saturday night? I don't think so."

"She could have gotten a flat tire."

"There, I just sent her a text," Tom said, putting his phone back on the table. "Hopefully, she kept her phone on."

"You know how Mom is. She's always running late to everything."

"But I specifically told her to be on time," Tom said, hearing his phone ring. He stared down at it and shook his head. "Goddamnit. She just texted back and said she's gonna be late."

"There you go."

"She had to go down to the basement and bring up that stupid cat."

Gwynn's ears perked up when she heard the word basement. She'd specifically told Callum about Susan's cat, Polly. Had Callum already killed Susan and sent that text message to Tom, only intended for her? Hopefully, Susan was lying dead on the basement floor, blood pooling around her dyed brown hair.

The host stood at the podium and introduced herself to the crowd. Forty minutes of speeches passed before the woman opened an envelope and announced Tom as the big winner of the night. It was no surprise, as Gwynn had known all along that he would win. He acted surprised at hearing his name called. She stood along with the rest of the crowd and applauded, her enthusiasm now intended for her dead mother-in-law instead of her husband. Tom delivered a surprisingly entertaining and funny speech, although she shouldn't have been surprised by this. He'd had lots of practice performing in front of large crowds, especially after playing lead guitar in

Dirt Fish back in college. Being alone with him much of the time, when he was mean and irritable, she tended to forget his considerable talents.

After Tom's speech, in which he thanked his company, his coworkers, his family, and even his loving wife, he palmed his plaque and returned to their table. Gwynn gave him a big hug as the crowd continued to stand and applaud. Surprisingly, she felt proud of him. Winning that award was quite an accomplishment. She could almost love him again if she could find a way to erase the painful memories and start anew. But of course she couldn't—and wouldn't. Too many things had passed for that to happen. Gwynn sensed his mother was dead—or soon to be dead. And next on her list was Tom, sitting squarely in her crosshairs.

The emcee gave one final speech, ending the ceremony. Tom handed his plaque to her and headed to the bar to hang out with his colleagues, leaving her to fend for herself. No way did she want to sit with Trish for the next hour, discussing house plants, rude coworkers, and celebrity gossip. It pissed her off that Tom had chosen to celebrate his victory with his friends instead of her. Gwynn glanced back and searched for Peters, but didn't see him anywhere.

"I'm going to get a drink, Trish. Would you like one?"

"I'd love a gin and tonic."

"Coming right up. Make sure you keep an eye on Tom's plaque. He'd be beside himself if someone walked away with it."

"I'll guard it with my life," Trish said. "Do you think my mother's okay? It's unlike her to miss one of Tom's events."

"I'm sure she's fine. I'll bet she lay down to take a nap and simply forgot to wake up in time."

"Yes, that's probably it."

"After all, she is getting up there in age."

"I know," she said. "Sometimes I don't want to admit that to myself."

"Don't worry about her, Trish. She's fine," she said. "I'll be right back with our drinks."

Gwynn headed to the bar and saw Kaufman standing with a few other people. Tom sat with a group of men on the other side of the room, all of them patting each other on the back and toasting his success. She reached the bar and saw the bartender making martinis for an older couple. She reached into her purse, pulled out her burner phone, and texted for Peters to meet her downstairs in five minutes. After ordering her drinks, Gwynn turned and saw Kaufman standing next to her.

"Hello, Gwynn."

"Hello, Dr. Kaufman. Thank you so much for helping me out this evening."

"You're welcome."

"I'm sorry about Tom's rudeness. That was totally uncalled for."

"No need to apologize. I knew from our discussions what to expect from him."

She laughed. "Try living with the guy."

"Helping you is the sole reason I came here tonight."

"Can I at least buy you a drink?"

He shook his head. "No, I'm about to head home."

"Thanks again for coming."

He nodded. "How are you feeling?"

"Much better now that you're here."

"Good. I'll see you at our next session."

"That you will."

Gwynn watched Kaufman head toward the exit. After taking her drink from the bartender, she headed back to her table, handing Trish her gin and tonic. Then she sat down next to her sister-in-law and tried to make small talk, but it soon turned into something more serious and not at all what she expected.

"Maybe I was wrong about you, Gwynn."

"Oh?" She sipped her drink. "In what way?"

"You've really come around on my brother."

Gwynn placed her Old Fashioned down on her coaster and grabbed a napkin. "I really do love Tom and understand how I screwed everything up. Thank you for giving me a second chance, Trish."

"I know I've been hard on you over the years, but it really hurt me to see my brother in such pain."

"I can't even imagine."

"Unlike you, I don't have anyone else in my life except for my family. I see the incredible love you guys have for each other, and I know I would kill to have that kind of relationship."

Gwynn scratched her nose after hearing the word 'kill'. "I guess I didn't understand what you were going through."

"I get so lonely at times." Trish sipped her drink and studied her. "I don't admit this to too many people."

"Hey, you can always talk to me if you need an ear to bend."

Trish's eyes became moist. "You don't know how good that makes me feel."

Hearing this broke Gwynn's heart, and for the first time ever, she viewed Trish in a sympathetic manner. It was no wonder she remained fiercely loyal to Tom and her mother.

Gwynn's burner phone buzzed in her purse. She excused herself and headed toward the exit, her eyes locked on Tom. He was still with his friends, charming them with some long-winded story, his back facing away from her. A colleague walked over and handed him a bottle of beer, and they all toasted. She estimated that he'd consumed nearly twelve beers since noon. Gwynn moved quickly into the lobby and raced downstairs. Once she reached the bottom, she turned and saw a door slightly ajar. Peters stuck his head out and nodded for her to come inside. She slipped through it and watched as Peters locked it behind her. It was a small office with a stunning view of the harbor. In the distance, she saw the walking path that snaked around the peninsula and led into the Back Cove. It gave her a private thrill seeing Peters down here, knowing how he'd humbled himself for her benefit. In the same breath, she suddenly felt an overwhelming desire to be with Callum.

"I've waited so long for this moment," he said, cradling her face in his hands.

"Same here. I can't wait until we can finally be together again." Did she really say that?

"How are you dealing with Ivy's death?"

"It's devastated me, to be honest with you. I want nothing more than to kill the person who did this to her."

"Be patient, Gwynn. I think I might have an idea who committed these murders," he said, kissing her neck and face.

"Who is it?"

"I can't say anything about it right now. You're just going to have to trust me."

She rolled her head back as he kissed her neck. It felt nice to be with Peters, but she wondered if she would ever stop thinking about Callum Frye and how he made her feel.

"I have to go back upstairs now," she said, her hands pressed against his chest. "Tom might be looking for me."

"But you just got here."

"We can't take any chances that he'll find out about us."

"Right," he said. "Do you know how hard it was for me to apologize to that asshole?"

"I know it was, and I can't thank you enough for doing that."

"Fuck him. I only did it because you asked."

"I know, and you did good."

His expression hardened. "Did you see the way he was rubbing it in my face?"

"That's Tom for you," she said, shrugging. "On the plus side, I'm getting closer to learning who he sent that video to."

"Really?" he said. "Who was it?"

"I can't tell you right now," she said with a smile. "You're just going to have to trust me."

"Fair enough."

"Don't go back upstairs, okay?" she said. "Walk out of here and don't look back."

"But I was going to have another beer."

"There's plenty of other bars nearby. Go somewhere else and drink. Just not here."

"Alright, if it means that much to you."

"It does," she said. "I'm going to walk out of this room first. Wait a few minutes before you leave here." She grabbed the doorknob and turned to him. "I love you, Peters," she said, more to convince herself of this than him.

"I love you too, Gwynn. I can't wait until we can finally be together."

She opened the door and started to head upstairs when she saw Trish coming out of the bathroom across the hall from her, clutching Tom's plaque. Her pulse picked up a beat, and she prayed that Peters would wait a few minutes before coming out.

"Where have you been, Gwynn? And why did you come out of that room?" Trish said. "Tom's been looking all over for you."

"Stupid me. I thought it was the restroom."

Trish pointed at the door she just opened. "It's right here. Didn't you see the sign?"

"Obviously not. I was so excited about Tom winning his award tonight that I wasn't paying any attention."

Trish laughed. "Tom was right about you being scatterbrained."

"Yup, that's me. Scatterbrained ole Gwynn," she said. "Would you mind going upstairs and telling Tom that I'll be right up? I really have to pee."

"Of course."

Gwynn went inside the restroom and collapsed against the sink. That was a close call. Her face appeared pink in the mirror. She took a few deep breaths to compose herself, hoping she wouldn't suffer another episode where she couldn't recognize herself. She was so tired of running around and lying to everyone that she wanted to throw her hands up in surrender. If only she could be free of Tom and live her life accordingly. No more lying or killing. No more worrying about death. Or Jack's wellbeing. Be happy and free of all that. Free and unencumbered to write stories and raise her son.

Gwynn took out her phone and checked her assets. Her portfolio had taken a big jump, now almost fifty thousand dollars more than when she started. Wonderful news. And Tom had no idea that she'd squirreled away that money, or that she'd authored those scripts that would soon premiere on Netflix.

After splashing water over her face, she left the restroom and headed upstairs, where she saw Tom talking to a few other couples. He clutched his plaque in hand and looked happier than he had in a long time. Trish stood next to him, a proud sister, staring up at him in awe. Gwynn pulled up next to her husband, gripping her purse while waiting for him to finish his conversation. After saying goodbye to everyone, he put his arm around her shoulder and escorted her and Trish toward the exit.

"I'm so proud of you," she said.

"I told you you would be."

"You most certainly did."

"I feel like everything is starting to fall into place for me. I have an amazing family, a good job, and now have received recognition for my professional achievements. What more could a man ask for?"

Gwynn shrugged. "Not much, I suppose."

They reached their car. Tom kissed his sister goodbye, directing her to call their mother once they arrived home. Trish said she would give her mother a good tongue-lashing for not attending his big event. Tom held the door open, and Gwynn slid into the passenger seat. He went around and got into the driver's side, even knowing he'd consumed a great deal of alcohol this evening. As frightened as she got when he drove in this state, she knew how mad he got when she asked for his keys. But she wanted no problems tonight. It would be difficult enough once he learned about his mother's passing. Then again, he might not even realize Susan had died until mid-morning, when his calls to his mother went unanswered. He glanced over at her with glazed eyes, smiling crookedly, one hand gripping the wheel.

"I know something else I would like."

"Oh?" she said, dreading what perverted act he was going to ask her to perform this time.

"What do you say we give Jack a little brother?"

His words stunned her. "You mean have another child?"

"Yeah. What else could I mean?"

The thought of having another kid with Tom made her stomach turn.

She was not against the idea of having more children, but certainly not with Tom. No way she'd allow that to happen. His genes were poisonous, inward-facing barbs that only traveled in one direction. Besides, after his mother died, Tom would be next in line, leaving her a single mother with two young children to raise. She needed to put an end to the vicious cycle of male domination that had plagued her throughout her life. And it needed to end with Tom. And start anew with Jack at the top of the chain, despite his own flawed genes.

"So what do you say, hon?" Tom said.

"Yes, I'd love to have another child with you. Let me get off my birth control, and then we'll start soon after."

"I knew you'd come around to my way of thinking," he said, pressing the ignition button. He pulled out onto the street and headed toward Falmouth.

Tom sped through the narrow Portland streets, driving way too responsibly for someone who had been drinking all day. She thought it entirely possible he might die soon, but in doing so, he would kill the both of them in a fiery, drunken crash.

Be careful what you wish for, Gwynn.

Chapter Fifty-One

DR. EZRA KAUFMAN

I return home, flustered by her husband's disparaging comments. But more than that, I could tell that Gwynn was up to something. She had that gleam in her eyes that I recognize after all these years counseling her. Why else would she invite me and that detective to Tom's award ceremony? I have this strange feeling that I'm going to wake up in the morning and read some disturbing news.

The house is dark when I go inside. How long will I be able to live in this spacious home by myself? Do I even want to stay here when a smaller one would be so much easier to care for? But I love it. This place in the West End has been my home for so long now that I'm not sure I'd be happy anywhere else.

I turn the lights on and study the photographs on the wall of my mother when she was a young girl, just after she'd been released from that death camp. I fight back the tears while staring at her smiling young face, already missing her.

Thinking of my mother forces me to consider all the things I've done, and a wave of shame rolls over me, knowing how she would disapprove of my actions. It's possible she might consider me a failure despite all the good I've done. Despite the nice home I've made for myself, the people I've helped, and all the money I've made. Why do I feel like such a fraud? She survived the worst, enduring hardship and famine, never expecting her only surviving son to be complicit with a murderer.

Yet I can't deny that the world is a better place because of the people she disappeared: rapists, murderers, pedophiles. Callum Frye is the prime example of her benevolent justice, and he has certainly lived a productive life. Even that dead girl, Ivy, might have had a fighting chance had her father left years ago.

All this moral ambiguity confuses me.

I pace the room, wondering if I have the courage to break away from her. To tell the police everything I know and, in the process, implicate myself as an accessory to murder. Admit to them that I aided and abetted a serial killer. Maybe they would have mercy on me and give me immunity, especially if I told them all that her father had done. It wouldn't matter whether they believed me or not, because it's not my responsibility to convince them of her guilt. At least I'll have done the right thing, even if doing so destroys my reputation—and my life—in the process.

For the first time in a while, I think about my younger brother. How I loved Chaim. Had he survived that ill-advised war in Vietnam, he would have been successful at whatever he undertook. I was sixteen months older than him and protective to a fault, but in many ways, he acted like the older brother to me. He often fought the tougher guys in order to keep me safe. I kept telling him that violence was not the answer, but he never listened. In high school, Chaim hung out with the ruffians in the school parking lot, smoking cigarettes and goofing around. He made my parents so angry at times, but I could tell that they admired his independence and strong will.

So it didn't surprise me when he joined the Army right out of high school, telling me he was going over to Vietnam for the adventure, as well as to defend the ideals America stood for. I told him he was stupid and that America's ideals had been corrupted long ago by greed and iniquity, but he disagreed with me to the point where we had a big argument the day before he left for boot camp.

I go into my study, take his framed photograph off the bookshelf, and study his chiseled profile. Leaving the office, I head up to my bedroom and get undressed. Come morning, will I do the right thing and go to the police?

Or will I continue to do nothing and behave like a coward? I think about the despicable things Tom does to her in the privacy of their home, acts designed to dehumanize and degrade her. It's more than just sex between two consenting adults, because Gwynn is not really consenting to it. What he's doing is a form of rape. But does that give her the right to kill him?

If only I had some chronic disease with months to live, then maybe I could escape this situation and make peace with myself. The doctor says I'm healthy as an ox and could live for a few more decades. But can I go on like this? Shouldering the guilt and shame?

I lay down on the bedsheet and curl up into a fetal position. It feels so comfortable nestled under the warm blanket that I feel as if I could stay like this forever. Like back in the womb, safe and protected, floating blissfully in a warm pool of embryonic fluid. It feels like a new life. A fresh start. Reborn to do good instead of facilitate the bad. It wouldn't bother me in the least if I died right now in this bed. But then I'll never have had the chance to redeem myself. But is redemption even possible this late in the game?

Who knew when I started out at Harvard, fresh-faced and eager to change the world, that I would one day aid and abet a serial killer? My only goal back then was to help people and make the world a better place.

This is my last thought as I drift into unconsciousness.

Chapter Fifty-Two

Tom turned off the exit and cruised through the center of town, past all the blinking orange lights. There was not much traffic this late at night, and the roads were dark and foggy. Despite drinking all day, Tom didn't swerve or drive erratically.

Instead of going home, he turned into a fast-food restaurant and went through the drive-thru, asking if she wanted anything. She didn't. Her intestines reticulated in her gut as if two pony-tailed trolls were using them for a game of double Dutch jump. At any moment now, she expected Tom to receive the call about his mother, and it left her on edge.

Tom ordered two double cheeseburgers, a large fry, and an apple pie. After paying with his phone and then driving to the second window, he grabbed the bag, reaching inside for a handful of fries before passing it over to her. He drove off, turning onto their street, and she noticed something alarming. Callum's Jeep sat parked against the curb, three houses removed from her own. During daylight hours, it would have stood out due to its stark green color, but at night it melded naturally into the suburban landscape. Tom didn't even notice it as he drove past, occasionally reaching into the bag for another handful of fries. The stench of salt and starch nearly made her gag.

He parked in the driveway and got out of the car, and they walked inside the house in silence, Tom clutching his plaque by his side. It reminded her of when he threw her own award in the trash: an award that she'd been proud of winning. Once inside, she turned on the lights, placing the greasy bag down on the kitchen island. Tom kicked off his shoes, slipped off his tie, and tossed his suit jacket over the sofa, all for her to pick up later.

"Will you bring that bag over to me?" Tom said, kicking his feet up onto the coffee table. "And grab me a beer while you're at it?"

Gwynn wanted to tell him that he'd consumed enough alcohol for the day, but she didn't care if he drank himself to death. Of course, cirrhosis of the liver would take way too long to kill him, and she didn't plan on waiting that long for him to die. She'd seen the negative effects of drugs and alcohol during her many years working at The Loft, and she'd do anything to keep Jack shielded from such pain.

Her mind spun as she reached inside the fridge to get Tom a beer. She cracked it open and then grabbed the bag off the island. After walking over to the sofa, she slipped off her shoes and sat next to him, handing him his beer and bag. She needed to be exceedingly nice when the call came in so he'd not blame her. Would it be tonight? Tomorrow? After seeing Callum's Jeep parked on her street, she wondered if maybe he'd chickened out. The possibility that her mother-in-law was still alive worried her. Then why had Susan failed to appear at Tom's ceremony?

Tom gulped down half his beer before opening the bag. He was red and sweaty and breathing hard. The stench of processed cheese and cheap ground beef filled the room. The way he ate after a long night of drinking repulsed her, spilling crumbs over his shirt and trousers, and chewing with his mouth open. He held out the bag for her, and she took a fry, although it was the last thing she wanted right now. She nibbled on the long shoestring, the grains of salt practically singeing her tastebuds. Orange burger wrappers lay crumpled over the coffee table, which she would later need to toss in the trash.

"I'm so proud of you," she said.

He turned to her and grimaced. "Did you know that dickhead was going to be there?"

"Honestly, Tom, I had no idea."

He reached over and squeezed her neck, pulling her toward him. It was the first time he'd ever been remotely physical with her outside of the bedroom.

"You wouldn't lie to me now, would you?"

"Let go of me," she said, pushing away from him. "You know I wouldn't lie to you about that. I couldn't care less about that guy."

"Better not," he said, stuffing the rest of the burger in his mouth. After he finished chewing, he said, "Did you see the look on his face when he was apologizing to me?"

"No, I was too busy talking to your sister."

Tom laughed. "I thoroughly enjoyed rubbing it in his face, especially with you sitting there in that hot dress."

She nibbled on the fry, trying not to be drawn into this conversation.

"I think I enjoyed screwing with his head as much as I did winning that award." He unwrapped another cheeseburger and shoved it past his mustard-stained lips.

"Serves him right for challenging you to a fight."

"Too bad he's never going to have what I have." He put his hand on her knee.

"And he never will."

"I gotta take a piss," he said, guzzling the rest of his beer. "Go grab me another, will you?"

"You finished that one already?"

"Don't ride my ass tonight, okay? I'm celebrating."

"Gimme," she said, taking his empty.

"Besides, I'm going to start dieting and hitting the gym tomorrow."

I'll believe that when I see it, she felt like telling him.

Still clutching his burger, Tom stood and staggered toward the bathroom, planning to eat the rest of his burger while tottering over the toilet. How disgusting. She pulled out her phone and saw that Trish had sent her a text message, asking if Tom had checked in on his mother. She texted back and told her no. After hitting send, she checked on her cryptos and saw another big jump in her portfolio. Her initial investment had now soared over two hundred thousand dollars. Callum had been right. But was now the time to sell?

Tom staggered back to the sofa, chewing the remainder of his burger. Once he sat down, she handed him his fresh bottle of beer. He'd sleep in late tomorrow morning, it being Sunday. That meant she'd have to pick Jack up from his friend's house and take him to church, and then finish all the household chores before Tom woke up.

"Why do you still see that leprechaun, anyway?"

"He helps me."

"Helps you with what?" He laughed. "How to deal with your asshole husband?"

"Actually," she said, "he was the one who advised me not to leave you."

"Yeah, you told me all that before."

"It's true."

He sipped his beer, spilling some over his shirt. "Why did you see him in the first place?"

"How many times have I told you this, Tom? I was diagnosed with a personality disorder when I was a young girl."

A weird smile came over his face. "Is that why you kill people?"

The question surprised her. "I'm not really sure why I do that."

"Whatever the reason, don't ever change who you are. It's what makes you special."

"You're bad, Tom."

"Not as bad as you," he said. "Does that shrink know about that part of your life?"

She laughed. "Of course not. I'm no idiot."

"I'd always pictured him to be taller and more effeminate."

"Dr. Kaufman is an accomplished and cultured man. He attended Harvard and Harvard Medical School."

"Whoop-de-doo. You and I went to Brooks, and that's one of the best liberal arts colleges in the country," he said. "He looked to me like a guy who can't get laid."

She punched his shoulder. "Don't talk about him that way, Tom. He's very nice."

"All the same, I felt like he was sizing me up as we talked."

"You're just being paranoid. And you only feel that way because he's a psychiatrist."

"Do you tell him about the things we do in the bedroom?"

"Oh no. He'd have a field day with that one."

"Good. Because what we do in the privacy of our home is nobody else's business."

"I agree." She yawned, wanting more than anything to get away from him. "I'm exhausted. You want me to get you another beer before I head up to bed?"

"Sure. After all, I am Citizen of the Year."

"They should have awarded you Husband of the Year, too," she said, leaning over and kissing his warm cheek.

Tom guzzled the rest of his beer.

"Now I want you to come up to bed right after you finish the next one. Remember the last time you stayed down here and gave yourself a bad hangover?"

"Tomorrow's Sunday. I can sleep in as long as I like."

"True."

"Besides, it's not every day that a guy wins Citizen of the Year. A little celebrating is in order."

"Will I have to come down here and drag you upstairs?"

"Take it easy. I'll be fine."

"I worry about you, Tom. Jack and I want you around for a long, long time."

"Go on upstairs. I'll come to bed when I'm good and ready."

Gwynn kissed him one last time before heading upstairs. It was all she could do not to laugh at the nonsense she'd just spouted. Maybe she should have become the famous actress and not Tift. And yet Tift had also fooled her, making Gwynn feel like she was her most trusted friend in the world, when in reality Tift had used her for her own personal gain. The more she thought about it, the more she had misgivings about her old college roomie. Like, why did she invite Sandra to her summer home last year and not her?

Why had Tift not told her that she'd be vacationing in Maine? Or sleeping with Tom and doing all those nasty things to him back at Brooks? Okay, maybe she could forgive Tift for not telling her about that. The rough sex play must have embarrassed her, not to mention the fact that she'd sung along to those racist rap lyrics. And yes, she and Tom had broken up when Tift hooked up with him. Yet the more she got to know the real Tift, the more underhanded and duplicitous her friend seemed to be.

The bedroom felt like a temporary sanctuary, quiet and safe. But this feeling of peace wouldn't last. Whenever Tom lumbered upstairs and crashed next to her, she'd have to listen to his snoring all night. And smell his beery breath, fight for blanket supremacy, and try not get kicked off the mattress. Because of that, she doubted she'd get any rest.

For whatever reason, her mind returned to Tift. She recalled that crazy night she'd comforted her after her 'date' with Townsend. Tift had been hysterical, and it was all she could do to keep her from doing something stupid. Had Townsend really raped her? Or had Tift agreed to sleep with him and then made a big stink afterward? Would Tift be so cold and callous as to lie about something as serious as date rape? She'd stolen her scripts and took all the credit for them. But lie about getting raped? That seemed too hard to believe, even for someone like Tift. But what if she had lied? Then all of Gwynn's actions were for…

No, she reassured herself, Tift couldn't be that evil.

She cleared her mind and resolved to get some sleep. Tomorrow, she would scoop Jack into her arms and squeeze him with all her might. Love and cherish her little wiggleworm like never before. He was the entire reason for her existence.

Chapter Fifty-Three

DETECTIVE PETERS

Peters left the facility and walked down Commercial Street. A thick fog had settled over the port. Despite not drinking much, he felt like throwing up. He needed to stop somewhere and get a few pops in him before he self-destructed. The meeting with Gwynn seemed hopeful on the surface, but it felt like she couldn't wait to get away from him. Was he imagining this? He remembered how he sabotaged his marriage to Beth and pushed her away. Would he push Gwynn away, too?

He slipped into the Commercial Street Pub and climbed up on a stool nearest the men's room. A basketball game played on the overhead screen. Celtics vs Lakers, and he didn't have a wager on it; his bookie wouldn't take anymore bets from him until he paid up in full. He couldn't shake the nausea threatening to overtake him. The bartender came over and took his order. A few seconds later, a double shot of Jack Daniel's sat paired with a Pabst Blue Ribbon. He quickly downed the shot and followed it up with a swig of beer.

Shame overwhelmed him. The memory of apologizing to Tom replayed over and over in his head. Why would Gwynn make him do such a thing? And why had he agreed to do it? Tom should have been the one apologizing to him. And someday he would, once they determined who he sent those videos to.

But what if, after all this had passed, Gwynn decided not be with him?

She did say she loved him before leaving that basement room. He slapped the side of his head, and the people around him stared at him as if he was crazy. Why was he torturing himself like this? Gwynn loved him; he was sure of it. She better love him because he had snuffed out four girls and one homeless dude in order to be with her. The things people did for love. He'd killed for it. Over and over and over and over. And he was planning to do it again. Maybe he'd even kill Gwynn if she decided to dump him.

He ordered another shot of Jack. Drank his beer. Watched the game mindlessly and without a care in the world as to who won. The shot arrived, and he knocked that one back, too.

Gwynn had invited him to that awards ceremony for a specific reason. And Dr. Kaufman, too. The look on her face when he'd apologized to Tom didn't escape his notice. Had she enjoyed watching her husband humiliate him? Something didn't seem right about that whole scenario.

He sipped his beer. Ordered a pickled egg. Tried not to beat himself up over that embarrassing apology. Watched the game mindlessly and without a care in the world who won.

He was so mad he felt he could kill someone.

Sometime later, Annabelle's face filled the screen. Two faces, actually, seeing as how he'd knocked back four shots of Jack and three beers. She seemed to be speaking directly to him. Annabelle was sitting next to Nguyen and asking her some pointed questions about the night in question. He stood off his stool and flipped her off, shouting at the screen, which surprised the few patrons inside the place. The bartender warned him to settle down as he knocked back the rest of his beer. Then he left a hundred-dollar bill on a fifty-eight-dollar tab.

He staggered out of the bar and headed back to his condo. Being alone felt like a curse. It was part of the reason he had killed those girls: to release his pent-up angst. Sometimes one had to be cruel to be kind.

Commercial Street was dark and deserted at this hour. He weaved along the sidewalk, hoping the pickled egg wouldn't come up on him. He was sweating profusely by the time he reached his condo. Was he having a stroke? A panic attack? Clutching his chest, he climbed the stairs and went inside his condo, heading straight for the personal items he'd taken off the dead girls' bodies. He dumped them over the comforter and collapsed into bed.

In seconds, he was snoring.

Chapter Fifty-Four

GWYNN

The blare of her alarm clock woke Gwynn the next morning. She usually got up well before it went off, but she must have really been tired last night. When she looked over, she saw that Tom had never made it to bed. What a surprise. He must have fallen asleep on the sofa after drinking too much. Maybe that was why she'd had one of her best nights of sleep in months. It being Sunday morning, she had a lot to do before they made their way to church, assuming Tom wasn't too hungover to go.

Gwynn showered and dressed before tiptoeing downstairs. Once on the main floor, she saw Tom passed out on the sofa. He'd probably sleep like that for a few more hours, or at least she hoped he would. It would give her some peace and quiet before she started in on all the chores. She gazed up at the clock and saw that it was almost seven thirty. Jack needed to be picked up from his friend's house at eight. She went into the closet and grabbed a blanket, spreading it over Tom's body. His face smushed up against the sofa's backrest. She picked up the half dozen beer bottles on the coffee table and all the burger wrappers and stray fries scattered along the floor. His tablet sat on the table, but she refused to open it, afraid of what she might find. After tossing the garbage in the bin, she headed out to retrieve Jack.

The early morning sun felt wonderful over her skin. Spring had sprung with a vengeance, promising a warm summer. Neighbors were out mowing their lawns, clipping hedges, and walking their dogs. Gwynn glanced down at her phone and saw that her portfolio had given up some of its recent gains, consolidating at a lower level, but that seemed like a normal development, because it couldn't keep going up forever. Still, Callum's advice to lock in profits echoed in her head. She couldn't afford to lose her gains.

She considered all the good things that were happening at the moment. Tom's mother was most likely dead on her basement floor, no longer a threat. Her time at The Loft was coming to an end, thanks to her dragon boss. After all this, she would land on her feet and come out even stronger. Maybe even come to her senses and get back with Peters, especially now that he'd identified the person committing these murders. He was a decent guy with problems like everyone else, and he had accepted her in full. Besides, nobody was perfect.

A fresh start in life was what she needed. Once Peters solved these murders, they could move out to LA. She could work on her writing and enjoy the nice weather, unburdened by her checkered past. Peters could be a TV personality and consult on all the true crime shows and detective series. There'd be no need for her to keep killing once she relocated out there. Unless she bumped heads with that LA serial killer that Tift had mentioned. It relieved her to know she could finally be a normal person like everyone else.

She drove over to Jack's friend's house. After parking, she went to the front door and knocked. When she stepped inside, she saw Jack playing video games with his friends, the four of them laughing and joking, which made her happy. Her son appeared to be a normal, well-adjusted boy, able to make friends and be social. It filled her with pride when Jack turned and thanked his friend's parents for having him over, especially when Debbie told her that Jack had been the perfect little gentleman. She grabbed his hand and led him to the car, buckling him into the back seat.

"Did you have fun with Carter and the other boys?" she asked.

"Oh yeah. His dad took us to Red's last night for ice cream. Then we went to Bug Light Park and threw Frisbees around."

"I'm glad you had so much fun."

"Do we have to go to church today?"

"We go to church every Sunday."

"Why?"

"We need to thank God for all the blessings he's given us in life."

"Okay." He seemed to think it over. "Why did Daddy call you a bad name the other night?"

So he had heard it. "Even grownups get mad and say things they shouldn't. That's why we need to ask God for forgiveness when we make mistakes."

"He shouldn't have said that." Jack furrowed his brow.

"No, he shouldn't have, but we both know that he's a good dad to you."

"I know he's a good dad, but he still shouldn't have said it."

"And you and I have said things we shouldn't have."

"Yeah, I guess you're right."

She turned onto their street. "Please be quiet when you get home, Jack. Your dad is still asleep on the sofa."

"Did he drink too many beers again?"

So Jack knew that his dad drank too much. What else did he know about his parents' relationship? Hopefully, not everything.

"No. We got home really late from the ceremony last night. Your dad won a big award."

"Cool. Can I go up to my room and play with my army guys when we get home?"

"Did you eat breakfast?"

"Carter's mom made us waffles with chocolate chips and whip cream."

"Sounds yummy," she said, looking at him in the rearview mirror. "Yes, you can go upstairs and play for a while. I'll call you when it's time for us to leave for church."

"Okay."

She turned into the driveway and parked. Once she unbuckled him, they walked to the front door and went inside. Tom was still asleep, which pleased her. Usually gruff and short-tempered when hungover, she knew Tom would be miserable all day. And she would be stuck with him unless she could make up some excuse to go grocery shopping or run errands.

Hopefully, he'd be lounging on the couch, watching golf or the Red Sox, and leave her alone.

Gwynn waited anxiously for the call to come in, informing them that Susan had accidentally fallen to her death. Both Trish and Tom would be inconsolable when they received the news. She thought of Jack, knowing how much he loved his grandmother. One thing about Susan: she loved Jack as much as she loved her own children. In that sense, she felt bad that her son would no longer have any grandparents left to dote on him.

She started the laundry, hoping to stay clear of the living room. After carrying the basket downstairs, she settled on the basement couch, watching television while she folded clothes. Someday, when she had enough money, she would hire a maid to do the laundry, wash all the dishes, and clean the house from top to bottom.

She stopped folding a pair of Jack's pants when she saw Annabelle on TV, standing in the living room of Nguyen's parents' home. Nguyen sat on the couch, under a blanket, staring blankly up at the camera. Annabelle squatted next to her and asked Nguyen some simple questions, which the cop had a hard time answering. But she did say that she believed someone had set out to hurt her that night. Gwynn grabbed the laundry basket and brought all the clothes upstairs, noticing that it was time to get ready for church.

Waiting for the news of Susan's death left her anxious and on edge.

Upon returning upstairs, Gwynn heard Jack laughing. She saw the boy jumping up and down on his father's shoulder and disrupting his sleep, which would cause Tom to wake up in an even worse mood and take out his frustrations on her.

"Get off your father and go upstairs, Jack. You need to get ready for church."

"Awwww. I want Daddy to wake up so we can play."

"You can play with him later. Now go on."

She debated letting Tom sleep a bit longer, but then decided against it. He prided himself on showing up to church every Sunday and acting like the consummate family man. If she didn't at least give him the option of going, he might become upset with her. Besides, she wanted to be by his side when he learned of Susan's death. Everything had to be just right. Oh, and the expression on his face would be priceless when he heard the news about his dear old mother's passing. She wouldn't miss seeing that for the world.

She went over and began to gently shake him, noticing that he'd barely moved from his spot. It seemed odd that he was not snoring because Tom always snored. She shook his shoulder a bit harder, turning his body toward her. That was when she saw his discolored face and purple lips. Then the foamy saliva on the cushion. She let go of him and dropped to her knees, placing her ear against his mouth. Nothing. Grabbed his wrist and placed her forefinger over the inside of it. No pulse, either.

Tom was dead.

And she hadn't killed him.

Not directly, anyway.

He must have suffered a heart attack or massive stroke.

Had God answered her prayers?

The discovery floored her. But to her surprise, she started to cry. Why? Hadn't she wanted this to happen all along? She thought back to all the great times they'd shared together back at Brooks College and their deep and abiding friendship before he turned into a monster. She remembered when she gave birth to Jack and watching as Tom held the infant boy in his arms, proud as a peacock. Was her mind playing tricks on her? She should be ecstatic, but it felt like a piece of her history had been ripped away from her. She hadn't even felt this way when her own parents died. And despite his bad behavior and perverted sexual practices, she no doubt believed that Tom, in his own sick way, loved her. He'd been one of the few people who'd fully accepted her for who she was: a cold-blooded killer. She'd finally become a free woman, so why couldn't she stop crying? Why was she being so weak and emotional?

Even though she'd recognized the signs of trauma bonding, she'd ignored all the symptoms and developed an emotional attachment to her abuser, which was rooted in love, murder, and their deep ties that went back to their years at Brooks. The family dynamic had in some ways become an integral part of her being, a security blanket, protecting her from her own demons. And now that blanket had been lifted off her, she and Jack were on their own.

Would she have been this way had she killed him herself? With her own hands? But in a way, she had killed him by serving him all those fatty foods and beer, and replacing his statins and blood pressure pills with generic pills.

The tears streaked down her face until she heard Jack trampling down the staircase. She needed to get her son out of the house before the medics came and took Tom away. She squeezed her husband's cold hand as if that might bring him back to life, although that was the last thing she wanted now. He'd died of natural causes, and she was partially responsible. She'd wanted him dead for a long time, and now that she'd gotten her wish, all she could do was cry when she should have been happy.

"Jack, we need to go over to the Mcloskeys' house."

"Why?"

"Don't ask why. Just do as I say," she said, reaching for his hand.

"Are you crying, Momma?"

"My eyes are just itchy."

"Can I say bye to Daddy?"

She tried to hold back the dam. "Not now. Let's let him rest a little while longer."

They walked over to their neighbor's house, hand in hand, and all she could think about was the good times they'd spent together. She rang the bell, and Cliff answered. His teenage daughter, Kelly, usually babysat Jack when she and Tom went out for the night.

"Everything okay, Gwynn?" he asked, a look of concern over his face.

"Would you mind watching Jack for a bit?"

"Sure. Anything we can help you with?"

"I have a situation on my hands. Please keep an eye on him," she said, wiping the tears away.

The first thing she did upon returning home was call 9-1-1. Then she sat holding Tom's hand, praying to God to forgive her, even though she knew she didn't deserve it. She remembered the good days when she and Tift would head down to the Rat to watch Tom play guitar in Dirt Fish. Her freedom from his controlling ways was a thing of the past, yet she couldn't shake the overwhelming despair that had now descended upon her. She sat with him until the authorities arrived. They came in and immediately pronounced Tom dead, draped the sheet over his body, put him on a stretcher, and then took him away, leaving her all alone in the house.

First Ivy and now Tom. She never thought death could be this painful. And yet death pretty much defined her entire existence. How would she break the news to Jack? Her phone rang while she considered this. Seeing Trish's number, she lifted it to her ear. Had her sister-in-law already heard about Tom's passing? But he'd been wheeled out of the house only minutes ago.

"Oh, Gwynn, I have such terrible news," Trish said, sobbing. "My mother is dead."

Chapter Fifty-Five

DETECTIVE PETERS

Peters stood at the back of the crowd, listening as the minister said a few words over Tom Denning's casket. The sky was gray and misty, a perfect day to celebrate the death of his nemesis. Yet he found himself filled with bitterness at the way things had turned out. He thought Gwynn would be elated at getting rid of her mother-in-law and husband in one fell swoop, but staring at her now, alongside her son and sister-in-law, he wasn't quite sure what to think. She looked devastated, weeping at various intervals, and he couldn't tell if it was an act or genuine emotion. If it was an act, it appeared to be a very convincing one.

But why would she be sad? Merely because Tom had died from a heart attack instead of foul play? What difference did it make how he died? Women were strange, emotional creatures, and he'd never been good at understanding them as long as he'd been alive. Maybe by convincing everyone she was sad, it would make her appear like a genuine victim.

Peters hated Tom almost as much as Gwynn did, eagerly looking forward to the day he could exact his revenge. Now he'd never get the chance, which would eat away at him for as long as he lived. He did, however, plan on coming back here someday and pissing on the asshole's grave.

The minister said a few kind words about Tom, proving he didn't know anything about the man. Surprisingly, Peters found himself begrudgingly respecting Tom because of his fierce love for Gwynn. All these people had gathered here to celebrate his life, which meant that they also liked and respected him. When he died, he'd be lucky to have three people at his burial, unless he died in the line of fire. Then the entire PD would be forced to attend, which wouldn't be the worst way to go. In a weird sort of way, he understood why Tom did what he did: he hoped to hold onto Gwynn forever. Tom's possessive and controlling behavior was because he loved her with all his heart, as misguided and wrong as that sounded, and because he never wanted her to leave him. He felt the same way, only he'd resorted to killing young girls to achieve the same goal.

Once the minister finished speaking, the casket was lowered into the ground. Tom's mother had been buried in this same cemetery just a day earlier. Peters glanced around at the large crowd and saw only a few other people he knew. Most of them were Tom's coworkers and college friends. He was surprised to see Tift Ainsley standing off in the corner, dressed in black and sobbing quietly into a designer handkerchief. For some reason, he couldn't take his eyes off her. She looked even more exotic and stunning in person. Although she was one of the most popular actresses on the planet, no one seemed to be paying much attention to her.

Peters saw the psychiatrist standing a few rows behind Gwynn and Jack. Kaufman looked older and more somber today. As Peters stared at the man, Kaufman turned, and their eyes briefly met. Did the shrink know something about him that he didn't? Kaufman's gaze bore into his soul almost as if he could read his mind. Peters watched Gwynn step forward, grab a handful of dirt, and toss it on top of Tom's casket. Then she turned and reached for Jack's hand, and together they walked toward the line of cars. Tift rushed over and embraced her old friend as everyone looked on. Had it not been for Townsend violating Tift back in college, all this carnage might have never happened. Strange how things had turned out. On the other hand, he never would have fallen in love with Gwynn had Townsend not committed such a despicable crime. His life might have taken an altogether different and depressing trajectory.

The one person he did not see here was Callum Frye.

Slowly, the crowd dissipated. It irked him that he couldn't be seen in public with Gwynn until an indeterminate period of mourning had passed. He felt frustrated, yet hopeful at the same time. Tom dying of a heart attack seemed like a cruel and fitting act of justice. Nature had stepped in and accomplished what he and Gwynn had been planning to do all along. Was that why she was sad? Because fate had interceded and stolen her valor?

Peters walked ahead, hands in his pockets, watching Gwynn stroll arm in arm with Tift. Jack and his aunt walked just behind them.

And what about Tom's mother slipping down those basement stairs? Two untimely deaths in the span of twenty-four hours, and no one was asking any hard questions? A heart attack couldn't be planned. A heart attack lacked intent or motive. Even he could see that Tom's health had been veering dangerously in the wrong direction. People were often their own worst enemy, and in the end, man's bad habits proved more lethal than all the world's serial killers combined.

Peters reached his car and stood at the driver's side door, watching as the crowd dispersed.

So who did push Tom's mother down those stairs? He was fairly certain he knew who. The thought of Callum Frye working hand-in-hand with Gwynn made him crazy with envy, and he couldn't help but feel a sense of betrayal. But what was he to do with these feelings? His first marriage had ended in divorce when he'd convinced himself that Beth had been cheating on him while he patrolled the streets of Portland. Despite her constant denials, he couldn't get the crazy idea out of his head. Would he be able to control his demons this time around? Or would he obsess over Frye and ruin another good relationship?

Now that he'd gotten a taste for blood, he wanted more. He'd come to enjoy having such vast power over another human being. It made him feel powerful and in control of his life. On some level, he understood Gwynn's compulsive need to kill, but maybe he hadn't fully comprehended all her motives. He had begun to kill to get back into her good graces, but had jealousy and insecurity added to the fuel? Was there some sort of psychosexual subtext behind his actions?

Peters tried to convince himself that she would never cheat on him like…

she had cheated on Tom. No, Gwynn really loved him. She'd told him time and time again that she did, and he had no choice but to believe her. Together, they were a force to reckon with. But apart, they were guaranteed to mutually destruct.

Had Gwynn used Frye for her own selfish needs? If so, the guy posed an imminent threat to him. Frye might even know all the bad things that Gwynn had done and where the bodies were buried. It was why he had to make certain this guy never had the chance to destroy the love he and Gwynn had cultivated between them.

He got inside his car and joined the funeral queue. Slowly, he cruised through the cemetery as raindrops splattered against his windshield. He turned on the wipers, knowing he had a lot of work to do in the coming days. Gravestones passed on either side of him, a constant reminder of death. He looked forward to getting his hands dirty in the pursuit of justice. Would his next victim be the one that finally cemented his relationship with Gwynn? He couldn't wait to find out.

Once the convoy hit the main road, he raced back to his condo, mentally preparing for what needed to be done next.

Chapter Fifty-Six

GWYNN

Gwynn returned home with Trish and Jack in tow, amazed at how brave Jack had been through all this. Last night, he'd cried at bedtime before she tucked him in. It would take time and much love to help Jack get over his father's death, but she would be there for him whenever he became sad and needed comforting. And she vowed to never speak ill of the boy's father. Only she knew the vile things Tom had done to her while he was alive, and she would take those secrets to the grave.

Trish walked over and gave her a big hug, and Gwynn couldn't help but feel guilty the way she'd treated her sister-in-law. Trish stood in front of the sofa, staring at it as if it might bring her brother back. Gwynn wished she could help her cope, but people would be arriving soon, and there was food and drink to set out.

"Is that where my brother died?" Trish said.

"Yes."

She choked back the tears. "How is it possible to lose two family members in one night?"

"Life is crazy and unpredictable," she said. "It's a reminder that we need to cherish every second we have on this planet and the people in our lives."

Trish turned to Gwynn. "You and Jack are the only family I have left now."

Gwynn placed her hand on her sister-in-law's shoulder. "And we'll always be there for you."

"Thank you."

"I'm so sorry for how I've treated you in the past, Trish."

"I'm sorry too. But that's all water under the bridge now." Trish turned back to the sofa, using a tissue to wipe away her tears. Dark circles ringed her eyes. "Poor Tom. My brother was the best person I knew."

Gwynn wished she could tell her the truth about her husband, but she'd vowed never to hurt her sister-in-law like that.

"He was so dedicated to you and Jack. He loved his family more than anything else in the world. Same with my mother."

"Why do you think she was going down the cellar?" Gwynn asked.

"She was trying to bring up that stupid cat of hers. I always told her to be careful when going down those stairs, because she wasn't getting any younger. And I told her to take her phone with her in case she needed to call for help."

"She was a good woman."

"She was the best mother a daughter could ever have had. And Tom was the best brother, too."

"I want to ask you something, Trish."

"Sure."

"If something were to ever happen to me, would you mind raising Jack?" She had thought about this long and hard. Besides herself, no one loved Jack more than Trish did.

"You know I will. I'm honored you would even ask."

"Jack loves you so much. You've been an amazing aunt to him."

"Jack's a great kid. He's going to be a special guy someday, just like his dad."

Gwynn swallowed her tongue.

Cars began to park in the driveway and along the street. She embraced her sister-in-law one last time before turning toward the kitchen. She went to the refrigerator and took out the trays of cold cuts and bowls filled with salads. The doorbell rang, and Trish walked over to answer it. Gwynn turned and saw Tift enter with a handsome male guest, most likely some model she'd hired to accompany her here. Gwynn placed the tray down and went over to her friend, seeing Tift dressed in all black, a bit over the top, but that was Tift. Still, she was excited to see her friend. It brought back happy memories of their four years together at Brooks. She hugged her, recalling all the good times they had together. Like the Saturday evenings when they slipped out of their dorm room to hit up the town and dance the night away. Or quiet times when they would walk around the tree-lined campus, talking about whatever was on their minds. It moved her that Tift would take time out of her busy schedule to fly here for Tom's burial.

"You don't know how much you being here means to me," Gwynn said.

"I will always be there for you," Tift said. "Oh, Gwynny, I'm so sorry for what you're going through right now."

"Thank you."

"Tom was such an amazing guy."

"Yes, he was." She recalled that video of Tom and Tift in that dorm room, and Tift rapping along to those racist rap lyrics.

"What will you do now that he's gone?"

"Honestly, I haven't thought that far in advance."

"Take some time for yourself, hon. Mourn. Cry. Let all your emotions spill out. Maybe when you're feeling better, you and Jack can come out and stay with me for a while."

"I just might take you up on that."

"It'll help you get your mind off these horrible tragedies."

"Speaking of that," Gwynn said, "what's going on with the TV show?"

"I think it's going to be a huge hit," Tift said. "I don't usually say that, but the buzz around town has been amazing. Even the cast and crew are sensing that we could be part of something special."

"I'm so happy for you."

"It's not just me, hon. It's you, too. After all, it was your baby. If this show manages to take off, and I think it will, it's going to help everyone's career."

She liked the sound of that. "Could we talk about this later? I have a lot on my plate right now."

"Absolutely. Just you and me over a bottle of Pinot and a box of tissues."

She gave Tift one last hug before returning to the kitchen island. The doorbell rang again, and when she turned, she saw Trish letting in a group of people. Some of them were Tom's coworkers and their families. Jack sprinted toward the door and welcomed in a couple of boys his own age. They raced noisily out to the backyard and started playing on the swing set. Kaufman had, somehow, slipped in with the group, dressed in a black pinstripe suit. He looked uncomfortable standing there, the crowd towering over him. He shook Trish's hand and offered his condolences. Then he made straight for the kitchen where she worked, setting out the food.

"Hello, Gwynn."

"Thank you so much for coming, Dr. Kaufman," she said, hoping Jack wouldn't see him.

"I'm so sorry for your loss."

"Thanks." She leaned over and gave him a hug.

"A heart attack?" he whispered in her ear. "Really?"

She let go of him and stood back. "Tom obviously had some health issues that went unnoticed."

"I don't know how you did it."

"It wasn't me. It was his unhealthy lifestyle that did him in," she said, studying his expression.

"Unhealthy lifestyle, right."

"It's true. I kept telling him to eat healthier and stop drinking so much."

His expression hardened. "It appears that you're a liberated woman now."

"I am, but even I never thought it would be so hard to say goodbye."

"Our response to death is often complex and confusing, especially when a person's abuser dies."

"Please, no psychobabble today, okay? I can't handle it right now."

He nodded.

"I'm going to change my life from here on out and be a good person, Doctor Kaufman. I swear on it."

Kaufman smiled and walked away. What did that mean? Did he not believe that she could change her life and be a better person? Did she even believe that herself? Could a tiger change its stripes midstream and become a lamb? She really wanted to change, even if she believed that her actions were warranted.

Change would take time. She had one more person to take care of before she'd be done with that part of her life. One more death in the grand scheme of things wouldn't matter now, especially if that person was a brutal serial killer. Besides, Ivy deserved it. Gwynn swore that it would be the last time she killed, assuming that Peters didn't beat her to the punch and arrest the culprit first.

The end of her old self was now in sight. Would the new and improved Gwynn be much better?

Chapter Fifty-Seven

DETECTIVE PETERS

Now that Peters knew where Frye lived, he followed the guy everywhere, and always at a safe distance. The fact that Frye drove a bright green Jeep made his job much easier. The entire week he'd dedicated to this task. Apparently, Frye didn't work a normal nine-to-five job, and he rarely left his large waterfront home before noon. A twenty-two-year-old guy owning a house in Cape Elizabeth seemed crazy and wrong. Peters planned on hiding his surveillance activity from Gwynn, in the unlikely event she did something stupid, and warned Frye that he was being watched. Could he trust Gwynn? Then again, everything was more complicated now that Tom and his mother were dead. He rationalized his need for secrecy, knowing in his heart that Frye had something to do with the death of George Fields and Gwynn's mother-in-law.

He made a mental note of everything he observed, careful not to write anything down. Frye met with the same blonde girl every afternoon and sometimes at night, and always on the Western Prom after she got off shift at Maine Medical. A pretty blonde nurse with long legs named Ashley Thornton. He knew it would be easy to lure Ashley into his car when the time came. Being a good-looking cop had its benefits, especially when you were famous for solving a notorious murder case. And even more so when you were a serial killer yourself and knew how to charm and persuade people.

Last night, he followed Frye to a well-known bar in Portland's Old Port. He sat in his car for three hours before Frye came out with a different girl on his arm. Cheating on Ashley made Peters despise him even more. He watched as the girl got in Frye's Jeep, and then the Jeep sped away. He had no desire to follow them because he had a good idea what they would be doing later on.

He followed Ashley the next night, feeling bad for the pretty young nurse, knowing that Frye had cheated on her. Her only mistake had been to date the wrong guy at the wrong time, a guy he hoped to set up for five murders. She worked different shifts at the hospital, sometimes doing a double and getting out before midnight. Peters imagined her to be a kind and caring person, cradling newborns in her arms and smiling at all the happy parents looking on. Some nights, Ashley walked alone back to her apartment on Spring Street, staring at her phone the entire way. Such a shame he had to kill her. But he'd grown accustomed to killing, and each time it got easier than the last. It helped him feel better when he remembered the real reason why he did it. Love turned men into crazed beasts. Love made men liars, thieves, and murderers. He remembered that line in the *X-Files,* and it had always stayed with him, especially after meeting Gwynn: *You're my one in five billion.*

Chapter Fifty-Eight

DR. EZRA KAUFMAN

I had planned on seeing Gwynn when I woke that morning to discover that both her husband and mother-in-law had died during the night. What a shocking development. I actually felt sorry for her, and for that reason, I didn't cancel our therapy session. Yet I couldn't help feeling that she had something to do with their deaths. But how does one cause a heart attack? And anyone who knew Tom could clearly see that his health had been trending in the wrong direction. The extreme weight gain and heavy drinking had put considerable stress on his heart, as did his high-stress job as a certified public accountant. Then there were the risky sex games they played. Did he ever wonder during these encounters if he might end up dead?

But what am I to make of her mother-in-law's death? Yes, falling down stairs afflicts many elderly people. It just seems too much of a coincidence that mother *and* son would die on the same night, knowing Gwynn's express desire to be free from both of them. Nothing I learn about their deaths would surprise me. No discovery would prove shocking. I wouldn't put it past her to have induced that heart attack, no matter how outlandish that theory seems.

But then Gwynn showed up in my office a week later, genuinely upset that her husband had died. I studied her closely and didn't detect any deception. Even knowing how badly Tom had been treating her, it surprised me that she took his death so hard. Was it because his death came out of left field, random and without warning? Would she have felt different had she been the one who killed him? Maybe Gwynn was the real control freak in the family and not Tom. I didn't say much during our session, content to sit back and listen to her talk about all the wonderful memories they'd shared together at Brooks College. Had she forgotten about all the bad things he'd forced her to do? Or that he threatened to go to the police and separate her from her son? Even at this advanced age, and with all my experiences and training, people's behavior still surprises me.

Gwynn is finally free from Tom. Now she can be the person she's always wanted. Her husband's untimely death has had another unexpected effect: she's the beneficiary of his generous life insurance policy. I'd assumed that Peters, her secret lover, would be the topic of discussion during our sixty minutes together. Instead, all Gwynn discussed were the good times she and Tom shared.

This confuses me.

Before she left my office, she told me that she'd been thinking about moving to California and starting her life over with Jack. In some ways, it would be a huge weight lifted off my shoulders if she did. She's the last patient I will ever see, and in many ways, I've failed her. More importantly, I've failed myself.

Chapter Fifty-Nine

GWYNN

A Month Later

The board members of The Loft had sent her a large bouquet of flowers, offering their condolences for the deaths of her husband and mother-in-law. They told her to take as much time as she needed away from work and get her life back together. But after burying Tom, she decided that it would be best to get back to a normal routine as soon as possible. So she returned to the office and resumed her duties.

Everyone at work approached her and offered their regrets for Tom's unexpected passing. Their gifts and heartfelt comments touched her and made her appreciate the people she worked with every day. The only person who didn't say anything to her was Denise, but she didn't expect as much from her. Denise locked herself in her office, not even having the balls to come face-to-face with her. She would have at least respected the woman if she'd approached and acted like the bitch she was, but she didn't even do that.

Not that it mattered anymore. Her days at The Loft were coming to an end.

Gwynn picked up Jack from his after-school daycare and returned home. She'd been surprised at how well he'd been dealing with everything thus far. His teachers and fellow students had been wonderful, giving him all the space he needed when he got sad. Otherwise, Jack's behavior hadn't changed dramatically, leading her to believe that he'd either bottled up his feelings or moved on. Would it manifest at some later point in time? She reminded herself to be vigilant and watch for any signs of trouble. Her worst fear would be for him to turn out like Tom, and because of that, she vowed to raise him to be a good person and be nothing like his father. Or her father. Or her.

The house felt empty these days. Tom's absence had finally started to sink in. Funny how her mind tended to repress the worst about him. Only now, after a month had passed, was she starting to fully appreciate the freedom she'd gained from his death. She felt able to reinvent herself and start anew. Maybe somewhere else. Free to raise Jack in a good home with morals and values.

She'd invited Peters over tonight to watch the pilot of *Bad Choices*. She felt nervous about seeing him for the first time since burying Tom, but she had to know if there was still any chemistry left between them. Trish planned on picking Jack up in an hour. The deaths of her mother-in-law and Tom had, surprisingly, brought her and her sister-in-law closer together. As far as Peters was concerned, she wondered if all those romantic feelings would ever return. Her grief had been such that she hadn't yet spoken to Callum about what he did that day at her mother-in-law's house. Or how he pushed her down those stairs. Oddly, he hadn't even tried to contact her. His lack of sexual interest in her made her feel old and unattractive. Still, the best strategy going forward was to cut ties with him and hope they went their separate ways.

She didn't need anything from anyone now. She had her freedom and could control her own future. Soon she would receive a nice check from Tom's life insurance policy, a policy she never even knew about until after he'd died. For the first time since Tom's death, she'd been feeling optimistic about her life moving forward. She'd started to grow into her authentic self, unchained from the obsessions that had consumed her since childhood. She was finally free from the two men who had the biggest influence on her life.

The doorbell rang as she flipped through some of the photo albums of her and Tom in better times, when Tom was thinner and cooler. Tom playing guitar in Dirt Fish. Tom holding Jack the day he was born. The three of them sledding down the Eastern Prom and skating in Deering Oaks, all wearing mittens and holding hands. Oddly, it made her nostalgic for those days. She moved to the door and let Trish inside. Her sister-in-law hugged her and then turned to catch Jack in her arms.

"What do you two have planned for today?" she asked Trish.

"Well, I was thinking about a stroll on Higgins Beach and then get us some ice cream afterward, unless you'd rather eat lima beans, Jack."

"Yuck! I hate lima beans."

"Then it's the beach and ice cream, kiddo."

"Thanks for taking him, Trish. He really loves hanging out with you."

"I'd be a basket case if you and Jack weren't around."

She thought of her plan to move to California and briefly experienced a pang of guilt. "I'm so glad you and I ironed out our differences."

"Life's too short to hold grudges, right?"

"I couldn't agree more," Gwynn said. "What will you do with your mother's house?"

"I suppose I'll have to sell it. Of course, I'll give half of the proceeds to you and this little monster."

Jack giggled. "I am not a monster, Aunty Trish. You are."

"No, you keep it," Gwynn said. "Your brother left us in good shape."

"Are you sure? You might need it for Jack's college fund."

"We're fine, trust me."

"My mother had a nice home with a lot of expensive things. And the market's hot right now, especially houses along the water. I'm sure it will sell quickly."

"If you need help with anything, please let me know."

"Will do, sis."

Gwynn squatted down to meet Jack's gaze. "You behave yourself, wiggleworm, and listen to everything your aunty tells you." Gwynn stood back up.

"I will," Jack said.

"I see that your friend's show is premiering tonight. Are you going to watch it?" Trish asked.

Gwynn stood. "Probably not. I don't watch much TV these days," she said, wondering if Trish would view the show and connect the dots back to her.

"I have no interest in violent crime shows. There's too much nastiness out there already."

"True."

"Besides, I can barely stay up past nine most nights." Trish turned to leave, holding Jack's hand.

"Hope you guys have fun," she said, waving to them as they left. Once Trish buckled Jack in the back seat, she pulled out of the driveway and disappeared.

Gwynn looked down and realized that her hands were shaking. She uncorked a bottle of Chablis and poured herself a glass, hoping to steady her nerves. Once sufficiently calm, she sat back down with a photo album and started to flip through it. After today, she hoped to never look through these picture books again. Had it not been for Jack and the fact that he might want to look at these someday and remember his father, she'd toss them in the trash. She reached the last page and saw a photo of Tift, Tom, and herself standing arm in arm at their college graduation, and it brought up a whole host of emotions. Snapping the book shut, she felt a tear dribble down her cheek, and she swore it would be the last one she'd ever shed for Tom.

She heard a knock at the door as she was sipping her wine. She took a deep breath and headed over to see who it was. When she opened it, Callum Frye was standing there.

"Hi, Gwynn."

"You shouldn't be here." She pulled him inside and quickly closed the door. "Where's your Jeep?"

"Don't worry, I parked it at the far end of the street."

"Why are you even here?"

"Not even a thank you for getting rid of that mother-in-law of yours?"

"I've been a bit busy as of late, if you haven't noticed."

"So I've heard," he said, looking around the room. "Looks like you caught a break with Tom keeling over like that."

His flippant tone angered her. "What do you want?"

"How in the world did you pull that off?"

"It was a heart attack, Callum. I had nothing to do with it."

He laughed. "Why don't I believe you?"

"You saw him with your own eyes. He was hardly the model of good health."

"Knowing how skilled you are, something tells me otherwise."

"What do you want?"

"You should have seen your mother-in-law's expression when I jumped out of that closet."

Gwynn hadn't the stomach to hear about this now.

"I'll give the old biddy credit, though; she put up quite a fight."

"I hope she died quickly."

"Oh no. She was still breathing when I went downstairs to check on her. And I shoved her really hard."

"Can we discuss this some other time?"

"I sat with her for a few minutes and told her the whole story about how you saved my life, and how you killed all those bad people. Then I told her about your plan to kill Tom."

"Did she say anything?"

"Her breathing was labored, but her eyes widened when I mentioned her son's name."

"Do you think she understood what you were saying?"

"Oh, I'm sure of it. I even cradled her head in my arms so she could hear me better."

Gwynn crossed her arms and stared at him, imagining Susan's final moments on earth, and feeling a warm glow of contentment growing inside her.

"When I was sure she understood, I covered her mouth with my hand

and finished her off."

"You think that was a good idea? You could have left behind some DNA?"

"Oh no, I was wearing gloves," he said. "She didn't have much time left, anyway."

Gwynn felt nothing for Frye and wanted him out of her life. It had been a mistake to get romantically involved with him, despite the pleasure she had received from their two encounters. Somehow, she needed to forgive herself and move on from him.

"I think we should go our separate ways now." She pointed toward the door.

"Is that it between us? We're done?"

"I lived up to my end of the deal. And so did you."

"Are you sure you want to be done with me, Gwynn?"

"Positive," she said. "Goodbye, Callum."

He leaned in and tried to kiss her, but she shoved him away. Laughing, he turned and loped down the street.

Gwynn closed the door and stood with her back against it, staring at the sofa where Tom had died. For a brief second, she thought she saw him reclined on it and waving a finger for her to come over. His skin was powder white, and he was thin like he had been back at Brooks. He smiled at her, although not in an evil way. Frightened, she closed her eyes and tried to breathe. When she opened them, Tom was gone. She reminded herself to replace that sofa with a new one. If she didn't replace it, she felt like Tom's ghost might haunt her for as long as she lived here.

Chapter Sixty

DETECTIVE PETERS

As Peters turned onto Gwynn's street, he saw that familiar green Jeep parked along the curb. The sight of it infuriated him. He parked against the curb and jumped out of his car, walking until he stopped next to it. Placing his hand on the hood, he realized the engine was still hot. Why was Frye in the neighborhood? Parked near Gwynn's house? His mind went to a dark place.

"Hey, what are you doing?" a voice called out.

Peters turned and saw Frye striding toward him. For a big guy, he moved with remarkable grace. Then he remembered that Frye had been a competitive figure skater back in the day.

"I was just admiring your Jeep. It's really cool."

"Yeah, bro, it's a one of a kind," Frye said. "Sorry for snapping at you like that. I'm kind of protective of it."

"I can understand why you would be," Peters said, standing back and admiring the Jeep. "I was thinking about getting one of these myself."

"Then you better put in your order now. It takes about six months to get a delivery on a model this limited, and you have to fill out all the forms online."

"Wow. That's a long time."

"Good things come to those who wait."

"Evidently."

"You look familiar. Do I know you from somewhere?"

"I don't think so."

"Wait. Now I recognize you," Frye said, pointing a long finger at him. "You're that detective who solved the Muddy River Killer case."

"Guilty as charged." He laughed and held up his hands.

"Wow. This is so cool. I'm Callum," he said, holding out his hand.

"Mike." They shook. He released first. "You live in this neighborhood?"

"Nah, just visiting a friend. You?"

"I was driving by when I saw your Jeep, and I just had to turn around and check it out."

Frye patted the hood. "Yeah, she has that effect on people."

"I'm terrible with all this computer stuff," he said. "You think you could show me how to custom order one of these so I can get all the options like you?"

"Sure, man. I can help you out with that. You know your way around Cape Elizabeth?"

"A little. I've been to The Cookie Jar a few times."

"Figures a cop would know The Cookie Jar. Tom makes the best donuts in Maine," he said. "I'll give you my number, and that way you can call me sometime, and we can set up a time to meet."

"Sounds great."

"I can't believe I'm talking to the famous detective who solved the Muddy River case."

"Let's not get carried away now. I'm not that famous."

"The hell you're not. You've been on all the news and true crime shows," he said. "Personally, I find serial killers fascinating."

This caught Peters's attention. "If you don't mind me asking, how does a young guy like you afford a vehicle like this?"

"One word, bro: cryptos," Frye said, opening the door and getting behind the wheel.

"You mean like Bitcoin?"

"Yeah, but that's just only one of the coins I own." Frye handed him his business card.

"I'm clueless when it comes to that kind of stuff."

"Come on over sometime, and we'll have a few drinks and talk. If you want, I'll give you a list of cryptos that will moon this cycle."

"Moon?"

"Blast off." He laughed. "As in make you a pile of money."

"Okay. That sounds good."

"Call me," Frye said, making his hand into a phone and placing it next to his ear.

Peters stepped back and watched the Jeep speed away. Staring down at Frye's cellphone number, he couldn't quite believe his good luck. The stupid kid had given him the perfect excuse to enter his house. Not even blood-gulping vampires had received such an enthusiastic reception. Now all he needed to do was plant the girls' personal items somewhere inside, and then everything else would fall neatly into place. How brilliant would he look when Gwynn finally realized that the kid she'd saved a long time ago—assuming Frye was that kid—was himself a serial killer?

Chapter Sixty-One

GWYNN

Gwynn had butterflies in her stomach when Peters finally arrived. She went to the door, trying to convince herself that this was the man she was meant to be with for the rest of her life. Would she ever feel the same passion for him that she once did? Somehow, she doubted it. But she had to know for sure. So how would she handle the situation if he wasn't?

She opened the door and smiled when she saw him standing there, holding a pizza box in one hand and a six-pack of Heineken in the other. The beer reminded her of Tom and immediately soured her mood. Peters looked ragged from all the hours he'd been putting into these murder cases. He reached out and pulled her into his arms, kissing her on the lips. She felt put off by his impudence. Would this be the night they reignited their romance and brought it back to life? Or the night their relationship fizzled?

"I've missed you so much," he said. "How about you?"

"You know I have."

"Good. It's about time we got reacquainted with each other."

Chapter Sixty-Two

DETECTIVE PETERS

Peters settled down on the sofa while Gwynn put the six-pack of beer in the fridge. It occurred to him that Tom had died somewhere in this house. Did it happen in the bedroom while he slept? Or did he die somewhere else? He decided not to ask and risk alienating her. But the fact that Tom was finally gone thrilled him. He only wished he could have been there to watch the prick die. The accidental death of his mother, on the other hand, seemed too coincidental. Knowing Gwynn the way he did, he couldn't help but feel that she had something to do with it. But Gwynn had been at that awards ceremony the night the woman 'slipped' and fell down those stairs. Maybe that was why Gwynn had invited him to the event, so he wouldn't suspect her. It convinced him more than ever that Frye had helped Gwynn kill both Gwynn's mother-in-law and George Fields. An athletic guy like Frye would have had no problem pushing the old woman down those stairs and then finishing her off.

Tift's new show would be debuting tonight on one of the cable stations, and he couldn't wait to watch it.

"A beer and a plate for you, sir?" she said, sitting down next to him.

"By all means," he said. "I know I didn't say it before, Gwynn, but I'm sorry about Tom dying like that. It must have come as a complete shock."

"I won't lie to you, the suddenness of it hit me harder than I expected."

"A heart attack. Who would have guessed?"

"It was horrible finding him like that. And I had my son to think about."
She turned to him. "Then again, just looking at Tom, you could almost see
it coming."

"He'd really let himself go."

Gwynn grabbed a slice of pizza. "Tom hadn't been treating his body like
a temple these past few years."

"No offense, but it served him right for the way he'd been treating you."

"I agree, but we did have a son together. And lots of history dating back
to our years at Brooks."

Peters grabbed a slice of pizza, sick of hearing about her years at Brooks,
an elite college he would have never in a million years gotten into. He
reminded himself not to say anything bad about Tom lest he ruin the mood.
"It just seems crazy that his mother would slip and die the very same night
he had a massive heart attack."

"It is an unusual coincidence."

"The two people in this world who knew about that video and could have
royally screwed us over ended up dying on the same night. What are the
odds?"

"Sometimes lady luck shines down on you when you least expect it."

"Thank God for lady luck, then."

"We should just be thankful they're gone."

"Believe me, I am." He took a bite of his pizza. "You're the only thing I've
ever wanted."

She smiled, but it seemed forced.

"Aren't you having a beer?" he asked.

"Not in the mood tonight."

Peters took another bite of pizza, waiting for her to say something nice
and loving, but she didn't, and so he tried not to think about Frye pushing
that woman down the stairs. Or Frye sitting in Gwynn's car at the bean
plant, conspiring with her to murder George Fields. And he didn't even
want to think about the possibility of Frye having sex with Gwynn beside
that fireplace, and on the very same rug they'd once made love on before
Tom barged in and ruined everything. Not that it mattered now because

Frye would soon be out of the picture once Gwynn learned that he'd killed all those girls.

***

They sat around and talked after eating pizza. He was careful not to drink too much, needing to drive home later, not sure if Gwynn would invite him to stay the night. He couldn't put his finger on it, but something seemed off between them. The chemistry they once shared wasn't quite there.

He tried to ignore the voice in his head warning him to be wary of her. Or that she once threatened to kill him. Would she threaten that again if she decided not to be with him?

Finally, Gwynn picked up the remote.

"The show is about to start," she said.

"I'm really looking forward to it."

She turned and smiled. "You and half the male audience out there."

"Please, Gwynn. You're way prettier than Tift Ainsley."

"You're just saying that."

"No, I'm not. To me, you're the most beautiful woman in the world."

"That's so sweet of you, but we both know that's not true," she said.

She turned on the TV and reclined against him, and Peters finally felt as if, maybe, just maybe, they'd turned a corner.

But would this last? He remembered the last time he sat down with her to watch a Tift Ainsley movie. Gwynn had spiked his beer and knocked him out. If he hadn't wrestled his gun back from her inside his car, she would have surely killed him. What a crazy, twisted relationship he'd gotten himself into. Never in a million years would he have thought his life would turn out this way.

***

The show ended, and the credits rolled. He couldn't quite believe what he had just watched. He stared at the flatscreen with his mouth open. Although the setting was West Coast, he recognized the show for what it was: a thinly veiled retelling of Gwynn Denning's life story. Of course, viewers would be hard-pressed to make the connection between Tift's character and Gwynn. Or between himself and Garth Fuller, the ridiculously handsome detective who played him to a tee. How did Tift know about all these murders unless…unless Gwynn told her about them. Did Tift steal Gwynn's idea and write the script herself? Then change the location and all the characters' names? Even the son's name sounded the same: Jett instead of Jack. Peters turned to Gwynn and saw her smiling from ear to ear.

"Did you like it?" she asked.

"Like it? I loved it. But…"

"But it reminded you of someone else's story?"

"How did they…"

"Not they. Me."

"You what?"

"I wrote all the scripts and sent them to Tift, never expecting her to like them."

"Wait. You mean to tell me that you came up with the idea for this show?"

"Yup."

"You know what this means, Gwynn? You're a real writer now."

"I am a real writer. Isn't that crazy?"

"But there's one thing I don't get. Tift's name was in the credits as head writer and creator of the show."

"And why do you think that is?"

He thought about it for a few seconds.

"Bitch stole my idea."

"Why would she stab you in the back like that?"

"She claimed the show wouldn't have gotten picked up otherwise," she said. "The good news is, I got paid for writing it, and if the show manages to get renewed, I get to write for a second season."

"Will Tift continue to get the credit for your work?"

"Sadly, yes, but she promised to get me into the screenwriters' guild if I help her out. That way I can get more work in the future, assuming I want it."

"That's amazing. And to be honest, Tift was great in your role."

"She was great, wasn't she?"

"I'm so proud of you."

"I'm proud of me too. I can't believe that I actually have a talent for something."

"Well, there is your other talent."

"That only you and I know about," she said. "And I hope to keep it that way."

"Now you have a talent that people will respect and appreciate."

"And pay me lots of money to do."

"You're amazing, Gwynn."

"Thanks, but I couldn't have done it without you."

He reached over and caressed her cheek. "Speaking of that, how long do we have to wait in order to be seen in public?"

"I think we should give it a few more months before that happens."

"I wish I could announce to the world that you're all mine."

"Be patient, Peters. Our day will come."

"I'm assuming you're done with that other thing?"

"I will be once we find Ivy's killer."

"I feel I'm getting closer to identifying the culprit. When I nail down this case, I'm going to put this guy away for good."

He stood to leave, waiting for an invitation to stay. But she didn't extend one. It wouldn't have bothered him as much if he could just stop thinking about her and Frye hooking up. For whatever reason, he couldn't help but feel that Gwynn's passion for him seemed to be waning. Was he imagining this? And with her burgeoning career as a writer, would she take Jack and move out to L.A. and leave him behind? Maybe she'd ask him to move out there with her? He would, too, if she asked. Nothing would please him more than quitting the PD and getting out of this frigid state, and then settling down in sunny LA with Gwynn and her son.

She kissed him at the door. Had she used him to get what she wanted? Like when she'd invited him to Tom's award ceremony so he could provide her with a convenient alibi. Just thinking about that pissed him off. Why couldn't she love him the way he loved her? After all, he'd killed four girls and a homeless guy just to be with her. That took sacrifice and dedication. It meant he loved her with all his heart. He even planned on killing that pretty nurse, Ashley, and pinning it on Frye.

He needed to meet up with Frye and get into his good graces, and the sooner the better. Only then could he set him up for the series of murders he'd committed. No need rushing things along. He could take his time and make sure and do the job right, all the while growing his relationship with Gwynn. And tonight was a start, he thought, as he settled behind the wheel.

His phone rang as he started the engine.

"Hi, Mikey."

"Fuck, Ruby. What do you want now?"

"Getting a little low on funds, sweetie. I think it's time we meet again."

"This had better not be what I think it is."

"Come on, boy. A girl's got the right to better herself now, don't she? And Ruby needs some bank, or this ole hoe's gonna be sick again."

Maybe Ashley wouldn't be his last victim, he thought as he pulled out onto the road.

Chapter Sixty-Three

GWYNN

Gwynn walked hand in hand with Jack along the banks of the Presumpscot River, pointing out the various plants and ferns. This was the exact spot where she found Ivy. She placed a bouquet of flowers by the ferns and stepped back to say a quick prayer for the girl. The day was spectacular, and her son had no idea about the terrible things that had taken place down here. Dressed in a UMaine white t-shirt, shorts, and blue Crocs, he ran to the edge and stared down at the moving green water. It appeared crystal clear today, and she could practically see down to the bottom. Small fishes darted between the fluttering reeds. Gnats darted out over the eddies that were spinning wildly in the flow. Jack shouted when he saw a school of fish swimming past. She pulled up next to him and pointed to a family of turtles sunning on a branch sticking out over the water.

It pained her to think about what had happened to Ivy. Because of that, she swore to do everything in her power to avenge the girl's death. It would be her last hurrah before she ended that sad chapter of her life. At least Ivy was not suffering anymore. She truly believed the girl was in a better place.

Jack turned to her, not seeing the tear trickling down her cheek. He grabbed her by the hand and pulled her toward the river, talking nonstop the entire time.

Life couldn't be better. Even her boss at The Loft had backed off and given her some much-needed space. Little by little, she'd begun to appreciate her newfound freedom and the identity she had hoped to carve out for herself. It was the little things in life she now looked forward to. Like not having to ask permission for where she went and whom she saw. No more did she need to perform acts on Tom that she found twisted and depraved. She didn't have to pretend to be nice to him all the time. Or dress and talk the way Tom wanted. She lived by her own rules now. Spent her own money. She'd even developed a better relationship with Trish, something she never thought possible.

The insurance company cut her a nice check, a portion of which she invested in more cryptocurrency. The rest of the money she used to buy mutual funds and bonds. Her and Jack's financial future seemed secure.

The first two episodes of *Bad Choices* had garnered huge ratings for the network. The critics raved about its grittiness and dark beauty, lavishing praise on the writing, saying Tift had created a complex cast of characters that viewers loved to hate. A few said it had been the greatest performance of her career and would surely propel her to new heights. The network, ecstatic with the ratings, ordered two more seasons. There was even talk of Tift being nominated for multiple Emmys, including one for acting and another for Outstanding Writer. Tift's influence in Hollywood seemed to be growing by the day.

Watching Jack throw rocks into the river, she realized that she was more than happy to let Tift take all the credit for her show. Dealing with her two-faced friend would require tact and patience, despite knowing that she had the upper hand in their relationship, thanks to that video she possessed. If she refused to write more scripts, Tift's reputation would surely suffer. And who better to write a show about a serial killer than someone who had actually done it?

Gwynn reflected on her relationship with Peters as she gripped Jack's hand and walked along the water's edge. She didn't feel the same way about him as he did for her. Their chemistry hadn't sizzled like it did when they first met. After her mind-blowing trysts with Callum, she didn't think she could ever settle for good sex with Peters. With Jack to raise, and a new career on the horizon, she didn't need a man to be happy. She needed to work on herself and building up her self-esteem. And not killing people would be a good start.

After an hour passed, Gwynn grabbed the blanket out of her backpack and spread it over the warm grass. She removed the turkey and cheese sandwiches, along with the bags of chips and two cans of lemonade, and placed them down on the blanket. Then she and Jack sat down to eat. A few ducks paddled close to shore, and Jack stood and threw them crumbs. The sound of his laughter filled her ears and made her happier than she'd been in a while. It made everything she had done worth it. Because without her son, life was not worth living. He motivated her to be the best person she could be. She would protect Jack and keep him safe. Watch as he developed into a fine young man. Unlike Tom. Unlike her father. Unlike her.

Maybe they'd move to LA and start life anew. She had a bright future out there if she chose to pursue it. Leave Peters and this life behind. Just her and Jack. And, begrudgingly, Tift Ainsley.

Yes, this was what she wanted to do. The only problem was, what should she do about Peters? He knew everything she had done.

Jack laughed and pointed at something in the water. She nibbled on her sandwich and craned her neck to see what he was looking at. It looked like the edge of a vinyl bag popping out of the river. She stood, caught the sun reflecting off what looked to be a metal zipper, and walked to the edge to get a better look. On the other side of the river, she saw something. Or someone. A sliver. An apparition. And then the apparition came into better focus, and she saw Tom. He was thin, and his hair was long, and he had a guitar strapped around his shoulder and was singing. He looked up from the neck of his guitar and smiled at her. Then he lifted his hand and sliced it across his neck. Had he learned, in the afterlife, that she had been responsible for him dying?

The reflection off the zipper momentarily blinded her. Jack laughed and grabbed her hand. When she looked across the river, Tom was gone. And the bag was drifting in her direction.

Acknowledgments

I'd like to thank the team at Level Best, especially Shawn Reilly Simmons and Deb Well. Thanks to my agent, Evan Marshall. Members of my writer's group, Tim Queeney and Julie Selbo. And mostly I give thanks to my wife, Marleigh, and two kids, Danny and Allie.

About the Author

Joseph Souza is the award-winning and bestselling author of twelve novels and a book of short stories. He's won the Maine Literary Award, the Andres Dubus Award, and was a runner-up for the Al Blanchard Award. He's worked as a teacher, cabbie, social worker, truck driver, editor, bouncer, barber, wrestling coach, paralegal, and intelligence analyst in the DEA (Organized Crime Unit), to name just a few jobs. He lives in Maine with his wife and has two children.

AUTHOR WEBSITE:
  josephsouzawriter.com

SOCIAL MEDIA HANDLES:
  Facebook: Joseph Souza, Author
  Twitter: @josephsouzafans
  Instagram: josephsouza2060
  Twitter/X: @josephsouzafans
  Goodreads: https://www.goodreads.com/author/show/4393351.Joseph_Souza
  Bookbub:
  NetGalley: Cruel & Bitter Things

Also by Joseph Souza

Unpaved Surfaces (Kindle Press)

Need to Find You (Kindle Press)

The Neighbor (Kensington)

Pray For The Girl (Kensington)

The Perfect Daughter (Kensington)

The Anchorman's Wife (Level Best Books)

Cruel & Bitter Things, Bad Choices Novel, Book 1